ACE

THE OUTLAW CHESS SERIES

HARLEY DIAMOND

Published by House of Books Press

www.harleydiamond.com

Edited by Karen Sanders Editing

https://www.karensandersediting.com/

PA Services by Arcane and Reverie

contact@arcaneandreverie.com

Proofreading Services by Proofreading by Mich

https://www.instagram.com/proofreadingbymichx/

Formatting Services by Irish Ink Publishing

https://www.facebook.com/IrishInkPublishing

PR Services by Peachy Keen Author Services

https://www.peachykeenauthorservices.com/

Cover Design by Vicious Desires Design

https://www.instagram.com/viciousdesires/

Cover Model: Kevin Creekman

https://www.instagram.com/thecreekman/

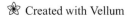 Created with Vellum

Blurb

MY DEVIL. MY ANGEL. MY HEAVEN. MY HELL.
Jason Steele. A bad boy biker placed on earth to tempt good girls like me.
The future Prez of the Angels of Hellfire didn't want the unattractive best friend he grew up with. Plain Jaine Jones.
At least not for keeps.
The reason eighteen-year-old me skipped California for New York?
Unrequited love.
Mr. Ace of Broken Hearts played me, then asked the bitch who made my life a misery to be his old lady.
It's been ten years. My father is dead.
I need to go home to lay him to rest.
Ace won't expect the ugly duckling who's transformed into a swan
—the badass queen who's no longer plain.
It's time for the fallen angel to be served his penance for what he did.
But not by God.
By me.

Playlist

Creep by Radiohead

Author's Note

ACE is NOT standalone.

ACE is BOOK 1 of a SERIES, which contains an ONGOING STORYLINE that CONCLUDES in BOOK 6, DIRTY PADRAIG.

These books contain MULTIPLE POVs from characters across the entire series.

Due to the nature of the CONTINUING STORYLINE, these books MUST be
READ IN ORDER.

ACE
DIRTY CILLIAN
RAZR
DIRTY DYLAN
DIRTY EOIN
DIRTY PADRAIG

CHAPTER ONE

JAINE

Ten Years Earlier (Age Eighteen)
The Angels of Hellfire Clubhouse, Rising, California

I HEAR THE GUTTURAL GROWLS OF THE HOGS BEFORE I SEE THEM.

He's back.

Walking across to look from his bedroom window, I take in the large group approaching the compound entrance, leaving a trail of dust hanging in the air in its wake. Each hog is loved and cherished by its rider, and the well-oiled machines gleam in the late afternoon sun.

"If only they looked after their old ladies as well," I mutter to myself.

I watch as Jefferson, one of the new prospects, swings the large metal gates open to allow the brothers through before slamming them shut afterward. He gives the heavy iron a thorough shake to be sure they're secure, causing the rusty hinges to creak loudly in protest.

Not that he needs to bother. It's an instant locking device, plus there's CCTV everywhere, with a coded entry system on the entrance door. The digits are changed every second day, minimum. Still, I guess it pays to be vigilant, although, who in their right mind would mess with a one percent club? Only fools with a death wish.

I inhale the long-familiar redolence of exhaust fumes emitting from the straight metal pipes. It's a smell that's permeated the very walls of the clubhouse through the years, to the extent where it's now ingrained.

Well, it's one of the ingrained things, at least. The only real welcome one. The other is DNA. Cum, to be precise.

Closing my eyes, I let out a long, audible exhale.

"What the fuck are you doing, Jaine?" I grumble to myself.

I can hear the blood pounding through my brain and in my ears. Thump. Thump. Fucking. Thump.

I suddenly feel nauseous with nerves.

The sounds of rock music and men hollering make up the background noise. The continual hum is only broken by their old ladies' loud shrieks as they pretend to laugh at crap jokes and repeated stories. Shit that wasn't even funny the first time around. Walking across, I push closed the heavy bulletproof door, which clunks solidly behind me.

Silence ensues.

Leaning my back against its dark grey surface, I shiver as the coolness of the metal sends shivers up my spine. I wander around his bedroom, my nervous fingertips trailing over the familiar stuff within easy reach.

Nerves cause me to bite the inside of my lip so damn hard I can taste the copper tang of blood.

I glance around the room at the blue-painted walls and the unmade double bed. Its black covers are now grey, and the white fitted sheet is pulling away from the mattress edges, having shrunk in size. Their visual wear and tear is a constant reminder—not that I ever needed one—of the number of times they've been washed on account of the fucking he's done in that bed ever since he's been legally able to.

Shit. Who am I kidding? He's been fucking cum sluts since he got his first boner.

And also Emilia.

The bedding is clean. I hope. The mattress? Well, it's a bit like everything else in the clubhouse. Avoid blacklight usage at all goddamn costs unless you want to be blinded.

The U.S. flag hangs on the wall above his bed, billowing gently as it's caught by the warm early August breeze seeping through the partially open window.

The faint trickle of air does nothing to disguise or dispel the combined scent of aromatic cologne, sex, and him, which lingers in the room.

Closing my eyes, I breathe in deeply.

I love his fucking smell.

But then, I love everything about him.

My gaze drifts along the shelves that line the walls that hold porn magazines, condoms, bike parts, and all the other essential stuff that any almost-nineteen-year-old male needs.

I run my fingers across the surface, then grimace when I look at the tips. Oh, and dust. Lots of dead skin cells belonging to fuck knows which skanky bitches.

He has no time for cleaning. Not with all the women he's servicing these days.

How many times have I been in this room? Too many to mention.

I'm the only female allowed in here unattended, and definitely the only one where the first thing on his mind isn't fucking.

Today. Tonight. Well, that's going to be different. At least, I hope it is.

Pulling my green velvet scrunchie from my hair, I drag my sweaty hands through its long, blonde length. I lick my lips. My mouth feels dry.

My pop was born in this town. We moved back here from Nevada when I was seven. I remember the first time I saw Jason Steele.

Ace.

A boy with eyes as blue as the bluest thing ever, and with inky hair as black as midnight. His smile made me melt. We've been thick as thieves ever since.

Best friends.

I've loved him from that first moment, and I fell in love with him as soon as I was old enough to understand what being in love felt like. What it truly meant. There hasn't been a day when I haven't loved him in some shape or form. There never will be.

Today?

Well, it's my eighteenth birthday, hence the get-together at the clubhouse.

We did cake and gifts earlier with some of the retired brothers, their old ladies, and their families.

I haven't seen him today yet, though.

I need to speak to him as the letter came. I've been dreading it, but at the same time, I haven't. I've been accepted into Yale. I'm following in my pop's footsteps. I never told Ace I'd applied to colleges, and definitely not that I'd applied to any out of state. He's never once asked about my future or what I plan to do with my life. He's selfish like that. All bikers are. Women are there to cook, clean, and fuck. The end of their usefulness stops right there. He likely thought I'd graduate, then hang around here forever. Become somebody's old lady. Maybe even his. But I need more from life than this club. I need to have career options.

I'm not sure how he'll react. Did he think I'd stay in Rising forever? Probably. Then again, maybe he won't even care if I go.

I have to leave California in a few short weeks and move to Connecticut.

Why am I so nervous?

I want him to be my first.

Does he know that?

Nope.

At least, not yet.

He will, though. When I throw myself at him tonight.

I rub my hands down my khaki cargo pants just as the bedroom door bursts open.

"What are you doing in here, PJ?" His voice has deepened over the years, and it makes me feel all kinds of fuzzy inside. Lust? Desire? All I know is that a shiver runs through me just about every time he opens his mouth.

I spin around and look at him.

He takes up the entire doorway with his six-foot-four frame, which gets broader each day. Icy blue eyes stare at me from a face that's naturally tanned from the sun, and with cheekbones any woman would die for. He runs his hands through his thick black wavy hair, which hangs several inches below his shoulders.

I fucking love a man with a mane.

I frown and then pout. "Just got a bit of a headache, that's all, Ace."

It's a blatant lie.

I'm the only one who calls him that. Ace. When he first introduced me to the game of poker, he deliberately removed all the aces every time it was my turn so I could never win. I was too young to

know any better. Or too stupid. Or too infatuated. I was too something, that's for sure. I only realized when they fell down his sleeve
as he leaned over when he almost kissed me that very same day.
That's another story. Anyway, the name's stuck ever since.

I walk across the room, kick off my white high-tops, then flop
on my back on the bed, pretending everything's normal. That I'm
not planning on seducing my best friend. Walking across, he lies on
his side beside me. Same as we've done a million times before. I
turn my head to look at him, and he grins at me. My eyes take in his
bright white smile with its slightly too-long canines that give him
the wolfish look that I love. They then drop to the dimple in his
chin.

No wonder women want him. He's so goddamn beautiful.

Not as much as I want him, though.

I smile back at him.

"Emilia's been looking for you." I huff when I mention her
name. I move my gaze to stare at the ceiling, my hands fidgeting
with the hemline of my white tank top. "Where's Jason?" I speak in
a breathy tone, trying to mimic her slutty voice and calling him by
his real name the way she does. She wouldn't dare call him Ace.

He leans up on one elbow and smirks down at me. My gaze
discreetly runs up the dark blue jeans that cling to his muscular
thighs and slim hips, then to the black muscle tee that caresses his
upper torso.

"Are you jealous, Plain?" he asks teasingly.

I hate that fucking name. He's called me that since our early
teens. Well, only after I called myself it, in fairness.

Plain Jaine.

Most of the time, he abbreviates it to PJ. That's if I'm lucky. I'm
plain and forgettable, you see. I have glasses and braces, and I'm
nothing much to look at. I'm five foot nine and skinny with zero
shape. I can't put on weight no matter how much I try. Maybe it's

because I practice MMA three times a week. I have an impressive six-pack, but teenage boys aren't interested in that sort of thing, are they? At least not on girls. Maybe one day I'll grow the tits or ass they are interested in. Maybe even both. I'm not holding my breath, though.

"You wish, weirdo!" I snap. Why? Because I am totally and utterly jealous of her.

Standing up with his back to me, he stretches, and my eyes automatically drop to his butt. They then sweep over the black leather prospect cut he's been wearing since he turned eighteen. The name of the club is emblazoned on the back. Angels of Hellfire. I know he's excited about being fully patched in next week on his nineteenth birthday.

It's his destiny to be prez, you see. Like his old man is now.

I raise my gaze just before he turns around and catches me staring at his ass.

"Anyway, it's time for me to give you my present, so let's go, sweetheart." He smirks and makes a come-hither motion with his finger, then holds out his hand for me to take. I raise mine reluctantly, rolling my eyes exaggeratedly. Grabbing it, he yanks me with ease to my feet.

I slip on my shoes, then he locks our fingers as we walk through to the communal area.

"Gusto, you got the kit ready, man?" Ace shouts over the top of the metal music that's now blaring in the background.

I shake my head and try to prize my hand from his.

"No fucking way. I'm not getting a tattoo," I whisper to him. "Gusto, put that kit away. It's not needed," I yell, shaking my head and dragging my heels.

Ace stops and turns to look at me. Raising one eyebrow, he moves his hand to grip my wrist determinedly. "We're both getting one."

I roll my eyes again and sigh, staring at him. "What are we getting and where?" I ask, feeling worried.

"Well, I'm going to get 'plain' tattooed on my dick," he replies with his wolfish grin.

I slap his arm with my free hand and try again to tug my other away, then I burst out laughing. "Plain dick?" I chuckle louder, just to be irritating. I love getting under his skin. He shoots me that familiar scowl of his.

"Isn't anything plain about my dick, PJ," he says huffily, yanking me beside him. His expression is now impassive, as he's no doubt annoyed at my offending his well-used appendage.

"Well, you said it. I was just repeating." I smirk, raising my eyebrows.

"Happy birthday, Chiquita. Now, what am I doing for you both?" Gusto interrupts our usual bickering as he unravels his kit.

I fucking hate needles.

I stare around the bar area. Most of the families have dispersed now, and the cum sluts will fill the place soon. The brothers that remain are drunk and laughing, sitting at the dark wood tables and chairs. The others are propping up the dark grey metal bulletproof bar with their heads together, discussing what they deem to be important shit. I've learned it's best not to ask or know. It's safer that way. Not that they'd tell a woman anything, anyway.

Bikers are chauvinist pricks.

"We both want the letter J scrolled behind our left ear," Ace replies, then looks at me for approval.

"You okay with that, Jaine?" Gusto raises an eyebrow at me, making sure I'm one hundred percent in agreement.

Anyone with half a brain knows you should never get a name inked on your skin. But an initial? Well, it could stand for anything, I guess.

I swallow. Inside, I feel all kinds of warmth, though. Ace is putting my initial on him.

I nod slowly. "Um, yeah, but could I have an A instead, please?"

Ace rolls his eyes, and I look up into his piercing blue gaze.

"You'll always be Ace to me," I say quietly.

He searches my face, and it feels like his eyes are looking into my soul.

He smiles and nods. "You go first, PJ." He motions for me to sit down.

I take a seat and stare at the short, stocky Gusto as he prepares the equipment. He runs his hand down his long beard before putting on a pair of white latex gloves, which he snaps in place across his wrists.

"This will sting, baby girl." He looks at me again before he starts. I guess if I want to back out, now's the time.

I nod, then swallow hard as the gun buzzes into life.

"Here, hold on to me." Ace offers me his hand for moral support and adds a reassuring smile. I clutch it as I sit and try not to move as I get my first ever tattoo. I grimace in discomfort and my mouth fills with the taste of blood as I bite the inside of my lip yet again.

Ace admires Gusto's work once it's done. "I've changed my mind," he announces.

I wrinkle my nose and slap his arm.

"I'm joking, PJ." He snickers, then ties his hair back, and I watch as Gusto inks a scrolled J behind his ear. He pulls a face, pretending to be in pain. I slap him on the arm again. It's not his first tattoo. Nowhere near. He has lots. Each one inked perfectly onto his beautiful body. Still, I'll bet mine is the only initial he has on him.

"Jaine, what's going on?" a questioning voice asks from behind me.

Shit.

"Pop! Um… it's my birthday present from Ace." I spin around as I take in the tall, slim, dark-haired man that is my dad. He's handsome but mars his features by constantly wearing a worried frown like the world is about to abruptly end. He's standing beside Ace's pop, Duke, the club prez.

My dad's a friend of the club and acts as their lawyer. He and Duke have known each other since their high school days. They were best friends, even though they're opposites.

My dad frowns even more if that's possible. His green gaze eyes my tattoo with distaste. Meanwhile, Duke laughs and pats Ace on the shoulder. "She's a keeper, this one, son."

My dad glares at him. It's his biggest fear. Me and Ace ever getting together.

I smirk as Ace's cheeks go pink.

"Happy Birthday, lil Jainie," Duke says to me as he kisses me warmly on the cheek. He looks like an older version of Ace.

"Thanks, Duke." I smile in response.

"You pussy-whipped, bro?" Ace's friend Clay, another prospect, walks across and butts in, like the dick that he is. Emilia has her arms wrapped around him. She'd no doubt have her legs wrapped around him too if there weren't children around. He smirks at me. He's not as tall as Ace, although he's not far off. He's handsome all the same, with a blonde buzzcut and big brown eyes.

"Shut up, Clay, or I'll whoop your ass on the range." I scowl at him threateningly.

"Bring it on, *Plain*." He smirks again as he emphasizes Ace's nickname for me while wrapping his arm around Emilia's waist. Jefferson walks over to join us with a matching smirk, tucking his long blonde hair behind his ear. Assholes. My eyes drift to him and then to Emilia.

I take in the voluptuous, dark-haired, olive-skinned girl. She's in all my classes even though she's Ace's age, as she was kept back due to poor attendance. We're worlds apart. She never talks to me at school. Seldom speaks to me here unless it's to say something bitchy about my looks. Jefferson's in my grade too, but he never talks to me either. I'm not cool. Too forgettable. Not good enough looking to be seen with. Emilia's wearing a tight black dress that barely covers her very generous assets. Tits hanging over the top, ass hanging out of the bottom. She's probably not wearing any panties either. She smiles at Clay, but her eyes constantly drift to Ace, and she gazes at him longingly.

He's mine.

"All done," Gusto announces as he wipes the blood from behind Ace's ear.

I walk across to look, and warmth surges through me. Ace got a tattoo for me. I must mean something to him, surely.

I smirk when Emilia frowns at the ink. "Right, let me show all you useless prospects how to shoot straight."

We go outside and do some target practice, and I whoop their asses, as I do every time.

"What did your pop get you for your birthday, Jaine?" Emilia asks as she drinks a beer while sitting on Clay's lap.

I look at her, my gaze drifting down to where she's almost rubbing herself back and forth across his dick. I turn around and continue to shoot.

"A Harley Softail Deluxe in all-black," I mutter quietly, not wanting to sound like a show-off.

"Wow. Shit, that's impressive." Clay looks surprised for a moment and then I watch as he drops his hands to Emilia's hips, encouraging her to grind against him even more.

I put my empty Glock down the back of my pants and yawn

My insides flip as I think about what I'm about to do. Or at least try to do.

Seduce my best friend.

"I'm tired. You mind if I go lie on your bed for a little while, Ace?"

He's still shooting. He's always trying to beat me, but he never fucking will. Duke says I have natural talent. A rare gift.

"Sure thing, PJ," he replies, without looking at me.

My eyes scan over him as he shoots. I'll never get tired of looking at him.

I can feel Emilia's glare on me. If I'm on Ace's bed, at least he can't fuck her on it.

Putting my hand on his shoulder, I whisper in his ear. "You'll never shoot better than me, so you may as well give up trying."

"Screw you, sweetheart." He growls in annoyance and shrugs my hand off. I make the L shape with my finger and thumb on my forehead and laugh even louder.

"You wish, loser," I yell back as I walk away, flipping him the bird.

"Well, you can now she's legal, Jace," Emilia announces with a smirk as she takes another sip from her beer.

She's looking at me with her eyes narrowed. It's like she knows exactly what I intend to do.

Making my way back through the clubhouse, I go into Ace's room, close the door, and collapse on the bed.

Shit. Am I going to be able to go through with this? Will he want to fuck me? I mean, I'm not like Emilia. I'm not pretty or curvaceous.

I'm Plain fucking Jaine, after all.

I strip down to my top and panties. Placing my glasses and scrunchie on the nightstand, I get under the covers and find myself drifting off. I'm awoken, I'm not sure how much later, when the mattress sinks beside me.

"Hey, sweetheart," he says quietly.

I frown as I open my eyes, feeling completely disorientated for a moment until I remember I'm in Ace's bed.

He's lying on his side, resting his head on his elbow and staring down at me with a small smile playing on his lips. The leathery smell of his cut is almost as intoxicating as the musky, aromatic smell of his cologne.

"Hey you," I whisper as my eyes drink him in.

I close them and roll onto my back, stretching out with my hands above my head.

When I open them, Ace's eyes are on my chest. I glance down, and my hardened nipples are pressed against my top.

I look at him, and his blue eyes search my green ones.

"Ace?" I whisper so quietly it's almost inaudible.

It's now or never, so leaning forward, I press my lips gently against his. I quickly lie back down, conscious that I have no real experience when it comes to kissing. Well, not proper kissing with tongues. My cheeks heat, and I bite my lip nervously. My fingers toy with the cover as I start to worry about how he'll react.

What if he doesn't want me?

He frowns and looks confused. "Do you want me to kiss you, PJ?"

I close my eyes in mortification and nod. "Yes," I whisper.

My heart is beating so hard I can feel it pounding against my ribs, and I'm sure they'll snap at any moment.

I'm not sure how long passes. Minutes? Hours? Eventually, he leans over and gently presses his mouth to mine. His breath is warm and his touch soft. His teeth scrape against my bottom lip, and his tongue trails across the seam of my closed mouth, asking to be let in.

My best friend is kissing me. Ace is kissing me.

I part my lips, and his tongue slips boldly inside to tangle with my own. I groan softly as I welcome the taste of tequila, minty tooth-paste, and everything Ace. Taking my reaction as a green light, he deepens the kiss, his mouth becoming more demanding. He quickly steals away my breath, my heart, and my soul. I run my fingers through his hair, relishing how soft it is. Lifting my top, he cups my small breasts in his calloused, rough hands. His fingers squeeze my nipples, causing them to pebble with the resultant jolt of desire trav-eling straight to my clit. I gasp, and my hips raise reactively.

"I want you, Ace," I whisper against his lips.

CHAPTER TWO

JAINE

Ten Years Earlier (Age Eighteen)
The Angels of Hellfire Clubhouse, Rising, California

ACE STANDS UP AND LOCKS THE DOOR BEFORE MOVING ACROSS TO lift my top over my head, pull my panties down my legs, then gently part my thighs.

"You're fucking beautiful." He stares at me with darkened eyes, and I feel my cheeks redden. I've never had a man look at me naked before. Joining me on the bed, he kneels in front of me and spreads my thighs farther apart.

Dropping his hand to my bare pussy, he gently runs his fingers up and down my entrance before pushing one inside.

"And so fucking wet." He smirks, then watches my reaction as he pushes another inside me. It feels tight and slightly uncomfortable. Turning his hand palm upwards, he slowly moves them back and forth, his thumb circling my clit at the same time.

"You want to come on my hand, PJ?"

I nod, my hips instinctively rising to grind against his fingers.

"Tell me." He stops temporarily. I know he wants me to be completely sure.

"Yes, I want to do that." I nod at him, my cheeks heating further.

I feel the pressure gradually build. It's so intense with him watching my reactions to what he's doing to me. It feels so goddamn good.

My stomach is coiled so tightly, and then the release rushes through me as the orgasm takes hold. My eyes widen as I scream out his name. I try to push his hand away and close my legs, but he doesn't let me, and the orgasm rolls straight into another.

As I lie there panting, he stands and removes his clothes, his eyes never leaving mine. I've seen him with no top on loads of times, and in shorts too. But I've always been shy when I've looked at his body, never wanting to be caught blatantly staring. Now I can relish in the sight of his defined torso, muscular build, and the V at the bottom of his eight pack. My gaze follows the trail of dark hair leading inside his shorts, his bulge straining against the front of them.

He wants me as much as I want him. That much is obvious.

I don't have to imagine what his erection looks like for very long, as he quickly removes his shorts and rolls a condom efficiently over his dick. He's body confident, unlike me. Why wouldn't he be? He's truly fucking beautiful. He stands proudly as my gaze drifts slowly over him. I lick my lips and panic inwardly. He's huge. His girth is almost as thick as my wrist. What if it doesn't fit?

He rejoins me on the bed and presses his upper body against mine.

"You sure about this?" His blue eyes search my face as he gently pushes my hair behind my ear before placing his lips softly against my tattoo.

"Yes, I'm sure." I nod. I've never wanted anything so badly in my whole life.

He leans forward and presses his mouth against mine again, his tongue exploring and tasting, deepening the kiss until I can scarcely breathe. Trailing his wet tongue down my neck, he moves further to take first one nipple and then the other in his mouth, sucking them in and biting them almost painfully. I never want him to stop.

His mouth moves slowly down my abdomen as his hands part my thighs. I gasp at the sensation when his tongue runs up my slit, and he parts my soft folds by sucking them gently into his mouth.

He thrusts his tongue inside me, and the sound of my slick wetness fills the room. His fingers circle my clit before he replaces them with his mouth, sucking it hard and nibbling it with his teeth.

The sensations are too much. I try to move away, but his hands grip my hips and hold me still as his mouth devours me. I drop my hands to his hair, pulling on it as I come loudly on his face.

"Yeah, that's it, PJ," he murmurs against my clit as he continues to lap at my release. "Damn, you taste so fucking sweet."

Lifting his head, he kisses me on the mouth, my cum now covering both our faces, my taste on both our tongues.

He positions himself between my thighs. Using one arm to support his weight, he grips his dick in the other, rubbing its blunt head up and down my folds, then using the tip to circle my clit.

"Tell me what you want, PJ. I need to hear you say it. I need you to be sure."

I feel my cheeks redden, but there's no going back now.

"I need you inside me, Ace," I whisper.

He rubs his dick up and down my entrance again. His eyes

never leave mine as he slowly pushes in, inch by perfect inch. I feel pressure and then pain. I clutch onto him, my nails digging into his back as I press my face against his shoulder.

"You okay?" He pulls back and looks down at me with a worried expression.

I nod. I'm not sure if he knew I was a virgin or not. Still, it doesn't matter. I'm sure as hell not one now.

"Yeah, you're just so… big," I say breathlessly, panting as I try to disperse the pain.

"Told you there isn't anything plain about my dick, sweetheart." He smirks as he kisses me gently on the mouth.

Staying inside me, he changes position and kneels, resting my feet on his shoulders. He pulls out almost entirely and then thrusts straight back in.

I gasp at how deep he's gone. It's painful, but there's pleasure mixed with it now.

"You like that?" His questioning eyes search mine.

I look up at him, my gaze taking in every inch of his handsome face before dropping to where he's buried deep inside me.

I nod. I clench around him, letting him know I want and need more.

He leans his head back and closes his eyes. "Jesus, PJ. You're so fucking tight."

He starts to drive in and out. Long, deep thrusts that fill me each time. He leans forward so my legs are against my chest as he continues to fuck me, his mouth sucking hard on my neck.

My core immediately starts to coil again as he connects with every single spot he should inside. I drop my legs and wrap them around his waist, and my arms snake around his neck, loving the feel of his body as he rocks against me.

"Ace," I groan loudly as my inner walls convulse around him.

"Fuck." He grunts as I pull him over the edge with me. I watch as his face contorts with pleasure. I don't think I've ever loved him more than I do right this second. Right when he's only mine and no one else's. His dick twitches inside me as he fills the condom with his cum in short, steady thrusts.

We lie afterward, a heap of twisted, sweaty limbs, his body still partially covering mine. I rub my nose against his neck, wrapping my arms around him, needing to feel him close. Eventually, he rolls onto his back, takes off the condom, ties a knot in it, and throws it on the floor.

"Ew. Remind me never to walk barefoot in here again, Ace."

He chuckles loudly, pulling me against him and kissing my forehead.

It's a perfect moment. He's perfect. It was perfect.

"You know what just happened changes everything, don't you, PJ?" he says quietly, exhaling at the same time.

I nod. I don't have the heart to tell him things will change anyway, as I have to move to Connecticut in a few weeks. I've worked out how I'll be able to travel back and forth, though, so it's not all bad. He's worth the effort it'll take.

Why? Because I love him.

"I know." I snuggle into his side and drift off to sleep.

I'm awoken later by voices. Not overly loud voices where I can hear what's being said, but at a sound level where I can hear mumbling.

Stretching out, I reach for Ace, but the other side of the bed is cold and empty, so he's been gone for some time. I press my face against his pillow, inhaling his familiar scent, a contented smile spreading across my face.

Naked, I walk to the door. Is it Ace who's talking with someone? It's not that late. Only around eleven p.m., so I'm guessing many of the brothers will still be here. The cum sluts will undoubtedly be out in full force, servicing all their needs now their old ladies have left and can't bear witness. It's not like they don't know what goes on, though.

I know I shouldn't, as eavesdroppers never hear good of themselves, but I put my ear against the door. I still can't hear anything clearly as it's way too thick. I open it a fraction, and I can make out that it's Ace and Clay talking.

"Jesus, tell me you didn't fuck Plain Jaine? Em said you looked like you were thinking about it, but I didn't believe her. There's no way you would…"

"Shut up, asshole," Ace hisses, interrupting him.

Clay laughs out loud.

"Holy shit. You really did. What the hell were you thinking? I mean, you're lowering your standards, Jace. PJ's a nice girl, but she's no looker, is she?"

"I said shut up!"

Clay snickers, refusing to let it go. "Well, I didn't have our future prez down for the type who hands out pity fucks. I mean, that's bad enough, but to fuck PJ, then move straight on to Emilia. Shit, even I wouldn't be that disrespectful."

There's a pause.

"It's PJ's birthday. I could hardly say no when she came on to me. Plus, I'm never going to turn down free pussy. Anyway, she's keeping my bed warm, so I may see if she's up for another round or two before morning."

I gently close the door and lean my back against it. Tears prick my eyes and a lump forms in my throat.

I mean nothing to Ace. That much is clear. Just another notch on his bedpost, despite being his so-called best friend. Worst still, he intended to stick his dick back in me after fucking Emilia. Gross.

"Asshole," I mutter out loud. I switch my gaze from the darkness of the room to the full moon outside the window. I can't spend my life standing on the sidelines, watching Ace fuck a conveyor belt of women. He's the future club prez. They'll be lining up with their legs spread, each waiting for their goddamn turn. My heart wouldn't be capable of watching that day after day.

It's barely surviving now, watching him with Emilia.

Ugh, I hate that bitch.

I go into the bathroom and clean myself up, then quickly get dressed. Opening the bedroom door, I scan the corridor to make sure the coast is clear. It is. He's likely fucking someone else now. He can't keep his dick in his pants, and he's happy to stick it in any warm, wet hole. Maybe I was no good and didn't satisfy him. Maybe that's it.

Humiliation and pain flow through me, and I bite back the tears. I make my way into the communal area. It's loud, and the men are in varying degrees of undress, either fucking or being sucked off by cum sluts. I've seen it all before, though. Nothing shocks me anymore about what goes on in this shitshow of a place.

The music comes to a sudden stop, so I walk across to the jukebox. I select my favorite song. The one that reminds me of me.

Creep by Radiohead.

Let's face it, the lyrics are accurate.

I am a creep. I am a weirdo. I don't belong here.

Turning to leave, I walk straight into Emilia. I take in her pretty face, made unattractive by the smirk covering it and the evilness seeping through her olive skin.

"Well, if it isn't little Plain Jaine." She takes a drag from the cigarette she's smoking and blows it right in my face. "Aww, what's the matter? Did Jace leave you all on your own after he fucked you? Maybe now you'll realize you mean nothing to him. Now he's had you, he'll think of you as just another cum slut."

"Get out of my face, Emilia!" I push her back, and she laughs.

"Everyone knows I'm going to end up his old lady anyway. He's already hinted at it. I mean, why would he want you? Have you looked at yourself in the mirror? You're ugly." She snickers, then looks at me almost pityingly.

I push past her and storm out of the clubhouse.

Jogging the three miles home, I pack immediately, tears streaming down my face, her comments and bitchy laugh still ringing in my ears.

I need to get away from the Angels of Hellfire.

I need to get away from Rising.

I need to get away from Jason 'Ace' Steele.

———

IN THE MORNING, I MAKE MY EXCUSES TO MY STUNNED POP, TELLING him I need to go to Connecticut sooner rather than later to get settled. Then, getting on my Harley, I set off, and I don't look back. My stuff will be sent separately by courier.

When I reach my destination one week later, I look at my phone and take in the countless missed calls from Ace. The voicemails I'll never listen to. The messages I haven't read and never will. I buy a new SIM card and put the other one in my pocket. Then I send my contact details to Duke and my pop with strict instructions to not pass them to anyone else.

They'll both realize something's gone down between him and me.

And Ace?

Well, I think of the lyrics of my song.

I only wished he had thought I was special. And I only hope he does notice when I'm not around.

Wishing and hoping don't mean jack, though.

That shit's for goddamn fools.

Tomorrow?

Well, it's the start of the rest of my Ace-free life.

CHAPTER THREE

JAINE

Present Day (Age Twenty-Eight)
NYPD

THE HARSH ECHO OF MY FOUR-INCH HEELS DEPICTS MY ANNOYANCE and agitation as I make my way through the NYPD headquarters. The stark white walls and grey tiled floor are bland and uninteresting, like most of the assholes who work here. Both coverings offer an easy-to-clean surface for wiping blood and other bodily fluids off. A clean down must have taken place recently as the rawness of the Lysol keeps catching the back of my throat.

I don't make eye contact with anyone. I know exactly where I'm going. I've been here a million times before. Same shit, different day. The receptionist, who looks to be around eighteen, glances in my direction. I hold my hand up, silently indicating that it's best not to speak. Not if she knows what's good for her. Her mouth opens and closes like a goldfish, but no words come out, which is just as well.

Interview room three is my destination.

I don't even bother to knock before I open the door and walk straight in.

"Ah, Ms. Jones. We've been expecting you." Detective Prescott moves to stand.

Is he trying to pretend to be a fucking gentleman? Laughable. I motion for him to stay seated. Looking around, I take in the round-faced silver clock on the wall of the non-descript room.

Nine-thirty a.m. Give me ten minutes with this asshole.

A basic pine-looking canteen table separates Prescott from my client, and each sits on chairs that wouldn't look out of place in a children's classroom.

Gabriel is handsome for a pig. I'd estimate him to be in his late thirties. He's well-dressed, his suit made to measure in dark grey. He must come from money, as the salary he gets paid for doing this shitty job wouldn't allow him to afford thousand-dollar suits. Either that, or he married exceptionally well. His crisp white shirt contrasts nicely against the dark grey, his NYPD tie, and his tanned skin. He looks a bit like Henry Cavill, but not as thickset. His eyes are laughing at me, which pisses me off further. One of these days, I'm going to shoot the fucker right between those piercing blues.

Both of us are about to play the same repetitive goddamn game.

"Take a seat, Ms. Jones," he offers in a condescending tone.

I don't sit. Instead, I get straight to the point.

"Detective Prescott, can I ask, are you charging my client with anything today, or are you merely trying to waste my valuable time?" I place my leather briefcase on the table and straighten my navy pinstripe suit. Leaning over, I put my hands flat on the cool surface. His gaze instantly drops to my cleavage, which is now at eye level and no doubt perfectly displayed by my low-cut white blouse.

I raise my eyebrows at him, and he smirks.

"There was a murder in Brighton Beach last night, Ms. Jones. A senior member of the Bratva was killed. Your man here," he motions his head towards him, "was seen leaving the vicinity not long after." He taps the eraser end of his pencil on the desk slowly and repeatedly. I want to grab the fucking thing and either snap it in half or stick it up his ass, but I stop myself. Just.

"Are there any witnesses, Detective Prescott? My client lives in New York, so it's not unreasonable to expect him to ride through Brighton Beach from time to time." My tone is clipped and professional.

Prescott and I glare at each other. We both know my client may well be responsible, but with no proof, he can kiss my ass.

"No witnesses, or at least none that will step forward." He glances at me, then looks back at the pencil.

He's pulled us in as a warning. To let me know they're the primary suspects.

"So, my client is free to go. Is that correct?"

"Yes, he's free to go." Detective Prescott presses down on the pencil, and it snaps in half.

I turn my attention to the other man in the room. My client is leaning back in his chair with his muscular arms folded in front of him, looking bored. His long wavy hair hangs a few inches below his shoulders, its blondness making him look rather angelic. In direct contrast, the sleeves of his Henley are pulled up, showing the plethora of tattoos he wears across his body. Some of them are obscene, and all of them depict violence, emphasizing the demon he *truly* is. The leather cut he's wearing displays his rank—enforcer—and the name of the MC he belongs to—the Iron Scorpions. Alongside is the easily recognizable one percent outlaw patch.

"You're free to go, Blaze," I mutter at him.

He stands up slowly and stretches like a cat before smirking at Prescott. "Nice seeing you again, Detective," he drawls.

He then turns to look at me with his eyebrows raised. I glare in response. This isn't over. If he is responsible, he's been way too fucking careless this time.

"Get the fuck out of here, and don't push your luck," I hiss at him.

He swaggers to the door and opens it, saluting Prescott before closing it behind him.

I immediately slam my hands on the table. "Stop wasting my fucking time, Gabe."

He ignores me, his gaze still directed at the remaining half pencil he's currently tapping against the tabletop. The other half is across the room somewhere.

"We both know he's as guilty as sin, Jaine. Or at least, the Scorpions as a whole are," he says in a calm voice.

"We know nothing." I lean forward, and his gaze immediately drops to my cleavage again. "My eyes are up here, Prescott." I glare at him.

He smirks. "Let's be clear. Every time I know it's one of those fucking MC outlaw bikers of yours, I will drag them in. Personally, if I have to."

"Of mine? Really?" I roll my eyes and shake my head. "What's the point in pulling them in if you don't have anything to pin on them?"

He leans back in his chair and looks me up and down, slowly undressing me with his eyes.

"Inconvenience? To let them know I'm watching? Or maybe I just want any excuse to see you," he rasps as he links his fingers across his torso and smirks.

I look at the time. Nine-forty a.m. Ten minutes, as predicted.

"Fuck you, Gabe." I pick up my briefcase and leave the room, slamming the door behind me as hard as I can. My heels make the same clipping sound on the floor as I exit the building.

Hailing a cab, I head straight for the Iron Scorpions' clubhouse, which is one hour out of town.

I message Delaney, aka Prez, aka Razr.

Jaine: *I'm on my way.*
Delaney: *Shit.*
Jaine: *You'd better not be fucking any of those cum sluts.*
Delaney: *Nope. I'd like to have kids someday, so I need to keep hold of my balls.*
Jaine: *What woman would be stupid enough to birth your seed, Prez?*
Delaney: *The one I'm messaging right now, hopefully.*
Jaine: *Oh, so you're messaging me AND some other bitch?*
Delaney: *Very funny. Get your ass here so we can practice baby-making.*

The Iron Scorpions' Clubhouse, Brightling, New York

"Here's the thing. I can get you off with a certain amount of shit, but if you get caught red-handed murdering a Russian, there's only so much I can do. If you want to act like you're more powerful than Jesus Christ himself and can walk on water, then have at it with your blatant disregard of the law but find yourself alternative legal representation!" I bang my hand on the table as I stand in front of the council. The top is carved with the club insignia. A scorpion and dagger.

"You sure Prescott wasn't pulling me in so you could pay him a visit, Jaine? That cock sucker didn't take his eyes off your tits the whole time we were in there." Blaze smirks and glances at the others, causing them to snicker immaturely.

I glare at him.

"Don't be so fucking disrespectful." Delaney points his finger at him.

"I don't need you fighting my battles thank you," I mutter. I direct my attention back to Blaze. "If it was you then you must have been seen. Or someone wearing a Scorpions' cut was. Prescott might be a lot of things, but stupid isn't one of them. He knows you're guilty. He pretty much fucking told me so. This was a goddamn warning. What the fuck's going on anyway? Why the hell are you going after Bratva? We don't need World War III kicking off in the center of NYC. That shit won't end well for anyone!"

"It's council business," Bomber mumbles.

I turn and glare at him, taking in his black buzzcut and even blacker demonic eyes. He sits hunched in a chair that's in no way large enough to accommodate his bulky well over six-foot frame comfortably. He's not a handsome man, or at least not to me, but maybe that's because I don't like or trust the fucker.

"Oh, it's council business, is it Mr. VP? Well, next time I get a call from NYPD, I'll let the council handle Detective Prescott, shall I? Let's not forget that I never asked to represent this club. I got dragged into this shit, remember? I don't need this, especially when I don't know what the fuck is going on half the time and have to act blindfolded. Screw you, and screw this." I pick up my briefcase and leave the room, slamming the door behind me again as hard as I can. It's satisfying if nothing else.

"Assholes," I mumble as I make my way past the clubhouse bar and communal area. The walls are white, contrasting against the gunmetal grey tables, chairs, and bulletproof bar. The floor is black and easy clean. Shitty soft rock music plays in the background. I grimace at the sight of one of the cum sluts being fucked on the pool table by a seriously obese brother. Excellent. On top of all the other crap I have to deal with today, I now need to bleach my fucking eyeballs. I thought I'd left this shit behind when I left Rising.

Nope. Apparently, I have a type.

Asshole presidents of MCs.

Not that I knew what Delaney was. He's a property magnate. Owns loads of New York and is a self-made billionaire. Little did I know when I met him that he wore a cut under that ten-thousand-dollar business suit of his. Before I knew it, I was representing his club.

I didn't need the business or the money.

He found out about my MC background through Duke and then discovered my pop was the legal representation for the Angels of Hellfire in California. Delaney managed to get me in front of him by citing he wanted to utilize my services to handle his property portfolio and other business ventures. He did. It wasn't a lie. But then the manipulative asshole asked if I'd also represent the Scorpions in exchange for them forming a mutually beneficial alliance with the Angels. It was tantamount to blackmail.

Duke, my pop, and Delaney all convinced me to do it, even though I was reluctant. That was four years ago. Delaney and I have been fucking ever since. Duke stepped down last year, although we still speak most days because he's still my point of contact.

He is now prez of the Angels. Him. Ace.

Inside Delaney's room at the clubhouse, I strip, my eyes scanning around the familiar space. The bed and furniture are all black leather and scream quality. There's a bookcase filled with first editions and books on business and economics. The room and everything it contains doesn't fit in this outlaw environment, and at times, I'm not sure the man himself does. I mean, he's successful. Why risk your life every day when you don't need to? Then again, he was born into this world. He's also a bloodthirsty fucker and extremely handy with a blade; his weapon of choice.

I inhale the sandalwood smell of his cologne, which lingers in the air.

I head for the shower, wanting to wash off the NYPD stench. Not long later, I'm aware of the screen opening and closing behind me.

"You okay?" Delaney mumbles in my ear, his arms encircling my waist and his erection poking me in the ass.

I shiver as he pours cold body wash on my back before rubbing my shoulders, his fingers pressing against my tense flesh to get rid of the kinks and knots. His hands move around to cup my tits, his fingertips squeezing my nipples almost painfully, causing pangs of desire to shoot straight to my clit. I groan and press my ass back against his hard-on, needing him inside me, seeking the release.

I turn around and kiss him, my mouth desperate for the familiarity of his. His tongue searches and tastes as his hands drop to my pussy, pushing two fingers deep inside as his thumb circles my clit. I groan loudly, throwing my head back as my body starts to soar.

"Come on my hand, Jaine," he growls against my throat as he sucks hard on my neck.

He pushes in a third finger and quickens his movements, and my body erupts as the waves of pleasure course through me.

"Fuck your fingers, Delaney. I need your dick inside me," I whisper against his mouth.

He lifts me and places his hands under my ass as I reach mine down to guide the blunt head of his erection between my swollen folds. He thrusts in and groans against my throat as my pussy clenches around him. He drives into me as the water cascades over us. My nails dig into his back as my body moves with his. Adjusting me so I'm pressed against the shower wall, he positions my legs so they're flush against his torso, allowing him to go almost too deep.

"God, yes," I groan as his dick bangs against my cervix.

"Fuck," he growls as his movements become faster and more erratic; a sign he's getting close.

The orgasm flows through me, leaving me dizzy, and my walls clench around his dick so tightly it drags him over the edge with me.

"Fuck. Yeah, that's it. Jesus, your sweet pussy's going to fucking kill me one of these days," he pants against my neck before lowering my feet to the floor, his cum running down the inside of my thighs.

I hang onto him as I regain my balance, then we finish washing each other in comfortable silence.

As we dry off in the bedroom, I look at the man I've spent the last four years of my life with.

Paul Delaney is handsome and then some. The thirty-two-year-old has pale skin due to his Irish ancestry, making him look like he's been sculpted from marble. His hair is long, straight, and strawberry blonde, and his eyes are green. He's tall at around six-four, which is just as well, as with my standard four-inch heels, I'm over six foot. His build is relatively lean, but he's pure muscle. His body is bumped and ridged to perfection, tattooed and scarred to fuck. On his back, he has a tattoo of the insignia for the Iron Scorpions. All the brothers have it, and they wear it with pride. My eyes drop to his dick. Even flaccid, it's still fucking huge. He smirks at me.

"Want some more?" He raises an eyebrow.

I shake my head and smile at him. "I need to get back to work, Delaney, so keep your cock away from me as I need to be able to walk." I chuckle as I wrap a bathrobe around my nakedness.

He smirks contentedly as he leans back on the bed with his

hands behind his head, a small towel now wrapped around his slim hips, watching as I sit and dry my hair.

I know what he's going to say before he says it. It's what he always says these days. Has for the past few months. I avoid answering when I can, but he's got me cornered.

"Jaine, are you going to agree to be my old lady? We've been together for four years now. I want to wife you, you know?"

I look at him in the reflection in the mirror. I mean, any sane woman would jump at the chance of being Mrs. Paul Delaney. A property magnate billionaire and Manhattan's most eligible bachelor. He also has a huge dick and knows exactly what to do with it. What the fuck is wrong with me? Why don't I just say yes?

"I'm not ready to ride bitch and wear a cut stating I'm the property of someone." I mutter the feeble excuse. One I've used several times before.

He rubs his hand across his face, exhaling loudly. "I've already said you don't have to do either of those things."

"What about my extra-curricular activities?" I bite my lip, looking at him.

"I've already said you don't have to give them up, either. Not if you don't want to."

I watch in the mirror as he gets off the bed and walks over to me. Pulling me to a standing position, he wraps one arm around my waist and tilts my chin up with the other hand, so I have no option but to look at him. Our green eyes connect.

"I love you, Jaine," he whispers, placing a soft kiss on my forehead. "Do you love me?" He looks down at me, his expression gentle. Hopeful.

There's an uncomfortable silence.

He drops his arms and starts pacing the floor, running his hand through his hair. "It's because of him, isn't it? It's always been because of him." he hisses.

I frown and pretend I don't know who he's referring to, even though I know full well.

"I'm not sure who you mean." I blatantly lie. I'm not proud of it.

"Jason fucking Steele."

I shake my head. "Don't be stupid. I've not seen Ace for ten years. He's probably married with half a dozen kids by now."

"You speak to Duke every other day!" His tone is accusing.

"Because of the alliance. I never ask about Ace, and he knows not to mention him. I'm not interested in what he's doing or who he's doing it with. Now, can we talk about this another time as I need to get back to the office?" I dress quickly, anxious to be on my way, fed up of having what's quickly becoming a way too frequent confrontation.

Pulling on my jacket, I pick up my phone and notice I have several missed calls from Pop. I stick it in my briefcase.

Walking over to Delaney, I snake my arms around his waist. He's tense, but he pulls me snugly against him, kissing the top of my head before letting out a long sigh.

"I'm just conscious I'm not getting any younger, and in this life, more so with all the Bratva shit going on you never know what day will be your last. I want a family before the chance of having anything normal is taken away from me. I want that with you, Jaine. No-one else."

"Let's talk about it over the weekend, okay?"

He deserves the honest to God truth from me. That I don't love him. Not like that. Never have, and after four years together, it's not likely I ever will. You can't force feelings, same as you can't switch them off.

Trust me. I've tried.

I've never alluded to love Delaney. Not once. What started as a purely physical and mental attraction has remained so. It's never progressed beyond. At least not for me. I think deep down he knows that. He just wants to hear me say the damn words. He needs the finality. Then he can make his own decisions.

Why haven't I told him?

I enjoy what he and I share. It's suited my purpose, at least until now. Until recently, it suited his too. And I don't want to hurt him. I may not be in love with him, but I love him all the same. I'm also fiercely protective of him. I know his past. He may be a fucking madman, but he wasn't born that way.

Deep down, I know he deserves someone who can give him what he wants. It's only fair. If it's a wife and kids he needs, then that person isn't me.

CHAPTER FOUR

JAINE

Jones & Associates Legal, Upper East Side, New York

"DID YOU HAVE SEX WITH YOUR PREZ BOYFRIEND AT LUNCHTIME, Jaine? You're walking like a cowboy." Cherry mutters dryly. She doesn't even bother to look up, so I'm not sure how she can possibly observe and comment on how I'm walking. Her face is stuck in a book as per usual.

"Shut up, Cherry," I grumble, not in the mood.

"Oh, you definitely did because you're hangry, which means the only thing you've had to eat today is dick." She turns the page of some reverse harem story she's reading. It's her current smut of choice. "Do you think I could borrow some of those biker boys? I need three to make all my orgasmic dreams come true, apparently."

I don't answer, resulting in her looking up. I cast my eyes over her long crimson hair and red, pouty lips. Her hair is dyed, and her lips surgically enhanced. Still, her skin is creamy and perfect, and her face heart-shaped and beautiful. She's hourglass perfection in a compact five-foot-five body, with long legs, massive tits, and a bootylicious butt which are all displayed to perfection by her little pink playsuit. She rolls her big baby blues at me as she waits for me to respond.

"I'm sure they'd be more than happy to take part in your sexual shenanigans, provided you don't mind that they've been sticking their dicks in the cum sluts at the clubhouse." I shake my head as I sit at my desk and fire up my laptop.

While I wait, I gaze around. Our offices are monochrome, with grey carpets, white walls, and black furniture. The JAL logo is circular and is displayed behind the reception area in full bronzed stainless steel. We have ten members of staff—eight lawyers, excluding me, and two admin. Cherry and Sasha, my two best friends, also work here. Well, work is perhaps an over-exaggeration on their part.

While we graduated from Yale Law School together, they much prefer to intern without pay. That way, Cherry can read filthy romance novels uninterrupted all day, then try to live out her sexual fantasies by using the bikers as very willing participants. Sasha, meanwhile, can take two-hour lunch breaks or just come to work when the mood takes her. Their families are loaded. Being lawyers merely adds to their marriage marketability. It proves to both their future intendeds and New York's high society that they're intelligent and can hold an adult conversation among like-minded peers and fellow professionals. That's all that matters. It was never going to be put to any use. They'll be married off to eligible bachelors in due course, so no need to work for a living or to earn a damn cent. Their future requirement in life is to look pretty and decorative, host coffee mornings, and produce heirs for their billionaire husbands. I let them share an office with me more for the entertainment value than anything else.

"I'm back! What have I missed?" Sasha sashays into the office laden down with designer shopping bags. She drops them on the floor, then collapses her tall, slim self onto her chair like she's just run a marathon. It's hard work spending vast sums of mommy and daddy's money. Pushing her long chestnut hair behind her ear, her hazel eyes drift over Cherry and me. She crosses her legs and adjusts her white trouser suit accordingly. She always looks immaculate.

"Jaine fucked the prez at lunchtime. Not the old one who runs the country, young Paul Delaney," Cherry mumbles, her face now back in her book.

"Really, Jaine? Was it just what the doctor ordered? Just as well it wasn't the old guy. You'd probably have killed him, and then where would we all be?" Sasha says, looking thoughtful. "Do they have to do the chimney smoke thing when the president dies?"

I look at her. "No, that's the Pope, babe." I rub my hand across my face. God help me. "Honestly, why the fuck do I put up with you two?" I can't help but chuckle.

"Because you love us, and fortunately for you, we love you too," Cherry says without looking up.

"Yes, because we're BFFs and will be forever," Sasha adds in a sing-song voice, standing up to wrap her arms around me and drowning me in whatever fragrance it is that costs a billion dollars an ounce these days. Shit, I can almost taste the vanilla notes, and I fucking hate vanilla.

My burner phone vibrates.

I don't need to check for the name of the message sender because only one person has the number.

Delaney: *Extra-curricular just in. Call me.*

"Excuse me, girls."

Cherry and Sasha both look up with wide eyes. They suspect I do something illegal out of hours, even though I've never told them what it is. I never would. That knowledge would put them in too much danger. When the burner phone goes, they know that's what it relates to, though. Without having to say a word, they know not to pry.

I go into the ladies' restroom, and I call him.

"It's me, baby. Sorry, I know you're not having the best of days, but this one's urgent—a known sex trafficker of young children. There's only one problem. Killing him may draw attention. He's another Bratva in the same location as the one Blaze is suspected of taking out. They're not related as far as I know. This one's got a two-million-dollar price tag on his head."

I exhale. "You read the details, Delaney? You're happy they're accurate, and the target is guilty as charged?" I always ask him. It's way too dangerous to email the information more times than is necessary. I trust his judgment implicitly. If he says the creep is asking for a bullet between the eyes, then that's what the fucker will be served.

"Yes. It all checks out. The area will be crawling with pigs, though, so are you sure about this one?"

"Provided they're not related, yes. Send me the image. I'll take out the trash this evening." I put the phone down, then wash my hands and face. Staring at myself in the mirror, I take a couple of deep breaths and make my way back to my desk.

"I need to go, ladies, but if you want a night at the clubhouse tomorrow, let me know. Cherry, if you need me to line up three of the brothers to fuck you over the pool table, I can make the arrangements." I say with a small grin.

"Ooh, live entertainment! How fab! Count me in!" Sasha says with a beaming smile.

Cherry rolls her eyes. "Well, if they're going to fill me up with their moonshine beforehand, I'm game."

I laugh. "It's not moonshine you'll be full of, babe. It's cum."

She's not lying—she's up for anything. Guess it comes from attending an all-girl convent school. She missed out. Then again, she probably still saw way more action than Plain fucking Jaine.

Switching off my laptop, I grab my briefcase and leave the office, taking the floor to the penthouse in the same building. My reasoning for living there? Why commute when you don't have to? Life's too goddamn short to spend it traveling between places. The whole building is owned by Delaney, except for my apartment, which I insisted on paying full price for last year.

Jaine's Apartment, Upper East Side, New York

I STRIP NAKED, THEN OPEN THE SEALED PACKAGES, QUICKLY changing into the brand-new black leggings, black long-sleeved top, and thick black socks. Black flat boots will finish my look, which I'll put on once I'm at street level. Opening the purpose-built safe room at the rear of my apartment, I select one of several guitar cases before closing the secure door behind me with a loud clunk. Lifting the lid, I inspect my rifle, load it, then change the scope for one more suitable for the time of day and setting. Satisfied, I close the case, put on the brand-new black puffer jacket, and shove my new balaclava in the pocket. Once outside, I put on the boots, pick up the case, and then take public transport to Brighton Beach.

It's dark when I get off the bus. Litter lines the streets, but fortunately, as it's cold, the smell of decaying trash is tolerable. I keep my head down and my hood up to not attract any attention to myself, then walk briskly to the location. There are pigs about, but it's not as bad as I feared.

"Hi. Sorry, I've managed to lock myself out. Could you let me in, please?" I speak into the door entry system in the building opposite.

"Yeah, sure." It's a gruff male voice. The tone of a man that never questions a woman when she says things like this since he thinks the female species is incompetent. It works in my favor. I make my way inside and up onto the roof of the building. I know from there I'll be able to see into the apartment of the Bratva target.

It's cold. I put on my balaclava and stick my hands in my pockets to keep them warm. My breath is visible in the cold night air. I take in the lights of the New York skyline, then prepare my nest and position my rifle. Then I wait.

Hours pass. My only distraction is watching the yellow cabs move like tiny ants across the streets far below. I'm about to give up and head home when the lights switch on in the target's apartment. I quickly lie down, look through the scope, and take in the greasy fat fuck with his comb-over hair. He's that type—the sort who can't get pussy without paying for it. I know you should never judge a book, but sometimes you just know when you're staring at the dregs of society.

He moves about the apartment. It's ostentatious and filled with huge pieces of furniture and expensive gold-colored crap. I watch through the scope as he pours himself a drink.

"Enjoy it, asshole, as it'll be your last," I mutter.

He sits on the sofa, and I watch as he unzips his fly. Jesus, he's going to get his dick out and jerk off. Filthy pedo fucker.

He grabs his tiny cock and starts to stroke himself. He lays his head back on the sofa as his hand picks up the pace. I can't watch anymore of this. I pull the trigger, and seconds later, his hand stops. There's a beautiful round hole in his forehead with a trickle of blood running down. Behind him, his brains are splattered across the repugnant room.

I quickly pack up and make my way out of the building. It's not likely the Russian will be found until morning, so I take my time, being careful not to draw any attention to myself.

I give my jacket to a homeless woman, along with my boots, not too far from where I live. She doesn't question why. She's just grateful for anything that will help her keep warm on such a frigid evening. I walk the rest of the short distance in my socks.

Once home, I remove my clothes outside the entrance door, placing them into a container for items I have incinerated. Naked, I walk to the shower, turn it on to near boiling temperature, then scrub myself until my skin is bright red and glowing. Once I'm sure there are no traces of the nest property on me, I get out of the shower, spray it with bleach top to bottom, and rinse it down.

Once I'm in my pajamas, I sit on the leather sofa and call Delaney.

"You okay, Jaine? Everything sorted?" he asks quietly.

"Yeah. Everything went as planned." I reply with the exact words every time, so he knows the deed is done. "I miss you," I add, wishing he was here, suddenly missing his presence and familiarity.

"I can come over if you want?"

"No, it's okay. It's late. I just wanted you to know that I miss you."

"I miss you too. Are you and the girls coming to the clubhouse tomorrow?"

I laugh. "Yes. Cherry's decided she wants to have a reverse harem, so apparently, she needs three willing brothers to help her fulfill her most recent sexual fantasy."

He laughs loudly. "Jesus Christ. They'll be queuing up for a taste of her posh pussy."

I snicker.

"What about you?" he asks quietly.

"What about me?"

"Do you need anyone else?"

"No. All I need is you." I tell him what he wants to hear.

"Good." I can hear the relief in his voice.

"Night, Delaney."

"Night, baby."

I stare at my apartment. Like the office, it's monochrome in shades of black, white, anthracite, and silver. It's immaculate.

The two-million-dollar price tag for tonight? As usual, half will be laundered through the legal businesses run by the Scorpions. The other million will be donated to charity via discrete means. In this instance, one that cares for the victims of child sex trafficking.

Their memories can never be eradicated, but at least we can help secure them a brighter future.

CHAPTER FIVE

JAINE

The Iron Scorpions' Clubhouse, Brightling, New York

ALL EYES ARE FOCUSED ON THE HEADLINE NEWS CURRENTLY showing on the huge flat-screen TV overhanging the bar area. It's all about the Bratva scum who was shot in the head by The Exterminator.

"They know it was him as his bullets have an 'X' engraved on them, and as it came out the back of the fucker's skull along with his brains, it wasn't too difficult for the pigs to locate and identify," Flame announces with a smirk to the others, their gazes all riveted to the screen.

I look across at the club secretary who's serving behind the bar, taking in the short white hair, translucent skin, and clear blue eyes of the slim-built albino. He's the quiet sort and quite stand-offish. This is only the second time I think I've ever heard him speak, so he must be enthused.

An image of the Russian appears, and the brothers all cheer and holler in celebration of his murder by the surreptitious sniper.

I'm sitting on Delaney's lap, sipping the warm beer I've been holding in my hand for the best part of an hour. I'm not much of a drinker, and it's flat now and tastes like shit, so it's lost whatever slight appeal it had.

Delaney and I make eye contact, and he smirks as the brothers get even louder. We watch the rest of the report, trying to feign interest and portray shocked faces. Thankfully, Flame switches the TV off pretty soon after. I don't like seeing the results of my handiwork all over the press, but it comes with the territory, I guess. Everything comes at a price, and the price that fucker paid was his life

The last of the old ladies eventually trickle out the door, and the music gets turned up. The cum sluts start to surface, wearing attire that leaves pretty much nothing to the imagination. The stench of their cheap perfume fills the air and catches the back of my throat. It leaves an acrid taste in my mouth that even the lukewarm beer won't wash away. In most clubhouses, the norm is to retire them out to pasture as soon as they reach thirty. Once everything starts to head south, it'd be even more of an unpleasant sight than it is now. In their minds, they have until then to convince one of the brothers to make them their old lady. Very few make it to those heady heights. Who wants an old lady who's been fucked by pretty much every other brother in the club?

They're currently not looking pleased that three of the most eligible brothers are at the beck and call of my friend Cherry. They're standing, heads close, and whispering with their arms folded and unflattering frowns marring their heavily made-up features.

Cherry's wearing the shortest of pale blue jean shorts and a red bra top that's got barely enough stretch to cover and contain her very generous tits. Blaze is face down between her thighs, inhaling her pussy through the material. Meanwhile, she's rubbing her hands up and down Bomber and Ripper's groins.

Ripper, the sergeant at arms, is a giant of a man, olive-skinned, with long, black hair down to his waist, and large golden eyes. He's rubbing Cherry's nipples through her top while Bomber has his tongue down her throat.

"Isn't the entertainment fab!" Sasha sing-songs as she watches the live sex show. Tucking her chestnut locks behind her ear, she sips daintily on a glass of rose like she's in a fancy wine bar instead of a cum-stained, smoke-filled MC clubhouse. She looks entirely out of place in a pale blue pantsuit, matching red-soled Louboutin heels, and a ten-thousand-dollar Chanel handbag clutched in her perfectly manicured hand.

"You want to dance, pretty lady?" Dollar, the treasurer, holds out his heavily tattooed hand to her. He's by far the sweetest of the council members. Average-sized, shaggy brown hair, blue eyes, and with the cutest pair of dimples when he smiles. He looks like butter wouldn't melt. From what I've heard about him, that shit would goddamn sizzle when he gets going, never mind fucking melt.

"Ooh, don't mind if I do!" Sasha beams up at him and claps her hands excitedly before making her way to the dance floor, aka the middle of the room. Dollar immediately starts spinning her around, and she shrieks with laughter. I can't help but admire her constant joie de vivre no matter what shitshow's going on around her. She's a breath of fresh air.

Meanwhile, rolling my eyes, I take in my other friend, who's almost having a four-way on the pool table.

"Cherry, can you take your reverse harem to a bedroom, babe? It might be your fantasy, but it isn't mine, and I don't need to watch you getting laid. My eyes definitely couldn't cope with having to bear witness to that visual three times over, that's for sure," I yell across at her.

Blaze snickers and pulls her up to a sitting position. She looks disorientated. Her cheeks are pink, and her red hair's a mess. He lifts her off the pool table and throws her over his shoulder in a fireman's hold before all four disappear to the bedrooms at the back.

"Jesus, she really is going to fuck all three of them." It's barely audible. I'm saying it more to myself than anyone else.

Delaney chuckles and presses a kiss to my neck, making my whole body shiver. The physical side of our relationship has definitely never waned.

I press my lips to his, and he growls against them. "I need to pay a visit to the little ladies' room," I say with a smile. I can feel his eyes on my ass in my dark blue Daisy Dukes, so I add a little sway to my hips.

After washing my hands and face, I head back just in time to catch one of the newly recruited cum sluts sitting on Delaney's lap. She's like twenty-one or something. At this rate, she won't see twenty-two, as she obviously has a fucking death wish.

"You want some fresh pussy, Razr, baby?" she says in the sluttiest voice she can muster while straddling him, facing him front on, and grinding her ass down on his dick. Her hands are rubbing up and down his chest like she's trying to make a goddamn genie appear. She's all blonde and has fake everything. You name it, the bitch has had it altered or filled. Why? Who needs shit like that at twenty-one? Well, one thing she's not having filled is her pussy with Delaney's dick.

Maybe it's a spike in adrenaline due to last night's killing. Who knows? What I do know is I see red. Fifty shades of the fucker. Including blood red.

I storm across and pull her backward off his lap by the hair. She yelps in pain and grabs at my hand, trying to loosen my vice-like grip. Half of her shitty, glued-on extensions come away when I loosen my hold, and I grimace and shake them off in disgust. I bang the heel of my hand against her nose, and it immediately explodes.

"Delaney's mine, bitch. Do you hear me? Now, just be grateful I didn't hit you as hard as I could have because the shrapnel from your face would now be lodged in your brain, and you'd be dead," I hiss in her ear. I throw her across the floor like a rag doll. With my training, I can take down most men. This plastic Barbie has no chance.

The brothers whoop and holler at the catfight.

Assholes.

"Clean Bailey up, Mojo." Delaney exhales exaggeratedly at the longest serving cum slut. She's around my age and wearing the equivalent of dental floss, which barely covers her nipples and clit.

"Thanks, Mojo. And sorry," I add, trying my best to sound and look apologetic but failing miserably. The little bitch deserved everything she got. Maybe it was an over-reaction on my part, but she was goddamn disrespectful.

Mojo smiles at me, then tugs Bailey's hand before dragging her away in a trail of blood. DeeDee and Chanel, two of the other cum sluts, try their best to mop it up with paper towels while tottering around on ridiculously high stiletto heels.

Delaney grabs me around the waist onto his lap.

"Calm down, my jealous little spitfire," he whispers hotly against my ear.

"You let her grind on your dick?" I look at him accusingly. "Why the fuck would you do that?"

He smirks. I can feel *that* piece of his anatomy harden beneath me, no doubt at my publicly staking my claim over him.

"You wanted me to react, didn't you, you asshole?" I can feel my temper flare, and I'm ready to slap him. The fucker let her do that on purpose.

Aware of my intentions, he grabs my wrists before forcing my hands behind my back. Picking me up, he throws me over his shoulder like a goddamn caveman before carrying me to his bedroom. Once inside, he tosses me on the bed and locks the door.

I immediately get up and run at him, wanting to scratch his fucking eyeballs out, but he grabs my wrists and turns me around, pushing me roughly against the bedroom door and knocking the wind out of me. I raise my leg to knee him in the balls, but he twists out of the way before it can reach its destination. Then he kisses me. Hard.

Adrenaline, lust, and desire flow through me, and my hands immediately reach for his hair, pulling on it, my tongue pushing into his mouth as I groan in desperation.

"Fuck me, Delaney. Hard and fast," I growl against his lips as his hands squeeze my tits through my top.

"You got it," He pulls my white tank top over my head, drags my shorts down, and his hands rip off the scrap of underwear I'm wearing.

Yanking his wifebeater off, I rub his dick through his jeans before unbuttoning him to freedom, my hand wrapping around his thick, hot flesh. He groans and curses as he pulls the rest of his clothing off.

Pushing me onto the bed, he drags me by the ankles towards the edge before resting my feet on his shoulders. Grasping his dick in his hand, he rubs the blunt head up and down my folds and through my slickness, lubricating himself before thrusting in.

"Oh, God, yes," I groan as he starts to drive in and out, his mouth biting and sucking on my neck, his hands holding tightly to my waist so he can hold me in place and penetrate as deeply as he can.

"Fuck, Delaney," I whisper as my insides immediately coil.

He pistons into me, his body quickly sheening with sweat.

Faster. Harder. The silence of the room is filled with the sound of his flesh slapping loudly against mine and our matching growls of appreciation.

"I'm coming," I pant as I feel the orgasm tear through my body.

I watch as his own face contorts with pleasure. "Yeah, squeeze out every last drop, baby. Jesus Christ, your pussy is fucking magical."

My insides grip him like a vice as his cum fills me, marking my inner walls with his wet heat.

He collapses on top of me, our sweaty bodies still connected, our hearts pounding. I pant against his neck.

He holds my face in his hands and looks down at me. "I love you, Jaine. So, fucking much." He places a sweaty kiss on my lips.

Moving to rest my head on his chest, I close my eyes and let my fingertips drift back and forth across his body.

My phone vibrates.

It vibrates again.

And again.

Cursing, I stand up to answer it.

"Pop?" I suddenly feel guilty as he's tried to contact me several times and I didn't call him back.

"Jaine, is everything okay there?" His voice sounds shaky, like he's worried about something.

I pull on a bathrobe, not wanting to be naked as I speak to him. It's not like he can see me, but still. It just feels all kinds of wrong. I sit on the edge of the bed. "Yes, everything's fine, Pop. Why?"

"Razr won't have told you as you're not council, but the Bratva are baying for blood. They've had two of their top men taken down this week, and they're blaming the Iron Scorpions. I'm not sure if you've seen the news, but The Exterminator shot the second Russian. It's common knowledge that he works closely with the Scorpions, so they're holding the MC responsible for both deaths. They'll likely target the Angels, too, due to the alliance. Right now, anyone connected with either MC isn't safe."

I exhale, trying to take it all in.

"I need to go as I'm meeting with Duke, but promise me you'll be careful, Jaine. Try to distance yourself from the Scorpions as much as you can, at least for now, until this blows over."

I nod, even though he can't see me.

"I will, Pop. You be careful too," I whisper.

"Of course. I love you, Jaine."

"Love you too."

I hang up, then turn to look at Delaney. "Do you want to tell me what the fuck is going on?"

CHAPTER SIX

JAINE

Jones & Associates Legal, Upper East Side, New York

Rubbing my hands up and down my face, I fire up my laptop.

"Asshole," I say out loud to an empty office. I'm referring to Delaney. Who the fuck else?

It's five a.m. on Monday. Sleep didn't come easily. Who am I kidding? It eluded me the entire weekend. Not because of what Delaney told me, but because of what he didn't. There's some serious shit going down, and the Scorpions are refusing to divulge.

"I can't discuss it with you as you're not council." I mimic his voice.

I mean, I'm *The* fucking Exterminator, for Christ's sake. I've killed hundreds of people. Money aside, each target was deserving of my engraved bullet between their eyes, and half of the bounty always goes to the relevant cause. Pedophiles, sex traffickers. You name it. If that piece of trash deserves to be taken out, who you going to call? No, not fucking *Ghostbusters*. The Exterminator, that's who. I'm trying to make a difference. Rid the world of the vermin of society. Be the vigilante it needs. Or at least one of them.

I need to phone a friend. I dial his number with a smirk on my face.

"Morning, Irish."

I lean back on my chair and take in the New York skyline out the window.

"Jaine, what the fuck? It's the middle of the night," he mumbles in a sleepy voice.

I snicker. "Hardly! It's five a.m.! You alone?"

"Why the fuck are you asking that? Are you horny? Are we going to have phone sex?" He yawns, and I can't help but laugh out loud.

What is it with the Irish? Everything they say sounds like a joke. They can read out loud the instructions on how to operate the microwave, and it would be goddamn hilarious and deserving of a spot at the local comedy club.

"Sounds good. What you wearing, big boy?" I say in a breathy Marilyn Monroe-esque voice, trying my best to sound sexy and likely failing miserably.

"I'm stark bollock naked, and I've got morning wood, so if you want to come over and ride my dick, I'd be forever grateful."

I laugh again.

"Ooh, morning wood. My absolute favorite. Would it give me pussy splinters? Oh, and just so you know, I'm not wearing any underwear, so we can skip the part about you asking me the color. I'm also wet, and my arousal is running down my thighs thinking about you fucking me." I put on my best sultry voice.

He laughs out loud. "You're not making my hard-on any easier to deal with. Now, as much as it's lovely to hear from you, what do you want at this time in the morning? Be quick now as I need to go fuck my hand."

"That's not a very nice way to talk to your ex-girlfriend now, is it, O'Connell? I thought the Irish were meant to be charming. It seems the big man upstairs missed you out. You should ask for a full refund on account of the personality he *didn't* give you." My smile widens.

"That's because he gave me a bigger dick than most. Given how good-looking I am, he thought the ladies would appreciate that more than an over-abundance of luck or charm." He chuckles.

We're like this all the time. Bullshit banter.

"Yeah, yeah, yeah. Okay, I need to know what's going on with the Bratva."

Padraig O'Connell, or Irish as I call him, is the youngest of four sons, whose father, Fergal, heads The Hudson Dusters here in NYC, aka the Irish Mob. They're single-handedly responsible for most of the bodies swimming with the fishes at the bottom of the river. Padraig and I went to Yale together. No one knows of our *outlaw* discussions apart from him and me. While Sasha and Cherry know him as my ex, they have no idea who he *really* is. Again, for them, it's just safer that way.

There's a pause.

"Your boyfriend hasn't told you?" He sounds surprised. Not sure why. MCs don't tell women anything. Chauvinist pricks.

"Which one?" I ask.

"Very funny." He yawns again. "That big bad prez you've got under your thumb. You know, the one that uses a switchblade as his weapon of choice hence his road name Razr."

"Shut up and spill, Irish."

I can hear his hand rubbing over his stubble.

"The Bratva intercepted guns meant for the Sicilian mafia. Your road captain, Knight, wasn't paying enough attention, and they vanished. One million dollars' worth of weapons, which is coming straight out of the Scorpions' pocket. Not that the money is the issue. We all know how wealthy Paul Delaney is. It's a pride thing. Blaze took the rap for the resultant retaliation attack by the Scorpions, as you know, and you got him off with NYPD by citing no evidence, but the Russian's throat was slit from ear to ear. It wasn't Blaze who killed him. It was your lover boy, Razr."

"Why the fuck would they steal weapons?" I ask, filing the information on Delaney away for now.

"The Sicilian mafia want to deal with us direct. They want to cut out the Bratva and, in turn, get better prices. The Scorpions add on a hefty sum to ours to make it worth their while handling the transport, and it also includes a share for the Angels. Rather than be removed the Russians would, understandably, prefer both MCs be taken out of the equation. The Bratva have always supplied to the Sicilians, so they think it's their God given right to remain involved. With their mark up on top the prices are no longer competitive, and the Sicilians are threatening to switch to the Chinese. The Chinese guns are shite in comparison, but the Sicilians are currently paying double the price. The Bratva have, understandably, taken offense at potentially being dropped and intercepted the weapons to get all of our attention."

"Right. I'm hearing that the Bratva is baying for blood now, though, after two of their men were killed. That right?"

"Yup. They have a new leader going by the name of Lebedev. He's young for a pakhan. Our age. He needs to prove himself worthy of leadership, so he's out for revenge for the two high-rankers the Scorpions allegedly killed."

Rubbing my hands across my face, I look out the window.

"Only one was killed by the MC, Padraig."

"Yes, I realize that, but The Exterminator is seen as being in Razr's back pocket these days, so the Bratva is holding them responsible for both targets."

"Between you and me, the fucker who was shot with his pants around his ankles trafficked children. He deserved to be shot, resuscitated, and shot again."

There's a pause. Shit, have I revealed too much?

"Yes, we're aware of that. He was also having them take part in porn before auctioning them off to the highest bidder based on their, shall we say, performance and skill level."

I cringe at that thought. Fucking kiddie-fiddling scum.

"Anyway, how do you know that? I thought the Scorpions weren't telling you anything. Have you got an *in* with The Exterminator, by any chance? Only a handful of people know the Russian was fucking his hand when he was shot between the eyes."

Shit. I pause, thinking how best to respond. "Let's just say The Exterminator and I go way back."

He pauses for thought. "Interesting. So, the bottom line is, anyone associated with the Scorpions, the Angels, or the Dusters is currently at risk. My advice? Keep away and distance yourself, darlin'."

I don't reply.

"So, can I go back to sleep now, or are you going to come visit me and let me fuck you at long last? I promise you won't be disappointed."

"In your dreams, my little leprechaun." I laugh at him.

"Hey, I may be a leprechaun, but there isn't anything little about me."

I laugh. "Padraig O'Connell? That's for you to know and for me never to find out. You blew that chance a long time ago when you stuck your dick in someone else. Anyway, thanks for the intel, Irish. Anytime I can return the favor, let me know."

"Be good to know who The Exterminator is. We may have a use for his services, and we pay extremely well."

I pause again. "I'll be sure to let them know. Top of the morning to you and all that!"

He laughs heartily. "And to you, darlin'."

Putting the phone down, I spin around in my chair.

Six a.m.

I change in the ladies' restroom and head to the gym for one of my MMA sessions.

CHERRY'S LEANING AGAINST THE WALL WHEN I RETURN TO THE office. She's dressed in a little red playsuit which highlights her crimson hair and scarlet lips. Her face is stuck in a new book. No doubt she's contemplating and reviewing her next sexual roleplay.

"Morning, babe. Are you standing there for a reason?" I place my briefcase on my desk and fire up my laptop before smoothing down my navy suit.

She looks at me, then looks away. "I can't sit down."

Frowning, I take her in. "What do you mean? Is the chair broken? Shall I get it swapped for another?"

Then it dawns on me.

I laugh out loud. "Fuck me... well, no, actually, it's you who was fucked, obviously. All three of them?" I lean back on my chair with my hands on the armrests, eyebrows raised, waiting for her to respond.

She nods. "Yes. Twice. They've broken my pussy. Ruined it. Fucking dirty bikers."

I laugh. "I'm sure it's not ruined. If we can squeeze a baby out of our vaginas, I'm sure it will be right as rain in a day or two. A biker's huge dick is nothing in comparison to a head."

Her phone vibrates, and she rolls her eyes.

"Who is it?" I ask, my curiosity piqued.

"It's Blaze. He's been messaging me all weekend, but I haven't replied. He wants to see me again. Just me and him next time."

I purse my lips. "You want to see him again?"

"Morning, my beautiful BFFs!" Sasha interrupts as she breezes in the door, the scent of Chanel No. 5 surrounding her and wafting through the room, its trail almost tangible. "I've brought blueberry muffins and caramel lattes. Yes, I know I'm the type of friend people would die to have! Well, not literally. Or at least I hope not." She frowns, then smiles. "Anyway, aren't you two so lucky!"

My stomach instantly grumbles at the thought of bad-for-you carbohydrates in any form. After fetching plates from the refreshment stand in the corner of our three-person room, she places a muffin and a paper cup of coffee on each of our desks.

Collapsing in her chair and smoothing down her navy and white polka dot dress, she breaks off a piece and pops it in her mouth before groaning loudly. Then she notices Cherry, who is still leaning against the wall, looking like she's holding up the fucking building.

"She can't sit down," I say as I inhale the smell of fresh baking and put a large section of the sweet delight in my mouth.

Sasha looks from me to Cherry and back again. "Why?"

I shrug. "She's been fucked. Well and truly. By three hairy bikers." Then I laugh so hard I accidentally spray some muffin across my desk.

Sasha frowns at her sympathetically and sticks out her bottom lip. "Oh, Cherry. Shall I get you one of those cushions? You know, the ones with the hole in the center? They're for situations like this, aren't they?" She looks at Cherry and then at me, as if for guidance.

I laugh, swallowing my mouthful before I speak. "Well, typically, they're not for cases of over-fucking. They're for people with hemorrhoids. Still, I guess it could work in cases of pussy abuse."

"Really? Was it abuse? Oh, Cherry, I'm so sorry."

Shaking my head, I rub my hand over my face. God, give me strength.

"Yes, and now Blaze is asking her to be his old lady," I add.

Cherry glares at me.

Sasha grimaces. "Oh, I hate that expression. Why can't they just say WAG?"

I roll my eyes inwardly. "WAG? So, wives and girlfriends, right? I'm not sure the kind of activities the bikers get up to would qualify for any trophies or medals, Sash. I'm also thinking they would fall more under the heading of blood sports. Anyway, how did you get on with Dollar?"

She smiles coyly and crosses her legs. "Well, he's the most caring and unselfish lover. I'm seeing him again on Saturday." She pops another piece of muffin in her mouth.

I message Delaney.

Jaine: *I have one friend who can't sit down and is convinced her pussy is broken. She must have been good, as Blaze is now stalking her with flower emojis. Then I have another who says Dollar made sweet, passionate love to her and now wants to date. What sort of MC shitshow you running there, Prez? Where have all the angsty bad boys gone?*

Delaney: *I love you.*

Jaine: *Oh, so it's your fault. You've turned them all gay.*

Delaney: *I'm far from being gay, baby. If you want me to ride across there right now and show you how not gay I am, I'll set off now. I can bend you over and fuck you across your desk. Your friends can watch.*

Jaine: *You can prove it to me tonight. A couple of times, at least.*

Delaney: *My pleasure, or should I say, yours.*
Jaine: *Go away. I'm extremely busy.*
Delaney: *You messaged me!*

I CHUCKLE AS I PUT MY PHONE ON MY DESK.

Switching off from the girls chatting in the background, I finish my blueberry muffin and drink my coffee.

I think back on my conversation with Padraig. I'm fortunate to have him as a confidant. We dated for a few months at Yale, and I was really into him. Like, I loved him, pretty much. That's how into him I was. I never thought I'd experience that connection twice in my life. Unlike Ace, Padraig and I never slept together, though. More my decision than his. I was on the rebound from Ace and was still worried I was shit in bed. Why else would he fuck Emilia straight after me? The longer I had to think about it, the more I convinced myself that was the case.

Padraig and I broke up when I found out he'd stuck his dick in someone else, likely as I wasn't giving out. Not that that's any excuse.

His Irish charm made it easy for him to get into panties, so he used it to his advantage, I guess. I wasn't interested in becoming another notch on his bedpost, nor in catching an STD so I cut him loose, even though I was inconsolable for a long time afterwards. To be honest, I never knew what he saw in me anyway. I was Plain Jaine, and he was tall, dark, and extremely handsome, with, as his ma called it, 'the gift of the Irish gab'.

Did I do the right thing by dumping him? I'll never know. But I'll always think of Padraig as the one that got away. That was nine years ago, and we speak every day. Sometimes several times a day.

My phone vibrates, interrupting my thoughts. It's Duke.

"Duke, how are you?" I answer with a smile.

It vanishes when he doesn't reply. It's then I realize it's not good news, and that something's happened to either Ace or Pop.

CHAPTER SEVEN

JAINE

Jones & Associates Legal, Upper East Side, New York

"Duke? What the fuck is going on?"

I can feel the dread swirl through my body, and my now cold blood is pounding in my ears.

Thump. Thump. Thump.

"Jainie. It's Jeremiah. It's your pop, honey. I'm so sorry."

He's sobbing. The ex-prez of the Angels of Hellfire is crying like a baby.

"What happened, Duke?" I ask, my voice sounding distant, like it belongs to someone else.

"He was shot, baby girl. It was instant. He didn't suffer."

I close my eyes and rub my hand across my forehead in disbelief.

This can't be happening. God, please tell me this isn't fucking happening.

"Was it the Bratva?"

He pauses, probably wondering how the hell I know.

"Was. It. The. Fucking. Bratva!" I repeat with a hiss.

"We… we think so."

I exhale loudly. Someone is going to pay for this. I will find the fucker who put my pop in an early grave, and I will end them.

"I'll set off for Rising as soon as I have everything in order this end." I put the phone down. What the fuck else is there to say? I have to go home.

This MC lifestyle has cost my pop his life. Unbeknown to me, my killing of the second Bratva must have unleashed fucking hell.

My phone starts to vibrate immediately. It's Delaney.

I ignore him.

He sends a message.

Delaney: *Answer the goddamn phone, Jaine.*
Jaine: *Fuck you, asshole.*

He calls over and over. I switch it off.

I look at my two best friends, who are standing beside the window side by side, having overheard every word.

"Do you know what, Jaine? We'll all three of us get on our bikes and ride to Rising," Sasha sings as she claps her hands, then walks across to clear up the plates and coffee cups like the shit going down is normal. Like I wasn't just told moments ago that the man who gave me life is now dead.

I look at her like she's insane. "Do you know how far it is and how dangerous it will be?

She nods as she stops and pats down the front of her dress.

"We're friends for life. Like the Musketeers. Were there three of them or four? I can't remember." She frowns, then shrugs. "Anyway, no matter. We're going with you. You're not doing this on your own. No way, Jose," she says, shaking her head vehemently. "It'll be like old times when we used to race around town on our Harleys."

I smile at the distant memory.

When I started Yale, all I had to get around was my Softail. Friends from day one, Cherry and Sash immediately decided they needed a hog and begged their folks accordingly. Money was, of course, no object, but both sets of parents were not impressed at my bad influence over their respectable and, until then, well-behaved daughters.

If looks could kill, I would have been dead that day. Twice over. Story of my life.

"It's hardly the same as riding around the streets of Manhattan, Sash. Rising is three thousand goddamn miles away."

She shrugs again. "So, we'll take it slow and enjoy the scenery on the way. I mean, I don't want to sound insensitive, but your father's not going anywhere, is he? And this..." She looks around the office. "Well, you've got eight proper lawyers working for you. They can cope, Jaine. Let us be there for you. I mean, I'd expect you to wait on me hand and foot if it were my daddy."

Cherry nods to signal she agrees with Sasha as she walks over and wraps her arms around me. "How soon do we need to set off, babe?"

I rub my hand across my eyes. "Well, we'll need to get the hogs serviced first as they haven't been used in a while, so the day after tomorrow, most likely," I say quietly, my mind distracted.

She nods and looks relieved. "My pussy should be okay to travel by then. I'll call Blaze and ask him to handle getting our bikes roadworthy by the end of tomorrow latest. I'll promise him a fuck when we get back. Just him, though. I'm not doing that reverse harem thing ever again!"

Even though the situation is dire and depressing, we all burst out laughing.

What the hell would I do without my BFFs?

———

DELANEY STORMS INTO MY OFFICE AN HOUR LATER. HE'S IN FULL MC presidential mode. To anyone else, he would be intimidating. To me? He's an asshole.

"Ladies, could you leave us." He can barely contain his fury as he looks at Sasha and then Cherry. The rage isn't directed at them per se. It's emanating from every single pore of his body and forming the words coming out of the thin line that makes up his mouth.

"You okay for us to go, Jaine?" Sasha tries her best to scowl at my uninvited guest but fails miserably. She hasn't got a nasty bone in her body. Instead, she looks at me sympathetically and rubs her hand up and down my arm.

I nod as I stand and walk toward the window. I look out, but I see nothing. It's all a great big fucking blur.

They close the door on their way out, glancing back only once to shoot daggers at the prez of the Iron Scorpions.

"Why the fuck didn't you answer your goddamn phone?" he growls from behind me.

I turn and glare at him. "I was busy trying to come to terms with the fact that my pop has been shot dead."

He runs his hands through his hair, then rubs one across his mouth as he thinks about what to say.

I spin around. I can't even look at him.

"Jaine, I'm sorry about your pop." His voice is full of sorrow. Do I detect a hint of regret? Guilt even? "He was just in the wrong place at the wrong time, unfortunately. A couple of Angels' prospects got gunned down too."

I nod. Like that makes it all better. I don't have exclusivity on grief as it wasn't only my pop who was killed. Two other families also have to endure the pain and sorrow of losing their loved ones in this shitshow of a fucking outlaw world we live in, never being able to see them again or tell them that they love them.

"The Bratva or the Sicilians?" I ask woodenly.

My question is met with silence.

"I know about the missing guns. I know it was you and not Blaze who killed the first Russian. I know everything, so don't treat me like I'm a fucking idiot, Delaney." My voice is quiet, contained.

"How?"

I laugh. It's forced.

"How what? How do I know about what's been going on? How do I know my taking out the second Bratva caused this to happen? How do I know you're the asshole that could have and should have fucking pre-warned me?" I spin around. "You knew my killing the second Russian would start a war, and you did it because your pride was hurt. A million goddamn dollars? I'd have gladly given you a million dollars, Delaney! My pop is lying on a slab in a mortuary freezer with a bullet between his eyes over this. He was only fifty-eight years old. You could have prevented this. I could have prevented this!"

I walk over to him. His face is cold. Impassive.

This isn't Delaney now. This is Razr. His insane alter-ego.

All of a sudden, he seems taller. Broader. More menacing. He fills the room with his dark presence.

This is the fucker who's killed hundreds of people. Well, guess what, sunshine? So the fuck have I.

"His. Blood. Is. On. Your. Fucking. Hands, Razr." I poke him hard in the chest as I emphasize each word.

He grabs my wrist, his fingers digging in. It will leave a bruise, I'm sure. "Who fucking told you?" His voice is low.

I smirk at him. "I have contacts too, you know? I know everything." I jerk my arm away from him. "Don't you touch me." I turn back to the window. "We're setting off for Rising the day after tomorrow."

"The hell you are." His tone is threatening.

"So let me get this straight. Your pride gets dented when the Russians steal some guns. You kill one Bratva, then leave me to deal with your sloppy mess with Prescott at NYPD. You then tell me nothing about what's going on and entice me to shoot a second Russian. As a direct fucking result of my hitting the depraved piece of shit, my pop gets murdered. And then you try to tell me I can't go back home to bury him? Are you for real? Well, guess what? Fuck you! I am going to Rising to deal with my pop's funeral and to lay him to rest."

"Duke can take care of it," he says quietly.

I turn to look at him. Can he even hear himself? Has he gone even more insane?

Then reality dawns, and I realize the real reason he doesn't want me to go.

I nod and smirk. "Aww, what's the matter, Razr? You worried about me seeing Ace again? Are you feeling insecure? Jealous, maybe?"

I can tell I've hit a nerve. I've hit *the* nail on the head. He knows all about Ace. He knows the exact reason I left Rising.

Unrequited love. The fact that Ace didn't want me.

He walks over and pushes my hair back so my tattoo behind my ear is showing. He traces the scrolled letter A with his fingertip before gently pressing his lips to it.

"If Steele makes a move on you, I'll cut his throat open, then rip his fucking head off, Jaine. You have my word on that."

I glare at him, knowing full well he means every word.

"You're unbelievable. Do you know that? Get out of my office and my life, Razr. You're no longer welcome in either." I point at the door.

His green eyes bore into mine, and his nostrils flare like he's considering responding.

He doesn't.

The warning is out in the open. I have no doubt he would kill Ace in a heartbeat.

He leaves the room, slamming the door behind him.

Only when I'm sure he's left the building do I finally allow myself to cry.

CHAPTER EIGHT

JAINE

The Iron Scorpions' Clubhouse, Brightling, New York

BLAZE HAS CALLED CHERRY TO CONFIRM THE HOGS ARE READY FOR collection. The club's motorcycle repair shop, which is one of their legitimate businesses and used illegally for money laundering, is booked for weeks in advance, but he's prioritized our rides. He's fully aware of how urgent it is. Everyone is sympathetic.

I don't want their fucking pity. I want revenge.

Cherry owes him one screw per hog, or so he says. They're at the compound, so she's driving us there in one of her mom's many SUVs, and we'll ride back separately. We can collect the cage when we get back or one of the bikers will drop it off. We've already packed and had our stuff couriered to Pop's house, where Anita, his elderly neighbor, will take delivery.

We'll make the just under three-thousand-mile road trip in around ten days. Taking only the bare essentials, we'll stay in quality hotels en-route so we can get a decent night's sleep. Worst case, we can always purchase more clothes if we need to.

We reach the compound, and I get out of the passenger seat and key in the entry code. It doesn't work. Delaney will have changed it so I can't get in. I punch the panel in frustration, cursing under my breath. Fucking dick. Having to ask for the code is his way of forcing me to speak to him. Well, he can kiss my ass.

I call Blaze instead.

"Can you let us in, Blaze? We're here for the hogs."

"No problem, Jaine. I'll let the prospect know to open the gates."

We watch as Jamie, the latest intake, jogs across and opens the iron bars. He reminds me of the last time I saw Ace. Wavy black hair, baby blue eyes, and wearing a prospect cut. Young and eager. Before the shit of looking over your shoulder every minute becomes tedious and wears you the fuck down. Before wondering if today will be the day you breathe your last. He raises a hand and waves as we drive through, then quickly closes the gates behind us before checking they're secure. Frowning, I think of the two Angels' prospects who lost their lives alongside Pop this week—gunned down at only eighteen years old. Same age as Jamie.

From the outside, the Iron Scorpions' clubhouse looks like a prison. Set in around sixty acres of nothingness, the exterior of the two-story building is depressingly grey with windows covered in bulletproof metal, and with bars over the top, just for good measure. Metal railings surround the perimeter, and there's only one way in or out. The top of the fencing is electrified and finished with barbed wire, and there's CCTV everywhere.

It's grim-looking, as is the scowl on the face of their prez, who's currently looming at the entrance. The sleeves of his Henley are pushed up, and his muscular, heavily tattooed arms are crossed in front of him, causing his pecs and biceps to bulge impressively.

Jumping down from the SUV, I feel the heavy weight of Delaney's stare as he looks me over. He'll appreciate the tight-fitting black leather pants and black thigh-high boots, I'm sure. My ancient bike jacket covers my tank top. It's patched to the Angels of Hellfire. I've had it since I was sixteen years old. I know the patch won't be appreciated on Scorpions' territory, even if there is an alliance between both clubs.

Red rag to a bull? You bet your goddamn life. Let him be pissed off. See if I care.

"Razr," I acknowledge him.

Sasha and Cherry quickly run over to look at their hogs. They know without me saying a word to give us space.

He greets me with a slight nod of his head. "We need to talk, Jaine."

I stand and look at him. He's a powerful, handsome man, and mine for the taking if I want him.

"Got nothing to say to you, Razr." I storm across to where the hogs are parked up, conscious he's following close behind. Cherry is flirting with Blaze, and Dollar is going all googly-eyed over Sasha. Both girls are dressed similarly to me, and the guys are almost coming in their pants. These bikers love independent women on hogs. They instinctively want to tame them and get them to submit to riding bitch. Maybe for Cherry and Sasha that'll happen one day, but I'll never be anyone's goddamn bitch.

My eyes drift to my HD Softail. Jesus, she's a fucking beauty. A shiny black classic with non-standard black wheels. Tears prick my eyes when I remember my pop giving me the keys on my eighteenth birthday. One of the best days of my life and one of the worst. I got my dream hog. I lost my best friend.

"Sorry to hear about your old man, Jaine." Blaze looks apologetically at me.

I nod at him in thanks. "Appreciated, Blaze. Thanks for sorting out the hogs at such short notice."

Swinging my leg over my ride and straddling the familiar leather seat, I take my half helmet from where it's resting on the bars and put it on. Then, taking my aviators from my jacket pocket, I slide them in place.

"Damn, you look hot, Jaine. Can I take a photo?" Young Jamie wolf whistles, then smirks as he runs his hands up and down the seams of his cut. His request earns him a scowl from Delaney, and his expression turns apologetic.

"Why, thank you, Jamie. And yes, provided you promise you're not going to print it off and then spill your cum all over my face." I wink at him and watch as he goes red, his cheeky smirk widening. That's precisely what he's going to do, and everyone standing here knows it. He'll probably laminate the fucking thing. You know, make it wipe clean. He takes a photo on his phone of me, Cherry, and Sasha like we're Charlie's fucking Angels.

Revving up the engine, I kick the stand up.

"I'll see you girls in the morning." I nod at Cherry and Sasha, who both wave me off before continuing their flirting with Blaze and Dollar.

Jamie opens the gates and I make my way out of the compound and take to the open highway.

Damn, I've missed the freedom of riding. The therapeutic hum of the engine and the feel of it throbbing between my thighs. The wind in my hair and the peace and tranquility that comes with being completely alone. Well, at least as alone as I ever can be. I'm conscious there's a hog following me and fully aware that it's Delaney.

Not wanting him to trail me all the way to my apartment and knowing he will otherwise, I pull over at a truck stop and wait and watch as he follows me in. He won't want to leave things as they are. With us not on speaking terms. He won't get another opportunity to see me before I set off on the long journey home.

I park up behind some trees in a relatively secluded spot. It's been raining, and the smell of petrichor is strong. I inhale deeply. The fresh scent reminds me of Rising. Kicking the stand down, I get off my hog and lean against the side before closing my eyes and raising my face to the warmth of the sun. Delaney pulls up beside me and leans against his ride.

We stand there in silence for a few minutes.

"If there had been any other way, I'd have taken it, Jaine." He pauses before he continues. "It wasn't about the money. It wasn't even about pride. I had to take a stand. If we'd let the Russians walk all over us, it would have created problems along the whole supply chain. You know that. It would have caused issues for the Angels and the Irish too. We'd have lost respect, and with that, even more lives would have been at risk, as all the fucking vermin would have crawled out of the woodwork to challenge our position."

I stare into the distance and exhale with a frown. "I realize you did what you had to do, Razr. But I'm still pissed that you didn't explain to me what was going on. That you used me as a pawn in your fucking game. There isn't anything acceptable about that in my mind." I take off my helmet and run my hand through my hair.

"No. I know, and you're right. But no one expected them to retaliate the way they did." he replies, exhaling loudly while looking at the ground and kicking at the loose stones with his boots. "I want you to know that I've approached the council to request they agree to you being involved in our discussions and decisions moving forward. It seems only fair when you bring in a shit ton of money too. Not that they're aware of that. I've got approval from everyone apart from Bomber. By the time you come back from California, I'll have him convinced. I may have to tell him about your extra-curricular activities, though. Just so he fully appreciates how important it is for you to be kept in the loop at all times and on all matters."

My stomach sinks. Telling Bomb? He fucking hates me with a passion. I immediately get a bad feeling in my gut. I glare at him. "You tell him that as a last resort, Razr. You hear me?"

He nods. "Can you quit calling me Razr? You only call me that when you're pissed at me, and I don't want to fall out, Jaine. Not when you're about to leave for Christ knows how long." He walks over to stand in front of me, snaking his arm around my waist. Pulling me against his hard body, he presses his nose against my hair. "I'm sorry about Jeremiah. He would have been the best grandaddy to our babies."

I nod and breathe out a shaky sigh in response, my heart immediately feeling like a heavy lump in my chest. What to say to that? Did I need reminding of that? Any children I have will never meet my pop. I mean, how shitty is that reality? I blink back my tears before Delaney can see them. It doesn't pay to show you have any fucking emotion in this life. It's a sign of weakness—nothing more.

"I know you are, Delaney. It's just one of those things. We're never safe when we choose to accept and embrace this godforsaken lifestyle, living day to day and never knowing which one will be our last. I know that. My pop knew that too. He lived and died for the Angels' patch." I lean my head against his chest and close my eyes, breathing in and taking comfort from the familiar smell of his leather cut and sandalwood cologne.

He tilts my chin up, his eyes searching my face before he drops his lips to mine. They're soft and gentle. Familiar. I wrap my arms around his neck, and as he deepens the kiss, our tongues tangle, his searching and filling my mouth. Cupping my ass, he pulls me against his hard dick, and I rub my hand against his erection through his jeans.

"Shit, Jaine. You feel what you do to me? No one is made for me like you are," he growls. He leans his head back with his eyes closed as I continue to stroke him.

Dropping to my knees, I unbutton him to freedom. His dick is rock solid, the tip purple, swollen, and leaking pre-cum. I lick away the bead of fluid before sliding my mouth down his entire length, taking him deep in my throat.

Fisting my hair, he thrusts hard and fast. My mouth is used to his sheer size and at dealing with how rough he can be. I hum against him, the vibrations causing him to curse and his movements to quicken. He thrusts deeper, causing me to almost gag and making my eyes water.

"Take my dick deep in that pretty little mouth of yours like a good fucking girl." He grunts as he tilts my head back so he can watch me deep throat his cock. I look up at him and drop my hands to squeeze his balls hard, and he explodes in my mouth.

"That's it. Swallow my cum, sweetheart. Every last fucking drop." I let his seed gather at the back of my throat, then drink down his salty thickness in one motion before licking clean his softening dick. Pulling me to my feet, he kisses me hard on the mouth. "I love you, Jaine," he murmurs against my lips.

I don't speak. In response, I just press my face against his cut and inhale his scent one last time.

It remains unspoken, but both of us know everything's about to change.

CHAPTER NINE

DELANEY

The Iron Scorpions' Clubhouse, Brightling, New York

"VP, A WORD, PLEASE."

Bomber's stacking bottles behind the bar. He turns and nods at me as I make my way to the meeting room. Leaving the door ajar, I take my seat at the head of the walnut councilors' table and switch on the grey banker's light. Staring at the surface, I run my fingers across the Iron Scorpions' insignia. Bomber joins me, closing the door behind him before taking the seat at the opposite far end and putting his feet on the tabletop.

"Don't disrespect the Scorpion, Bomb," I grumble warningly as I glare at the boots resting on the heavily engraved wood.

He nods, removing them and placing them on the floor. "So, your old lady is on her way to California, then, Prez." He's wearing a smirk like it's fucking hilarious. My fingers twitch, itching to get my blade out and cut it from his face.

"She's not my old lady," I grunt at him. She's never agreed to it. Never agreed to let me wife her either—goddamn frustrating woman."

"And now she's heading straight onto the dick of Jason Steele?" Bomber snickers. I knew I shouldn't have told the fucker the whole story of why Jaine left Rising.

In three paces, I reach him and pull his head back. I press my switchblade against his neck, and a drop of blood pools on the tip. One movement and I could end this fucker. If he continues to disrespect me, I won't hesitate.

"You got a death wish or something, brother? Any more talk like that, and I'll cut you from ear to ear," I whisper at him.

He raises both hands in submission. "Only messing, Razr," he says with another annoying smirk. Is he fuck only messing. He doesn't like Jaine. Never has. Never will.

Discussing the subject of her with him always makes me reactive. Today, even more than usual. I always knew she'd have to return to Rising at some point. I was kind of hoping when it happened, it would be as my old lady or wife. Even better as both.

"Try to find out discreetly if Ace has a woman." I pray to the Almighty he has because if he goes near Jaine, I'll be forced to cut out his still-beating heart and shove it down his throat. That shit won't be good for business.

"Will do, Prez. Anyway, I'm guessing that's not what you want to talk to me about." Bomb raises his eyebrow.

I pick up the gavel and stare at him, moving the lump of solid wood around in my hands.

"She needs to be part of the discussions moving forward. She has a right to know what's going on, Bomb," I say quietly, hoping he'll accept it without question but knowing the fucker won't.

He pounds his clenched fist on the table. Frustration is etched on his face at my continued insistence on this. He probably thinks I'm pussy-whipped. Maybe I am. All I know is that given what she does in her *spare time,* she deserves a say. She's earned it. We all benefit financially from the money her hits bring in. It lets us enjoy a nice lifestyle without having to get involved in the drugs trade, which we relied on heavily in the past. Bomber knows I need a yes from him. The Scorpions is a democracy. We all need to vote, and we all need to agree. Together, we're judge, jury, and where required, executioner. It's the way it is. The way it's always been. The only way.

"I'm sure it hasn't escaped your attention, Prez, but Jaine's got a pussy, and last I heard, women are not allowed to sit on council meetings or in church, so I say nay."

I exhale loudly. "Bomb, there's something you don't know about her. Now I'm going to tell you what that something is. It will make you the only other living person in this whole goddamn world that knows this shit aside from her and me. If it gets out, I'll know exactly where the leak is. You'll immediately become a dead man walking, mark my words. Then I'll cut you so bad and into so many pieces they'll need to reconstruct your corpse like a fucking jigsaw to work out who the fuck you are. Understood?" He knows I mean every word. Where she's concerned, I'd end every fucker.

"Understood, Prez." He nods once, sitting with his arms crossed in front of him, a trail of blood running down from the blade wound on his neck.

I pause, uncomfortable with the reveal, but if I can't trust Bomb, who the hell can I trust? We went to fucking school together. At thirty-two years old, we've known each other most of our lives. My old man got himself killed by the pigs in a shoot-out when I was twenty-five. It was my duty to the club to step up and become prez, and it made sense to have my friends, those closest to me and who knew me best, take up the other council positions. Aside from them, I only have my sister, Sarah, who's Jaine's age. I haven't seen her in years, as she wants no involvement in the MC life after what happened to our old man. Who can blame her? With money being no object, she decided to travel the world. Fuck knows where she is. Shit like that never appealed to me. Not that this life did to begin with, but when you're born into it, it's impossible to get out. The only way to do that is in a wooden box unless you have someone who can take the reins from you. For that, I need an heir.

My mom died birthing Sarah. I don't think she's ever forgiven herself for that. Not that my continually blaming her for my mom's death helped. Will I ever see my sister again? Who fucking knows?

I exhale.

"Jaine is The Exterminator." I say it slowly and quietly.

You could hear a pin drop. Then he laughs, disturbing the silence.

"Good one, Razr. Now tell me the real reason you want her on council." He's leaning back in his chair, thinking this is all one big joke. I hold his gaze, and the smile slowly leaves his face. "Jesus, you're serious." He looks shocked as hell. Then again, why wouldn't he? Everyone assumes the best sniper in our parts is a man and that works in our favor. No one would ever suspect Jaine.

"She's pissed that her last hit was the Bratva scum, which caused the war to break out. She says if she hadn't taken out the target, her old man would still be walking, and she's right. She has no fucking kin left now. That shit's on me. I should have given her a choice. I have to live with that. Moving forward, she wants to be involved in who she hits based on what's going down, and I can't blame her. Even if we don't tell her, she has a contact. She knows exactly what's going on without me saying a goddamn word. Not sure who they are, but let's try to find out which team they're playing for. My guess is it's the Irish." I stare out the office window. It's early, and there's no one else around yet. If there was, I wouldn't be having this conversation, as even the walls have fucking ears.

"Will do, Razr. And based on what you've just told me, I'd like to change my vote to a yay," he mutters. I hear him push his chair back and stand.

"Appreciated, Bomb," I say, not looking at him.

The door closes as he leaves.

My thoughts drift to her. We've had her followed. She'll be aware of the tail. Aware it's to keep her and her friends safe. She's observant. Misses nothing. It comes with being a lawyer and a sniper. The tail will leave as soon as she enters Rising. Steele will be waiting for her at the other end, and she'll then be under the protection of the Angels.

I run my hand through my hair in frustration. Shit, I should have had her tied down by now with a baby in her belly. I've had long enough. It's difficult to do with someone who's so fiercely independent, though. My woman drives me insane in more ways than one.

Should I say mine? Is she mine? Or is she Steele's? Or does that little spitfire belong to neither of us?

I know she was in love with him. She left home without a backward glance because he didn't love her back. How could he not love her? Fucking fool.

Taking my phone out of my pocket, I message her.

Delaney: *I love you, baby.*

She'll reply when she parks up. She never says she loves me. Why? Likely because she doesn't. It's that simple. If she said it, she'd only be saying what I want to hear to shut me the fuck up. She knows it. I know it. She'll do anything to stop me from pestering her about becoming my old lady.

Shit, I'm thirty-two. If I want kids, I need to have them soon. I don't want that with anyone but her. In this game, we're living day by day. Our next breath could be our last. We need to take what we want or risk never having it.

If she goes to Rising and there are no feelings between them, or if Steele's married, then I know she's mine. No one can take her from me then. I hope.

Niggling at the back of my mind, though, is that he won't be. He's been waiting for her, as she has for him. What they shared isn't over. For her to leave everything she ever knew, her only living relative, the feelings she had for Steele must have been strong ones. If she were over him? If she loved me? She'd have gone back to visit her pop because seeing Steele wouldn't have mattered. She didn't because it does matter. He matters.

If he touches her, I'll cut out the fucker's organs one by one.

She may not have agreed to be my old lady yet, but everyone knows that in every other sense of the word, she's just that. He'd better not fucking disrespect me.

There are two people in this world I'd die for.

My sister and Jaine.

So what if Jaine doesn't love me back? If she doesn't now, she never will. Still, call me a selfish fucker. I'm not prepared to give her up without a fight to the death. There isn't anyone who knows me like she does. She accepts me, even knowing my past and what I'm capable of. How many I've killed. How I kill. There isn't a woman I will ever respect as I do her. She's fearless and strong, intelligent, and beautiful too. And the way she looks after my dick? Hell. No, she's mine all right, and I intend to keep it that way.

"Luc. What can I do for you?" My phone goes, interrupting my thoughts. There's a pause as the Sicilian Don, Luciano Ruocco, switches from thinking in Italian to thinking in American. Sometimes he forgets and talks in his mother tongue, and I can't understand a goddamn word. Still, I cut him some slack as he's new to this game.

I wait.

"Razr. Good morning. I'm just calling to let you know that our hands are clean regarding the recent issues you have experienced with Lebedev and his men. We would never dishonor you in such a way. Or the Irish, for that matter. We do not wish to be dragged into your battles. As you know, we are trying to regroup at this time."

"Yes, Luc. I was sorry to hear about your recent bereavement. You do know my woman's old man was killed during the recent hit in California?" My tone is quietly threatening, so he's aware he'd better not be lying to me because I will find out, and I will slit him, then dice the fucker.

"We have heard, yes. Please give Jaine my condolences. As you know, I have met her on several occasions previously when we attended the same charity functions in Manhattan." His response sounds sincere.

Yes, she has met him, but he wasn't the Don then. He was merely the younger son. His father and elder brother were blown up by a car bomb six weeks ago. It's strongly suspected the Mexicans, La eMe, planted it. Issues with drugs going missing or quantities being under or some other shit these lowlife fuckers tried to pull.

"Appreciated, Luc. I'll be sure to pass on your regards to her," I reply, still not fully trusting this wet behind the ears Sicilian bastard. Yet another one taking over a powerful mantel at a young age, like Lebedev.

I'm getting old. These fuckers are all in their twenties.

"Thank you, Razr. Please tell Jaine that if she needs me for anything, assistance or otherwise, she's to call me, pronto. Pass my number to her if you will," he offers a bit too enthusiastically.

"Will do. Thank you, Luc." I put down the phone.

I won't pass his number to her. I don't need any more competition where she's concerned. Still, I appreciate his call. It may be that we'll be supplying to the mafia direct in due course. The asshole

Russians wanted to cut us out of the picture, but it's likely they'll be the ones to be bypassed. Lebedev has a lot to learn if he thinks he can fuck around with the Irish. Old Fergal O'Connell is all about gentlemanly handshakes and pride. He'll kill the fucker with his bare hands if he thinks Lebedev is harming The Hudson Dusters' reputation in any way. Then he'll say half a dozen Hail Marys as penance and move on.

I run my gaze over the Scorpion table.

I didn't ever think normal was for me. Women were for fucking. Just three holes. I never thought I'd want any of the marriage and family shit.

I never used to.

Not until I met her.

Pushing thoughts of Jaine aside, I focus on the more pressing matter at hand. The Russians and what those fuckers are going to get up to next because, mark my words, the shit going on is far from over.

CHAPTER TEN

ACE

The Angels of Hellfire Clubhouse, Rising, California

"WE NEED TO BE FUCKING VIGILANT. CHECK EVERY STRANGER WHO comes into town and question any suspicious fuckers who stop to loiter. Male or female. You got me? We're in the middle of a goddamn war here! If they give you shit, shoot them in the head and move on to the next. We're not taking any chances."

"Got you, Prez."

I hang up on the brother and run my hand down my face. Everyone's on duty. There's a fucking biker rally taking place two towns along in Fielding, which is typical when war has just broken out with the Russians. There are strangers everywhere, and not all of them with good intentions.

Running my hand through my hair, I think about *her*.

I've waited years for her to come back. To come home. Perfect timing. I'm not sure what the fuck I'll say to her. What can I say to the old lady of Razr of the Iron Scorpions that won't see him wanting to cut my fucking dick off and shove it down my throat?

I stick my Glock down the back of my jeans under my cut. We're expecting her tomorrow with two of her loaded friends. She's here to bury her old man.

Trying to find them will be like trying to find three needles in a haystack with the number of bikers in town. She won't call me. She'll go out of her way to make it difficult for me to locate her. She's stubborn as a goddamn mule. Then again, she doesn't have my number, and I don't have hers. She changed hers the minute she landed in Connecticut ten years ago. While my bed was still warm and smelling of her. Probably never gave a shit about or listened to the voicemails I left. Or read the messages I sent. She likely never gave a fuck about me in truth.

Best friends? Fucking joke.

I was only there to scratch an itch. Just good for a bit of rough before she headed off to start her new life three thousand miles away. She didn't think I knew about that, but I did. The offer from Yale. Her pop told mine, and my old man told me. She never bothered to tell me she was moving away. Like I didn't matter in her grand plans.

Still, I was never good enough for her. She knew it. I knew it. No matter how much I wanted to be.

I only wish she'd left my goddamn heart behind when she went.

Resting my hand on the council table, I stare at the club insignia. An engraved skull head with flaming angel wings.

"Ace, you good to go?" My VP, Clay, sticks his head around the door. He grins widely. "It's getting close now. Tomorrow's the day. Little PJ returns to Rising. *First love never dies,*" he sings to me with a smirk.

"Shut up, you fucking idiot." I glare at him, not prepared to rise to his immature banter. The asshole has never grown up.

"She's with Razr, so mind how you go. He won't hesitate to carve you into small pieces and feed you to the dogs, alliance or not. He's a mean motherfucker," I warn him.

"Gotcha, Prez." He mock salutes.

My phone goes.

"Steele." The voice is gruff.

"Razr," I reply. Speak of the devil.

"Change of plan. My woman and her friends will be arriving in Rising today. You make sure nothing happens to her. To any of them." His tone is menacing. "Oh, and Steele?"

"Yup," I say again, already bored with this one-sided conversation.

"You make sure to keep your fucking hands to yourself." He hangs up.

In my book, people who try to intimidate are full of empty threats and bullshit. I don't see the need to threaten to end someone's life to get them to do my bidding. It should come down to mutual respect. That's where Razr and I differ. He threatens me like he's this great big fucking murderous machine. I've taken as many souls as he has, if not more. I use a gun. He uses a blade. A weapon's a weapon. I'm one of the best shooters I know. Not as good as the Scorpions' sniper, The Exterminator, but close enough.

I call my old man. "PJ's arriving today. Razr just called." I look out the window at some of the kids playing in the compound, pretending to shoot each other, dust flying as they kick up their innocent heels.

"I know, son. I've just spoken with Jainie. She can't give an ETA due to the volume of traffic because of the rally, but she'll let us know when she hits town." He sounds nervous. Maybe worried about incurring the wrath of Razr should a hair on PJ's precious little blonde head be harmed. I'm surprised she's not insisting on riding bitch these days, being a wealthy, swanky lawyer and all. Or turning up in a limousine. She's probably all designer clothes, make-up, and false fucking nails. Drinks tea with her goddamn pinkie in the air.

"Keep me posted, Pop. I'll do the same." I hang up.

The clubhouse is empty on the inside, and the music's down low. It's early afternoon and still family time. The aroma of fresh bread lingers as the old ladies sit outside, giving out sandwiches, cakes, and other baked goods. Kids and grandkids run around, chasing each other and playing football, their shrieks and giggles filling the air. I smirk at the teenagers who are all hanging around behind the building. The girls are looking for their first kiss, and the boys are looking for their first lay.

Meanwhile, the cum sluts are in their rooms, waiting for night to fall so they can get themselves filled with cum in both ends. Nothing changes. New old ladies. New sluts. All still with the same old shit going on day in, day out.

Walking outside, I take in a deep breath and raise my face to the summer sun. The women have planted some flowers around to try to pretty up the place and make it easier on the eye. It doesn't work.

Most of them remember PJ, and all of them loved Jeremiah. He wasn't patched in or anything due to his profession, but he was a loyal *friend* of the club and my old man's best friend from school. I think everyone's looking forward to seeing her again. The one who managed to escape this life and go on and make something of herself. Although, did she escape, given who she's seeing? Sometimes it's better the devil you know. Still, the Angels can't complain. The alliance with the Scorpions has made us a wealthy charter. I guess we have her to thank for that.

"You want a snack, Ace?" Emilia interrupts my thoughts and walks over wearing a long, white summer dress that displays her curves and compliments her dark hair and olive skin. She's not an old lady or a cum slut. Some say she's mine. She isn't. Sometimes I fuck her. She wants me to wife her, but I never will.

"On a diet, Em," I reply as I straddle my ride.

"You don't need to diet, baby. You're a hunk of lean, sexy muscle." She runs her hand down my torso and keeps going. I grab her wrist before she reaches my dick.

"There's a time and a place," I say firmly as I motion my head towards the young children running around.

"Maybe later, then, big boy," she says coyly as she licks her lips.

"Yeah, maybe."

"I hear PJ's coming today now." Her expression changes to one of distaste.

"Yup."

"You good to go, Prez?" Clay yells across.

"Yup," I reply.

Lincoln, our newly recruited prospect, swings open the gates. Clay, our enforcer, Jefferson, and I make our way out.

He salutes us, and I take in his long, bright red hair and smiling blue eyes. I can smell his cut from where I'm sitting on my hog, the leather smell solid and potent, the black skin not even cracked yet due to its newness. Won't take long for the pressure of this life to show on both his cut and in his eyes. Not even knowing what happened to the previous prospects put him off working towards a patch. At eighteen, it wouldn't have put me off either. Then again, I was born into this. I had no say in the matter. Not sure it would have made a difference if I had, as it's all I've ever known.

We rev up the hogs, then ride into town to meet with some of the others and find PJ.

CHAPTER ELEVEN

JAINE

Twenty-One Years Earlier (Age Seven)
Rising, California

I LOOK AT HIM AND SMILE SHYLY, MAKING SURE MY LIPS DON'T
part. I deliberately don't show my teeth, as the boys at my last
school said I look like Bugs Bunny.

What's up, Doc? they used to say, then they'd roll around
laughing when I cried. They also made fun of my glasses. They said
I was ugly and skinny too. They were really mean.

This boy has shoulder-length wavy hair that's as inky black as
the midnight sky. His eyes are as blue as the bluest thing ever on a
scowly face that's been turned brown by the sun. He has freckles
and a dent in his chin that makes it look like a little butt. He's
wearing navy shorts and a white wifebeater, and his knees are
bruised and dirty.

I'm tall for a girl, but he's still a full head taller than me.

I've decided that he's beautiful. The most beautiful person I've ever seen.

"I'm Jason, and I'm eight," he says as he holds out his hand politely. He kicks the loose stones at his feet while smiling crookedly. He has two pointed teeth that make him look like a wolf.

"I'm Jaine, and I'm seven," I say, almost breathlessly, running my hands down my pale blue summer dress before taking his clammy one in mine. My eyes drop to his dirty nails, a sure-fire sign that he likes to play outside a lot. I like to play outside too, but I never really had anyone else to play with before.

Shielding my eyes from the brilliant sunshine with my hand, I look over at both our pops, causing Jason to turn to look at them too. They're smiling, slapping each other on the back, laughing real loudly and looking like they haven't seen each other in forever.

"My pop hasn't smiled in ages. Not since my mom went to heaven," I say quietly, and I feel a tear run down my face.

Jason studies my face intently, taking in my distress, and then walks closer. I look up at him with tear-filled eyes, and he wipes the fallen ones from my cheeks.

"My mom's in heaven too, so maybe they're best friends now."

I smile. "Yes, for sure they are." Then, forgetting, I accidentally show my teeth. I instantly blush and put my hand over my mouth.

"What you hiding your smile for, Jaine? It's real pretty," he says, showing me his wolfish one.

I grin at him, my cheeks feeling hot at the compliment.

This beautiful boy thinks my smile is pretty.

"You think if our pops are best friends, and our moms are, that we could be best friends too?" he asks, looking at the ground while waiting for my response. I can just tell my saying yes is really important to him.

"Sure." My voice is almost a whisper.

"You want to go to the river? I can show you how to skim

stones." He looks at me, his face full of longing, desperate for me to go play with him. Maybe he needs a friend as much as I do.

I nod and smile, showing my teeth.

"Race ya, then, slow poke!" He takes off at full speed, kicking up dust from the worn track as he goes and leaving me running after him.

It was right then I knew I loved Jason Steele.

Present Day

"Wakey, wakey, sleeping beauty." It's Cherry's voice.

Shocked, I sit bolt upright and look around, completely disorientated. Then it all comes flooding back to me. Yes, my pop really is dead. Yes, I am almost home, and right now, we're about twenty miles outside Rising.

We're currently sitting in Pete's Diner, having a muffin and a latte. It's Sasha's staple. Go figure. The smell of home-cooked food fills the air. The tablecloths are red and white check. A vase of fresh daffodils sits in the center of each, along with every sauce and condiment you could ever possibly need. Pete sings along with gusto to Planet Rock in the background as he cooks from the menu. It's clear he loves his job.

"I'm awake," I mutter, even though I hadn't been. I wipe the back of my hand across my mouth on the off chance I've been drooling.

"Are you eating that?" Sasha asks as she stares at my untouched chocolate chip muffin.

I shake my head and grimace. I'm way too nervous to eat. She immediately leans across the table and breaks a chunk off before popping it in her mouth and groaning loudly with her eyes closed. It's reminiscent of the orgasmic scene from that old movie *When*

Harry Met Sally. I'm just waiting for another customer to yell out, 'I'll have what she's having'.

I roll my eyes. Lifting the muffin carefully, I move it across to her side of the table.

"If I'm not having the damn thing, I don't want to be covered in its crumbs, thank you," I mutter.

I frown as I stare out the window, taking in the familiar sights of my youth. The dream I had threw me. Are my old childhood memories, the ones that I'd buried away in my subconscious, coming back to haunt me as I near home? As I near Ace? Picking up my latte, I take a sip, but it's lukewarm now, so I drink down its caramel flavor in one go.

"You said I could have a ride of the Softail when we were on the final stretch, Jaine," Cherry looks across the table at me. Like me, she's wearing tight-fitting black leather pants and a black tank top. She's also wearing my old leather jacket as she forgot to bring her own. I'm wearing one with fringes. She finds them too distracting, apparently, so declined my offer of this one, even though it's designer and cost a fortune. Maybe it's just as well she's wearing the Angels patched one as I'd sooner not draw attention to myself.

I nod. I was kind of hoping she'd forgotten. Reaching into my pocket, I pull out the keys and pass them to her.

"You damage my baby, and I'll kill you," I warn her. I'm candid. That hog is my pride and joy, and my pop's greatest gift to me, aside from life itself.

She rolls her eyes. "It's only twenty miles. I'll be careful."

She passes me her keys in return.

"First time I'll have had a Fat Boy between my legs," I say with a smile, and we all giggle.

I can feel Sasha's eyes burning into me, the half-eaten muffin no longer of interest to her now she's had her chocolate fix. It's been discarded and pushed to the side.

"Are you nervous, Jaine?" Her eyes are huge as she tries to gauge my reaction to her question.

I frown at her.

"About going home?" I shrug. "No, why would I be?" I know fine well that's not what she's getting at.

"No. About seeing... you know, him. Jason. Ace."

Now both of them are staring at me.

I bite my lip. "Yes and no." There's no point in being anything other than truthful with these two. "I mean, he's probably got a wife now, or at the very least, Emilia will be his old lady. It's been ten years, remember? He's also most likely obese and bald." I chuckle, my hand instinctively reaching up to touch the tattoo behind my left ear. "Delaney will also have threatened Ace's life should he so much as look in my direction, so I might not even see him the whole time I'm in Rising."

Cherry rolls her eyes. "Razr's such a chauvinist pig. He wants you barefoot, pregnant, and riding bitch. You do know that, don't you?"

I nod. "I'm well aware of that, but what Paul Delaney wants and what he gets are two entirely different things where I'm concerned. He's been pressing hard to get me to commit for months now, and here I am, still only using him for sex. Delicious sex, I have to admit, but still just sex."

"Do you think you'll ever be *in love* with him?" Sasha asks, using air quotes. "I mean, as much as I agree with Cherry that he's a chauvinist, he really does love you, Jaine."

I raise my eyebrows at her. "Jesus, Sash. I never thought I'd see the day you'd be feeling sorry for Paul Delaney." I lean my head back on the booth seat and consider the question, then I shrug. "Honestly? If I don't love him after four years together, it's never going to happen. That aside, I think I have to make peace with my past before I can move forward with anyone. To do that, I need to exorcise the ghost of Ace. I'm hoping this trip will see me able to do that." I stand up and stretch. "Anyway, shall we get going?"

We leave payment on the table, along with a very generous tip and Sasha's crumbs.

Once outside, I raise my face to the summer sun, put on my helmet, and straddle the Fat Boy.

My heart's in my mouth for two reasons.

I watch as Cherry straddles my beloved Softail, which is the first one.

"Be careful," I mouth.

"I will," she mouths back.

The second is the impending confrontation with my beautiful boy.

With Jason Steele.

We rev up the hogs and head the short distance into Rising to meet Ace.

CHAPTER TWELVE

JAINE

Rising, California

WE REACH THE SIGN FOR RISING WHAT FEELS LIKE SECONDS LATER. It's been ten years, but it's still not been long enough. It's still far too soon for me to be confronted by *him*. I'm not ready for my brain to drag up the past and go through what he did to me line by line. Not sure I'll ever be ready.

The town itself hasn't changed. The good folks of Rising probably haven't either. Still the same old butchers, bakers, and candlestick makers. I look around, and it's like time stood still, but with a fresh coat of paint thrown over the top.

Rising has its own unique smell. Petrichor and wildflowers. I inhale the sweet air deep into my lungs in an effort to swap the oxygen of New York that's running through my blood for that of this place. To turn me back into the girl I used to be.

Plain Jaine.

Not that I'd ever want to be *her* again. At least she fits in here. I don't. Not anymore.

As soon as we enter Rising, I immediately take in the group of bikers sitting on their hogs outside Ned's cigar shop. I can clearly make out the Angels of Hellfire patches on their leather cuts. They swing their heads around as they hear our rides approaching, taking in the three women entering their sacred domain on custom-built hogs.

My heart pounds in my chest. I instinctively want to flee from the unknown that Rising and Ace offer me. To turn around and ride back to the safety and security that Manhattan and Delaney offer me.

I switch on my indicator as I ride up the main street and pull into the parking bays in front of old man Nelson's post office. There's a small package to be collected, and I told Anita I'd pick it up on my way to the house. The girls pull in behind me. I'm conscious the bikers' eyes are on us now, looking at us warily. They'll be on high alert after what happened with the Bratva. I guess they'll be expecting Razr's old lady to arrive today too.

Given the rally going on in Fielding, I'm surprised by how few bikers there are in Rising compared to the numbers we encountered on the road. It's late afternoon now, though, so maybe the volume of passing traffic has died down. Rising doesn't like to attract tourists. Unwelcome folks that might want to stick their noses into the MC's illegal business affairs. So, there are no hotels or other sources of accommodation for passers-through to spend the night, just to encourage them not to stop and keep right on going.

We dismount our rides and head into the post office. It's the same old glass-paneled door, and the same old bell that dings when you push it open.

The girls make themselves scarce by going into the small shop attached to the rear. They can take in the products on offer in there, most likely with distaste, as the majority is canned.

Tears immediately spring to my eyes when I take in Mr. Nelson standing behind the familiar old walnut counter. He's got to be eighty years old, but he still looks the same, only with greyer hair and more of life's experiences etched on his face. He looks at me and smiles, but there's no recognition there. I walk across, and my eyes drop to the glass frontage underneath the counter, which still displays the largest selection of colorful sweets and gobstoppers I have ever seen. Then my gaze turns to the old-fashioned weighing scales. How many times did Ace and I come here at every age for our daily bag of sweets? We'd accuse old man Nelson of robbing us by adjusting the mechanical scales in his favor. Then he'd laugh and add another little helping for our cheek.

"Afternoon, Mr. Nelson. I'm here to collect a parcel."

I feel like a teenager all over again. Worst still, I feel like Plain Jaine all over again. I stand at the counter and look at him. The sounds of local radio play tunelessly in the background. He peers at me over the top of his reading glasses, his eyes watery with age, shuffling from foot to foot and trying to work out who the hell I am and how I know his name.

"It's me, sir. Jaine Jones." I make it easier for him. I can hear the tears in my voice.

"What? Oh, dear sweet Lord, it's little Jaine Jones! Sylvia, Sylvia... come out here! Jaine Jones is here. She went all the way to Connecticut, do you remember? Left Rising and made a name for herself as a bigwig lawyer."

Sylvia, his tiny wife, who's almost as wide as she is tall, waddles through. She sees me and immediately starts crying while wringing the bottom of her crisp white apron in her hands and patting the grey bun on top of her head.

"Oh, Jaine! Look at you! Why, you're so beautiful! Oh, and poor Jeremiah! I'm so sorry! We're so sorry! Oh, Jaine."

We hug and sniff. Eventually, I'm allowed to leave with my package after I promise faithfully to return the next day to let them know what I've been doing these past ten years. I'll need to leave the majority out. I can't say I'm a vigilante who shoots vermin in the head in my spare time, and as part of my proper job, I get MC outlaws off the hook like my pop did.

The girls and I leave the store and stand at the entrance so I can compose myself. The bikers have moved and are now directly across the street from us, eyeing our rare hogs with interest.

"Cherry. Sasha," I whisper.

"Yeah, BFF?" Sasha says, looking at me and then across at them, her arm now linked through mine.

"Cherry… you got the jacket from eBay if anyone asks. The Softail is yours. The Fat Boy is mine. I want to see if they recognize little old Plain Jaine. Shall we give them a show, girls?" I say with a wink.

"Yeah. Let's show these one-percenter bad boys we will *never* ride bitch." Cherry smirks at me, then holds her head up defiantly.

"You want to go first, girlfriend?" I raise an eyebrow.

Cherry winks, then takes off towards the Softail, sashaying her perfect hour-glass body, while Sasha and I pretend to look at magazines at the store entrance.

From the corner of my eye, I watch as jaws almost hit concrete as they take in Cherry. That girl just screams posh pussy. She flicks her flame-red hair over her shoulder and turns to face us, giving them a view of her great ass. The Angels' patch will almost definitely be on display now. They sit upright and watch as she straddles the Softail, rubbing herself over the soft leather seat like she's riding a goddamn dick.

"You next, Sash?" We both giggle.

My tall, leggy friend makes her way down in low-rise dark denim jeans. She looks like a fucking supermodel with her tall, slim build, and her dark tresses framing her perfect features. She leans down to tuck her jeans into her boots, so all eyes are on her ass. While she hypnotizes them, I use the opportunity to check out the pack. I scan the faces. I see Clay and Jefferson immediately.

Where the fuck is Ace?

Sasha straddles her Sportster and lowers herself down real slow as she smiles across at them. The girls then look towards me.

I take off my jacket and sling it over my shoulder.

I know I look good in skin-tight leather pants and a tank top. I'm also braless, and my nipples will be on show as they're so hard you could hang coats off them. I walk towards the hog like I'm on a fucking catwalk. A wolf-whistle greets me, followed by another.

I slowly straddle the Fat Boy.

"Here we go, ladies. In 3, 2, 1."

Right on cue, the bikers cross the road head in our direction. We smirk at each other.

"How you ladies doing this fine day?" Clay speaks as he stops in front of us.

The years have been way too kind to this man. He looks hot as hell. Still blonde, but no longer sporting a buzzcut. His hair is way past his shoulders now, and wavy, his eyes the color of chocolate molasses. His handsome face has matured, so it's all lined and defined. Any boyish features have long since faded. He's all fucking man.

"We're doing fine, Mr. Biker Boy." Sasha smiles at him coyly as she sucks on the arm of her designer aviators, running her tongue along the edge.

Clay watches her, then clears his throat. No guessing where his mind's just been. "What brings you to Rising? You ladies just passing through our town?"

It's then I hear the other hog approach. I'd recognize that sound anywhere. It's a classic Super Glide Sport, and I know exactly who it belongs to. My eyes drift to the rider. He's helmetless, and his long black hair flows behind him. His eyes connect with mine, but I see no recognition in them, thankfully.

Everyone looks at him. It's hard not to. Some folks are just born to be stared at. Sasha uses the opportunity to turn to me, and I nod to acknowledge.

Yes, it's Ace.

He pulls up beside the others and dismounts his ride before walking over to us.

I feel like I've been sucker-punched, the oxygen stolen from my body. My heart thumps in my chest as I take him in. This boy. This man. Ten years ago, he was the center of my whole fucking universe.

My mouth is suddenly bone dry. He's taller, or at least he's filling my world with his larger-than-life presence. He walks like a panther with a lean build that you just know is taut and rock-hard underneath his clothes.

Yup, he's definitely confident.

His blue jeans cling to his muscular thighs and slim hips, and his white Henley is pulled up to his elbows, displaying the plethora of tattoos that caress his arms. I find myself wondering if he's had any bitches' names inked on him, and I immediately feel a pang of jealousy. It looks like the Henley's one size too small. Probably deliberately so he can flaunt his toned physique.

Yup, he's definitely vain.

My eyes scroll up to his face, which is tanned and more chiseled and defined than it ever was, likely with age and life's experiences. A small beard caresses his jaw. It's welcome addition making him look dirty. Really, really fucking dirty.

You'd like to get dirty with him, wouldn't you, Jaine?

Shut the fuck up, brain!

Yup. Hard to believe my beautiful boy is even more beautiful.

"Where did you get the jacket?" His rich, dark, and smooth like melted chocolate voice is directed at Cherry.

My gaze eventually locks with his, and he's staring at me suspiciously like I'm a piece of shit on his fucking boot.

Yup, he's definitely an arrogant asshole with a capital A.

"eBay? Why?" she replies haughtily as her eyes drift slowly over him.

He turns to look at her, completely ignoring her blatant ogling.

"I was just asking these beautiful ladies if they're just passing through our town, Ace." Clay smiles at Sasha, who's still sucking on the end of her glasses, flicking her tongue over the end like she would tongue a dick.

"Nope, we're here for a few days at least." Cherry smiles saccharine sweetly.

"Who you here to see, and what business do you have here in Rising?"

Who the fuck does Ace think he is? I step off the Fat Boy and stride across to him.

"It's none of your goddamn concern why we're in this here town," I reply, staring at him, my blood now boiling in my veins. I'm pissed at his tone, but I'm also pissed at how he treated me in the past. The culmination of both is going to result in an explosion any minute now.

"My town, my business, sweetheart." He stands over me, trying to make me cower.

Fuck him. Then the familiar smell of his aromatic cologne envelopes me, which only agitates me further as my panties suddenly feel soaked, and I don't know whether I want to punch the fucker or kiss him.

"Fuck you, you arrogant asshole." I glare at him, my gaze dropping to take in the word *President* on his leather cut.

"Well, much as I wouldn't mind having a taste of your sweet pussy, I really don't have time for a fuck right now. So, instead, I'll ask you again. What are you doing in Rising?" He growls.

"And I told you it's none of your goddamn business, Prez." My voice is quiet and level. Our faces are inches apart. His eyes? The ones that were bluer than the bluest thing ever? Well, I never realized until that moment how many shades of blue there are. His eyes contain every single shade, and some that possibly haven't even been discovered yet.

Usually, I wouldn't, but I break eye contact first. Only so I don't turn into a puddle in front of him. There's no way I'm giving the asshole *that* satisfaction. I walk across and straddle the Fat Boy. One of the younger brothers reaches out and tries to take my keys from the ignition so I can't drive off before answering the question. It's a step too far. Before he knows what's happening, I'm off my ride, and his arm's twisted up his back. If I push it just a little bit further, it'll snap.

"Don't you *ever* touch my hog again, you hear me? Next time you try dumb shit like that, I will break your fucking arm," I whisper in his ear.

He nods, and I push him away. The others laugh and holler, no doubt amused that he's had his ass whipped by a female.

I walk back over and take in the thirty or so bikers in front of me. I recognize many faces, but there are only two others I remember the names of.

I turn to stare at Ace. "It's good to see you, Clay. You too, Jefferson," I say without looking at them. Then I walk closer, so *he* and I are almost nose to nose. "Can't say the same about seeing you again, though, Ace. Once an asshole, always an asshole." I smirk at him and raise an eyebrow.

He stares at me, and I watch as it finally dawns on him exactly who I am.

"PJ?" He pushes my hair back from behind my ear as he takes in the scrolled letter A. This brief touch has the oxygen leaving my body for the second time. I feel my insides gush, so aroused I'm only glad I'm wearing leathers instead of jeans as it would definitely be fucking noticeable by now.

He steps back like he's been burned and frowns. His eyes scan me from head to toe, probably wondering where the braces, glasses, and poker-straight body have gone.

I see every emotion flick through his eyes as he looks at me in wonderment before they go impassive and cold.

"Why didn't you just say who you were instead of wasting everyone's fucking time? You know we're on high alert. We haven't got time for silly games when lives are at stake." he's looking at me like I'm a piece of shit again.

His eyes drop to my nipples, which are almost waving at him and demanding his attention, preferably from his hands or mouth. Even better, both. He must be able to read my mind as it causes him to lick his lips in response.

Did I hear a slight growl? If so, was it him, or was it me?

"I'm surprised you all didn't recognize me, Ace. Sorry, I'm no longer *plain*." I smirk at him, but I know deep down he's right. My pop is dead because of the danger we're all currently in, and here's me messing around like a fucking kid. I should know better.

I pass Cherry the keys for the Fat Boy and take my seat on my Softail.

"Well, I'll be damned." Clay lets out a long wolf-whistle and rubs the back of his neck. "Holy shit, PJ. Would you look at you," he utters when he finally finds his voice.

I nod at him. "Anyway, we'll be seeing you guys. Tell Duke I'll drop by this evening if he's around, Clay. If not, I'll see him tomorrow. He's got my number, so he can let me know when's convenient." I hand him my phone. "Put your number in there and call yourself so you've got mine. Probably best I have two points of contact whilst I'm in town."

Clay takes the phone and types his number in, then calls it just to be sure. He smirks at Ace as he hands it back to me.

Sticking it in my pocket, I put on my helmet and jacket and start my hog, with Cherry and Sasha following.

"Jefferson, Rebel. You go with them," Ace orders.

I don't argue with him. I know Delaney will have him under strict instructions. We're now under the protection of the Angels as we're on their territory.

I nod at Ace, and he nods back. Then I set off for home.

Frowning, I think of what Clay called him earlier. It must be his road name these days.

Ace.

Why the fuck did he choose that? For sentimental reasons? Not likely. Maybe he still cheats at poker.

I snicker to myself as I ride to my old home.

My grin leaves my face when I remember Pop isn't going to be there when I arrive and never will be again.

My mouth sets in a grim line. My worry is the only way I'm ever going to be able to exorcise Jason Steele out of my system is to fuck him.

CHAPTER THIRTEEN

ACE

The Angels of Hellfire Clubhouse, Rising, California

WE RIDE BACK TO THE CLUBHOUSE IN SILENCE.

I'm still furious. What the fuck was she thinking messing around like that? We're not kids anymore. This is serious shit we're involved in. Her old man's just been shot dead over what's going on with the fucking Russians.

My mind's full of her. I'm cursing myself over that too. The way she looked. Her smell. Her confidence. Her skin almost set me on fire when I touched her. Jesus, if I thought I wasn't worthy of her then, there's no way in hell I am now. She looks better than any woman I've ever seen in real life or in any magazine. She's success-ful. She's made something of herself. She's the old lady of the billionaire prez of one of the most successful charters in the US.

Why did I think she'd even spare me a second glance?

More importantly, she's clean. Pure. Her hands aren't covered in the blood of countless vermin's souls sent straight to hell with my bullet in their heads.

I'm not Razr. It doesn't sit right with me. The thought of willingly tarnishing her with my fucked-up shit.

Lincoln opens the gates, and we file in and park up.

Em's sitting with the old ladies still. It's late afternoon, and they're starting to pack up their free wares, no doubt swapping recipes so they can make more of what was popular next time around. I look at Em. She's pretty in her own way, with her olive skin, dark hair, and curves in all the right places. But she needs to stop waiting for me. She deserves better. I've promised her nothing. I never will. Still, she waits around, wasting her time, possibly because I've not committed to anyone else, so she still has hope. She still thinks there's a chance for us.

Both of us are fucking fools. There's no chance for either of us —her with me or me with PJ.

Getting off my hog, I storm towards the clubhouse and motion for her to follow me to my room. Adrenaline is flowing through me, and I need a release.

She closes the door behind her.

"Get on your knees." My tone is flat. She knows what I want, and I just need her to get on with it.

She does as she's told and sinks to the floor before unzipping me and pulling out my already rock-hard dick. I watch as she licks the pre-cum from the tip. She trails her flat tongue slowly underneath from my balls right up to just under the crown, where she sucks against the nerve endings. I hiss at the sensation when it makes my balls tighten further.

"You know what to do, Em. Spit and suck."

She knows I like it wet. I watch as she grips my shaft and spits, then she takes my cock deep between her lips. I immediately thrust hard and fast into her mouth, making her gag when the tip connects with the back of her throat. My dick hardens further. I fist her hair, taking in her watering eyes and the mixture of pre-cum and saliva running down her chin and dripping onto her dress.

I pull her to her feet, then shove her backward onto the bed. Lifting her dress to her waist, I push her panties to the side, then run my fingers up her slit. She's drenched. Her pussy juices coat my hand as I fuck her with three fingers, my thumb pressing against her clit, causing her to come almost immediately. I don't even bother to remove my jeans or her underwear. I sheath my length with a condom and thrust straight into her. She's hot and tight. I fuck her hard and fast, and like the asshole I am, I close my eyes and imagine it's PJ beneath me. Her blonde hair spilling over my pillow, her long legs wrapped around my hips, her perfect little pussy welcoming back my throbbing dick.

Em screams in my ear as she comes again, her walls gripping onto my dick like a fucking vice. My balls feel like they're going to explode, and then I finally come. I grunt loudly as the pressure releases from my balls as well as my brain, and I keep driving into her deep and fast as I empty until I'm bone fucking dry.

Standing, I pull my jeans up and go to the bathroom to take care of the condom. Em is sitting on the edge of the bed when I return.

"I need to go speak with Duke, so you need to leave," I announce, feeling like a complete dick for using her and then telling her to get out. Still, she knew what she was signing up for with me. I've never promised her anything.

She leaves with an annoying smirk and closes the door.

I wash my hands and my face and change my Henley for a clean one.

I sit on the edge of the bed and think back on my only time with

Jaine. When I popped her fucking cherry. I should have known she was a virgin. It's not like I'd ever seen her with anyone else. I just shoved my dick in her when I should have been gentle. I didn't realize until the following day when I saw blood all over the sheets. I wanted to apologize for hurting her, but by then, it was too late. She'd already gone. Set off for Connecticut. She gave my almost nineteen-year-old asshole self the most special part of her, and I took it with no consideration. The memory is stored in my mind. I can still smell her. Taste her sweet pussy on my tongue. Hear her cry out as she came.

There's not much I wouldn't give to replay that moment over.

I KNOCK ON DUKE'S DOOR. IT STILL SAYS PREZ ON IT, BUT I'M NOT bothered about shit like that. I wait for him to answer. Sometimes he fucks Darla, the old lady of a brother who recently passed. I walked in on them recently. There's no way I want to witness that shit going down again. Guess he's only in his fifties, though, so he's still young enough to want to get his dick wet from time to time.

"Come in," he bellows.

I open the door, and he's sitting at his desk with his reading glasses perched on the end of his nose, his hands among a whole pile of receipts and invoices. He's the treasurer for now. At least until we can find someone else. The last one, Notes, got shot in the head by a ricocheting bullet during a previous run. If that asshole had any luck, it was bad.

Looking around, I take in the familiar walnut desk and the pair of dark grey leather tub armchairs at either side. The walls are filled with photos of brothers, past and present. So many images of men in Angels' cuts it's difficult to see the white walls underneath. The picture above his head is a photo of him and Jeremiah. It was taken around the time Jeremiah moved back to Rising with Jaine, just after his wife died.

The curtains in the room are drawn. It's like my old man doesn't want to see the light of day now his best friend can't witness it with him. Jeremiah's death has hit him hard. They were complete opposites, but like brothers more than friends all the same.

"Has she contacted you?" I ask him as I collapse in the chair facing him. He removes his glasses, placing them on the pile of papers, and leans back in his chair.

The smell of cigar smoke lingers in the air. It catches my breath, so I can almost taste it. He doesn't have many, but it's top-shelf tobacco from old Ned's shop in town when he does.

I look at him. He's still handsome, even approaching sixty. Same height, build, and eye color as me. His black hair is peppered with grey now, and it's cut short. His face is lined. It's doesn't take many years to rack those up living this kind of lifestyle.

"I'm guessing you mean Jainie?" He raises an eyebrow at me.

I nod, my gaze turning to the window that overlooks the rear courtyard. There's nothing to see, but any distraction is better than nothing, even if it is only scrubland and fucking tumbleweed.

"Yes, I've just spoken to her. She's coming to the clubhouse tomorrow with her friends. She said you'd been a bit unwelcoming, but that was more a reaction to how she behaved, which she knows was wrong. She said to apologize to you on her behalf. She'll also apologize in person when she sees you."

I nod. In a way, I'm glad she realizes my responses were due to the dangers we're all facing. She's under my protection now. I have a duty to keep her and this town safe.

He sighs. I know what he's going to say before he says it.

"You know, it was always my dream for you and her to end up together. I always said she was a keeper. The way she ran after you from when you were kids. Put you on a goddamn pedestal, she did. She loved you from the moment she met you, son."

"Yup, and now she fucking hates me. Today's proof of that."

He chuckles. "You know, I think she's still hankering after you. I mean, she's not settled with anyone else now, has she? And it's been ten years since you last spoke."

I look at him, narrowing my eyes and focusing on what he's just said. "She's Razr's old lady."

He shakes his head. "Nope. He wants her to be, but she's always turned him down. From what I hear, he's offered her marriage, the works, but she's turned that down too. She won't commit to him. Some of the other Scorpions say it's messing with his head and that he's pussy-whipped as a result. Can't think clearly no more. Not prioritizing club business. Well, they say that to me. They'd never say that to him because he'd slit their disrespectful throats." He laughs. "And look at you. You fuck Em, and she keeps waiting around. You need to let her go, son. Let her find someone else while she's still got youth and beauty on her side. You'll never commit to her. Just like lil Jainie will never commit to Razr. You're in each other's blood. Always have been. Always will be. You both just lost your way a bit."

I listen to what he's got to say.

"If I so much as look at her, Razr will cut me personally and with great pleasure."

He just shrugs. "Better to die fighting for what you want than to live a life in limbo thinking about what might have been. And that's what you've been doing these past ten years, isn't it? Not fully living. You went from being an outgoing sort to becoming melan-choly and withdrawn overnight. When Jainie left town, she sucked the soul right out of you and took that with her. Not intentionally, but she did all the same.

"Now, I didn't raise no damn coward. You might never get this opportunity again, so if you want the girl, you've got to fight for her or let her go once and for all and move the fuck on with your life. I don't know what happened. What it was that resulted in her skipping town all those years ago, but the way I see it, mistakes were made on both sides. You should have gone after her, but she should never have run off in the first place. Not without an explanation. As her best friend, you deserved that at least. But you were both so young and headstrong then, so maybe it was for the best. This time apart will have done you good. You'll both have had time to grow and mature and become the people you were meant to be. Now, as adults, you can see if you can make it work. See where life takes you. Just don't have any regrets, son. That's all I ask.

"I know Jeremiah frowned on the idea of you two being together, but in these later years, he was always saying that if Jainie were going to live this life, he'd rather it be with you here in Rising than with Razr in New York. It was his dream for his little girl to come home to him. He never got to see that happen, but maybe, if it's God's will, he'll get to witness it happen from where he's resting now."

His voice breaks, and I walk over and rub my hand across his shoulder. He reaches up and squeezes it with his.

I don't have the heart to tell him I think he's got it all wrong. He's always loved her like a daughter. PJ doesn't want me. She applied to schools across the country to get away from all this. To get away from me. To go off and make something of her life. I would just have held her back, and she knew that. If we'd stayed in contact, I'd have been able to convince her to return, so she cut me loose. Burned her bridges with me and this town. Bridges that are only being reinstated temporarily because her pop's been killed. Once he's been laid to rest at Rising Cemetery, she'll no doubt sell up his property and leave. There'll be nothing to bring her back then, except to return fleetingly to visit his grave.

Meanwhile, I'm stuck here. Prez of an MC. A life that was mapped out for me before I was even fucking born.

Nope. There's only one thing for it. I need to face reality. I need to fire up PJ's hatred of me and get her out of Rising as soon as I can. She sure as hell doesn't belong here anymore, and I sure as hell don't belong anywhere else.

CHAPTER FOURTEEN

JAINE

Sixteen Years Earlier (Age Twelve)
Jaine's House, Rising, California

"WHY CAN'T I EVER WIN!" I YELL AS I THROW THE PLAYING CARDS at him.

"'Cos you're rubbish at poker and 'cos you're a girl." He laughs at me as he rolls over on the floor to lie on his back while staring at his phone screen. He's always staring at that damn thing these days. I'm not allowed a phone yet. Pop says I can have one for my birthday.

I look around my pink girly bedroom, which is filled with all things sparkly, feathery, and glittery, along with a white metal princess-style four-poster bed. My pop keeps saying I need to change the décor to something more suitable for a teenager, but I'm still only twelve. I've got a few months yet.

"I hate you." I glare at him as I sit with my arms wrapped

around my shorts-clad legs. He's gotten all gangly because of some growth spurt he's had going on, and he's got some pimples too. I've offered to squeeze them, but he just looks at me in disgust and tells me I'm gross. He's going through puberty. I heard Duke telling my pop. Pimples or not, Jason still looks beautiful in his dark blue jeans and black Henley. It's impossible for him not to look beautiful. He was born to be the center of attention.

"No, you don't. You love me," he replies nonchalantly, his face still in his phone.

I stand and walk across to stare in the mirror hanging on the back of my bedroom door. I smile exaggeratedly at myself and then grimace. I've been in such a bad mood this week. The dentist pulled some of my teeth due to overcrowding in my mouth. I've had to have a brace fitted that makes it look like I've got train tracks running across them.

I sigh. As if I'm not ugly enough.

"Why am I so plain, Jason? Why am I plain Jaine?" I fidget with my brace, then exhale loudly.

"You're not plain. You're just growing into yourself. I am too. My pop says it's the ugly duckling stage. And don't be messing around with that brace. You'll look back one day when you've got straight white teeth and you'll be glad you wore it, trust me," he says, still not even looking at me.

"And meanwhile, you'll still look like wolf boy with your pointy fangs." I laugh at him through the reflection.

"Right, that's it." He tosses his phone on the floor, stands up, and stretches. Grabbing me, he throws me on top of my bed before using his *fangs* to bite the delicate skin on my neck.

"Ow," I shout out, even though it didn't really hurt.

"Aww, let me kiss it better, Jaine." He presses his lips gently against my neck, and I suddenly feel breathless. Neither of us moves, then he slowly pulls back and looks down at me. I stare at him, not sure what to say. Not sure what's just happened.

"Have you ever kissed anyone before, Jaine?" he asks quietly as his gaze drops to my mouth.

I shake my head, as no words will come out. He's still leaning over me, his face only inches from mine.

"Have you?" My voice is almost a whisper.

He shakes his head.

Do I want him to kiss me? Do I?

Yes, I want him to kiss me.

My eyes drop to study his lips. They're pink, and they have a nice shape. They look soft and pillowy. He flicks out his tongue to lick them, and I look now as they glisten.

Jason's going to kiss me.

He leans his head forward, and I close my eyes in anticipation until I can feel his warm breath mingling with mine and smell the peppermint of the gum he's been chewing.

My heart is pounding in my chest with excitement and apprehension. What if I accidentally bite him with my braces and staple his lips closed? That's what the boys in school say will happen if I kiss anyone.

Will he put his tongue in my mouth like the girls say the bad boys do, and will that mean I want *it* if I let him?

"Jason, we need to go," Duke yells from outside the door, causing him to jump up almost guiltily.

I stare up at him, and he stares down at me. Something just happened. Well, it didn't, but it almost did. Things changed between us. He's my best friend. He'll always be my best friend. But maybe he's meant to be something else too. Like a boyfriend? I think I'd like that. For beautiful Jason Steele to be *my* boyfriend. I wanted him to kiss me. He wanted to kiss me. He really did. Didn't he?

I so want for us to be each other's first kiss now—more than anything.

I bite my lip and stare at him.

His eyes are downcast, and his face is pink. He's embarrassed.

That's when I see it. Or should I say *them*?

The aces from the deck of cards that he'd obviously hidden up the sleeve of his black Henley had fallen onto the bed when he leaned over to kiss me.

Picking them up, I stand and slap them into his hand.

"You took the Aces from the deck. You're a big fat cheat, Jason Steele!" I yell at him as I push him and playfully pummel his chest.

He laughs and grabs my hands.

"From now on, I'm going to call you Ace!"

"Yeah? Well, from now on, I'm going to call you Plain!"

Same Day

The Angels of Hellfire Clubhouse, Rising, California

POP AND I ARRIVE AT THE CLUBHOUSE JUST BEFORE SEVEN P.M. We're only staying for an hour because some of the ladies who come here after eight p.m. don't wear very many clothes, and he doesn't want me to see anything inappropriate.

Meatloaf is playing on the jukebox in the background. My pop grimaces as the song goes on about dashboard lights. I'm not really paying attention. I take in the familiar space with the dark grey bar. Families are sitting around at the dark wood tables and chairs, and the kids are complaining and crying that they want to go home, tired out after a long day of playing tag or football.

I can't see Ace. I smirk at the name.

My mind is still racing over the *almost-kiss* moment he and I shared earlier. Maybe he still wants to kiss me. I've put on a pale-yellow summer dress and brushed my blonde hair. I think I look pretty, even though I have glasses *and* braces now. I know I'm too thin, but I can't put on weight no matter how much I eat. Pop insists I go to the stupid MMA classes three times a week so I can always protect myself no matter what. He says I'll thank him one day.

I'll be thankful for a lot of things one day, it seems.

Duke comes over to sit beside us.

"Pop, I'm just going to find Ace," I say brightly.

He frowns. "Who's Ace?"

I smirk. "My new name for poker cheating Jason Steele." I smile at him, and Duke chuckles.

"Is he in his room, Duke?" I ask as I flatten the front of my dress down with my clammy hands.

"I think I saw him go outside." He smiles at me.

I rush out the door and into the yard. It's still warm, but there's a gentle breeze now that makes my skin prickle. I hear voices and a girl giggling.

Peering around the corner of the clubhouse, I see Emilia and Ace. He's wearing what he was earlier, and she's wearing a pale blue dress that's really short and tight and makes her butt look like two balloons.

He's leaning against the wall, and she's leaning against him.

I suddenly feel sick. I don't want her to be leaning on Ace.

He's my beautiful Ace.

She smiles at him and swishes her hair around her shoulders and then she puts her arms around his neck, and she kisses him, and he kisses her right back. He even puts his tongue in her mouth, and she lets him, which means she wants *it*.

I gasp. They turn and look at me, and I run back inside.

"Pop, we need to go." I pull at his hand.

He looks at me and frowns. "Why? What's wrong, Jaine?"

"I… I don't feel well," I lie, pulling even more determinedly on his hand.

We leave just as Emilia and Ace are coming inside. She smirks at me like she's won the top prize at the fair, and I just glare at her.

I hate her.

Ace grabs my arm, but I pull it away. I don't even look at him.

I didn't speak to him for a full month after that. It was the longest month of my whole life and the first time my heart got broken.

CHAPTER FIFTEEN

JAINE

The Angels of Hellfire Clubhouse, Rising, California

I TAKE IN THE FAMILIAR CLUBHOUSE FROM MY YOUTH AS WE approach. It's still bland and black. It seems to be one of only two color options available for this type of establishment, the other being grey like it is in New York. These buildings are all bullet-proof and built like Fort Knox.

Someone's tried to brighten up the outside by adding tractor tires, filling them with soil and then planting some colorful flowers, but it's the equivalent of putting lipstick on a pig. It's a nice finishing touch, but it does nothing to disguise the overall unattractive appearance. This shit can never be made to look pretty. The ugliness and evilness it contains seep out of every fucking crack.

The gates to the compound have been changed, or at least they've been taken back to bare metal and re-painted. Probably the latter, as the creak the hinges give out is still the same reluctant sound it was ten years ago.

"Thanks for picking us up, Jefferson." I smile warmly at him as he gets back in the cage after dealing with the iron bars. Riding the hogs was too much risk. Cherry and Sasha like a drink, and I have zero tolerance where that's concerned. No matter the reason, drink driving is not acceptable on my watch. Not under any circumstances.

"No problem, Jaine." He grins back at me.

Jefferson ignored me at school. I wasn't beautiful or cool enough to hang with. I guess it's a time in your life filled with peer pressure, and when appearances mean everything. He used to hang with Emilia's lot. I take in the green eyes dancing on his handsome, tanned face as they trail over me, now appreciatively, and his long blonde hair that hangs straight to mid-back. With his coloring, he could be my brother.

Cherry's got her eye on him. I've seen her sneak several sideways glances. Maybe she wants a guy in each port like a sailor. Blaze in NYC. Jefferson in California.

"Let's go, girls." Sasha pours herself out of the SUV and waves her finger at the clubhouse door.

Who knew Pop had such a large selection of fine Irish whiskies? Sasha does now, and she's sampled most of them. Gifts from The Hudson Dusters, maybe? I'll ask Padraig.

"Whoopsy!" She giggles as she almost falls flat on her face and is saved from eating dirt by Jefferson, who grabs her by the elbow to steady her. I roll my eyes and smile.

The girls are wearing short skirts with tight tops and heeled ankle boots. I'm dressed down in dark blue jean shorts, a white crop top, and high tops. So what if I have a six-pack, and it's noticeable? So what if it's not deemed feminine? At least I also have tits these days, so it balances out the boyish elements. Not massive at cup size

B, but still a handful and all my own. There's nothing fake about me.

It's past eight p.m. The cum sluts will be coming out in full force shortly. We've seen it all before, so I'm not worried about what shenanigans will be going on around us. Cherry and Sasha will probably be in the middle of it all anyway, knowing them.

I find my thoughts drifting briefly to Emilia. Is she still hanging around Ace? Is he still fucking her? Is she his old lady now? That same flare of jealousy from earlier sparks up inside me. I don't like it. I haven't felt jealously like that since Padraig stuck his dick in someone else.

I still fucking hate her. That bitch doesn't know the meaning of girl code. Likely can't even spell the damn words. She never paid attention at school. She was always too busy lying on her back with her legs spread. She flaunted her sexual relations with Ace in my face, despite knowing how I felt about him. I'd gladly put a bullet between her eyes given any opportunity.

We push open the door and make our way inside. All eyes turn to us, many of which I recognize, many I don't. The communal area is still the same grey bar with dark wood tables and chairs. The familiar smells of smoke, tequila, and sex immediately accost my olfactory senses, the combination bringing back so many memories. Some good. Some not so good. The place is busy with a mixture of brothers and old ladies still. The cum sluts are hanging around the edges like there's an invisible line drawn in salt that they can't cross over. Guess they know better than to try to attach themselves to any of the menfolk whilst their better halves are still present. I'm conscious I'm being stared at and realize I'll have no choice but to make the rounds. Might as well get it over with.

My eyes drift to the bar and immediately connect with Ace's. He frowns at me and looks tense. To his right is Emilia. She hasn't changed. She looks good. As I look across, she puts her arm through his. He glares down at the connection before pulling away. I glare at her, and I'm about to walk over. To do what? Snap her fucking neck? Say hello? I've no idea. I'll decide when I get there.

"Chiquita!" Gusto bellows and stops me in my tracks.

"Gusto!" I yell in response, wrapping my arms around his broad shoulders. I look down at him. His skin has more lines, he has less hair, his dark beard is longer with lots of added grey, and he's more portly, but still the same old Gusto—the man who gave me my one and only tattoo.

"Wow, look at you, pretty girl. Never mind being a lawyer like your old man, you should be on the damn catwalk, princess." He looks me up and down in a non-creepy way.

"I think I'll stick to the legal profession, Gusto, but I accept your compliment graciously." I smile at him, kissing him on the cheek.

Making my way around the place, I introduce myself and accept condolences from the brothers I know, the ones I don't, and all of their old ladies and girlfriends. I even introduce myself to the cum sluts. They don't know how to react to that. Some fucker's actually being nice to them, and it's not because they want something in return. I remember some of their faces, but not many. Most are new. Like in New York, they show them the door at thirty. And like prospects, there's a continual queue forming at the entrance to join the ranks. There's never a shortage. Young girls eager to be filled in all three holes with the cum of hairy bikers.

Just as I'm finishing my rounds, my phone vibrates.

"Delaney." I answer with a smile.

All eyes turn in my direction when they hear who I'm talking to. His reputation precedes him. He's a powerful, murderous bastard and is very important to this club, given the strong, financially advantageous alliance.

My eyes connect with Ace's again, and he scowls. He looks like he's been sucking on a bitter lemon from old man Nelson's store.

"Jaine. Jesus, I miss your voice." He sounds rough as fuck.

Maybe he really is missing me. "I miss yours too," I reply softly. "What have you been getting up to while I've been gone?"

He exhales. "Just taking out some of the trash in your absence. Listen, I'm thinking of visiting. I'm not sure I can go much longer without fucking you. Blaze and Knight have a meetup with the Angels, so I may come along. How does it feel being back home?" I know he's referring to the place *and* the people—one person in particular.

"It's not really home now, is it? New York is home to me. You know that."

Ace looks away. Probably relieved I'm saying that, as he'll be glad to see the back of me for sure.

"Anyway, it's difficult to say since we've only just got here. I haven't had a chance to catch my breath as we've spent so much time on the goddamn road. Listen, I'll give you a call tomorrow from Pop's house, okay?" I'm conscious the entire clubhouse is listening to at least one side of my conversation, maybe even both.

"Yeah. Okay, baby."

I walk towards the jukebox, where I'm less likely to be overheard. "Anything happening with the Bratva situation?" I ask quietly.

I'm not sure if he'll tell me anything, so I also make a mental note to call Padraig ASAP to check his end. Delaney won't go out of his way to lie to me unless he has to. I know he definitely won't put me in harm's way. After everything that's happened, though, I'm conscious I need to keep my own eyes open and my ears to the ground.

"It's not good news. There's still a lot of unrest. A lot of movement without any real action, like it's a ticking time bomb waiting to go off. My main concern is they've bought someone off, so they've now got someone on the inside." I can detect the worry in his tone. "We've got the green light from Bomb, though. I had no choice but to tell him about your extra-curricular activities to get him on board, but he's happy with you sitting on council." He says it matter-of-factly, like all he's done is tell his best friend I've changed the color of my hair.

I'm not sure I'm comfortable with Bomber knowing what I do out of hours. I'm not sure I trust anyone else knowing, but least of all him. Plus, he's old-fashioned. Women shouldn't be allowed an opinion or have input into anything important like decision-making. He already doesn't like me. Now he probably resents me on top.

I put the uneasy feeling to the back of my mind. I need to tell someone else just in case something happens to Delaney. He would die protecting me. I know that. I'd willingly do the same for him. But I wouldn't warrant I'd get the same level of protection from Bomber. That fucker would gladly turn me in. Usually, I'd tell Padraig as I trust him completely. Always have, always will. Strange, given we only dated for a few months, and I last saw him nine years ago when he'd only just started wearing long pants. This isn't something you just reveal over the phone, though. *'Oh, hi. How you doing, Irish? By the way, you know that famous sniper who kills the scum of society for scandalous sums of money? Well. Tada! It's me.'*

That means it needs to be Duke and/or Ace. I'd trust both of them with my life. Even if they wouldn't do it for me, they'd protect me to the nth degree for my pop, who was loyal to their club and died for their patch.

"Listen, I need to go. I'll speak to you tomorrow," I say quietly.

"I love you, Jaine."

"Miss you, Delaney," I answer before hanging up.

I'm standing right in front of the jukebox now. It's the same one.

The same colorful lights flash at me as though in welcoming recognition, and the same initials are engraved in the top right-hand corner. JS and JJ. I smirk at the memory. I have so many memories here.

"Where the fuck is it?" I mumble to myself, frowning, my finger trailing across the flashing glass screen, my eyes searching. The number is missing, and there's a white card placed over the original space where song number forty-two used to be.

I shrug and press the blank space regardless. Fingers crossed. I also press song number eleven.

Creep by Radiohead immediately springs into life. The song's been hidden from the jukebox like a dirty secret. Why, I wonder? Who would do that? Ace? Emilia? I lean my head back slightly and let the lyrics envelop me.

"You dancing, Jaine? It's your song." My thoughts are interrupted by Cherry, who's pulling on my arm. I've no idea where Sasha is—probably throwing up in the restroom after consuming way too much whiskey.

It's not my song, though. Ace and I used to mess around dancing to this song. I always said the lyrics reminded me of me. But it's *our* song. He knows it. I know it.

"Sure thing, babe."

She drags me into the center of the room, and we start to slow grind to the music, much to the delight and hollers of the bikers, who gather around to watch the all-female virtual sex show. Their admiration and adulation just spur Cherry on even more, and our moves become even raunchier. I'm surprised they don't start shoving money down our bras.

Song number eleven comes on next. *Naughty Girl* by Beyonce. Ace and I used to laugh at the cum sluts as they tried to dance sexily to this song, tottering around and almost breaking their necks in sky-high stilettos. Now? Well, I can dance to it better than the songstress herself.

I watch as Jefferson grabs Cherry around the middle. She shrieks with laughter, then immediately starts grinding her ass into his groin.

I shrug and start dancing by myself. Someone grabs me around the middle. Usually, I'd end them for doing that. Or at least Razr would. I turn around and take in the tall, lean man with dark brown curly hair almost down to his waist and eyes of amber.

Shit, he's hot. He smirks at me staring at him. Yup, and he fucking knows it too. I snake my arms around his neck and start to grind against his thigh.

I read his cut. "Nice to meet you, Mr. Sergeant At Arms. And you are?"

"They call me Chase, pretty lady." His smile widens, displaying perfect white teeth.

"Chase, huh? Why do they call you that, handsome?"

He snickers. "On account that the girls like to chase after me."

I can't help but laugh at his smug face. What is he? Twenty? Maybe twenty-one? "Oh, well. I won't be chasing after you... Chase."

"Oh, I'm sure I can convince you to, baby girl." He drops his hands to my ass.

I'm just about to break his fingers when someone grabs my wrist and pulls it hard.

"You need to come with me. Duke wants to speak to you."

It's Ace, and he looks furious. He drags me across the floor then through the door leading to the offices and the bedrooms.

"What the fuck are you doing?" I jerk my hand away and stop dead in the corridor, rubbing my now probably bruised wrist.

"You shouldn't be dancing like that. Not with him." I can tell he's trying to hold back his anger.

"What the fuck do you mean? It's how people dance these days! It's not like I was going to fuck him!" I look at him incredulously. "And even if I were, what business is it of yours?"

"You shouldn't disrespect your old man by behaving like that," he says dryly, his hands slung low on his hips as he stares at me.

"How the fuck am I disrespecting my pop by dancing, Ace? I'm also twenty-eight years old, so it's not like I'm a fucking virgin. You'd know that better than anyone, though, wouldn't you!" I hiss.

He closes his eyes and exhales slowly. "The people here respect you, PJ. They won't do that if you behave like a cum slut."

He's gone way too far. I slap him hard, leaving a red handprint on his cheek.

"Don't you ever call me a slut, asshole. Women can dance how they goddamn want. It doesn't make them a slut or easy." I point in his face as I emphasize every word.

He grabs me and pins me against the wall so hard he winds me and the wall pictures shake.

"You were fucking grinding on him! Why? Do you want dick? Is that what you want? If you want to be fucked, I'll happily oblige." He holds me by the throat as he hisses hotly against my ear, then he rams his front against mine. His dick is rock hard. "You want me to fuck you, sweetheart, you just let me know. You know where my bedroom is, or I can fuck you right here."

I twist my face to look at him. His eyes are filled with lust. The Devil's fucking lust. The sort that's a complete and utter sin. He smirks as he grinds his dick harder against my pussy. I know I'm wet. I'm fucking drenched. I want him. I want him to fuck me. I know it. He knows it. His eyes drop to my lips and then he kisses me.

CHAPTER SIXTEEN

JAINE

The Angels of Hellfire Clubhouse, Rising, California

ACE'S TONGUE FORCES PAST MY CLOSED LIPS TO STAKE ITS CLAIM, and I melt. My arms instinctively snake around his neck, and I cling to him, causing him to deepen the kiss, sucking my tongue into his mouth.

Someone growls. I'm not sure if it's him or me. I hear it again and realize it's me. I'm losing control of my sanity—God, how I've missed him.

Fisting my hair, he tilts my head back to expose my neck, trailing wet kisses up its length before finding my lips once more and filling my mouth with his tongue. His other hand drops to my tit, circling the outline of one nipple before squeezing it hard. A rush of pure desire shoots straight to my clit, and wetness pools in my underwear. I groan against his mouth, my hips instinctively pressing against his with a *please fuck me this instant* invitation, which causes him to curse under his breath.

He accepts my crude offer, dropping one hand to grip my hip painfully to hold me still. The other cups my pussy through my shorts, massaging my clit through the rough material. He tastes so fucking good. Of tequila and everything Ace. The combination with the smell of his aromatic cologne quickly causes all the carefully boxed-away memories to come flooding back like a tsunami.

Pulling his Henley free from his jeans, my hands reach underneath to touch his smooth skin, relishing in the feel of the jagged scars that now cover his body. My beautiful boy is now imperfect. But he's still fucking perfect to me. I drag my nails hard down the taut flesh of his torso, eliciting a groan of carnal pleasure from his throat, mine issuing one in response. My fingertips drop to his waistband and dip beyond until I can almost feel the heat from his hard dick. Almost touch it.

I'm completely lost in him. He's completely lost in me. How can a kiss be so fucking powerful? I'm drowning in everything Ace.

I can't let myself. Not yet. Not again. Not ever.

Common sense finally prevails. I push him firmly away and stand there with my chest heaving.

We stare at each other. I'm wondering what the shit just happened. Him? Likely the same. What the fuck is there to say? There's definitely no point in denying the chemistry we have. A connection so strong it's almost tangible.

"That can't ever happen again," I pant as I lean against the wall before running my hand through my hair. "I refuse to disrespect Delaney. He deserves better. From me. From both of us." I close my eyes and try to slow my heart rate. It's difficult as, when I open them, I'm drowning in the bluest eyes staring back at me, searching my soul for answers.

Answers to what?

He doesn't speak, but I can tell what I said has resonated. He has a conscience. I do too. If anything were to happen between him and me, it could only be if I ended things with Delaney first. I owe Delaney that much. More even. There's also the fact that he wouldn't hesitate in slitting both our throats if he thought I was cheating on him. Especially with Ace. That would be totally un-fucking-forgivable.

"I need to speak to Duke. Can you take me to him, please?" My voice is breathless and husky. I smooth down my hair and my clothes, not wanting his pop to look at me and know at first glance what's just happened between me and his son.

Ace runs his hands through his hair, then rubs them down his face before walking farther along the passageway. I follow.

We stop at a nondescript wooden door that says Prez on the outside. He knocks. It's met by a loud voice bellowing, "Come in." I'd know that voice anywhere, and tears spring to my eyes.

Ace opens it and motions for me to go inside.

"Jainie?" Duke stands when he sees me.

"Duke." I stumble over to him, this man who's like my second father, and throw myself into his arms as tears engulf me. The door closes behind me. Ace has left, no doubt to let us catch up. I cry non-stop for I don't know how long as Duke cradles me in his arms and smooths my hair.

"Hush, Jainie. It's going to be all right now. There, there, baby girl." Time passes, and he holds me as I let the pain and emotions flow for the first time since my pop passed. It only seems fitting to share this private moment with his best friend. Both of us united in our grief. Eventually, my crying subsides.

"Sorry, Duke." I lift my head from his now tear-stained cotton shirt. He wipes more tears from my face with his thumbs, then kisses me gently on the forehead before passing me a tissue.

I look at the man in front of me, who's now wiping tears from his face too. His similarity to Ace is incredible. The only difference is Duke keeps his hair short these days, and he's got more lines on his face.

"So, how have you been, lil Jainie? It's good to see you in the flesh after... what is it? Ten years?" He looks down at me, his eyes soft, scanning over me and taking in every detail. "Can I just say, Jeremiah must have been so proud. You've turned into a fine-looking young woman, and a very successful one too, by all accounts. Tell me, is Razr treating you well?"

I send him a watery smile as we move apart to sit. "Yes, Delaney treats me well, Duke. If he didn't, I wouldn't be with him. I'm nobody's fool. Nobody's goddamn bitch either."

"You're not his old lady, then?" He leans back in his chair.

I shake my head. "No. He wants me to be, though, and he's very persistent." I chuckle as I gently blow my nose.

I change the subject to the pressing one I need to discuss. I'm still filled with unease over The Exterminator revelation to Bomber. I've got a feeling in my gut that no good will come of it, and I never ignore my instincts.

"Anyway, Duke, I have something I need to tell you. Do you want Ace to be party to this?" I look at him, my hands playing nervously with my tissue.

Do I want Ace to be here? Do I trust him? He's hardly been communicative with me, and the way he looked at me when I came into the clubhouse earlier made it abundantly clear that I wasn't overly welcome, even if he did just stick his tongue down my throat.

"Do you want him to be here?" He frowns as he looks at me.

He'll think it's something unimportant. Some stupid female thing. So why bother dragging Ace away from important club business? There's no way he'll expect to hear what I'm about to say.

"Duke, I trust you with my life, and it could come down to that. Only two other people know about this. One I trust, the other I don't, hence why I needed someone else to know—someone who's on my side."

"Let me fetch my boy, Jainie. You wait right there." His chair groans in protest as he stands.

While he's gone, I stare around the room, taking in the larger-than-life desk, which matches the larger-than-life personality of the man who sits behind it. A man who looks kind and gentle on the outside. Looks can be deceiving, though. Duke will have way more kills than me. He's a murderer and an outlaw, although he'd never harm me.

The office walls are adorned with photos of brothers, many of whom have passed now—some due to natural causes, the majority while on duty for the club. I walk across and stare at the picture of Pop and Duke that's hanging behind the desk. It must have been taken not long after we moved to Rising.

The office door opens, and Duke walks back in. Ace follows, closing the door behind him. I cast my eyes over him, my gaze stopping to linger on his lips, which are red and plump from our make-out session. I find myself wondering if mine look the same and instinctively reach up my fingers to touch them, which doesn't go unnoticed.

"Ace." I nod.

"PJ." He nods back.

Both of us act like nothing's happened. Like we didn't just eat each other's faces off minutes before.

"Damn, there are only two chairs. Let me fetch another." Duke excuses himself.

Silence ensues.

I clear my throat. "I'm sorry about earlier. You know. In town.

Behaving like a kid instead of a grown-ass woman. More than anyone, I know how serious all this shit is," I say clearly, meaning every word.

"Apology accepted."

Silence ensues again.

"So, what do you want to talk to us about? I'm busy planning the next run." His tone is impatient. It's clear he doesn't want to be anywhere near me.

Frankly, right now, the feeling's mutual. It's too goddamn dangerous.

I try to contain the rage building inside me. It's also clear he thinks what I have to say isn't important. I can feel myself becoming a petty teenager again.

Shit. Why does he bring out the fucking worst in me?

"Why don't you go do that? I'll just speak with Duke. What I have to say is obviously not something that's worthy of your precious time."

He narrows his eyes at me. "I haven't got time for your high-maintenance bullshit, PJ. If you've broken a nail, tell your BFFs or Razr or someone who gives a shit."

I stare at him. I mean, I'm trying here. Really. I am. But he's not giving me anything to work with.

"Well, I suggest you take your conceited ass and that massive chip you have on your shoulder, and you leave. There's no way on God's green Earth that I'm telling you jack shit now, even if you begged me to!" I yell.

He runs his hands through his long black hair and hovers as if to add something. He then changes his mind and storms out, slamming the door behind him.

I sit on the tub chair just as Duke brings in a third, which is obviously no longer needed because the resident asshole has gone.

"Ace left. Said he didn't want to be wasting his valuable time with stories about what color I'm going to paint my nails or some other shit. I told him he needs to offload that giant chip on his shoulder. No one asked him to be the MC equivalent of Atlas," I huff, realizing I sound like a petulant teenager and cringing at the knowledge.

Duke sighs. "I'll have a word with him, Jainie. We're having some issues. It's not really for womenfolk to get involved in, though, as you'll appreciate. It's council business."

I immediately stand up and pace the floor, pissed off at the chauvinistic approach all these bikers seem to take.

"What areas do you mean, Duke? Like porn and sex clubs? Prostitution? Regular guns? Ghost guns? Hits for hire? Money laundering? Drug smuggling? I mean, for Christ's sake, do you think I don't know what the fuck goes on? I've only ever lived the MC life. For the record, I've just been accepted to sit on the goddamn council of the Iron Scorpions, so please don't think mentioning your illegal activities is going to harm my delicate feminine ears."

Duke frowns at me. "A woman on the council in one of the largest charters in the US? What the hell is Razr thinking?"

Anger floods my veins. "I'm not just any woman, Duke." I say it slowly and quietly. I take a breath and close my eyes to compose myself. "Have you ever heard of The Exterminator?"

He stares at me. "The sniper? Yeah, of course. Everyone's heard of him."

"Him." I smile, then laugh out loud.

I slam the palms of my hands so hard on his desk the room feels like it's shaking.

"The Exterminator isn't a 'he', Duke. The Exterminator is a 'she', and you're looking at her."

He looks up at me in disbelief, but when my expression doesn't change, he leans back in his chair, his face paling.

I bring up Delaney's contact details on my phone. "Delaney will answer within three rings. No matter where or what he's doing, that's how much I have *his* attention. Call him if you're in any doubt about my revelation. Ask him the question and get the confirmation you need." I offer him my phone.

Seconds pass, then he slowly shakes his head from side to side. To decline my offer or in disbelief that 'lil Jainie' could be a vigilante serial killer? Who knows?

"Why?" he asks, staring at me like I'm a whole new person and someone he doesn't even know anymore.

"Why what?" I ask as I retake my seat and slip my phone into my pocket. "Why did I take on the role of wiping vermin off the face of the Earth, or why did I tell you?"

"Both." His voice is quiet, and I suddenly feel guilty. Christ, he's old, and I've almost shocked the rest of his goddamn life out of him. My anger isn't meant to be directed at him. It's all meant for his asshole son.

"You know how good I've always been with a gun, Duke. My first hit was an Italian who raped a girl who was only ten years old. Shit like that shouldn't go unpunished. It didn't. After my first target, I figured I was going straight to hell, so I'm just making sure all those fuckers take a ride on the fiery helter-skelter before me. The last target? The Bratva? He was part of a group that was sex trafficking young children. Worst still, he was making porn stars out of them first to auction them off to the highest bidder based on what skillset they had to offer. I shot the asshole in the head while he was fucking his microscopic dick with his own hand." I exhale loudly. "So, that's why I do it. Why tell you? Well, up until last week, only Delaney and I knew about what we refer to as my extra-curricular activities. The shit hit the fan when I took out the second Bratva, as you know. Unbeknown to me at the time, there was already unrest after Razr took out the first one…"

"Wait, I thought it was Blaze who made the killing," Duke interrupts me, how brow furrowing.

I shake my head. "I have it on very good authority that the deceased was slit from ear to ear, which is Razr's mark."

He shakes his head again. It's a lot to take in. I realize that.

"Anyway, given the close relationship between The Exterminator and the MC, my hitting the second Bratva brought war to the Scorpions' door. The alliance is probably what resulted in my pop being killed. I told Delaney I wasn't doing it anymore. Not unless I was kept aware of what was going on. You know, so I could make informed decisions. The Scorpions' council approved my involvement moving forward, all bar one. They operate on a unanimous decision basis, as you know. To get the final party to agree, Delaney had to tell him about my vigilante role. I trust Delaney with my life. I don't trust the other person as far as I could throw him. I just needed to tell someone else because the other party has no loyalty to me whatsoever. If something happened to Delaney, I need him to know he's still being watched."

"Who's the other person?" Duke asks, his eyes narrowed.

"Bomber."

He shakes his head. "He's their VP. Razr and Bomb went to school together. They've known each other their whole lives. Bomber would never do anything to hurt Razr's old lady, surely?"

I look at him. "See, that's the problem right there. I'm not Delaney's old lady. Many of the Scorpion brothers think he puts me ahead of the club, and they don't appreciate that, given I've not shown my commitment to him. They think he's pussy-whipped. That my constantly turning him down is making him not always act in their best interests. Of course, that's complete bullshit. Delaney always puts the club before anything else, just as I'd expect him to, but rumors gain momentum. Shit stinks, and it also fucking sticks. Bomber resents me. Always has."

There's a pause.

"I have a confidant I'd normally tell this sort of thing to, so I'm really sorry to involve you, Duke. He also keeps me informed about what's going on. I can't run the risk of letting him know this from here, though, in case my calls are monitored or intercepted. That's why I'm telling you."

"Who is he?" He frowns at me.

"Someone I've known since I was nineteen. An ex-boyfriend. I'm not prepared to betray his trust, so please don't ask me to."

"How do we know he's trustworthy?" He focuses on me, his eyes narrowing.

"You have my word that he is. He's not MC, but he's on our side."

He raises one eyebrow. "So, one of the Irish, then."

I look at him but neither confirm nor deny.

There's a knock on the door.

"Come in!" Duke bellows, clearly frustrated at the interruption when he undoubtedly has a plethora of questions still to ask.

Emilia steps into the room. My hackles are immediately raised. I take in her short black dress, which compliments her olive skin. God, I wish she had aged badly or gotten really fucking fat. Smug bitch. Maybe I should just shoot her anyway. She smirks at me.

The thought of her and Ace together makes me want to choke the life out of her, revive her, and then do it all over again. Jealousy is a goddamn curse.

"Duke, Clay needs to speak to you and Ace. He's on the phone in the compound. It's urgent. One of the brothers has been arrested." She leaves, quietly closing the door behind her.

Who the fuck is she to call him Ace? Then I remember it's his road name.

I stand. "This goes no further, Duke. Delaney's convinced that the Bratva has bought someone off, so now we possibly have a person on the inside. Given Ace's attitude towards me earlier, it's clear my well-being is of no concern to him, so I don't want him to know either. That means, aside from me, only you, Delaney, and Bomber know. Can I have your word that it goes no further?" I ask, needing his confirmation.

"It will go no further, Jainie."

CHAPTER SEVENTEEN

JAINE

Rising Police Department

"Not what I wanted to be doing at eleven p.m. on a Friday fucking night," I mumble as I straighten my grey pinstripe jacket, only glad that I had two suits and my briefcase sent to Pop's house. Somehow, I just knew I'd need them. The Angels have no lawyer now, so I'm not sure what they're going to do. It's not like I can fly from New York every time one of the bikers ends up in trouble with the law.

My four-inch heels click on the tiled surface. It's reminiscent of NYPD with its stark white walls and grey tiled floor. Color charts are obviously not necessary when decorating the inside of pigsties. I'm sure I can smell the shit they wallow in, but it's likely just my imagination. I can, however, clearly smell vomit and Lysol.

It's obviously past the balding, middle-aged on-duty officer's bedtime as he's asleep at the reception desk. I slap my hand loudly against the wooden countertop, smiling as he wakes with a jolt. Poor bastard. He probably has a wife and kids at home, and this is the only rest he gets. I look at Ace and he smirks at me. I'm suddenly reminded of the almost nineteen-year-old boy I left behind.

It's good to know he has an expression other than the miserable, broody one he wears these days. Then again, he does suit the angsty bad boy persona he's got going on. Maybe a bit too well. My nipples instantly agree with my brain, and I have to adjust my jacket accordingly. I change my expression to a serious one before the pig looks my way.

"Excuse me, Officer. I'm here to see Detective Simons. My client is in custody, and I want him released immediately. You have no grounds to either hold him or charge him that I'm aware of. Ms. Jones from Jones & Associates Legal." I hand him my card.

"Ahh, Ms. Jones." I take in the detective who's just turned the corner and now stands in front of me. He's a muscular giant of a man with greying black hair and all-seeing piercing blue eyes. He looks to be in his late-thirties and is dressed well in a crisp white open-necked shirt and a pair of dark grey pants, teamed with expensive leather-soled shoes. His quirkily handsome face smirks at me, likely underestimating me as I'm female. I roll my eyes inwardly.

I hold out my hand to introduce myself. "Detective Simons. A pleasure to make your acquaintance. I'm the legal representation for Nathaniel Baker. I understand you have him in your custody."

He nods. "Yup, we do."

"Are you charging my client, Detective?"

"Nope."

"Any witnesses to anything you deem to be breaking the law?"

"Nope."

"Then, as we both know, if you're not charging Mr. Baker with anything, you can't hold him. I'll wait while you bring him to the front desk."

He stares at me, and I watch as his cheeks flush in what can only be annoyance at my abrupt tone.

"Officer Smith, please bring Mr. Baker around." He motions to the newly awakened officer, who's still wiping the sleep from his bleary eyes.

"Can I have a word, please, Detective Simons?" I motion for him to follow me to a quiet spot. "Listen, Detective," I start, lowering my head.

"Peter, please... Ms. Jones."

"Jaine."

"You were saying… Jaine."

"I was saying, Peter, that I don't want you to waste my time bringing these guys in when you've got nothing on them that will stick. If someone is telling tales out of school, I don't want to know. Having me dress professionally to come here on a Friday night will only antagonize me. Trust me, you don't want to do that. You may see a female lawyer in a pencil skirt and think I'm some sort of bimbo who's going to be easy to manipulate. I'm not. If you don't want to end up with your balls as hairy fucking earrings, don't mess with me. Don't play games with me. You will lose, I promise you. If you have something that will stick to one of my clients, then you'll have my undivided attention. If not, don't bother me unless I ask you to. Hopefully, we're clear on that." I smile as I pat his arm. "Enjoy the rest of your evening, Detective," I say as I walk away. I look at Ace, and it's clear he overheard every word.

Good. It's best he knows not to fuck with me either.

"Oh, Ms. Jones… Jaine?"

I roll my eyes before I turn around to face him again. "Yes, Detective?"

"Dinner tomorrow? Seven p.m.?"

I can't help but laugh out loud. Fair play to him. He's got bigger and hairier balls than I thought. I wag my finger at him as I'm about to reply.

"She's not available for dinner with you at any fucking time, Simons." Ace growls a response as he walks across and stands between us.

"You threatening me, Steele?" The detective glowers at him. I can't see Ace's face as he has his back to me, but his stance is menacing. My eyes immediately drop to his ass.

"Just stating a fact, Detective."

I roll my eyes at them as they posture, then turn as Nathaniel Baker, I'm guessing, approaches the front desk. Or Saw as he's more commonly known. I don't need any explanation or to imagine what he does with a saw. He looks disorientated, his long ginger hair mussed up like he's been sleeping. Lucky him.

I turn back to look at Ace and Simons.

"When you boys have finished comparing the size of your dicks and seeing who can piss highest up the wall, I'd like to get back to my evening. That's if you don't mind."

Ace turns and smirks at me. I ignore him and look past him. It'll take more than a couple of smiles to get me to even tolerate him. Grumpy, beautiful asshole that he is.

"Pleasure meeting you, Peter. Let's hope our paths don't cross again anytime soon. That is unless I decide to take up on your offer of dinner." I snatch the business card he's holding out of his hand, and I look at Ace, who looks mighty pissed off.

"My number is on the card. I look forward to hearing from you." He smiles smugly at Ace.

"Ace, let's go." He doesn't move, he just glares at Simons. In the end, I grab his arm and drag him away. My stilettos clip across the flooring as they did on the way in.

"What the fuck was that all about?" He stops once we get outside.

I roll my eyes. "Not that I have to explain myself to you, but I've just ripped the guy a new asshole and then tossed him a bone to make him feel better. I flirted a little, so he's thinking with his dick now. It's the lasting impression I want him to have. He thinks of me now, and he feels horny. He sees me, and it leaves him panting and wanting to fuck either me or his hand, so he's disadvantaged and incapable of making sensible decisions because all his blood's gone to his cock. There's also an old expression, Ace. Keep your friends close and your enemies closer. Never forget that. There are some days where your only hope in life may be relying on an enemy. Peter wants to fuck me. Let's keep him hoping he's in with that chance. Then, when I need him on my side, he'll be easily led there by his leaking dick." I get into the cage and close the door.

We pull out of Rising PD's car park and head down the main street towards the compound. It's been warm all day, but the sky's clear, so there's a cool crispness in the air. It causes a shiver to run through my bones like someone's walked over my grave. That feeling's either been caused by the temperature or because, as we're sitting at the single set of traffic lights outside Ned's cigar shop, there on the sidewalk is fucking Bomber. Or at least it looks like him. A doppelganger, maybe? Surely no other fucker could be unlucky enough to look like that asshole. I thought it was Blaze and Knight who were coming to California. Maybe I misheard Delaney.

He's talking to someone shady-looking who's wearing a flasher's mac and an NYC baseball cap. They walk around the side of the store just as the lights change. I want to turn around just to be sure it's him, but I don't want to draw attention to myself. I won't be seen by Bomb as the windows are blacked out. I just don't need Ace to realize how suspicious I am of Delaney's VP. He'll want to know why, and the identity of The Exterminator needs to remain a well-kept secret. Call me suspicious, but something doesn't feel right. I make a mental note to speak to Delaney about it.

We travel back to the compound in silence. Well, except for Saw snoring on the back seat and sleeping like a baby, likely because of the rocking motions as the cage moves along the uneven ground. Seemingly he was drunk, but he didn't do anything wrong. The officers of Rising saw a cut and pulled him. They'll no doubt have been trying to fabricate a case that would stick, at least for a couple of days. That way, they could hold him and squeeze him for intel on club business. I see it all the time. They'll be trying it on now the MC's lawyer is dead, and it'll only get worse. The club needs to find alternative legal representation and fast. I can't be that for them. Distance will prohibit it, and there's no way I'm staying in Rising. My life is in New York.

The Angels of Hellfire Clubhouse, Rising, California

WE WALK INTO THE CLUBHOUSE TO BE MET WITH THE DELIGHTFUL vision of a brother anally fucking one of the cum sluts over the pool table as she sucks another one-off. It's truly amazing what the eyes and the brain become accustomed to. Shock long ago ceased to register. Meanwhile, Cherry is dry humping Jefferson, and Sasha, who must have sobered up, is in a booth sucking Clay's face off.

I walk across to the jukebox and select hidden song forty-two, instantly feeling soothed as the familiar melancholy words wrap around my brain. The adrenaline pounding through it when I had my altercation with Simons has vanished, and I now feel mentally drained.

Walking back to the bar, I take a seat.

"You really like that song, don't you?" Ace asks.

I frown at him. He used to like it too.

"It takes me back to the past. As you already know, the lyrics remind me of me. Who I am. What I am. A creep. A weirdo. Plain fucking Jaine. I learned long ago to embrace that shit rather than try to hide it anymore." I don't ask why it was blanked out. It's obvious he was trying to eradicate the memories of me from his life. Or Emilia was.

"Can I have a bottle of room temperature water, please, Rio?" I smile at the barman warmly as he passes me an unopened bottle.

I can feel Ace's eyes on me, eyebrows raised. I answer before he asks.

"I don't drink alcohol often. It dehydrates me too much, and my coach gets annoyed when my muscles stiffen up." I open the bottle of water and drink half of it.

"You still do the MMA shit?" He looks towards my stomach, which was on display earlier.

I roll my eyes and lift my top to display it again. "Yeah. As often as I can. It helps keep me sane. I can take my frustrations out on my opponent by kicking the shit out of him and pummeling the smug grin off his face. You know, the one he's wearing when he steps into the ring thinking how easy it's going to be to take down a female." I finish the bottle of water as he takes in my six-pack. It always impressed him how a girl could have one. Not enough to stop him from preferring a big ass and tits, but still. At least I have *something* he admires. Something Emilia *doesn't* have.

His fingers reach out to touch my exposed skin, but I quickly pull my top down. His eyes meet mine knowingly. Dangerous territory. Way, way too dangerous. After earlier, we both know if we start something, we won't stop—no point in tempting fate now.

I turn my attention to the clubhouse and take in the sexual shenanigans going on. What sort of life is this? Criminals who engage in debauchery. Meanwhile, here's me. A lawyer. A person who's meant to uphold everything that is legal. What do I do? I do everything I can to get these outlaws away with murder, quite liter-ally. Then again, I'm a serial killer, so who am I to pass judgment?

I watch as Cherry drags Jefferson towards the bedrooms, his hard-on straining against his jeans. I chuckle as she salutes me before she vanishes and then I sigh out loud.

"She's got this reverse harem thing going on at the moment, so I'm surprised it's just Jefferson she's fucking with. Recently, she screwed Blaze, Bomber, and Ripper at the same time and couldn't sit down for days." I smile as I rub my hand over my tired face.

Ace smirks as he throws back a tequila. "What about Sasha?"

I look over at my other BFF, who's got her tongue down Clay's throat. "Dollar's taken with her, but I think it's one-sided. He wants to *date* her." I use air quotes. "Guys think Sash is strait-laced and stuck up. She isn't. She likes bad boys, and she's not afraid to eat those angsty fuckers up and spit them out." I smile as I look at her.

It's then I see *her* from the corner of my eye. Hanging around and waiting for *him*. Story of my fucking life. Jealousy courses through my veins. I need to get out of here or I'll smash her smug face against the goddamn bar. The thought of Ace fucking her is making my trigger finger itch.

"I'm going to take a spare hog and head home. I'll borrow a pair of joggers and a jacket and shoes from the store for tonight and return them in the morning." I drain the other bottle of water that Rio passed me before standing.

"What's the rush?"

I motion my head to where Emilia's standing. "Your old lady's waiting, and I don't like the feeling of her eyes drilling holes in the back of my head. I'm not sure they'll look quite as pretty with a bullet between them."

"She's not my old lady, PJ." He exhales before throwing back another shot.

"Bullshit," I say as I step down from my stool. "You've been treating her as just that since you were thirteen years old and you got your first boner." He attempts to speak, but I hold up my hand. "You know I'm right. If you don't want to admit it to me, at least admit it to yourself. Anyway, it's late. I'll see you tomorrow."

I nod at Emilia, who tilts her chin at me defiantly. I clench my fists and count to ten in my head to stop myself from walking over there and throttling the bitch with my bare hands.

"Thanks for the water, Rio." I smile at him.

The native American ties his long hair back in a ponytail and grins back. "No worries, Jaine."

I wonder what Padraig is doing right now. I smile as I take the short ride home.

Maybe I'll give him a call.

CHAPTER EIGHTEEN

JAINE

Thirteen Years Earlier (Age Fifteen)
The Angels of Hellfire Clubhouse, Rising, California

I HAVEN'T SPOKEN TO ACE ALL WEEK. HE'S AN ASSHOLE. IT'S JUST another classic sign that I'm a weirdo, though, when I don't get my first period until I'm fifteen. All the other girls in my class have had them for years. The lady doctor says I'm just a late developer. That's why I don't have tits or an ass either, apparently. I whispered it to Ace in confidence, and he started laughing like it was the funniest thing he'd ever heard. Shark week's not anything to laugh about. Neither is being a late developer. He's so immature.

I slapped him right across the face in front of everyone in the clubhouse. His look of shock made me feel so much better. I stormed home, and he hasn't even bothered to come to check on me since. I mean, I could have bled to death or something, and he doesn't even care. Some best friend he is. Maybe I shouldn't have slapped him quite so hard, but still. Pop says it was most likely my hormones making me act like a hissy cat.

I don't feel any different than I did before now that I'm supposedly a woman, and my tits and ass haven't grown any either. I put on a pair of pale blue jeans and a pink halter top and tie my hair back in a long ponytail. I haven't been training this week, so I'm going to take my bike to the clubhouse to get some exercise and to see Ace since he seems to have forgotten all about me.

It's Saturday, so all the old ladies are out in full force, offering me cakes, sandwiches, and other home-cooked foods. I decline them all politely as I already feel bloated. Walking through the communal area, I notice Duke.

"Hi, Duke. I'm just going to see Ace," I shout out as I jog past.

He looks up from the bar, his face going pale. "Jainie, wait..."

I push open the door of Ace's bedroom to find him naked on top of Emilia, his mouth on her tit. I stand there and stare at her legs wrapped around his hips. I see him naked for the first time, and it's then I realize he's not a little boy anymore. He has the body of a man, and with that comes a fully functioning dick, which he's sticking into the bitchy girl I hate with every breath in my goddamn body.

She smirks at me smugly from under him, causing him to turn his head and his eyes to connect with mine. What do mine show? Embarrassment, pain, hurt, anger, betrayal. I feel all of that and more. His widen in shock and realization that I now know his dirty secret.

Sex with Emilia is obviously way more important than our friendship. That's why he's not been bothering with me.

I turn around and collide with Duke.

"Jainie..."

I look up at him as tears run freely down my cheeks. Even he kept this from me. I run. I even leave my bike. I just run home.

I don't speak to Ace for six weeks. That was the second time my young heart got broken, and I swore it would be the last.

Nine Years Earlier (Age Nineteen)
Yale University, Connecticut

"HE'S LOOKING AT YOU, JAINE." CHERRY STICKS HER ELBOW IN MY ribs and nods in his direction while swishing her bright red bob around her shoulders.

I shake my head. "Why would he look at plain old me when he can look at you or Sasha?" I try to look at him discreetly over the top of my glasses. My face goes crimson when he catches me and smiles cockily in response.

Sasha looks at him, then at me. "Nope. The new Irish boy is definitely looking at you like your vagina is the pot of gold deserving of his rainbow end."

Cherry chuckles and elbows me in the ribs again, causing me to lose my grip on my pen, which falls off my desk. In my attempt to grab it, my entire pencil case follows suit, the contents of which lands on the floor and rolls downhill in the huge auditorium we're sitting in.

"Fucking great," I mutter to myself as the other students turn to glare at the person disrupting lessons. Everyone present has signed up for extra classes so we can graduate quicker. They won't appreciate my apparent lack of consideration.

"Have you been hit by the clumsy stick today, Miss Jones?" Professor Young asks loudly. He peers at me over the top of his spectacles, which are attached to a multi-colored lanyard. His cheeks are rosy, possibly caused by way too much alcohol consumption due to him having to do a job he hates. Teaching the likes of me. His face is getting redder by the minute, waiting for me to respond. He raises his head, making his ill-matched hairpiece wobble precariously on top. I swallow nervously. Shit, I hope it doesn't fall off, as that will no doubt be my fault too.

"No, sir," I reply, my face warming. I hate being the center of attention.

"Pick them up at the end of class, Miss Jones."

"Yes, sir. Sorry, sir."

———————

WHY IS IT WHEN YOU DROP SOMETHING, IT ROLLS INTO THE tightest of spaces? Tiny gaps that are also just ever so slightly out of reach, so no matter how far your stretch your fingers, it's a futile exercise. I'm crawling around the floor in the auditorium. It smells of urine for some strange reason. Did someone piss their pants, or did they just pull out their junk and let loose on the floor? I try to avoid the discarded pieces of chewed gum as I gather the contents of my now empty pink fluffy pencil case.

"You need some help?" The deep, laughing voice has a lovely Irish lilt and is coming from behind me. I'm on my hands and knees, and that means my ass is taking up the owner of the voice's entire view. In my rush to quickly remove said visual, I bang my head on a chair.

"Oww," I complain loudly as I sit on the floor. No doubt my ass is now being covered in the discarded gum, along with the dried traces of piss. Avoidance of both is no longer a priority, however, as I rub my aching head and take in the laughing blue eyes of the boy in front of me.

"I'm Padraig, by the way. Padraig O'Connell." He holds out his hand to help me up.

I pick up the last of my gel pens and stand up with his help before wiping down the back of my blue jeans. Padraig is taller than me by a good five inches, so he's easily over six feet. His hair is black and messy on the top with shorter sides, and his eyes are the piercing color of blue you'd associate with the Irish. He smiles, and they dance and sparkle on his face. He oozes cheekiness out of every pore. And he's beautiful. He's only the second boy I've ever thought that about.

"I'm Jaine. Jaine Jones." I'm conscious he's still holding my hand, and I can feel my cheeks go bright red.

"It's a pleasure to meet you, Jaine Jones. Can I buy you a coffee? Or a tea? Even better, can I kiss you?" he asks teasingly, his face breaking into a broader grin.

I laugh. "I'll take the first offer, thank you."

And that was it. From then on, I spent all my waking hours with Padraig when I wasn't with my BFFs or in class. We studied together. He was funny and intelligent. Like a breath of fresh air after what happened with Ace. I told him about my MC connections after he recognized the Angels of Hellfire patch on my leather jacket, and he told me about his Hudson Duster background. I never went into any detail about Ace. There was *a boy* I loved who didn't love me back was all I ever said. We never told anyone else about our backgrounds. It was safer for people not involved in *the life* not to know.

"YOU WANT ME TO ORDER PIZZA?" I ASK AS WE SIT SURROUNDED BY books. I'm lucky I don't have to share my room with any other students. It costs more, but Pop thinks it's for the best, so I can concentrate and not be distracted by the wild shenanigans of other teenagers. I stand up from the floor, sit on the edge of my bed, and reach for my phone. Padraig's eyes graze over my legs in my white jean shorts, then he pounces on me and pushes me back against the pillows.

"We can eat later, Jaine," he whispers against my neck with a soft chuckle.

He lifts his head and presses his lips to mine, his tongue immediately asking for entry. I open my mouth and it fills the space, tasting and searching as his confident hands run down the sides of my body. I shiver, my skin breaking out in goosebumps, and I groan against his lips.

Pushing his slim hips between my thighs, he presses his erection against me, and I can't help but rub myself against him.

"I want you, Jaine," he growls as his hand caresses my nipple under my top before his mouth drops to cover it. He suckles it, then bites it almost painfully, causing a bolt of desire to shoot straight to my clit. I know he has a lot of experience with girls. I can just tell. Whereas I've only ever had sex once before. And I was a disappointment.

Our mouths part only for the length of time it takes me to pull his tight white tee over his head, my hands needing to feel his firm flesh beneath my fingertips. Every day, he gets larger and more muscular. I'd be a fool not to notice how many female heads he's turning these days with his good looks and gift of the Irish gab.

He drops his hand to my pussy and starts rubbing me through the material of my shorts, and my hips grind against him instinctively. When he starts to unzip me, I freeze.

He groans against my neck and lets out a frustrated sigh. "No, Jaine. Please don't do this to me again." He lifts his head and looks down at me, his hair messed by my hands, his lips swollen by my kisses. "We've waited three months, darlin'. I've shown you how committed I am by not pushing things and going at your pace. But I'm a man, Jaine. I need physical interaction as well as mental stimulation. My doc says I have the worst case of blue balls he's ever seen." He runs his fingers through his hair and smiles at me, but I can see the dejection in his blue eyes.

"I'm... I'm sorry, Padraig. I'm just not ready." I turn on my side, tracing the outline of the horseshoe birthmark he has on his inner wrist that all the O'Connell men have. The truth is, I am ready. I want him. I love him even. I'm just worried that I'm so crap at sex he won't want me afterward. Same as Ace didn't. I mean, I must have been bad at it if he needed to go straight from me to Emilia.

We study and eat in silence.

A week later, I heard through the school grapevine that Padraig had fucked another girl on campus. She was dark-haired and olive-skinned. It was like God was punishing me all over again. For some reason, I deserved shitty karma. A day later, I sent him a message telling him we were done.

I never expected to care for someone else after Ace, so I didn't see Padraig coming. It was the third time my young heart had gotten broken. It was definitely going to be the last time. He asked if we could stay friends, and for some reason, I agreed.

I'm so glad I did.

Present Day
Jaine's House, Rising, California

I CHANGE INTO SOME BUTTONED BLACK SILK PAJAMAS, THEN LIE ON my princess-style white bed and look around my pink, girly bedroom, which is filled with all things sparkly, feathery, and glittery. We never got around to changing it, and I'm so glad. It smells of home and memories.

It's past midnight here so it's the middle of the night there, but I message him anyway. Like I do several times a day since we split up nine years ago. I'm grateful he's not married or anything. I realize that's a selfish thought, but I'm not sure a wife or even a serious girlfriend would be so understanding of our weird, dysfunctional relationship. I don't want to lose him.

Jaine: *You awake?*
Padraig: *Nope.*
Jaine: *You trained your phone to answer on your behalf?*
Padraig: *Nope.*
Jaine: *You trained it to give the same answer over and over?*
Padraig*: Nope.*
Jaine: *Do you want to fuck me?*
Padraig: *Yup.*
Jaine: *Ha! Call me, or I'm calling you, Irish.*

My phone goes straight away.

"Listen, I've had a busy evening and have only just washed off the blood. I'm now in bed trying to sleep like a normal person," he says with an exaggerated yawn.

"I'm sorry about before."

There's a pause.

"Stop talking in riddles, Jaine. Say what you mean. What do you need to get off your chest that means you can't sleep and you need to call me as your unofficial shrink?"

"When we were at Yale. When I was frigid."

He sighs. "It was nine years ago, darlin'. And we've stayed friends, haven't we?"

"Yeah. I don't blame you for fucking that girl, you know?"

"Well, I blamed me, so you didn't have to. I went to confession, so at least God would forgive me when it was clear you weren't going to."

I chuckle. "What was your penance for not being able to keep your dick in your pants, Padraig O'Connell?"

"Four Hail Marys and having to abstain from sex for a month."

"Ouch. That must have hurt."

"Yup. Worse than when I broke my leg. I abstained for three months, waiting for the perfect girl to let me inside her pussy. I got laid once accidentally while waiting, which I've regretted ever since. Then I got told to do without for a month as punishment. All the thanks I get for trying to behave like a gentleman."

"You regretted it? Why?"

"Jesus, are we really having this conversation now? In the middle of the night and nine years after the event?"

"Well, it's important not to rush these things, Irish."

He laughs. "Of course, I regretted it. I lost you over it, Jaine."

"Right. Well, I never knew that bothered you. Losing me."

"Course it did. If you weren't important to me, I'd never have hung around when you didn't give me immediate access to your sweet pussy. I had that on tap. If it was just sex I wanted, I could get that anywhere."

"So, you didn't just want me for sex?"

He sighs. "No. I wanted the complete package. We were the same, you and me. Everything fit perfectly. Well, apart from my dick in your pussy, as you refused to let that happen. I'm sure that would have been the perfect fit too, though. I got drunk one night. She offered hers to me, and I stuck my dick in it. She told you because she wanted me all for herself. Now, here we are talking on the phone nine years later about the reason we broke up."

"Why are you only telling me this now?"

"You never asked before."

"Oh, right."

"Right. Anyway, what did you need, darlin'?"

"When was the last time you saw me, Irish?"

"Nine years ago."

"You mean you haven't seen me in photos or anything?"

"No. Why would I?"

"Do you not want to see what I look like now? I could be ugly and hairy."

"Ugly and hairy like me, you mean?"

I laugh out loud. "You got Facetime?"

He sighs. "Yes, I've got Facetime, Jaine."

"Call me on it."

"Nope." He pops the P.

"Why?"

"Because next time I see you, I want you to be standing in front of me."

"But then we may never see each other again," I say huffily.

"Then that would be God's will."

"Irish?"

"Yeah?"

"I'm going to come to see you as soon as I'm back in New York."

He chuckles. "Looking forward to it, darlin'. So..."

"Yeah?" I reply.

"In the meantime, you want to have phone sex?"

I laugh out loud. "You're such a dick, Padraig O'Connell."

"You've just given me an idea. What about if I send you a dick pic? You could tell me how impressive my cock is over the phone, and I could fuck my hand at the same time?"

"You're an idiot!"

"You love me anyway, right?"

"I do, Irish." I laugh.

And who knows? Maybe I still do.

CHAPTER NINETEEN

ACE

The Angels of Hellfire Clubhouse, Rising, California

I RUB MY ACHING HEAD—TOO MUCH TEQUILA. MY TONGUE'S STUCK
to the roof of my mouth as it's so goddamn dry. Looking across my
bed, I take in Emilia lying there, sleeping. I fucked her hard last
night, and every time I stuck my dick in her, I thought about PJ.

My old man's right. I need to do the decent thing and let her go.
All we are to each other is a bad habit. She's a pretty girl. She needs
to find someone who'll love her and care for her while she's still got
youth and beauty on her side. That someone isn't me.

I also have to face the reality that what Jaine and I had is over
for good. Jesus Christ, we're bickering like a couple who need to
go for counseling and heading for divorce, and that's without a
physical relationship on top. She's so damn fiery. No good will
come of us getting together. We've both changed too much. We'd
kill each other within five minutes. Plus, her life is in Manhattan

now, not here in this two-bit town. There's no way she's going to give up all her success to come back here and be my old lady. Be my wife.

I should have gone after her when she left. My old man's right about that. Instead, I left countless voicemails. I sent numerous messages. I poured my heart out in every single one. I doubt she listened to any of them.

I should have made her listen. I didn't. I can't change that.

I shake Emilia.

"Come on, get going. I have stuff I need to do." I give her another push, then throw back the covers before walking into the bathroom and turning on the shower. Standing underneath the scalding water, I wash away the smell of the night before. Turning the temperature up further, I let the alcohol sweat out of my pores. Em's gone when I come out. The bedroom stinks of sex and tequila. I open the window, but there's little air movement, so the smell will probably linger all day.

There's a knock on my door.

"Come in." I tighten the small white towel around my hips, expecting it to be one of the brothers or my old man.

My eyes connect with her green ones the moment she enters. Shit, she's so fucking beautiful. I mean, she always was to me, even if the others said she wasn't. Especially Clay. That fucker was always saying how unattractive she was. I went along with it most of the time. I guess it's what you do with peer pressure. I learned just to say what the brothers expected me to. Shit was easier that way.

Surely PJ must have known when I insisted we get matching tattoos that she meant something more to me?

"Sorry. I can come back." Her eyes drift over me as she rubs her hands down the front of her shorts. Her gaze lingers on my scars and tattoos, and she licks her lips. I'm tempted to ask if she likes what she sees, but I don't think that will help our already terse communications. I can already tell that she does.

"It's fine. You can watch, or you can turn around. I don't mind either way. It's nothing you haven't seen before." I smirk as her cheeks redden when I start to untie the towel.

She quickly spins around. "Um... I just wanted to let you know Delaney is coming to California this weekend." Her voice is hesitant. She's telling me because she has no choice.

I'm not sure how I feel about that. I'm not a fan of Razr, truth be known. He's an arrogant son of a bitch who, from what I can see, gains his respect from his brothers by demanding it instead of earning it. I also don't know how I feel about seeing him with PJ. Them as a couple. His hands on her. Her hands on him. Then I realize I'm a complete hypocrite. She's well aware I'm fucking Emilia. She left the clubhouse last night so I *could* fuck her. The smell of our sex is still lingering in the room, for Christ's sake.

She gets up and closes the door, then sits back on the bed, still facing away from me. I look at her dressed in white jeans and a white halter top. Her blonde hair hangs straight down her back like it always has. Nothing added—no fancy colors or highlights. Everything about PJ is natural. She makes the best of what God gave her, and she looks after it well. My eyes drift down her back to the slight curve of her slim hips. I can feel my length start to grow as I imagine running my hands down to her ass, then dropping them to her pussy, parting her soft folds to find her warm, welcoming wetness underneath. I can still remember her sweet taste, and my mouth waters at the thought.

I pull on a pair of dark blue jeans and stick a white Henley over my head before putting on my cut.

"Duke mentioned you're friends with the Irish." Maybe I shouldn't say anything, but it's bugging me which of the O'Connells it is.

She stands and spins around to stare at me accusingly, like I somehow forced my old man to tell me her secret.

"What the fuck else did Duke say?" Her eyes narrow defensively.

I shrug. "Nothing, just that you had a confidant who was on our side, which means it has to be one of the Irish. Do you mind telling me who it is? Which one? It's not an unreasonable question."

"It's none of your goddamn business," she hisses at me like a fucking viper. Her hands are clenched at her sides.

"Duke's worried about you, PJ. He wants to know so we have all the facts. So we can keep you safe like your pop would have expected us to. He wasn't trying to betray your trust by telling me."

I try to be calm and reasonable, but it's like running a cage through a minefield where she's concerned. She's a little spitfire.

She turns away again, then sits on the bed. I can almost see shit whirring in her brain as she thinks about whether or not to tell me. Minutes pass. I lean against the window ledge, fold my arms, and wait.

"Your room's hardly changed," she mutters as she gazes around. "In fact, I'm sure there are several things that haven't even moved since I was last in here."

I shrug, even though she can't see me. "If it isn't broken, why fix it?"

"Hope you've changed the mattress." She looks down at it in distaste. I don't reply. She's looking for a fight, and right now, with my aching head, I don't have one in me. Plus, I'm waiting for the answer. She's trying to piss me off so I'll react, so she can fly off the handle and slam the door on her way out, taking her secret with her.

"Padraig," she mutters after several more minutes when she realizes I'm not taking the bait. "And please keep that to yourself. We've been friends for nine years. Almost as long as you and I were friends." She spits that last part out to remind me that we haven't been friends this past ten years. We've been nothing. Less than nothing, if that's even possible. "We dated for a short time at Yale when I was nineteen. He's a lawyer too, in case you didn't know. And if you're going to warn me off him or something, please don't bother."

"No. I like Padraig. I'm just surprised is all. You don't seem like his type." I say it, then realize I shouldn't have. That comment was the equivalent of using a blowtorch to light a firework then not moving back out of the way before it explodes in your face.

She immediately jumps up and spins around again, her eyes narrowed. Her hands form fists as she rocks back and forth on her feet like she's trying to decide whether to launch herself at me and scratch my eyes out.

"Are you referring to how I look now or how I looked then, Ace?"

I grimace as she yells. "What did he dump you for?"

Her green eyes are flashing with rage. Holy shit, what the fuck have I said now?

"Is it so fucking hard to believe that maybe I dumped his Irish ass?" She storms out of the room, then the door reopens. "Oh, and you might want to spray some air freshener in here as it stinks of tequila and fish. Tell Emilia she needs to wash out that bottomless pussy of hers occasionally. Either that or she needs to go get checked out at the nearest clinic as that stench is not fucking normal."

She slams the door again.

I sit on the edge of the unmade bed. So, PJ's ex-boyfriend is Padraig O'Connell. A billionaire Irish mobster and the youngest son of Fergal, who leads up The Hudson Dusters in New York.

Christ, I need to mend my bridges with her before I end up with my throat slit courtesy of Razr or sent to a watery grave in a concrete coffin courtesy of Padraig.

I smirk as I finish getting dressed, then I call him.

"Padraig."

"Ace? To what do I owe the pleasure?"

"I was just wondering when you were going to let me know you used to date PJ."

"PJ? Who the fuck's PJ?"

"Plain Jaine... Jaine."

"Plain fucking Jaine?"

"Yeah. Jaine Jones."

"Jaine Jones? Since when was she ever plain?"

"She referred to herself as it once. The name stuck." I admit it reluctantly.

"You're shitting me, right? No wonder the girl's got fucking confidence issues. Next, you'll be telling me you're the asshole she left Rising over. The one she loved, who didn't love her back."

My silence speaks volumes. "She told you she loved me?" I reply eventually, my heart pounding in my chest. Shit.

"Jesus, Mary and Joseph, tell me this isn't happening. So, it was you all this time?" He's furious, and I find myself wondering why. "You do realize you fucked her up good and proper? All she'd tell me is that she slept with some guy who popped her cherry and then he immediately went and fucked another girl. She loved him, and he didn't love her back, so she left her hometown as she couldn't face watching him be with someone else."

"Shit. It wasn't like that, Padraig." I run my hands through my hair. Suddenly, it all makes goddamn sense.

"No? Well, I dated that girl for three months, and she wouldn't let me touch her because she thought she must be useless in bed. Why else would someone fuck her then leave her lying there to go fuck someone else? I stupidly stuck my dick in another girl when I was drunk, desperate, and feeling sorry for myself, and Jaine dumped me because of it. It's the biggest single regret of my fucking life. I've spent nine years being her shrink on account of what you did to her. I'm meeting with her in Manhattan when she comes back home. I'm hoping to God she'll see sense and realize I'm the one she's meant to fucking be with." I can hear the frustration in his voice.

Jesus Christ, he's in love with her.

"She's as good as being Razr's old lady, Padraig," I remind him. It's best we don't forget that murderous bastard who will slice and dice anyone who goes near her.

"She'll never be his old lady. She doesn't love him. Not like that, anyway. She's not the type to just settle. That's why she's never committed to him."

"If that's the case and you say she loves me, what makes you think she'll settle for you?"

There's a pause.

"When we were together, she told me she was surprised she'd been lucky enough to fall in love twice in her life. Once with the loser who treated her like shit, which is you, and the other time with me. I'm hoping the latter is still the case."

I put the phone down. Or he does. One of us does.

PJ left Rising because she loved me and she thought I didn't love her back. It wasn't because she wanted to escape.

I RUN MY FINGERS ACROSS THE ENGRAVED COUNCIL TABLE WHILE waiting for the others to turn up.

Jefferson's last. He comes in and closes the door with a massive grin on his face.

"Anything you want to share, Jefferson?" I ask so we can get it over with and get down to business.

"Nothing important. My posh princess Cherry just wanted to give me a morning blowjob." He shrugs as he takes a seat. "Who am I to turn down wearing that scarlet lipstick of hers around my dick?" He smiles smugly, and the rest of the guys snicker.

I shake my head. "Anyone else? Clay? Something to say about the other bit of posh?"

He shifts in his chair, a lazy grin covering his face. "I'm not one to kiss and tell. You know that, Prez, but let's just say she knows exactly what she's doing with every hole in that pretty body of hers. Anyway, what about you? What's going down with you and PJ? How's that first love business treating you?" He laughs. He knows fine well all we're doing is yelling at each other constantly.

"There's nothing going on with me and PJ, and even if there were, I wouldn't share it round this goddamn table. That's not what this room is for," I mutter.

Chase looks at Clay and me and frowns. "Are you saying the pretty little thing who was grinding on me was PJ? Your Jaine? The one who wears your mark behind her ear?"

I narrow my eyes at him. "Yeah, that's right. You got a problem with that?" I'm about ready to shoot the fucker in the head for reminding me that she was grinding on him.

He shakes his head. "No, no problem, Prez. It's just... she's the opposite of plain. Dang, that girl is mighty fine."

"It's been ten years, Chase. She's changed. I've changed. Everything's changed. We've all moved the fuck on. Now, has anyone else got any questions they want to ask about PJ or any intel they want to share on her friends before we move on to important council business?"

Silence.

"Good. Can we get started, please, as we need to call church. Clay? Anything to report?" I look at him.

"Nothing on the shops and sex-related side of the business. We do have the next run taking place. Two million dollars' worth of guns coming in from the Irish via the Scorpions. Blaze and Knight are bringing them in a cage. They're due to arrive tomorrow night. There's talk Razr will be flying into California to meet with them. I spoke to Bomb this morning. Says Razr's missing his old lady and that the fucker's pussy whipped. He doesn't sound too happy about it." He snickers.

I scowl at him. I don't want to think of PJ with Razr or the fact that he's fucking her.

Jefferson speaks up. "The guns are ear-marked for the Mexicans. Ink and I are meeting them just before the border, and they'll take charge of the vehicle from there. They've paid off border patrol, apparently."

Ink interrupts him. He's a recent appointment to council. He's a huge fucker. His head is shaved completely bald, and he's covered in tattoos and piercings. "Let's just make sure they get every single weapon that's due to them. We all heard about what happened to Luciano Ruocco's father and brother when the late Don served them up a heroin supply that was under." He drags his finger across his neck to remind us they were killed. A car bomb, apparently, and suspected to have been planted by the disgruntled La eMe.

The door opens, and a worried Duke storms in, closing it behind him.

"I've just had Cillian O'Connell on the phone. Two teenage Irish girls have been raped and had their throats cut. Their bodies were discovered this morning after their parents reported them missing. The rapes were videoed. The link was sent to Cillian's personal email just before the girls were found. It's a suspected Bratva retaliation attack. It seems the new pakhan, Lebedev, wants to let us all know he's the new king of the hill." Duke takes a seat and runs his hands through his hair. "My thinking is the only way to end this is to take out Lebedev himself. They'll then be forced to regroup." He exhales, rubbing his hand over his mouth.

"Sick, twisted fucks." I can feel the bile rise in my throat. Jesus, what those girls' poor parents must be going through. "We need to speak to Razr. We need to employ the services of The Exterminator to take this asshole out. Put an end to this bullshit," I say quietly. Everyone nods in agreement.

Duke's face pales for some reason. "Let me handle that, son."

CHAPTER TWENTY

PADRAIG

The Hudson Dusters' HQ, Manhattan, New York

I'M SHATTERED. I STRUGGLED TO FALL ASLEEP AFTER TALKING TO Jaine and ended up fucking my hand. Twice.

"Ain't that right, Padraig?"

"Sorry, Da. What was that?" My eyes go around the table, taking in my brothers and my da. All of us wear tailored suits and ties. Da insists we look like business folk when we meet at the office. We're like something from *Reservoir Dogs*. The boardroom is impressive, with priceless artworks hanging from the walls, a white marble floor, and a central leather-topped round black table that could seat twenty or more. The matching leather chairs cost ten grand each and are uncomfortable as fuck. The floor's had to be replaced once already when Da shot at it with a machine gun. He says it was an accident, but we all know better.

"I said we need to put more protection on the womenfolk now the Bratva has attacked two of our own!" he yells, throwing his glass paperweight at my head, which only just misses and goes on to make an impressive dent in the wall behind me.

"Jesus Christ, Da. You could have brained me with that fucking thing." I look at the damage and fully appreciate I'd have either ended up dead or, at the very least, in the emergency room.

"Aye, well, it might have knocked some sense into you and got you to listen to me when I'm fucking talking to you. We need to take down this new pakhan, Gorbachev."

"He was the president of Russia, Da. It's Lebedev." I don't make a joke. He'd likely throw something else at me for being an insolent little fecker.

"Aye, him. We need to get him out of the picture. He's new and getting way too big for his boots walking around our fucking city like he's Billy Big Bollocks. We need to employ the services of The Exterminator. He'll be able to take him out. The Bratva will have to go into hiding and regroup, so we'll all have a chance to do the same. Eoin, find out who this Exterminator fella is. We'll put a price of five million dollars on this little arsehole's head. Ten if that's not tempting enough for the sniper." He grumbles as he looks at all of us over the top of his reading glasses. At sixty-five, Da's still a handsome fecker, even if his once black hair is now pure white. We know it's with age, but he insists it's the stress of having to put up with our combined incompetence.

I look at my eldest brother. All of us look like Da with our black hair and blue eyes, apart from our Cillian, who's got Ma's red hair and green eyes. At thirty-six, Eoin's still never taken a wife, but then, she needs to be the real deal as he'll have to inherit all this shite one day, and she'll need to be able to cope with being the big ma of The Hudson Dusters. He's definitely got the skills for the job as he's a financial analyst and economics guru as well as being a murderous bastard. Then again, all of us are the latter. I've stopped counting the number of souls I've taken and dropped in the Hudson.

"I'll put my feelers out, Da, but I'm not sure how easy he'll be to find."

Da scowls at our Eoin. He doesn't like the word no. In his mind, that word shouldn't exist. No equals an excuse in his book.

"Find him and fast, son." He ignores what Eoin said as the answer wasn't what he wanted to hear. If he's not careful, he'll get something flung at his head too.

I interrupt. "Da, I've got good communications with both MCs as has our Cill. The Exterminator and the Scorpions have a close kinship, if you didn't already know. I'll do some asking around. See if I can get access to him."

"Good thinking. You see, Eoin, you need to think outside the box like our legal guru Paddy here rather than inventing excuses at every fucking turn."

Eoin knows better than to reply. Instead, he scowls at me, and I flip him the bird.

"Cillian, you get the foot soldiers rounded up and make sure the women are protected. I don't want to hear about a hair on any of their heads being so much as fucking disturbed, you hear me, son?" He points at him, wagging his finger. It's a sight when he does that, but fuck me, if you laugh, you'll be encased in a concrete coffin and chucked in the river faster than you can say Jack Robinson, blood or not. I'm surprised they're not almost reaching the surface with the amount we've dropped in there recently.

"What do you want me to do, Da?" our Dylan pipes up. He's a year older than me and the quietest of us all. He's fairly good with IT and shite like that. Stuff he can do on his tod. He's an anti-social little fucker.

"Just make sure security is tight, Dylan, CCTV and the like. We need to stop the fucking Russian vermin from getting in like the rats they are. If anyone does get in, we need to see their faces so we know who we're putting a bullet in." He passes out our duties like Moses, giving each of us a commandment to look after.

"Will do, Da," Dylan replies dutifully. He's still got a scar from when the last flung paperweight hit its intended target.

"My thinking is that if we get shot of the Russian swine, we can get the Sicilians and also the Chinese on our side and build more alliances. Maybe even the Mexicans too, although I'm not too sure about that lot. That car bomb malarkey is a coward's way out, in my humble opinion. Stinks of old Ireland before The Good Friday Agreement. Anyway, it's best for us all to keep things harmonious. It saves killing unnecessarily and losing innocent lives. I don't like to see the widows of our brothers crying at church on a Sunday because their men have died because we've pissed someone off. I definitely don't want to be seeing grieving fucking parents. No father or mother should have to bury their children. If I have to spend the rest of my life saying Hail Marys, I'll hold you boys responsible."

Which basically means he'll shoot us all personally and with great pleasure unless we pull up our pants.

"Padraig, your man is key. The Exterminator. We need him to get rid of Gorbachev as soon as possible.

"Lebedev, Da."

"Aye, him."

I SEND A MESSAGE TO JAINE.

Padraig: *Why didn't you tell me Ace was the guy you were running from, darlin?*

She calls me immediately.

"You've been talking about me with fucking Ace?"

"He phoned me. Asked if I knew you."

"Jesus, Padraig. I mentioned I knew one of the Irish to Duke, and he mentioned it to Ace. He insisted I tell him which O'Connell brother I knew. The Angels and the Scorpions will be having me tailed. I didn't want them to think I was just randomly meeting up with a member of the Irish fucking mob!"

"He called you PJ and then explained the abbreviation, and it all sort of unfurled."

"Oh, it all sort of fucking unfurled, did it? And what did you talk about when you were discussing me and this was all unfurling."

"Oh, this and that."

"This and that? Could you be any more vague? Would you care to enlighten me on your this and that chat?"

"I said that you left town because of unrequited love and, in fairness to the boy, I think he was shocked to know that you love him."

"What the actual fuck, Padraig? Is my life a shitshow of a Harlequin novel? And you told him I love him?"

I hold the phone away from my ear as she's yelling now.

"It was ten years ago, so it's *loved*, not *love*. Past tense. Well, I'm glad you and Ace had a nice conversation about me. I'm so happy you and he were able to compare notes. Did he tell you where his road name came from too?

"No. He never told me that. Where did it come from?"

"He's a poker cheat. I called him it. I guess it stuck. Anyway, I don't think I want to know anymore. One thing I do know is that you're a fucking asshole, and he's a fucking asshole too!"

"Now, darlin', there's no need to get quite so agitated."

"No? Well, screw you, Irish, because we're done. Don't call me again. Ever."

She hangs up.

I call back. "Now, that wasn't very nice, Jaine ..."

"Go away. I said I'm not talking to you ever again."

She hangs up.

I call back. No answer. I message her.

Padraig: *I need to speak to you about The Exterminator.*

She calls back. "What do you need to know?"

"You know him?"

"You could say that."

"Want to tell me who he is? I could approach him directly."

"I could tell you, but then I'd have to kill you."

"Like you could ever kill someone, darlin'."

"Try me."

"My da wants to hire him for a five million dollar hit. Ten if that's not enough."

"Who's the target?"

"Lebedev."

"The new pakhan? He'll be difficult to get at. Has he got any history that deserves him to be taken out? The Exterminator doesn't do out and out hits for hire. Any target needs to be deserving of the engraved bullet. It's not all about the money as half is donated to charity."

"The Russians are responsible for the rape and murder of two young Irish girls. Their bodies were found this morning. I thought Ace might have told you."

There's a pause. I can almost feel her anger coming down the line.

"I'm telling you to fuck off, Irish. I'm telling Ace to fuck off. The Exterminator will also tell both of you to fuck off."

She hangs up again.

I mean, all I did was have a friendly chat with Ace about her.

Talk about over-reacting.

CHAPTER TWENTY-ONE

CHERRY

The Angels of Hellfire Clubhouse, Rising, California

"What am I going to do? I wail into my shot glass. It's only two p.m., and I'm already on tequila. I'm drinking way too much. I'm glad my parents can't see me now. They'd be so disappointed. All the money they've spent turning me into a marketable commodity with the best education money can buy, and what am I? I'm no better than a biker cum slut.

I blame Jaine. She introduced us to this sordid way of life. Well, I don't *actually* blame her. I look across as she sips from a bottle of water. She really was the proverbial ugly duckling. What a transformation. She's beautiful now. I like to think Sasha and I helped, but, in truth, Jaine had a natural beauty that was always going to shine through no matter what.

Me? Well, I've had my lips done. Not that anyone would notice. I paid a fortune to ensure no one would. So far, so good with everything else, although I will need to review matters in a month or so. My parents are insisting I attend some debutante ball later in the year to secure myself a billionaire husband before I get any older. Sasha's been told pretty much the same thing by hers. I used to enjoy going to those sorts of events. Dressing up, wearing designer dresses and expensive jewelry, rubbing shoulders with Manhattan's elite.

Now I realize it's all fake. Fake husbands, fake friends, fake lives, and then producing children who, in turn, will also become part of a fake world. Then history will just repeat itself.

This MC life? It couldn't be any more *real*. Living in the moment and taking nothing for granted. I mean, look at Jaine's father. Fifty-eight years old and shot in the head. Gone. Just like that. Poof!

These days, I wear as little as possible, have sex on pool tables, and have even taken part in a reverse harem. Well, the latter would have happened regardless. I mean, that sort of thing goes on which-ever circles you mix in.

"Cherry, you've been hanging out with Jefferson way too much. You've been virtually living at the clubhouse since we got here." Jaine looks at me. She's not complaining. She never does. She's the sensible one. She's just concerned I'm getting in way over my head. Still, I suddenly feel guilty. We came here so she didn't have to be on her own after her father died, and Sasha and I have spent all our time fucking our new biker boyfriends. I'm slumming it in slumsville with random people who have sex right in front of my eyes.

And I love it.

"You should clone yourself?" Sasha offers a response that isn't at all helpful.

"Why does he have to bring Blaze with him?" I mumble, ignoring her useless advice.

"Um... because he's the Scorpions' enforcer," Jaine replies with a small shrug.

She takes in my appearance. She's not judgmental. Usually, I'm pristine. Today? I'm wearing a tiny pink playsuit with my red hair tied up in a messy bun. I would never have dared to be seen in public wearing anything *messy*, let alone something that's physically attached to my body and perched on top of my head. I'm even wearing flats, for goodness sake. I really am turning into a biker's old lady.

My problem is, which biker do I want?

"But Jefferson will be here," I wail, then cringe inwardly at my whiny tone.

"Umm... yes, because he's the Angels' enforcer," Jaine replies, stating the obvious.

"You've obviously got a type, Cherry," Sasha offers, again, most unhelpfully as she inspects her perfectly manicured nails. I roll my eyes at her.

"Maybe you can get it on with Bomber as well as Clay, Sasha. You know, if you want to have a type too. VPs?"

I look at her as she sips from her glass of wine. She's dressed respectfully in a floaty Laura Ashley dress in pale blue with a daisy print. She doesn't look like she belongs here, unlike me. I blend right in these days. I watch as she sneaks a peek at Clay, and he smirks and winks at her. It causes Ace to turn around and look at Jaine. It's clear those two love each other, even if they can't see it themselves. I mean, Delaney adores her too, but he's a chauvinist pig who wants her pregnant, barefoot, and riding bitch. He wants to control her, and she's not the type that can be controlled. She's much too highly spirited.

"Well, maybe you could get together with Mr. Ace of Hearts over there, and you could have a type too. Presidents," I say to Jaine.

"I'd sooner change my name to Monica, give old Bill Clinton a blowjob, then let his cum spill all over my dress, thank you." She rolls her eyes at me.

I chuckle. Jaine says it how it is. I love that about her. She's so direct and bold. I also think she kills people in her spare time, although she's never said as much. It's all a bit *American Psycho*.

She stretches. "Let's go outside and do some target practice. Come on, Cherry. I'll show you how to fire a gun. Take your mind off Jefferson and Blaze. I've brought my Glock with me, although I'm sure there'll be others you can use."

I roll my eyes at her. I'd much rather not handle a filthy weapon. I'd sooner just sit here and fret over my Blaze and Jefferson dilemma.

We wander out. The sun is shining, and I raise my face to its warmth. Jaine sets up the mechanical shooting targets and the paper ones while Sasha and I sit at a table close by.

I notice Emilia sitting in the corner with two of her friends, watching us. I look at Jaine, who's wearing a white tank top and grey cargo pants. She looks fresh and comfortable. Emilia, meanwhile, is dressed for a night on the town with a full face of make-up troweled on. I roll my eyes inwardly. What does Ace see in her?

Putting on a pair of earmuffs, Jaine loads up her gun and shoots.

"Want me to check how you did, PJ?" Clay, who's come to watch, asks her with a beaming smile. I can hear Sasha's heart pounding from where I'm sitting as she takes in her biker lover.

"Sure thing," Jaine says as she loads up again. "I'll pass the gun to Cherry once you get back here as Christ himself only knows where the bullets will land. Probably in your head, Clay." She chuckles as she winks at me.

He changes the targets and brings back the used ones.

"Goddamn it, PJ. You created one perfect hole dead center, and every other bullet's traveled through pretty much the same spot. I mean, shit, I thought Ace was good. Where the hell did you learn to shoot like this?"

She shrugs and plays it down.

She shoots scumbags in the head. I just know it.

"Practice makes perfect, Clay."

Good answer.

"Plain Jaine can't be as good as Ace. You're just being nice." Emilia adds her two cents which is neither asked for nor appreciated.

"I've always been able to shoot better than Ace, Emilia, and that's not likely to ever change," Jaine replies dryly without looking at her. Her hands clench. With her martial arts training, she could easily kill Emilia.

I wish she would. Put us all out of our misery.

Jaine passes the gun to me. It feels heavy and lumpy in my small hands, and I don't know what to do with it.

"Here, let me help you with that, sweetheart." Jefferson appears at my side, and my heart flips in my chest. He's so handsome, with his muscular, tall frame. His face is tanned from the sun, causing his green eyes to sparkle, and his long blonde hair is tied back using one of my spare scrunchies. He's adorable. He sits down and pulls me onto his lap, wrapping his arms possessively around my waist.

"Be careful with that gun, Cherry. It's a dangerous piece," Jaine warns me, then looks at Jefferson so he knows to keep me safe. He winks at her, then takes the gun from my hands and lays it on the table.

Emilia interrupts again.

"Well, I'll bet you couldn't shoot the target that's on the water tower. It's been up there for months, and no one can hit it. If you're that amazing, you should be able to hit that easily." She's almost sneering. Jaine looks at her like she's going to smack her across the face and then snap her neck.

She stares Emilia up and down. Jaine will never back away from a challenge. She's far too competitive. "You got a sniper rifle with a scope, Clay? I wouldn't want to disappoint Ace's old lady now, would I?" she asks, her eyes never leaving Emilia's face. ·

I know Ace will have heard that comment, and he'll be furious. I so love it that Jaine keeps antagonizing him. But then he did treat her shabbily, so deservedly so.

"Sure thing, PJ. I'll fetch the best one we have."

He returns with a green rifle and passes it to Jaine. She nods in acceptance, then asks Clay to fetch her some screwdrivers so she can make minor adjustments.

Jaine lies on the ground and balances the rifle accordingly, looking through the scope thing at the top. There's a small crowd of brothers starting to gather now, and it looks like they're gambling on whether Jaine will hit the target. Emilia thinks not and will think it's great that more people will see Jaine fail. She really doesn't know Jaine very well. She seldom, if ever, fails at anything she takes on.

Just as she's aiming, Emilia laughs loudly, which causes Jaine to curse. The bitch is probably doing it deliberately.

"Can you shut up her damn cackling?" Jaine yells without moving her eyes from the scope. "Stupid fucking bitch," she adds quietly. I giggle, and Jefferson pulls me in even tighter, kissing the side of my neck. I can't help but sigh contentedly.

Taking her time, Jaine gently squeezes the trigger, and the shot fires. She then stands up, steps back, dusts herself down, and motions for Clay to lie on the floor and check the scope.

"Well, I'll be damned, PJ. Are you sure you haven't been taking lessons from The Exterminator?" he jokes, then stares in wonderment through the scope again.

"Don't be stupid, Clay." She laughs out loud while deliberately avoiding eye contact with Ace. I know my friend, and I know that look. She's lying. Does she know The Exterminator?

The brothers congratulate her as they take it in turns to look through the scope in disbelief

"Delaney, hi." She answers her phone. I try not to listen. My heart sinks. "So, we'll see you, Blaze, and Knight tomorrow, then." She smiles as she talks, but it fades after she hangs up. She needs to end things with Razr. She cares for him a lot, but she doesn't love him.

Jefferson starts to run his hand up and down the outside of my thigh, and I can feel him grow beneath me. He's insatiable. I want him too, though, so the feeling's mutual. The problem is, I also want Blaze, and I can't decide between them.

They'll both be here tomorrow, and I have no idea what I'm going to do as they both want me to be their old lady.

JAINE

The Angels of Hellfire Clubhouse, Rising, California

My phone vibrates again, and it's Irish. He just never gives up.

Padraig: *Talk to me.*
Jaine: *No. Go way.*
Padraig: *I'm sorry.*
Jaine: *No, you're not. Don't lie.*
Padraig: *Well, I would have been had I realized it was such a big deal.*
Jaine: *You told Ace I was in love with him. That's kind of a big deal.*

Padraig: *Well, you were.*

Jaine: Were *is the operative word in that sentence.*

Padraig: *You don't still love him?*

Jaine: *That's beside the point.*

Padraig: *You do still love him?*

Jaine: *I never said that.*

Padraig: *Do you still love me?*

Jaine: *That's none of your business. You don't deserve to know anything about me as you can't be trusted to keep your big fat Irish mouth closed.*

Padraig: *You used to love me?*

Jaine: Used to *are the operative words in that sentence.*

Padraig: *So, you don't love me?*

Jaine: *I never said that.*

Padraig: *Then you do?*

Jaine: *I never said that either.*

Padraig: *Right, I'm flying to California on the first available flight.*

Jaine: *Don't you dare!*

Padraig: *You won't talk to me.*

Jaine: *Why are you so bothered?*

Padraig: *We speak every day.*

Jaine: *Not every day.*

Padraig: *Every day.*

Jaine: *I'll bet there have been days we haven't spoken.*

Padraig: *Nope. In nine years, we've spoken every day.*

Jaine: *You liar.*

Padraig: *I swear on the Bible.*

Jaine: *You don't believe in God.*

Padraig: *I'm a good Irish Catholic boy.*

Jaine: *You're not good.*

Padraig: *How would you know? You've never tried me. You were frigid. Said so yourself.*

Jaine: *You know what I mean.*

Padraig: *Nope, explain yourself.*

Jaine: *You're not a good boy.*

Padraig: *My ma would disagree. She says I'm her favorite.*

Jaine: *Being her favorite doesn't mean you're good, Irish.*

Padraig: *Define good.*

Jaine: *Well, you can't be good. You kill people.*

Padraig: *What if they deserve to be killed? Surely that makes me good?*

Jaine: *Nope. That makes you a murderer.*

Padraig: *But what if I murder a murderer. Two negatives make a positive, no?*

Jaine: *Shut up, Irish. You're not good.*

Padraig: *Define good.*

Jaine: *Nope. Delete my number and go away forever.*

Padraig: *No point. I know it by heart, so deleting it from my phone won't delete it from my head.*

Jaine: *Go away.*

Padraig: *Where do you want me to go?*

Jaine: *Now you're just being a dick.*

Padraig: *Want a pic?*

Jaine: *I'm not replying anymore.*

Padraig: *If you don't speak to me, I'm booking a flight.*

Jaine: *You wouldn't dare.*

Padraig: *Try me.*

Jaine: *Goodbye, Irish.*

Padraig: *Consider my flight booked, Jaine.*

He wouldn't dare. Would he?

CHAPTER TWENTY-TWO

JAINE

Four Years Earlier (Age Twenty-Four)
Delaney Enterprises, Upper East Side, New York

"MR. DELANEY WILL SEE YOU NOW." I DON'T KNOW IF THIS BITCH IS his personal assistant or what. An employee with benefits, maybe? What I do know is if she doesn't quit staring at me down that conde-scending fucking nose of hers like I'm a piece of shit, I'm going to slam dunk her make-up-caked face off her desk and shatter the fucking thing.

"Thank you." I force a polite smile as I smooth down the front of my expensive grey pinstripe suit before walking confidently to the office door. Plain Jaine has gone. She doesn't exist anymore. Or at least not in Manhattan. Corrective eye surgery has gotten rid of the much-hated glasses. The braces are no longer – my teeth are now white and straight. I've also *finally* grown some tits and an ass. Not much, but still a handful in each of these essential areas.

Cherry, Sasha, and I threw a party once I had enough to fill a B cup as it was such a momentous occasion. We spent the evening drinking wine and tequila, and I spent a fortune online at Victoria's Secret. With one of their bras and enough effort, I can even create an impressive cleavage.

Paul Delaney owns this entire building. A very successful businessman, he's a billionaire at the age of twenty-eight, and his portfolio includes many prestigious properties in several very swanky areas of Manhattan.

He'd better not try to convince me he's earned all his money legally. I'm nobody's fool. If he tries to treat me as one, I'll be straight out that door, Duke recommendation or not.

The bronzed sign says CEO. I enter and close the door firmly behind me. He's standing, looking out the window. Who can blame him? The view is magnificent. Even a rental in this part of Manhattan would cost a fortune, never mind being able to afford to own a whole goddamn building. I take him in from behind. He's well over six feet, and he radiates power. It's almost tangible. A man who knows what he wants and takes it, or so I'm told. He expects you to hand it over. No questions asked. Well, that might apply to other people. Not to me. His hair is long, past his shoulders, and strawberry blonde. His frame is lean—panther-like. I'll bet he has a body to die for underneath the suit he's wearing that will have cost as much as a small family car.

"Please take a seat, Ms. Jones." His voice is deep, rich, and one hundred percent masculine. The type that makes your ovaries contract and you immediately want to offer to have his babies. I remain standing. I'll take a seat when he turns around and does the same.

I grew up in the MC life. To not stand your ground is the first sign of weakness and leads to manipulation. I will not be told what to do. Not a fucking chance. I'm a lawyer now. I've worked hard for this shit. My client base will be *my* decision. No one else's. No fucker will decide for me. I already have a waiting list, so if Manhattan's most eligible bachelor turns out to be an asshole, then he can find someone else. Simple.

He'll be fully aware that I haven't moved as footwear of any sort would make a sound on this white marble floor, let alone my four-inch stilettos. The furniture is dark wood. Walnut, I think. Everything else is black leather. Works of art hang from the walls. Nudes. Tasteful ones.

He turns around, and my gaze is instinctively drawn to his face. A pair of arrogant green eyes stare back at me. His nostrils flare, I'm guessing at my insolence at not doing as I'm told, on what can only be described as a perfectly chiseled face. He's handsome. And then some. More so in the flesh than in any photos I've seen. I'm not a creeper, but in this game, it pays to read up on who you're going to be working with. If you decide to deal with them, that is. Be prepared. Always. The online images don't do him justice. Stubble caresses his jaw and frames his well-shaped lips. I let my eyes trail down him, as that's precisely what he's doing to me. It doesn't faze me. He's tall, lithe, and his overall demeanor is menacing, but I'm used to men like that.

I walk across and take a seat, then I cross my legs. His gaze drifts slowly up their length. He's looking at me like a wild animal stares at a fresh piece of meat. He probably does this with every attractive woman he comes into contact with, save his own kin. Most of them, I'm sure, will welcome the attention from the billionaire and will spread their legs as soon as he clicks his wealthy fingers. Well, I'm not one of them.

"If all you want here is someone to sexually objectify, Mr. Delaney, then you can bring in the pretentious blonde that's sitting right outside your door. I'm sure she'll let you fuck her too, during company-approved break times only, of course. You do have to protect your billions, after all." I stand and walk towards the door, but a hand grabs my arm and pulls me back before I can reach it.

I spin around, and he smiles down at me, his white teeth as perfect as the rest of him. Annoyance flares in his eyes. "My, my. You're quite the little spitfire, aren't you, Ms. Jones?" He raises an eyebrow at me, and a smirk crosses his face, which I immediately want to slap off.

I jerk my arm from his grasp. "Not at all, Mr. Delaney, but this is, or should I say was, a business meeting. I don't appreciate being so blatantly mentally undressed. If those are the sorts of *professional* services you're after, then find them somewhere else," I hiss, glaring at him. "Now, if you don't mind. I'm leaving."

"I apologize, Ms. Jones." His eyes stare into mine. Green on green. I'll bet he never fucking apologizes, especially to the fairer sex. Paul Delaney 0, Jaine Jones 1. "It's not often... people... surprise me."

I nod. "Women, you mean. It's not often women surprise you. And let me think. They'd never dream of answering you back either." We both know that's true. We stand here, trying to figure each other out. One thing I now know for sure is that he's a chauvinistic prick.

"Shall we start again?" He motions towards the seat facing his.

I nod. "Provided you contain your arrogant asshole chauvinistic tendencies, then, of course," I say defiantly as I walk across and take a seat before crossing my legs once more.

He chuckles, and it's a lovely, deep sound. Again, he glances at my legs, albeit only briefly this time. "I can't promise to always contain them, but I shall do my very best around you, Ms. Jones."

He sits across from me and smiles, and no matter how hard I try, I can't help but offer a victorious smirk in return.

"Two months ago, I agreed to take on the legal aspects of your portfolio, Delaney! Everything's been going smoothly. Too smoothly. How did I know it was only going to be a matter of time? Hmm? I should have listened to my gut. It told me you were involved in illegal shit. Now tell me why I need to go to NYPD to speak to a Detective Prescott, and why the hell is he holding one of your employees in a cell?" I hiss at him as I get dressed. "It's seven p.m. on a Friday night, and I have a date that I'm now going to have to cancel."

"With a man?" he asks, sounding pissed off.

"No, with a fucking monkey. Yes, of course with a man," I answer, wondering why he's so bothered.

There's a pause.

"I need you to get him out, Jaine. Unfortunately, I won't be able to go with you, but I will, of course, make it very worth your while."

I roll my eyes. "As I've told you before, Delaney, it's not about the money, so don't think you can bribe me to do your bidding by dropping Benjamin Franklins into the mix. I'm not a goddamn prostitute. I can't be bought."

I step outside my rental apartment block only to find it's raining.

"Great," I mutter as I quickly hail a yellow cab.

I walk through the doors of NYPD. The purple-haired girl on reception looks like she should still be in high school, and she's chewing on a piece of gum like her life depends on it. The whole place stinks of Lysol, piss, and sweat, and not the hard-working kind. I wrinkle my nose in disgust.

"Detective Prescott, please." She looks me up and down, no doubt trying to work out if I'm worthy of her summoning her boss. I hand her my card. "Ms. Jones, of Jones and Associates Legal. You're holding my client here. Mr. Jackson Parker."

The detective rounds the corner. "Ah… Ms. Jones."

"Detective Prescott. Mr. Parker's lawyer. If you have no charges to press, I want my client released immediately." Straight to the point. Zero bullshitting. Hand him over. Or else.

He frowns at me, and after a brief altercation, he relents. He has nothing to hold him on.

Ten minutes later, my *client* turns the corner wearing a biker's cut with his club name and rank emblazoned on, alongside the one percent badge. It was the first time I met Blaze, the enforcer of the Iron Scorpions.

Once outside, I immediately call Delaney.

"Fuck you and fuck Duke. I am not spending my precious time getting your goddamn outlaw bikers off with fucking murder or anything else for that matter." I hang up then turn around, and Blaze is staring at me with a smirk on his face. I raise my eyebrow at him. "Well? You're free to break more laws and murder more people. Off you go!" I usher him away with my hand as I hail another taxi and head home.

Once inside my apartment, I change into pajama shorts and a camisole and pour myself a large glass of wine, even though I seldom drink. Needs must.

I stare around the place. It's expensive and very tastefully decorated. It's minimalistic and all in monochrome with black leather sofas, white walls, and silver and anthracite furnishings finished off with crystal fittings and lights. It's a grown-up place, unlike my bedroom back home in Rising.

Not five minutes later, there's a knock on my door. Pulling it open, I find Delaney standing there. His face is dark and brooding, and his arms are folded in front of him, causing his pecs to strain almost indecently against his Henley. It's then I see the plethora of tattoos that are usually hidden beneath his business attire.

"How the fuck did you get in?" I ask, but I quickly work out the answer. I nod slowly as it dawns on me. He owns the goddamn building. My eyes drift to his biker cut.

President.

It was the first time I met Razr.

Rage and adrenaline flow through me as I storm back inside. I spin around, raising my hand to slap the fucker, and he grabs my wrist painfully. It'll be bruised tomorrow. He holds the other as I try to scratch him and then pins both hands behind my back so my chest is pressed firmly to his. I pant against him, my heart pounding. I want to kill the asshole. Or I at least want to maim him.

He stares at me, his eyes boring into mine before he lowers his gaze to look at my lips. *Please do not kiss me.* I lick them reactively.

I shake my head. "Don't you fucking dare," I warn him.

But dare he does. His lips find mine, and they are hard and demanding, his tongue forcing its way into my mouth. Desire rips through me as my insides turn molten, and I groan, resulting in him deepening the kiss. He smells of sandalwood cologne and everything Delaney, and his mouth and tongue taste of what I only imagine to be raw, undiluted testosterone. He bites my bottom lip until I can taste blood. Using one hand to keep my hands firmly behind my back, he uses the other to jerk my hips forward so they're flush with his, his erection pressing deliciously against my clit. He's fucking huge. I groan again, yanking my arms free this time so I can snake them around his neck. Laying me back on the sofa, he drops his hand to my pussy and immediately begins to rub me through the thin layer of my pajamas. I can feel the material dampening more with every touch. My hips raise, and I grind against his hand like a bitch in heat. He uses his other hand to take off my top before quickly removing my bottoms. His mouth moves to suck and bite on my nipples, and my hands instinctively grab onto his hair, my back arching, wanting more of his mouth on my hot, needy skin.

Trailing his fingers up and down my slickness, he thrusts two fingers inside. I gasp. I'm only partially aware of a zip being pulled down and a wrapper being opened because I'm too far gone. He pushes in a third finger, and it starts to feel uncomfortable until his thumb begins to circle my clit. Shit. I'm almost there. My head's dizzy, and all I can think about is reaching my orgasm. My body is sheened with sweat, and I'm panting at being denied it. Removing his fingers, he positions his slim hips between my thighs and thrusts into me. I mewl loudly with the combination of pain and pleasure, and the unfamiliar feeling of being filled with dick. There hasn't been anyone since Ace. Delaney's movements are fast and precise. There's no talking. Neither of us utters a word. The only sounds are carnal groans of pleasure and skin slapping against skin. This is pure, raw sex.

Forni-fucking-cation.

The stuff the Bible warns us against, that will see us sent straight to hell for partaking. Right now, I don't care if Lucifer himself wants to fuck me next. It's a small price to pay. Delaney's dick is hitting all the right spots, and he's playing me like a pinball machine.

I use him. He uses me. And when I finally come, I see stars. He picks up the pace, nearing his own end and then curses as his cum fills the condom. The erratic thrusting of his movements drags me over the edge a second time, and I groan loudly in appreciation.

Lifting me from the sofa, he carries me into the bedroom. I'm naked, and he's still fully clothed. Typical fucking biker. Why undress when all you want to do is get your dick wet? After the day I've had, I immediately fall asleep. I wake in the middle of the night alone, and the familiar feeling of inadequacy washes over me. Did he leave? Like Ace did? Was I no good again?

It's then I hear the bathroom light click off. Delaney gets under the covers in the dark and pulls me to him until my head rests on his chest. I know this is the start of something. Our relationship has changed, and there's no going back. It's been building for weeks, this *thing* between us, so we were always going to wind up here. That doesn't mean I have to be his old lady or anything like that. We can just enjoy each other physically as well as mentally. He stimulates me in both areas, and vice versa.

It's not going to be all chocolates and flowers, that's for sure, but then, I never wanted that shit.

I'm annoyed about the deceit, though. Pissed off with him and Duke for misleading me. Delaney wanted me to be the legal representation for the Iron Scorpions like my pop is for the Angels. That much is clear now.

I thought I'd escaped the MC life when I left Rising. It turns out that shit follows you around like a bad smell. You can never leave. There's no escape. Our kind drift towards each other like pack animals because it's all we've ever known.

My pop tried to escape the life by moving to Nevada, but the calling was too great, and he returned to Rising. I tried to escape by moving to Connecticut, and now I'm involved with the Iron Scorpions.

It was then I knew I'd always be an outlaw and that I just had to accept that the one percent badge was engraved on my very soul.

CHAPTER TWENTY-THREE

DELANEY

Los Angeles, California

"Listen, I've just landed, Bomb. What the fuck's up, and it better be good." I'm pissed off that I have to put up with his shit when all I want to do is fuck my woman.

"I think Jaine may be working against us, Prez. I've heard a rumor she's in bed with the Irish, and they're planning to remove both MCs and the Russians from the supply chain so they can deal with the Mexicans and the Sicilians direct." He's whispering like he's somewhere public and doesn't want to be overheard. Either that or the asshole doesn't believe what he's saying. He forgets how well I know his bullshitting ways.

How the fuck would the Irish distribute? See? There are fucking holes in his accusations already.

I storm through the airport, restless to get out of its confines. I'm used to open roads, and this flying shit makes me feel claustro-

phobic. "That's bull. Jaine would never betray me, and she'd definitely never betray Steele or Duke," I reply dismissively. I mean, I
know Bomb hates her, but this is taking it to the extreme.

"Did you know she used to date Padraig O'Connell?" I can hear
the smugness in his tone because he knows something I don't.

I stop dead in my tracks. "Right, you've got my attention."

"Well, I have it on good authority that Jaine used to date him
when she was at Yale. Not sure why they broke up, but apparently,
he's still in love with her. He's currently on his way to California."
The words tumble from his mouth like he can't wait to give me all
this shitty news. He'd turn me against her any fucking way he can.

"Even if she did date him, there's still no way she'd betray
either MC. She knows what would happen if she did. She's not
stupid," I say threateningly, meaning he best be on the right track. If
what he's accusing her of turns out to be bullshit, he'll be the one
feeling my blade, not her.

"Hey, I'm just telling you what I'm being fed, Prez. I can't guarantee any of it." I can visualize the asshole holding his hands in the
air submissively. He's always happy to stir the shit but never willing
to lick the spoon. "Why else would O'Connell be flying to California at the same time you are? If he wanted to stake his claim on
her, he didn't have to wait nine years to do it, did he? And he could
just have waited until she was back in Manhattan."

The fucker has a point. If O'Connell wanted Jaine that badly,
he's had years to go after her. She was single for over five before I
met her. And why go all the way to Rising? "So why is he flying
out, Bomb? What the fuck are you getting at?"

"Personally, I think she's brainwashed him. Got him to agree to
do her bidding because he's still in love with her and wants access
to her pussy. I think she wants to kill you, Ace, and Duke, as she
holds you three responsible for her pop's death. She wants him to
help her. If she has all of you in one place, it makes her job a whole

lot easier as there's no time for either club to react. Bang. Bang. Bang. An Exterminator bullet in each of your three fucking heads. As I've said, Prez, this is pure speculation on my part. I just thought it was worth mentioning."

I exhale loudly. When he puts it like that, though, it's believable.

"But she's in love with Steele. Always has been. So why the hell would she want him dead?" I ask curiously.

"It's unrequited, isn't it? He's got an old lady he's been with all this time. Since even before Jaine left. She fucking hates her with a passion, and she's been heard threatening to shoot her between the eyes. Maybe she's completely lost it now she has to bear witness again."

I rub my hands up and down my face. On the surface, it makes sense. Why the fuck else would the Irish be flying in? And why Padraig when it's usually Cillian we deal with? And why did Jaine never tell me about what went on between her and the youngest Duster like she's got something to hide? Like it's a goddamn dirty secret?

"Who's this *good authority*, Bomb?" I ask, my tone threatening. I need to fucking know.

"I can't tell you that, Prez. Not yet."

"You're telling me all this about a woman I've been with for four years, and one I was hoping to wife. If you want me to treat what you're saying as gospel, you tell me, or I'll slit your throat. Theirs too when I find out who they are." I take my blade out of my pocket and flick it open, imagining I'm doing just that.

"Let me glean them of info first, Prez, and then I can tell you."

"You've got twenty-four hours. In the meantime, no one does anything without my say-so. No one harms a hair on Jaine's head. If her disloyalty turns out to be fucking true, then it'll be me and my blade she answers to before she meets her maker. No one else.

Understood? If anyone touches her, they'll lose their neck way before she loses hers."

"Got it, Prez. I'm just thinking it may be an idea for you to book into a hotel for tonight until we know for sure what the Irishman is up to."

I hang up and run my hands through my hair before putting my knife back in my pocket.

"Blaze."

"Prez."

"Pick me up before you meet with the Angels. I'll message you the details."

"Sure thing, Prez."

I disconnect the call and message the information. Stepping outside the airport, I inhale the sweet smell of aircraft fuel so deeply I can almost taste it. Minutes pass before I finally dial her number.

"It's me, baby. I've just landed." I speak quietly, my head still reeling.

"You want me to pick you up?"

"I'll get one of the brothers to drop me off. I've got a few emails I need to catch up on, so I'll do them before I leave." That's all I can muster in reply. She'll know for sure something's on my mind. Stupid, she isn't. She'll be wondering what the hell is going on and why I'm not desperate to see her. I can't tell her my blade hand is twitching at the thought of her betrayal. I need to calm down, so I at least give her a chance to explain when I see her face to face and before I decide whether to cut her ear to ear.

I hang up. There's no way I'm hiding out in any goddamn hotel. Not sure why Bomb would even suggest it. Like I'd ever avoid a dance with the fucking devil.

I hail a cab and make my way to a safe pick-up point, given the cargo we're carrying and its value. We don't need to attract any unnecessary attention. I stare out the window, but I don't see shit. My mind's too preoccupied with what that asshole said, which stacks up in so many ways. I still can't believe Jaine would ever betray me. Then again, she's just lost her pop, and responsibility for his death lies partially at my door for letting her take down the second Russian. If she's then gone home to find Steele still shacked up with the woman he's fucked since before he was legal, the woman he left to go fuck that night, that could have pushed her over the edge.

My other concern is who the fucker is on the inside. My gut's never wrong. The Bratva definitely has someone watching and waiting as Lebedev is way too quiet.

Something big is about to go down.

PADRAIG

Los Angeles, California

Jaine: *Please tell me you're not coming to California.*
Padraig: *Already here.*
Jaine: *You know you'll go straight to hell for lying, Irish.*
Padraig: *Going there anyway. You called me a murderer.*
Jaine: *You are.*
Padraig: *That's beside the point. That comment hurt my feelings.*
Jaine: *Bet what you did to the people you murdered hurt them a lot more.*
Padraig: *I didn't hurt all of them. Some I just gave concrete shoes. So officially, the water hurt them, not me.*
Jaine: *St. Peter still won't let you in those pearly gates. Not with that shitty excuse.*

Padraig: *He will. He's more forgiving and less judgmental than you. He knows I'm way too sensitive a soul for hell.*

Jaine: *You? Sensitive? Heard it all now. Sorry, I can't stop laughing.*

Padraig: *Twist the knife now you've stuck it in, why don't you? Kick a man while he's down.*

Jaine: *You're not down.*

Padraig: *Not yet, but I can be if you want me to be.*

Jaine: *Jesus Christ.*

Padraig: *You'll enjoy it. Women like my cunnilingus.*

Jaine: *Likely because your mouth never stops.*

Padraig: *Now, now. As my ma says, if you haven't got anything nice to say, don't say anything at all. No, it's because I have a long tongue. I'll show you when I get there.*

Jaine: *Please tell me you're not coming to California.*

Padraig: *Already here.*

Jaine: *Whatever. Anyway, there's no need for you to come now because I'm talking to you again, see?*

Padraig: *It's too little too late.*

Jaine: *I didn't message you for twenty-three hours and fifty-five minutes. It wasn't even a whole day.*

Padraig: *You were deliberately pushing the boundaries of our dysfunctional relationship.*

Jaine: *So? You betrayed my confidence.*

Padraig: *And I'm coming to ask for your forgiveness. And to show you my long tongue.*

Jaine: *I don't want to see it. Christ knows where it's been.*

Padraig: *Jealous?*

Jaine: *No. Why would I be?*

Padraig: *You are. I can tell.*

Jaine: *I'm not, and how can you tell even if I were?*

Padraig: *Because your replies will drop down to two-word answers shortly.*

Jaine: *Shut up.*

Padraig: *See? I'll get the 'F' word soon.*

Jaine: *What the fuck are you talking about?*

Padraig: *Swearing at me now? You're thinking of me using my long tongue on someone else's pussy. It's making you jealous, and so you're being reactive and saying mean things to me.*

Jaine: *Am not.*

Padraig: *See? Another two words.*

Jaine: *Fuck you.*

Padraig: *Another two. I know you better than you know yourself.*

Jaine: *Fuck off, Irish. There, that's three. Oops, I said the 'F' word again, didn't I?*

Padraig: *That's not the 'F' word I meant. I mean the one you say when you're really, really angry and really, really jealous. How you feeling right about now?*

Jaine: *I'm fine.*

Padraig: *Really. You sure?*

Jaine: *Yes. I. Said. I'M FINE!*

Padraig: *Gotcha.*

Jaine: *Fine is the 'F' word?*

Padraig: *Yup. Women say it when they're the opposite of fine. Which means you're angry, and guess what else? You're jealous.*

Jaine: *I hate you.*

Padraig: *No, you don't. You love me.*

Jaine: *Asshole.*

Padraig: *Charming.*

Jaine: *Please tell me you're not coming to California.*

Padraig: *Already here.*

Jaine: *Liar, liar, pants on fire.*

Padraig: *Mature. Really mature.*

I SMILE AS I MAKE MY WAY THROUGH THE AIRPORT.

Padraig: *I've just landed.*

Ace: *I'll pick you up in a cage.*

ACE

The Angels of Hellfire Clubhouse, Rising, California

"Jefferson, there's been a change of plan. Blaze and Knight are meeting Razr on their way to you, so they'll be later than anticipated. Can you give Blaze a call to discuss the new ETA? I won't be able to attend as I've been called to an urgent meeting with the Irish. After what happened with the Bratva, they want to discuss operations and security at our end. They're meeting with the Scorpions in New York once Razr returns to Manhattan." I say it matter-of-factly. I don't want to cause any unnecessary worry. Not that I'm sure there's anything to be concerned about, but there's a goddamn niggle at the back of my head that just won't go away.

"No worries, Prez. Will do."

I hang up, run my fingers over the skull on the council table, and wipe my hands down my jeans. They're sweaty. Something's not right. Call it a feeling. Why is Razr not getting PJ to pick him up? Bomb's words were he was pussy-whipped, so why delay? He's flown all this way just to see her. And why the fuck has Padraig turned up all of a sudden? We're in an alliance with them both, so the Angels can't show a lack of trust, but I've got a feeling something's going down that I'm not party to.

I haven't been bedding Emilia these past few nights either, and she's been going out a lot more as a result. She's not happy. She knows it's about PJ and my feelings for her. She's just been going into town. I had Jefferson follow her. Just suspicious, I guess. He had nothing to report back. Just that she's been on her phone making some private calls.

Truth is, I'm done with her. I'm letting her go, as my old man suggested. Even if PJ doesn't want me. *Especially* if she doesn't want me. I need to change my life. Start living. Start over.

I haven't spoken to PJ since she came into my bedroom. She's already said we've nowhere to go unless she breaks things off with Razr, and it doesn't look like that's happening anytime soon since he's on his way here. Then there's Padraig sniffing around her. What a fucking mess. Still, the ball's in her court.

Picking up my keys, I leave the clubhouse to go collect Padraig. We're meeting just outside town in Fielding.

If the Bratva shit doesn't cause an explosion, this thing with PJ fucking might.

CHAPTER TWENTY-FOUR

JAINE

Jaine's House, Rising, California

"SO, THEY'RE NOT ARRIVING UNTIL LATER, THEN?" CHERRY'S dressed in a flowing long white dress with spaghetti straps, her red hair hanging down her back. She looks *almost* back to her usual self. You know. The posh person she was before Rising infected her blood. Like it does with everyone.

I say almost. Apart from her nails. She's chewed each of them down to the quick. She's currently staring into space while nervously biting her bottom lip and rocking back and forth on Pop's old chair. The hypnotic effect of the repetitive motion is almost lulling me to sleep.

She's referring to Blaze and Knight, who are now arriving later than planned due to having to detour to collect Delaney. He didn't want me to pick him up for reasons known only to himself at this stage.

I'm dying to find out. Hopefully not literally.

"No, although it is just delaying the inevitable, babe," I remind her. I'm sitting on the porch swing, my hair tied back in a long ponytail. Sasha is beside me, looking her ever-glamorous self in a pair of fitted black pants and a crimson silk blouse, her perfectly manicured nails colored to match.

"Why don't you fuck them both and be done with it, Cherry?" Sasha says as she sips at her small shot of Irish whiskey. "You know, do that harem thing again."

Cherry rolls her eyes at her. "It's a reverse harem, and you need at least three men for that." She exhales frustratedly.

"You must know which one you like most," I say quietly, regretting the words the instant they leave my lips.

She glares at me. "Do you, Jaine?" I can tell she's still annoyed. They both are.

You see, I told them all about Irish and my plans to meet up with him once we're back in Manhattan. So now Cherry's turned the tables, knowing I'm in the same predicament. Ace and Irish. Both are in my thoughts constantly, and I don't know which way to turn. Delaney's rattling around in there too, of course, but only because I know I need to end things with him. I should have done it some time ago when he started talking about making me his old lady. Will he accept the rejection? Will he slit me ear to ear? Will he slit Ace or Irish ear to ear? Both? All? It depends what mood he's in when I tell him, I guess, and given that he's holed up somewhere, my current concern is there's a problem. A goddamn big one. If Delaney doesn't want to fuck, then someone's said something condemning about me, and he's not sure whether to believe it or not.

Fuck knows what. Fuck knows who.

But mark my words, Delaney's deliberating, and Razr's sharpening his blade while he does so. I know both the Jekyll and Hyde side of the prez of the Iron Scorpions so fucking well.

I shake my head. "Nope."

Sasha stares at me, her expression one of disappointment. "Jaine, I still can't believe you kept it from your two BFFs that you've been talking to Padraig O'Connell every day since you split up. For nine years you've kept him a secret!"

"I've explained all this already. I didn't mention it as I didn't want you to find out he's a fucking Hudson Duster. I didn't want to put either of you in danger." I sigh, getting annoyed that I have to keep repeating myself.

"Well, we're already in danger. We're involved with two MCs, and we're fucking their bikers. It's better to know about all three rather than only two. Although wasn't there a song that said two out of three isn't bad?" She frowns, then shrugs as she takes another sip of the amber-colored liquid. "Anyway, it's Delaney I feel sorry for. He loves you. He has for years. He worships the ground you walk on, and you're going to toss him aside like an old shoe." She shakes her head at me and rolls her eyes.

Fucking hell. I'm a real disappointment to Sasha today.

"But I don't love him. Plus, you've said yourself, he's a chauvinist pig who just wants to control me. We all know I'll never be able to accept that. Even if I wanted to. Rightly or wrongly, I've only ever used him for sex and conversation because he stimulates me in both areas. I've never promised him anything else. I never pretended to be something I'm not. Most importantly, I'm not what Delaney needs, even if he thinks I am. I'll be doing him a favor, I assure you. He might not see it straight away, but he'll thank me in the long run," I say with honesty, and we all know it's true.

I take her hand in mine. There's something I need to ask her, awkward or not. It's been bugging me for a while. No time like the present. They would just come right out with it if the shoe were on the other foot.

"Sash, you've always defended Delaney. Always stood up for

him. Are you in love with him or something?" I ask. I mean, Cherry never defends him. Why would Sasha unless she genuinely cares about him? I fully expect her to turn on me and deny it vehemently, but the opposite happens. Her cheeks go red, and she looks down at her glass, nervously swirling her drink so high it almost spills over the side.

"Well, he ticks all my parents' boxes, plus, he's kind and sweet most of the time, even if he does kill people. And he is extremely handsome. I could do a lot worse than Delaney and definitely could do no better. I wouldn't mind being his WAG," she concludes quietly. "Plus, yes, I do like him." She takes a larger sip of her whiskey.

We sit there in silence. What the fuck to say to that? One of my BFFs is in *sort of* love with the murderous biker I've been fucking for the past four years.

I stand up from the swing and walk across to lean on the railing. The white paint is chipped. I make a mental note to get someone in to quote throwing a coat of paint over the whole property, inside and out. Make it look new on the surface, even though its bones are old, creaking, and probably beyond repair. The house is set in fifty acres of nothingness, and Anita's property, Pop's elderly neighbor, is the only other in the vicinity.

I take a long, deep breath. It's hot and dry, and the air smells of wildflowers and dust. It's a scent that reminds me of being here. Home. I look around, and many of the bare tracks are still visible. The ones Ace and I created over the years, so the grass no longer grows in those areas. Stomped down forever by our ever-growing feet. I smile at the memories. So many of them filled with my beautiful boy.

I turn and look at the house. It's a ranch-style property with white walls and a dark, red-tiled roof. It's all on one level and sleeps seven, so it's a good size, and it also has a somewhat dilapidated pool, which is unusual in these parts. I've decided to keep it. I can't fucking let it go—the thought of strangers living here and changing the place. Putting their mark on it, and, in turn, eradicating the memories it holds of Pop and Ace.

Maybe I'll rent it out. Perhaps I won't. Likely the latter. I don't need the money, thankfully. I'm wealthy in my own right, and Pop was wealthy too. Extremely so.

Who knows, maybe I'll move back to Rising and live in it. Right now, I'm not making any rash decisions. I'm not making any decisions at all. Like tumbleweed, I'll see where the wind takes me. It all depends on what the future holds, and right now, I have no idea what that is. Or who it's with. If anyone.

"If you want Delaney, Sash, he's all yours," I say finally, giving her my blessing. "I'll never be able to make him happy, but you will for sure. You're exactly what he needs, even if he doesn't know it." I walk across and sit back down on the porch swing.

I pour myself a glass of the lemonade Cherry made earlier. It's lukewarm now, and it's also way too sweet for my tastes. I stop myself from grimacing unappreciatively.

Sasha snorts, which is unladylike for her. Cherry and I both turn to stare. "He loves you, though, Jaine, and you're a lot to live up to. I'm not sure I could ever come anywhere close. You're intelligent and bold and brave and so many other wonderful and powerful things. You're everything I'm not. I'm sure Delaney will want more than someone who just looks pretty and decorative. The thing I do best is shopping, let's be honest. He can have anyone he wants. He's Manhattan's most eligible bachelor. Why would he settle for me?" She frowns and drains her whiskey. I've never seen or heard my friend so down on herself before. She typically oozes self-confidence.

Shit. How long has she felt like this about Delaney?

"Listen, Sash. You're everything you've just said I am. You're the same profession. You're bold and brave. You came all this way on a fucking hog, for Christ's sake. You mix with bikers and danger every single day. Don't put yourself down. The only difference between you and me is I come from an MC background. I grew up in *the life*. Not many people do. I was just unlucky," I mutter and sigh. "And anyway, you've been exposed to it way more than most. Way more than any of those fancy pieces who attend those shit debutante balls. You've frequented MC clubhouses for the past four years." It's true. She's witnessed a lot of shit she really shouldn't have.

She sighs. "Yes, but am I, Sasha Preston, enough for a man like Paul Delaney?"

I smirk and shrug. "Only one way to find out. Suck him and see. Even better, just lick him and say he's yours!"

All three of us giggle hysterically.

My phone vibrates in my pocket, and I take it out.

"Duke?" I answer.

"Jainie, sorry to have to call you, baby girl, but Ace is being held at Rising PD." He sounds apologetic. I roll my eyes at Sasha and Cherry. What he's trying to say is, *can you put on your lawyer guise you wear when you pretend to uphold the goddamn law, then go break him out of jail?*

I sigh. "I'm on my way, Duke. I'll take the cage I have here. Could you ask Clay to come pick up the girls, and we'll all meet back at the clubhouse?"

"Yes, I'll make the arrangements. And thank you," he says gratefully.

"No worries, Duke." I hang up.

"So, anyway, Sasha, if you want Delaney? Once I give him the bad news, he's all yours. You can console him with lots of sex. The man's insatiable. I can't guarantee it will all work out for you, but you have my blessing. Not that you need it or that you asked for it, but you have it all the same. On that note, I have to go and break President Ace out of jail."

"Ooh, is it a bit like Rapunzel?" Sasha asks, clapping her hands excitedly.

Cherry and I just stare at her.

I roll my eyes. Inwardly, of course. There's no need to be rude.

Rising Police Department

I SMOOTH DOWN THE PANTS OF MY NAVY SUIT BEFORE I ENTER. MY blouse is low cut deliberately as, depending on what Ace has been up to, I may need to allow Simons a sight of my cleavage.

My four-inch heels click on the tiled surface. I try not to breathe in as the overwhelming stench of Lysol and piss assaults my olfactory senses, making my nostrils burn.

"Do they not have fucking urinals in this place?" I mutter to myself as I walk along the grey floor.

It's the same balding, middle-aged pig who's on duty. He's sitting behind the reception desk, awake this time, but only just. I'm sure I can see dried drool on his chin. A clear indication he's been asleep at some point this evening.

"Excuse me, Officer. I'm here to see Detective Simons. My client is in custody, and I need him releasing, please. A Mr. Jason Steele. I'm Ms. Jones from Jones & Associates Legal." I hand him my card.

I consider taking a seat, then decide against it. They'll have been pissed on or worse. I turn around with a grimace of disgust on my face as Simons appears.

"Jaine, it's good to see you. Can I have a word privately, please?" I frown at him, then nod. He shows me into the small room just off reception. It's the relatives' room. The one they use to tell people their kin has died.

My blood runs cold in my veins. Jesus Christ, please don't let anything have happened to Ace. Tears prick my eyes, and my heart suddenly feels heavy in my chest. They'd have asked Duke to attend, surely. Not me.

Simons looks at me, taking in my concerned expression. "Don't worry, Jaine. Steele isn't dead or harmed in any way." I breathe a sigh of relief inwardly. "Take a seat." He motions for me to sit on one of the two high-backed grey chairs. Grey and white. Everything is grey and white. My eyes scan the white table in the center containing the details of the local funeral parlor. Even their brochure is grey and white.

Talk about complementary.

"What's the problem, Peter? What the fuck is going on?" I ask, my tone terse.

He looks at me and frowns. At my language or at what he's about to tell me? "We had a tip-off tonight that Steele was going to be involved in some sort of illegal activity. He gives me his word that's not an accurate statement."

I nod. Inside, I'm worried. What if someone's tipped them off about the guns on their way to the fucking Mexicans? Two million dollars' worth of weapons that are scheduled to cross the border at some point this evening.

"Now, I'm not naïve, Jaine. I know the MC gets up to no good a lot of the time, but we've always had a tolerant relationship with them. You know how it is. We overlook certain things provided they help protect the town and its inhabitants and donate to the various local causes."

I nod.

"Now, if something is going on that's not within the vicinity of Rising, then we're happy to overlook this from time to time. But if the MC is bringing trouble to the good people of this here town, then we'll need to do something about that. Both of us. You and I. We, after all, uphold the law." He looks at me, knowing full well that statement's fucking laughable at times given who I'm here defending.

"With the information I have, Peter, I can assure you that nothing illegal is taking place within the vicinity of Rising that the MC or I am aware of." It's an honest answer.

He nods and looks relieved.

"We are all here to protect our community, Jaine. So long as we have your client, the MC's agreement on that, and we work together to uphold that, then we shouldn't have any problems living in harmony together. Do I have your word that you will try to maintain that status quo for all our sakes?"

I nod. "Yes, you do. Let's not forget that the MC are also towns-folk and their parents and grandparents helped build the infrastructure of this community, as did my own father. It will always be their wish and mine to ensure the safety and wellbeing of our locals and also those of the neighboring towns."

"That's good to know. I'm glad we have a mutual understanding. I'm confident you'll be able to keep those boys in line." He stands and opens the door and motions for me to step back into reception. I don't have the heart to tell him I'll be returning to New York after I've laid my pop to rest in Rising Cemetery.

"I'll have them fetch your clients now." He smiles warmly at me and motions to the sleepy pig, who stands, yawns, then wanders off.

"My clients?" I look at him and raise an eyebrow. "I thought it was only Ace… I mean, Jason."

It's then I hear voices.

Ace turns the corner. He doesn't look happy in the slightest, and I frown at him, trying to figure out why he's scowling even more than usual.

Then I hear the other voice and the laughter that goes hand in hand with it.

It's *him*.

God, no.

This was never meant to happen. Not here. Not now. To be confronted by both of them together. At the same fucking time.

He turns the corner, and my eyes fall into the blue eyes of Irish.

"Padraig," I whisper.

CHAPTER TWENTY-FIVE

JAINE

Rising Police Department

THE NINETEEN-YEAR-OLD BOY I KNEW IS GONE. I MEAN, WHAT THE fuck did I expect? It's been nine years. Well, I guess he's still in there somewhere. Underneath the exterior of what is now a fully grown hot-as-fuck man. Padraig's tall. Both his long legs and slim hips are flattered by the snug dark blue jeans he's wearing. A fitted white short-sleeved Henley covers his jacketless upper body, displaying the plethora of ink he's gotten over the years and emphasizing the fact that he's worked out.

A lot.

His once short black hair is now shoulder-length and wavy. Familiar eyes of piercing blue illuminate his face as he looks down at me. They always did sparkle most when he was wearing a smile. Precisely what he's doing now. He's fucking beaming.

Stubble caresses his jaw. Does he wear it like that all the time these days, or is it because he's been traveling? He suits it.

He's striking.

Fucking beautiful, in fact.

Even more so than before, which I never thought possible.

I'm conscious and well aware that I'm staring.

"Cat got your tongue, Jaine?" The deep, laughing voice of the boy from my youth fills the room. The familiar Irish lilt now comes from the mouth of the unfamiliar man standing in front of me. He smirks. The asshole knows he looks good. That much is obvious.

He always was a cocky fucker.

"Sorry, Jaine. I should have explained. When we picked up Steele, he had his Irish *friend* with him. I'm assuming you two know each other." Simons looks between us both.

"I've never seen this asshole before in my life, Detective," I reply dryly, my eyes never leaving Padraig's.

"Ah, I see you've never lost any of your wonderful charm or sense of humor, Jaine." His smile widens, and I feel the corners of my mouth twitch upward in response.

"Well, the big man upstairs saw fit to provide me with an abundance of both, Irish, which is more than can be said for your good self."

"Ouch." He clutches his hand to his chest dramatically, like I've wounded him in the heart. "I see that barbed tongue of yours has also gotten sharper over the years."

I roll my eyes at him, my mind flashing back to our earlier conversation concerning that piece of *his* anatomy and where the fuck he's been sticking it lately. "Can you just stop with all the tongue comments, please?" I smirk and roll my eyes exaggeratedly.

He throws his head back, laughing heartily. "I'll show you mine if you show me yours. What do you say?" he replies with all the cheek I remember so well.

"I say you're an asshole, Padraig O'Connell."

"I'll be anything you want me to be, darlin'."

"Somewhere else? Or if I can't have that, can you come with a mute button?" I laugh as I shake my head.

"Let's go. You two can play catch-up once we're out of here. I've got a shit ton of stuff to be getting on with," Ace butts in, the gruffness of his voice letting us know he's beyond pissed off.

At being arrested or at mine and Padraig's flirty behavior, I wonder.

The scowl he's wearing makes him look like he's been sucking on a sour candy from old man Nelson's store.

Padraig glances at him, then laughs. "I have to say, green is definitely not your color, Ace."

His scowl deepens. I rub my hand over my face so he can't see my smirk. Padraig's right. He's jealous. He storms towards the exit, and we follow him, lagging behind like naughty children who've just been told off.

"Oh, Jaine?"

I roll my eyes dramatically before turning around to look at Simons.

"I'm still waiting for you to call me. Dinner? Remember?" He holds his hand up to his ear to give the pretense he's holding a phone.

How fucking lame.

"Sure thing, Peter. I'll get back to you when I have my calendar to hand."

Turning back around, Padraig raises an eyebrow as he looks between the detective and me. Ace simply glowers in my direction. I look between them both, my expression telling them to say nothing. I've already explained, at least to Ace, why I need to keep the pig sweet.

We open the doors and step outside. It's been raining while I've had my *talk* with Simons, and the familiar smell of petrichor and wildflowers fills the air. I breathe in deeply until I can almost taste their floral sweetness against my tongue.

"Give me the keys. I'll drive," Ace says. He holds his hand out, a frown marring his forehead as he stares at me. My eyes graze over him. I can't stop them. His brooding bad boy demeanor only adds to his attractiveness, and doesn't he know it. He wears a stinking attitude so fucking well.

I reach into my jacket pocket and take out the keys. It didn't make much sense bringing my briefcase when it was only ever going to be a talking exercise with Simons.

Or a slapped wrist.

Or a warning.

It turns out, it was a combination of all three.

"Any idea who gave Simons the tip-off?" I ask Ace as I pass the keys to him.

"Nope," he replies reluctantly, taking the keys from me, then turning and striding towards the vehicle.

Asshole.

I exhale loudly. Padraig really couldn't have picked a worse time to show up. Things are already terse between Ace and me. His somewhat unexpected arrival hasn't helped matters.

I curse myself for making him react to the extent he's flown all the way to California. It's my own fault. All this because I didn't speak to him for a goddamn day, though? Surely not.

"Irish, tell me you didn't come to Rising just because I didn't speak to you." I frown at him as we walk towards the cage.

He chuckles and snakes his arm around my shoulder. "I'd like to say that was the case, Jaine, but it's not. It's only partially for that reason. Cillian was meant to come to discuss the ongoing Bratva situation with Ace, so I offered to come in his place. That way, I could kill two birds with one stone since you were being a mardy arse."

I smile. On the one hand, I'm grateful he didn't come all this way just for me. On the other, I feel disappointed that I wasn't the *sole* reason for him paying a visit.

"Maybe me being here will make *him* realize what he stands to lose if he doesn't sort himself out, though," he whispers in my ear, his head motioning towards Ace, who's glowering at us from inside the cage.

"Anyway, Jaine, can I please have a hug? It's been nine years, after all." He stops and stands there with arms wide-open, and I walk straight into them with no hesitation. It feels like I've come home when he wraps them around me.

He looks down and takes me in. "God, you're so fucking beautiful," he whispers against my hair as he pulls me tighter against him.

"You're not so bad yourself, Irish. You've aged well." I chuckle.

"Want to date?" He smirks down at me and winks.

"Been there. Done that. You couldn't keep your dick in your pants last time if I remember correctly." I laugh as I inhale the scent of him. Every time I tried to remember what he wore, it always eluded me for some reason.

The memories suddenly come flooding back. "Irish, please tell me you don't still wear Old fucking Spice."

He snickers. "My da swears by it, Jaine, so who am I to argue? I mean, it got him the love of his life, or so he says. Our Cillian says it was more likely because he has a big cock like the rest of us O'Connells. Apparently, when he was a young man, all the girls were after him because he was hung like a horse, but he's only ever had eyes for my ma."

I lift my head and stare into his laughing blue gaze. "Well, Cillian's wrong. Tell him from me. I agree entirely with you. It was definitely the Old Spice that sealed the deal." I press my nose against his white Henley before exaggeratedly inhaling the smell. "It can't have been the size of your O'Connell dick that swayed me as I never saw it, and I've no intention of ever doing so either," I add with a teasing smirk.

"Well, it's way bigger than my tongue, and my tongue is mighty impressive. You want to see, darlin'?"

"No. Keep that thing in your mouth." I laugh.

"Oh, come on. You're dying to see it. I brought it all this way especially."

"What do you mean you brought it all this way? Is it detachable? Keep it in your goddamn mouth, I said!" I chuckle as his hand snakes around my waist.

"What if I stick it in your ear? Would you like that?"

"Your dick or your tongue?"

"My tongue. My dick is way too big. But if that's what gets you going, I'm game for anything."

He tightens his grip around my middle and tries to stick his tongue in my ear, and I shriek with laughter.

All of a sudden, I feel like I'm nineteen again. We're interrupted when the horn on the cage is blasted. We're having fun, but Ace is letting us know he sure as hell isn't having any witnessing our almost juvenile antics.

I wipe the saliva off my cheek, wrinkling my nose in disgust as I rub my hand down my jacket.

Padraig grabs me by the wrist. "Come on. Your grumpy, jealous ex is going to have us re-arrested for disturbing the peace at this rate. We can sit in the back and make out while he drives."

I chuckle as he drags me to the waiting vehicle. "In your dreams, Irish!"

"Oh, we do a lot more than kiss in my dreams, Jaine, let me tell you." He snickers.

"Padraig O'Connell, you need to wash out your filthy mind." I pretend to be shocked.

"Let's get in the shower together, and you can wash every inch of me, darlin'. Inside and out."

We get in the back, laughing like old times. When I sit, I'm conscious Ace is glaring at me in the rearview mirror. I squeeze Padraig's hand and raise my eyebrows, silently letting him know we should quiet the fuck down.

I'm not sure how long he'll be here, but I'm sure we'll have time to catch up before he returns to Manhattan. A destination I'll also be heading to in the not-too-distant future.

We're driving along, and I take in the familiar sights of my hometown. Well, as much as I can in the dark. Out of nowhere, a black vehicle suddenly pulls in front of us and jams on the brakes, screeching to a standstill. Ace has to swerve to avoid rear-ending it. The roads are deserted, so I'm not sure why the driver felt the need to cut us up. Maybe he has car problems and wanted to make sure he got our attention.

Then my gut tells me something is wrong. This is something else.

Leaving the door ajar, Ace curses and gets out of the vehicle, no doubt to talk to the driver and find out what their problem is.

Seconds later, all of the doors are thrown open, and we're confronted by several balaclava-covered faces.

"What the fuck's going on?" Padraig says threateningly.

There's no time to react.

My hair is grabbed, my head is yanked back painfully, and a cloth is rammed over my face. I quickly lose consciousness.

CHAPTER TWENTY-SIX

JAINE

Location Unknown

I WAKE UP. IT SHOULD HAVE BEEN WITH A START, BUT I DIDN'T HAVE one in me. I feel exhausted. My mouth is parched. I feel sick. Of the three, the latter is currently most prominent—no doubt a reaction to the chloroform. Bile rises in my throat, which I swallow down. It still manages to burn like acid and leaves a sour taste in my mouth. There's a faint smell of floral disinfectant. Rose-scented, I think.

I'm in a cell. Or a room. It's a combination of both, I guess. It's rectangular. Just large enough to hold a non-descript single bed, a small table, a desk, and a chair. There's no writing paper or pen, so maybe you're just expected to sit there and stare at the goddamn wall in the absence of anything better to do. It's the type of pine furniture you buy flat-packed for next to nothing. You think you've got yourself the bargain of the century. Then, when you attempt to build it, you discover half the screws are missing. I take in the three white painted walls and the one made up solely of floor-to-ceiling metal bars.

I'm currently lying on the bed where I must have been placed. The sheets are the same as those used in a hospital. The type that either get boil washed or incinerated after use. Maybe there's a reason for them being that sort here. Maybe not. Perhaps I'm reading way too much into this situation. Then again, probably not. My guess is everything needs to be disposable. Like the clothing I wear when I take out the trash.

The small table holds a pitcher filled with water and a matching clear beaker. The pitcher is full. Raising myself to a sitting position, I place my feet on the concrete floor then notice the white painted door opposite, facing the bed. That's where I need to be, I've decided, but I'm unsure why. Call it gut instinct. I stand, then fall back on my ass. Shit, I'm so dizzy. Rubbing my hand across my face, I close my eyes, then re-open them with renewed determination. I finally push myself upright and manage to stay standing, even with the room spinning. My guts are heaving, and that takes priority. Beads of sweat form on my upper lip caused by the intense feeling of nausea. Walking across to the door, I open it to find a small washroom. It contains the basics. Toilet, a washbowl with a small mirror, a compact shower, and some basic toiletries. Shampoo, soap, a toothbrush, and some toothpaste.

I lift the lid on the toilet, kneel on the floor, and throw up until my throat's raw before leaning my back against the wall. Pulling my knees up to my chest, I wrap my arms around them, resting my head on top. It's safest to stay here until the need to heave passes.

Seconds pass, or minutes. It could even be hours.

My ass is numb and cold. My brain too. The place is still. Silent. Am I dead? Is this what purgatory feels like? It's not as if my corrupt soul will be offered a place in heaven, let's be honest, so it's not likely. I stand gingerly, brush my teeth, then walk back through to the other room. I empty the pitcher and scrub it out as best I can, then fill it with tap water. Two glasses later, only then do I allow my brain to think.

My shoes are missing, as is my jacket. I curse at the latter and can only hope *they* don't find what's hidden in the lining whoever they are.

I walk to the metal bars and look through them. I'm faced with a corridor filled with a sea of similar-looking hell holes.

"Ace? Padraig? You in here?" I say it quietly. Not sure who will hear me. Not sure I want anyone to.

Silence greets me.

Welcome. Unwelcome.

I grip the bars.

Please, God, let nothing have happened to them. I rest my forehead against the cold metal and close my eyes, then return to the bed. Lying on my side, I fall asleep.

Again, seconds pass, or minutes, or hours.

Can I hear groaning? I stand, grimacing as my bare feet come into contact with the cold floor. I'm not sure how I missed that unpleasant feeling the first time around. Walking to the bars, I press my face against them, letting them imprint on my skin so I can see as far along the corridor as I can—still no sign of life.

"Ace? Padraig?" My voice sounds alien to me. Shaky. Like my brain realizes this is it. Game over. *The* fucking end. I'm not scared. Just full of regret.

For what, though?

For not fixing things with Ace.

For not fixing things with Padraig.

I have no regrets about Delaney, though. About how he'll feel having invested four years of his potentially short life in a dead person walking. Does that make me a selfish asshole for not caring about his feelings?

Most likely, yes.

Maybe when you're faced with your own mortality, you become an egocentric fucker.

Who knew?

I turn to face my cell and notice the small fridge in the back. If there's food in there, I won't be touching it. It'll probably be laced with fucking poison or some sort of truth drug.

No one needs to know about *my* secret. About what I do in my spare time.

I lean my back against the cold bars, then slowly sink to the floor. A shiver runs through me. Someone's walking over my grave.

My fists clench at my sides. Who betrayed us? Who tipped off Simons? Whoever it was must have known full well Simons couldn't hold them. That I would go in and save the day. Is that what they wanted? To take all three of us together? Was this all pre-planned?

It must be some asshole with a death wish, that's for sure. Taking on two MCs and The Hudson fucking Dusters? Or is Delaney behind this? Was that why he'd gone all distant? Ace and me aside, surely he wouldn't be insane enough to take on old man Fergal O'Connell by kidnapping his youngest?

Then again, maybe he would. Sometimes there's no reasoning with the fucker when he's in Razr mode.

I wrap my arms around my middle. I'm freezing. My cream blouse is flimsy and offers no warmth. My feet are bare. I'll be cold when I'm dead, so what the hell difference does it matter if my bones are chilled now?

Tears prick my eyes. Not ones of self-pity. Or maybe they are, knowing I won't get to see my pop even in the afterlife. If there is one, that is. I guess that's why you're meant to have faith. Better to have hope and believe in and worship false idols than to have fuck all to cling on to. Just hanging around and waiting for the moment when you're launched into fucking nothingness. I never got to say goodbye to him. My pop. He was one of the good guys. It would have been the pearly gates for him. Whereas, me? I'm going for a ride on the fiery helter-skelter straight into the bowels of hell to burn for all eternity.

A single tear runs down my cheek, and I wipe it away with the back of my hand. In the MC life, showing emotion is a sign of weakness, unless it's anger or hatred. But then, who's here to see this solitary tear? Who's here to witness my one godforsaken moment of reflection and fragility?

Did I want marriage? Children?

Truthfully, I never gave it much thought. I figured I had all the time in the world to make that decision. I mean, I'm only twenty-eight, for fuck's sake.

I guess Delaney was right. You need to grab hold of what you want with both hands while you can and before it's too late. But who would I have wanted to share all of that with? I've loved Ace my whole life. Unrequited love. The worst possible kind. What if he had loved me back, though? My life would have been so different. I'd never have found Padraig.

My Irish.

Things happen for a reason, or so they say. Maybe so. Maybe life is just an exercise of exploring every avenue but still being clueless about which one to go down. Who you want? How would I ever have been able to choose anyway?

Between *them*.

Obviously, my ability to do so would have been limited if they didn't want me in return. Padraig did. Does. Or at least, I think he does. Whereas Ace? I'm not so sure.

I'd likely have spent my life in fucking limbo, never able to take the plunge with either. Fence sitting like I have this past decade. Playing eenie meenie miney mo until it was all too late. Until they'd both moved on with someone else. Until life really had passed me by.

Or until they were both gone.

Maybe the decision has been taken out of my hands.

I hope not. I hope they're okay.

In reality, my own life is over if theirs is. Even though Ace and I never spoke, I knew he was alive and well, existing in this shitty outlaw world somewhere, even if not with me. I could live with that. The knowledge was enough for me. Same with Padraig. We spoke every day. He was alive. Safe. Well.

A world without either of them in it isn't a world I want to be part of.

I exhale loudly.

Who? Why? Where?

Who took me? Why did they take me? Where am I? Where are they?

Have I been left here alone to perish?

How long have I been here?

I have no answers.

What I do know is that, given any opportunity, I will kill the fucker with my bare hands if he or she or they has harmed either of them.

"Jaine."

Am I hearing things now? It sounded so faint, I must be. My mind is playing tricks on me.

"Jaine?" It's louder.

My heart pounds in my chest as hope floods my veins, and I gasp.

He's alive.

CHAPTER TWENTY-SEVEN

JAINE

Location Unknown

"Irish?" I whisper.

I stand and press my face against the bars, my hands gripping them so tightly my knuckles are white. Am I hearing things?

"Irish! Is that you? Walk to the bars. Let me see you." I'm conscious my voice sounds teary, but right now, I don't give a fuck.

"Padraig!" I yell, frustration taking over.

And then I see him. My Irish. Two cells down on the opposite side. Looking a bit worse for wear but unharmed, or at least there's no sign of injury and no visible blood.

"Irish," I laugh sob. "Thank God you're okay."

"I'm fine. I've just woken up," he replies in a hushed tone.

"Do you know who's taken us?" I ask, hoping he's at least seen some sign of life.

"I've no idea. I'm guessing it must be the Russians."

"I'm so fucking glad to see you." I smile at him weakly.

"Ditto, darlin'," he replies quietly, but the sparkle has gone from his eyes. He looks subdued.

I need to ask the question, but I'm scared to. My heart's pounding in my chest as there are only two possible answers, and one doesn't bear thinking about. "Is Ace here?"

He exhales slowly. "I've not seen him. Not since he got out of the car. You know, before we were taken."

Dread flows through me. Regrets flood my veins. *Please, God, let him be okay. I'll do fucking anything.* I close my eyes and sink to my knees.

"I'm sure he'll be fine, darlin'," Padraig mutters as he takes in my devastated reaction, but he doesn't sound convinced.

We sit there in silence, both of us lost in our own thoughts.

Who? Why? Where?

I stand, then move across and lie on my bed.

"You want to play I Spy, Jaine?" His beautiful smiling voice interrupts my morose thoughts, and I can't help but smirk in response to his question. Always lightening the mood, my beautiful Irish.

I laugh out loud. "Only if I get to go first." I look around, but what's there to fucking spy? B for bars? C for cell? "I spy with my little eye something beginning with D."

I hear a deep chuckle, and I can tell his eyes are sparkling again. I need them to. It makes everything feel normal. Well, as much as it can be given we've been kidnapped and are currently being held hostage by fuck knows who.

"Devastatingly handsome Irishman."

I guffaw. "I've never met one of those in my life, so nope."

"Aww, Jaine, you're hurting my feelings."

"You don't have any feelings, Irish."

"I do."

"Only for yourself. I always did think you were a bit of a narcissistic asshole." I chuckle.

"No… for you. I have feelings for you, Jaine," he says quietly.

I don't reply immediately. All sorts of shit flies through my head. Do I want to talk about this sort of stuff? Open *that* can of worms. Right here, right now? With the grim reaper himself looming around the corner? I stand up and pull back the covers on the bed, knocking the plastic beaker off the cabinet in the process and spilling water all over the floor.

"Shit." I grab a handful of tissues from the bathroom and mop it up.

"What are you doing, Jaine?"

"I was pulling back the covers and I knocked over the beaker. I'm cold." I crawl under the scratchy material. "The thread count in these sheets must be a minus, by the way," I say with a small laugh.

"I wish I could keep you warm, darlin'."

"I wish you could too, O'Connell." I sigh.

Silence follows. I know he's waiting for me to comment on what he said.

"Guess we're crossing *that* bridge, then," I mumble quietly.

"Don't you want to cross it? Talk about things? We might never get another chance."

I nod to myself and pull the covers up to my chin. "What do you want to know? Is there anything you want to ask me? I'm no good at talking about this sort of shit. I'm not even sure where to fucking start."

"Did you love me when we were at Yale? Like, seriously. And I don't mean love like a brother or friend. Were you in love with me? I know you said you were, but did you really mean it?"

"Why do you want to know that now, Irish? It was nine years ago."

"I don't know. Humor me. I just need to know. Before I meet my maker if that's what's in The Almighty's plan."

I stare at the walls. I don't need to think about it as I already know the answer.

"Yes, I was in love with you."

There's a pause.

"Do you still love me? Are you still in love with me?"

I close my eyes. Do I tell him the truth, or do I lie?

What difference does it make when we could have the barrel of a cocked gun forced down our throats at any minute?

"Yes, I'm still in love with you, Irish. I never stopped." I close my eyes. He can't see me, but I still feel awkward as hell.

Exposed. Naked. Vulnerable.

"Why didn't you ever say anything? Never mention it these past nine years?" His tone is aggrieved now.

"I had my reasons. I wasn't enough for you back then, and I'm still the same person. If I wasn't enough nine years ago, why would the progression of time change anything?" I reply quietly. He knows what I'm referring to—his inability to keep his dick in his pants. He didn't love me enough to stay faithful to me then, so why would he now? Nothing's changed.

"Jesus Christ, Jaine. I was nineteen years old. I made a mistake. I said I was sorry until I was blue in the face, but it made no difference. I thought you didn't want to sleep with me because you didn't love me, or at least not as much as you loved the other fella! I thought that's why you kept making excuses." He's speaking candidly now. There's no smile in his tone. He's getting it all off his chest—the frustration of the past nine years. I can hear the pain in his voice.

"So, that's why you cheated? You thought I didn't want you because I didn't love you as much as I did him?" I question.

"Yes!"

"Well, it had nothing to do with my feelings for Ace. You know what happened between him and me. I guess I just couldn't understand why someone as popular as you would want to be with someone as unpopular as me. I also thought I was shit at sex, so I was nervous. Scared. When you cheated, I thought history was repeating itself, so like I did with him, I stopped things before I could be hurt more than I already had been. I thought I couldn't hold your attention because *I* wasn't good enough. That skinny, unattractive Plain Jaine wasn't good enough. That I'd never be good enough for anyone, so I'd always be someone's second choice. I gave up on boys then as an act of self-preservation, much to the frustration of my friends. It was just easier. There weren't any I was remotely interested in anyway."

"So, wait. You never dated or had any boyfriends after me?" he asks in disbelief.

"No. I just focused on my studies, then left Yale."

"What about Delaney?"

"What about him?"

"How did you meet him?"

I shrug, even though he can't see me. "Duke introduced us. I didn't know at the time, but Delaney was looking for a lawyer for the Scorpions. He, my pop, and Duke convinced me it was a good idea. I came from *the life*, so I guess I was a good fit. It's how the alliance between the MCs came about."

"Right."

There's a pause.

"So how did Delaney...? Shit. I don't know how to phrase it."

"How did Delaney convince me to fuck him?"

"Well, I was trying not to be quite so crude, but yes."

"Why change the habit of a lifetime?" I chuckle. "When I met Delaney, I looked pretty much like I do now. No glasses, braces, and I'd even managed to grow a pair of tits. Plain Jaine was gone.

Well, at least she was no longer visible on the outside. He wanted me, and what Delaney wants, he simply takes."

"You mean he raped you?" I can tell he's agitated now.

"No. He never raped me. It wasn't like that. He knew I wanted him too, so he didn't ask permission. He just took what he wanted, and I let him. We never discussed my past and my insecurities. Not until way after."

"So, what you're saying is, if I'd persevered and gone after what I wanted, you would have given in?"

I don't want to say the answer as I know he'll curse himself and be filled with regrets, but I'm not going to lie.

"Irish. I wanted you. I wanted to have sex with you. There's every likelihood that you could have kissed me into submission or got me so aroused I would have relented. So, yes, there was always that chance."

"Jesus fucking Christ." I can hear him quietly cursing and can tell he's running his hand through his hair.

"There's no point in dwelling on it now, is there?" I ask.

"You don't love Razr, though, so why would you fuck him?"

I laugh. "Delaney stimulated me mentally at first. He's a highly intelligent man, if you didn't already know. The physical stimulation stemmed from there. He's a sensual person, and, well, he knows exactly what he's doing when it comes to women. But you're right. I don't love him. I won't be his old lady, and I won't marry him, even though he's asked me to several times."

There's another pause.

"What about Ace? Are you still in love with Ace?"

I don't hesitate with my response.

"I will always be in love with Ace. Nothing will ever change my feelings for him."

I'm only glad the moody asshole can't hear me.

"But how can you be in love with us both?"

He's asking me something I ask myself most days. Something I have no answer to.

"I have no idea, Irish, but I am."

"Would you marry me if I asked you to?"

I laugh. "Is that a proposal? If it is, it must be the shittiest, least romantic one I've ever heard in my life."

"Well, it's difficult to be romantic in this setting, isn't it? So, I'm asking you, Jaine Jones. If we get out of here alive, will you be my wife?"

He's serious. I run my hand over my face. Now is not the time to be asking life-changing questions like that. Especially when everything could end abruptly. Especially when he doesn't know everything there is to know about me.

My thoughts are interrupted, and I'm saved from having to reply.

"Maybe PJ would prefer me to wife her instead, O'Connell," a dark smug voice says from further down the corridor.

Silence follows.

That fucker just heard every goddamn word.

CHAPTER TWENTY-EIGHT

JAINE

Location Unknown

"Look, we're just reacting to this shitty situation we've found ourselves in and saying things we wouldn't normally. Let's drop the subject. Impetuous offers and rash decision-making never end well." I can't undo what's been said or overheard, much to my extreme annoyance, so I'm doing my best to ignore it for now. "When this shitshow is over, and *if* we get out alive, we can revisit it or sweep it under the carpet as we see fit."

The latter is most likely.

"Oh, and Ace? You're an asshole for listening in to a private conversation." I sound angry, but I have every right to be. That was uncalled for.

Still, it's all out in the open now. Well, at least my feelings are. And Padraig's.

"I'm not deaf. I had no choice but to listen," he replies matter-of-factly.

"You should have made your presence known and you know it!" I hiss.

"Thought I did."

Asshole.

"Enough!" Padraig's voice is loud and firm, letting us know he's reached the end of his tether with our constant bickering. "We'll pick this matter up *when* we get out of here, not *if*. So, now that we're all present, let's discuss the pressing matter at hand. Who took us, why did they take us, and how the fuck do we get out of here?"

"It's got to be the Russians." Ace sounds convinced. It's the obvious answer, so to disagree entirely, which I'm itching to do just to be fucking awkward, would be plain petty. Why the fuck does he always bring out the immature teenager in me?

"I agree," Padraig confirms. "What about you, Jaine, darlin'? Any thoughts?"

I get out of bed and walk towards the bars. The floor feels colder than before, making me wish I had my shoes. Why the fuck did they take them? Did they think I was going to use them as a goddamn weapon? Then again, I would have given any opportunity. Four-inch stiletto heels could do a lot of damage to a skull.

Padraig is leaning against his bars, but I can't see Ace. He's probably lying on his bed because standing is too much of an effort. Either that, or he's on the same side of the corridor as me.

"I tend to agree, but I think there's a slim chance it could be someone else entirely," I mumble.

Padraig frowns at me. "What do you mean? Who?"

I pause before I speak. I'm in two minds whether to say what's in my gut or not, but I realize I have no choice.

"Delaney's been acting weird since he flew into Los Angeles. I offered to pick him up from the airport, but he turned me down. Some shitty excuse about having emails to do, then he couldn't get off the phone quickly enough. He said he'd wait for Blaze and Knight. I haven't heard from him since."

"Is that out of character?" Padraig asks.

I shrug. "Well, he came to California for one reason only. To see me. Yet when presented with that very opportunity, he turned it down."

"Was he acting normal before he left Manhattan?"

"Totally, and when I spoke to him on the phone the night before."

"Razr wouldn't be stupid enough to target the Dusters," Ace interjects.

"See, normally I'd agree. But maybe he's heard about Irish and me. The fact that we used to date and that we've been in contact all this time. I've never told Delaney any of that. It wasn't a secret per se. It just never came up in conversation. We all have skeletons in the closet. No offense, O'Connell." I snicker.

"None taken, Jaine." He chuckles back.

"If Delaney thought for one moment that I'd betrayed him with either of you, he'd kill us."

"But you haven't betrayed him?" Ace adds, his voice raised, like it's a question.

"No, I haven't. As I've already said, I'd need to finish things with Delaney before I could ever get involved with someone else. I owe him that much. I would never disrespect him like that."

"So, we have to consider that Razr may be behind this, then." Padraig blows out a long sigh.

"Yes, I think we do, or we definitely can't rule it out," I reply. "The only positive we can take from it is if Delaney is responsible and it's because he thinks I've disrespected him or betrayed him, then he'll want to kill me personally. He won't allow anyone else to do it. My end will be by his hand and his blade. That at least guarantees me a face-to-face with him beforehand. He'll allow me the chance to plead my case before he makes his final judgment." I say it like it's no big deal. Like the potential for getting your throat slit by your loving boyfriend is a regular occurrence.

"Do you think he could be working with the Russians?" Ace asks.

I shake my head, even though he can't see me. "That would be disloyal. There's no way he'd do that. If he wants me or any of us dead, it's purely down to him believing we've disrespected him or the Scorpions in some way."

"So, we've either got the Russians after us or an insane jealous biker with a fucking flick knife. Is that it?" Ace asks.

"That about sums it up, yes. The other currently unknown risk is the person who's whispering sweet nothings in Delaney's ear. Someone's said something about me to make him think I've betrayed him or that I'm about to, hence why he's avoiding me. Delaney's currently deliberating while Razr's sharpening his blade."

We sit in silence, all of us no doubt dwelling on this third party. I have my suspicions, but if I mention Bomb, it means telling them about my *other* role. Is now the right time to spill my guts?

"Is there anything else any of us needs to get out in the open? Any other potential reason the Russians could be after one or all of us? I mean, they could have gone after the Scorpions in New York. Why come all the way to California, and why target us three specifically?" Ace asks a pertinent question.

My blood runs cold at the sudden realization.

What if the Bratva have somehow found out about my extracurricular activities? Only three other people know. I'd trust Duke with my life, and even if he did want me dead, Delaney would never hand me over to them. It leads me to Bomb again. Has he got the ear of both Delaney and the fucking Bratva? What the fuck would they want with Irish and Ace, though?

Shit, I need to tell them. About my suspicions and my part-time job.

"Guys, there *is* something I need to tell you..."

I'm interrupted by movement at the far end of the corridor. We stay as we are.

Firm footsteps make their way towards us down the concrete floor, and I take in the visual of the slim-built man they belong to as he approaches. Wearing a black wool overcoat that only seems to lengthen his tall frame, he stops right in front of my cell. The first thing I notice about his face is his eyes. Black and bottomless, and looking like they lead to the bowels of fucking hell. In contrast, they're on a face that's pale with a sallow complexion, like the color of someone at death's door.

Maybe that's what happens when you've murdered as many as the man stood before me has. Perhaps, for each soul you take, a fraction of your own life disintegrates until you're a walking, talking grim reaper. His lips form a thin line on his insipid face, and his hair is slicked back and shiny. It'll be some expensive product, but it may as well be black grease. He's followed by two other men dressed the same, their faces impassive. No doubt they've been trained to be devoid of any emotion at all times.

"Ah, Miss Jaine Jones." His voice is deep and dark. Bone-chillingly so. His accent is Russian. So, we finally have our answer.

"And you are?"

He smiles. His teeth are yellow. He smokes a lot.

"Sokolov. I am the obshchak of Pakhan Lebedev." His smile widens. Does the fucker expect me to look impressed that he's one of the pakhan's right hand men.

He turns and looks at Padraig. "Mr. O'Connell." Then he turns to look at what I can only assume to be Ace's cell. "Mr. Steele.

"Leave us." He speaks to his goons without looking at them, and they turn and walk away. He doesn't speak again until we hear a door close in the distance.

He then turns to look at me. "I am sorry for inconveniencing you in this manner, gentlemen. To explain. Miss Jones has committed some very serious crimes against our organization. In normal circumstances, such actions would be met only by death. The pakhan, however, feels that we may have a use for Miss Jones' currently unrivaled capabilities for our own purposes. The pakhan has therefore decided that Miss Jones' life will be spared. Instead, she will be auctioned off and wed to one of our three main benefactors, thus tying her to us. Before that can occur, however, they have requested sight of Miss Jones and of what she has to offer."

He knows. The Bratva fucking know.

Delaney or Bomb has betrayed me.

"Sorry, but I'm totally confused," Padraig interrupts.

"Irish, let me handle this," I interject firmly.

"What sight do they require, Sokolov? Photographs? A video call? What the fuck are we talking about here?" Deep down, I already know. I know now how these dirty assholes work.

"A video of your, shall we say, talents." He smirks. Disgusting fucking scum.

My blood races in my veins. What the fucker is saying is that he wants me to star in my very own sex tape so they can decide whether my services are worth paying for. Like the fuckers do with the children they kidnap straight from their beds who are then sold on to the highest paying dirty pedophile after they've all jerked off to their performance.

Before he has the chance to react, I reach out my hand and grab him by the collar, pulling him tightly against the bars.

"You let your pakhan know that I'm coming for all of you sick assholes, but more so for him. Definitely for him. You mark my fucking words, that motherfucker will die at my hands." My tone is deadly.

His expression doesn't falter, but he swallows. He knows I could snap his neck right now if I wanted to, and I would if his goons weren't outside the damn door.

I let him go with a push, and he stumbles backward.

"What the fuck is going on, PJ?" Ace asks. Padraig is staring at me, looking equally confused.

"These fuckers make sex tapes of the children they traffic before they place them up for auction. The bidders watch said sick show, and the kids are then sold off to the pedophile who pays most. You know that, right?"

"Yes, I'm aware." Padraig looks at me.

"Well, they want to make one of me and then auction me off to the highest bidder." I rub my hand up and down my face.

"What sort of sex tape?" Ace asks, trying to mask his building rage.

"Come now, Mr. Steele. You've watched porn before, have you not?" Sokolov replies with a smirk. He's moved slightly farther down the corridor now. He won't make the mistake of standing so close to me again.

"Who the fuck with? And why? What do you want with Jaine? She's just a fucking lawyer." Padraig is pacing behind the bars now.

"We believe as you're both infatuated with her that you could be the willing participants. Think of it as your last goodbye." He smirks again.

It's what I expected him to say, but by saying it out loud, it's now confirmed. This is why the three of us were specifically targeted.

"So, you want us to fuck PJ while you film it? Is that it? Are you insane? On what planet do you think that's acceptable?" Ace hisses at him.

Sokolov shrugs. "We thought it would be kindest as you are all old friends, but if you're not willing, then we will find others only too happy to take your place. I may even put myself forward." His eyes trail slowly over me.

"You put one greasy finger on me, and I'll kill you with my bare fucking hands," I snap.

"But why!" Padraig shouts. "What the fuck do you want with Jaine?"

Sokolov raises an eyebrow at me. "My, my, Miss Jones. I can't believe you've never told your oldest friends about your *other* job."

I close my eyes and breathe deeply.

"Gentlemen, I'd like you to meet The Exterminator."

CHAPTER TWENTY-NINE

JAINE

Location Unknown

SILENCE.

Minutes pass. It feels like hours.

You could hear a fucking pin drop. I'm sure my pounding heart is audible. Well, at least it is in *my* goddamn ears.

"I shall take my leave now. I shall come for you and Mr. O'Connell in the morning, Miss Jones. In the meantime, we shall have an evening meal prepared and served for you all. It is, of course, your decision whether to eat it or not. We cannot force you. We shall also provide fresh clothing and suitable footwear." The smirking asshole who's just dropped the motherfucker of all bombshells turns to leave.

"Sokolov?"

"Yes, Miss Jones?"

"What happens if I say no? What happens if we don't go

through with this?" I've decided I need worst-case answers.

"Then, as I've said previously, replacement participants will be sourced, most likely myself and one other. The desired result will be achieved either way."

I nod. They'd resort to rape, then. Bile rises in my throat at the thought of any part of him touching any part of me. I swallow down the acrid taste. "And the wedding to the Russian benefactor? If I don't go through with that?"

"You don't have any choice. Although they are not yet aware of who you are, your sniper past, or your future role within our organization, they are fully aware of your importance. Each bene-factor has been given the same date to keep free. That is when the wedding will take place. If after the event you try to harm them or anyone else, or if you attempt to flee, then Mr. O'Connell and Mr. Steele will feel our wrath and pay the price for your rebellion."

I nod.

Nothing further is said until the door closes in the distance.

"I was about to tell you," I mumble.

Well, it's the truth.

Padraig stares at me through the bars, looking at me like he doesn't even know who I am anymore.

"You were about to tell us that you've killed hundreds of goddamn people in your spare time?" Ace rasps.

I start to pace on the cold concrete floor. I can't maintain eye contact with Padraig. Is he disappointed in me? For the killings? For not telling him? For some reason, his disappointment bothers me more than anything else.

"Well, I've never actually kept a running total, so I'm not entirely sure how many," I reply, suddenly feeling annoyed. "But anyway, every fucker I've ever killed deserved my bullet in their skull and a one-way ticket straight to hell."

"Who else knew about this?" Padraig speaks quietly. It's barely audible.

"Me, Delaney, Duke, and Bomb." I stare at Padraig through the bars again, but I still can't read his expression.

"You told my old man?" Ace sounds angry. He's got every right to be. By telling Duke, I've implicated him and put him at risk.

I immediately pace again. "Look, until I left Manhattan, only Delaney and I knew. It was safest that way—the fewer people who knew, the better. After what happened with my pop, Delaney thought it best I sit on the council at the Scorpions. Even though he assured me they weren't linked, if I'd known beforehand about the missing guns and the reason behind the first killing, I would never have gone after the second perverted fucker. Well, at least not immediately. Not until the two deaths didn't look like they were connected.

"The last time I spoke to my pop, he told me the Bratva held the Scorpions accountable for both deaths and were going to retaliate. He paid the ultimate price.

"All the Scorpion council members approved me joining, but the only way Delaney could convince Bomb to yay me in was to tell him everything. I guess I panicked when he told me that. Bomb hates me. He thinks I've got Delaney pussy-whipped.

"I was going to tell Irish, but I wasn't sure how secure my call would be, so I told Duke instead. I needed to tell someone who was on my side in case anything happened to Delaney. Bomb would have no hesitation in handing me over to the pigs if he thought he was the only one who knew my secret. I did try to involve you, Ace, but you seemed to think I was just looking for recommendations on what color to paint my nails that day or something else equally as condescending."

"You should have insisted I listen if it was this fucking important!"

I roll my eyes. "Yeah, well, you and your old lady didn't exactly welcome me into your clubhouse with open arms, so I wasn't too sure if I could trust you given where your loyalties lie."

"How many times, she's not my old fucking lady! And how could you think I'd ever betray you? I'd never do anything to hurt you, goddamn it." His frustration is evident.

"You betrayed me once before, and let me tell you, that shit stung."

There's a pause.

"You can believe what you like, PJ. I said all I had to say on the voicemails I left you and the messages I sent ten years ago. If you didn't listen or pay any attention to them, that isn't my problem. You always were too stubborn for your own good."

"Fuck you, Ace."

"No, fuck you, PJ."

"Oh, well, that'll be happening real soon, won't it?" I reply, then I realize how childish I sound.

"Holy Mary, Mother of Joseph, can we get back to the matter at hand?" Padraig interrupts. "So, this means for the Bratva to know, only one of three people could have told them?"

I nod. "Yes."

"My old man would die before he'd say anything," Ace says.

"I know that."

"What about Razr?" Padraig asks.

I shake my head. "He's too loyal. Even if he hated my guts and wanted me dead, Delaney would never stab me in the back. He's no traitor."

"So, that leaves Bomber as the party entirely responsible for our situation?"

"Well, yes and no," I reply.

"What the fuck do you mean?" Ace asks.

I can just tell the asshole is rolling his eyes, probably thinking

I'm trying to be an awkward bitch. "What I mean, Ace, is that there may be another informant."

"How do you figure that out?" Padraig asks, frowning at me.

"Well, until I went to California, only you and I knew we were in communication. I told Duke about my Irish contact when I told him about my vigilante role. Then, after Ace found out, I told Cherry and Sasha."

"Yeah, and your point is?" Ace snipes.

"Who told the Bratva about Padraig and me? I mean, Sokolov clearly knows we have a past. Bomb didn't know about it, and neither did Delaney."

There's a pause.

"So, there's more than one person involved, then?" Ace suggests.

"Well, I guess so, as the only person who knew absolutely everything before now is Duke, and there's no way he'd stab me in the back," I say quietly. "So, yes, it can only mean there's more than one person involved as the Russians know everything."

WE'RE EACH QUIET AND WRAPPED UP IN OUR OWN THOUGHTS. I'M lying on my bed. The meal the Russian scum served up remains untouched. No matter how much I attempt to cover it with the lid provided, the stench of some awful over-seasoned stroganoff dish still manages to seep through and pollute the air.

I push the tray to the far end of my cell, shower, and change into the clothes provided. A white tank top and a pair of regular cut, way-too-big blue jeans, which keep falling to my hips. White sneakers finish my almost teenage boy look.

"I'm not sure I can do this," Padraig mumbles.

"We don't have any choice unless we can come up with a means of escape beforehand, or unless you're prepared to let Sokolov fuck me personally." I know he's referring to the fact that he and I are *performing* tomorrow.

I could make a joke. Say that at long last he's going to get to fuck me, but I'm not sure Irish would see the humor in that, so I keep my mouth closed. For all his light-hearted cockiness and upbeat demeanor, the rivers of his Irish soul run deep.

Women are almost sacred in their community and protected at all costs. When they wed, they wed for life, and they take the line *'til death us do part* seriously.

This will be going against everything he believes in because he'll think I'll be doing this under duress.

I guess I'll just have to convince him otherwise.

CHAPTER THIRTY

JAINE

Location Unknown

It looks like a hotel room sans all furniture, apart from a queen-sized bed covered in pale grey silk sheets. It dominates the space. It's difficult not to look at it and for my mind not to fast forward to what's about to happen next.

It all feels fucking surreal. I try not to dwell on it, but it's not like I can put it off much longer. It's inevitable. We don't have any choice in the matter.

The walls are in a silver flock paper, and the floor is white-washed wood. A Venetian-style bedside cabinet holds a white ceramic pitcher and two clear glasses. That's it. There's nothing else.

Just me. And him.

There's a plain white door at the far end of the room. Walking over, I try the handle, but it's locked.

My natural curiosity has me wondering what the fuck's behind it. My common sense tells me that, given my recent run of luck, it's best not to investigate.

Fuck it. I still want to know. I'll try again next time.

Next time. With Ace.

Sokolov explained before leaving that there are recording cameras throughout, so there's no need for anyone else to bear witness. No need for anyone to be here to ruin the fucked-up atmosphere. Apparently, they'll edit everything once all the taping is in place. The tiny dots of red lights, I'm guessing, signal where the cameras are. They're easy to miss. I'm not sure if that's a good thing or a bad thing. That it doesn't feel like anyone else is intruding. That there's no escaping the fact that we're here alone. I'm not sure how I feel about it. This set-up. It's far too intimate. I feel way too exposed. Scared even, which is fucking stupid.

This isn't like being with Delaney. The feelings I have for Padraig surpass any I've ever known or felt for anyone. Apart from Ace.

Our eyes connect, and I quickly look away. I feel myself blush, something that hasn't happened to me in years. Jesus Christ, am I turning back into Plain Jaine? Insecure. Nervous. Awkward. Or is it because I love him that my hands are suddenly so sweaty? Because it means so much more than just fucking for the sake of fucking.

We've agreed not to speak or to say as little as possible. Just in case we say something we shouldn't, as it's being recorded.

I laugh inwardly. Let's see how long that lasts. He even talks in his goddamn sleep. Mr. Gift of the Irish Gab can't stop his mouth from running away with him most of the time.

I'm wearing my clothes from last night; the white top and the way too big jeans I keep having to yank up.

Padraig's stood looking at me. Is he waiting for me to say some-thing? Do something? Because right now, my mouth won't form words, and I can't move. He looks uncomfortable. Like he'd rather be somewhere else. Anywhere else. I don't know whether to feel flattered that he wants to protect me from all this or insulted that he'd so obviously rather pass up on the opportunity to fuck me.

It's not because he's nervous. Nope. He'll have fucked hundreds of women, I'm sure. Maybe even thousands. The issue is the circumstances. Why he has to do this. That it's for all the wrong reasons. That it's against my will.

Casual sex with a stranger is a walk in the park in comparison. We're both about to fuck someone we've loved for nine years. It's nerve-wracking.

My concern is that this might make our feelings stronger. Less easy to walk away from. Impossible to return to how we were. Confidants. Friends.

I need to speak to Padraig every day as much as I need oxygen to breathe every day. I need him to survive this fucked-up, crazy outlaw world I live in. And I know the feeling's mutual. I am to him what he is to me. We are each other's life raft, sounding board, best friend.

But I already have a best friend. Don't I?

Will everything change after this experience? I fucking hope not.

I take a deep breath and walk over to him, my eyes focusing on the buttons of his Henley. Reaching out my hand, I press my palm flat against his chest. I can feel his heart pounding. Is it beating so fast for me or because of this situation? If we were anywhere else, doing this for any other reason, would it still be as erratic? Then again, would we be doing this at all if not for this reason?

Blurring fucking lines.

He reaches his hand up to cover mine, and the warmth of his touch causes heat to course through my body. Holding my breath, I look up at his face. He's beautiful. His stubble has grown, but it emphasizes his perfect features and full lips more. Its darkness contrasts magnificently against those glorious blue Irish eyes of his. I reach my other hand up and tuck his inky black hair behind his ear. He closes his eyes as my fingertips trail slowly down his jaw, which he clenches in response. He swallows thickly. He's nervous. His eyes open slowly, and they're brighter than they were. I can feel his heart rate increase under my palm as desire flows through him, and it ignites the same response in me. Excitement pools in my belly, and it takes everything in me not to groan out loud, and he hasn't even laid a finger on me yet.

I reach my face up and press my nose against his neck. He smells of soap and raw masculinity. He smells of Padraig. All my memories of him flood my brain as I press my lips against his skin, breathing him in. He moves both hands down to circle my waist and pulls me tight against his hard body, and I move mine to circle his neck, pressing my tits against his chest, causing my nipples to pebble in response, pleading for his attention. Pulling back, I look up into his face, and his eyes are dark. My gaze drops to his lips, and he licks them, making them glisten. My insides feel molten as I move my mouth towards his, letting our hot breaths mingle momentarily, smelling and almost tasting the mint of his toothpaste. I gently press my lips against his.

His are soft and pillowy, and my mouth immediately remembers their feel and his unique taste. His tongue pushes past my lips, searching and rediscovering, our mouths reconnecting like they've never been apart. Dropping his hands to my ass, he pulls our fronts together, and I can feel his erection pressing against me. I groan into his mouth, letting him know I want this. Want him. He steals it from me, deepening the kiss further in response. His tongue fills my mouth before sucking mine into his. My hands pull at his hair as he grinds against me, causing my whole body to come alive. Lust and desire pound through my veins, causing my clit to throb almost painfully.

Our greedy mouths part only for the time it takes for him to lift my tank top over my head. I'm braless. There didn't seem any point in putting one on. Our mouths reconnect as his hands cup my tits, tweaking the nipples and causing a jolt of desire to rush through me. I groan loudly in disappointment as he pulls his mouth from mine, then moan in appreciation as he drops it to my nipple, sucking it in and biting it with his teeth. My hands clutch his hair, and I arch my back, pressing myself against his mouth. Demanding more. Needy. Greedy.

He bites and sucks at my nipples as his fingers drop to the button of my jeans. We're both aware we've reached the point where I usually freeze. He pauses. Hesitant. Remembering. I step back, and a look of rejection and disappointment crosses his face as he runs his hand through his hair in frustration. Then he watches as I undo the button and slide down the zip, causing the baggy jeans to drop to the floor. Stepping out of them, I stand before him naked for the first time.

I watch as his gaze drifts over me and his nostrils flare. Goose-bumps cover my flesh as his eyes cover every inch of my skin. I don't think I've ever felt so aroused. Is it the circumstances, or is it just because it's my Irish?

I need him to know how much I want him. That this is in no way forced. Walking towards him so we're inches apart, I take his hand and place it on my pussy.

"Feel how much I want you, Irish," I whisper in his ear. "Feel how wet I am."

His eyes never leave mine as his fingers stroke my folds, parting them to circle my clit, causing me to curse and my legs to almost buckle beneath me. He chuckles softly against my hair as he snakes his arm around me to keep me steady. Small circular motions bring me to the very edge. I start to pant, now desperate for the release.

Moving his head back, he stares down at me, watching my reactions to his touch.

"Do you want to come on my hand, Jaine?" he whispers against my ear.

"Yes," I hiss. "And be damn quick about it."

He laughs as he adds more pressure to my clit before thrusting two fingers inside me, knocking the wind out of my body as the mother of all orgasms ravages my very soul. I cling to him, saying his name over and over as the pulsing sensations work their way through every fiber of my being.

"Are you licking them clean or am I?" He smirks as he holds up his wet fingers.

"Let's both do it, Irish." I suck one into my mouth, and he sucks the other into his before our lips reconnect, both our mouths now tasting of my cum.

"I need you inside me, Irish," I say hotly against his lips.

Walking me backward to the bed, he pushes me onto the silky surface before removing his clothes. At least the Russians have given him clothes that fit. His Henley is a little too small, but I'm not complaining at how well it defines his pecs and biceps.

He whips it over his head in one movement, and it's then I can see the volume of tattoos that now caress his pale skin.

"I want you to talk me through every one of them when this is over, Padraig," I say as I admire the artwork that's inked on a body that's bumped and ridged to sheer perfection.

"That's a date." He smirks as he drops his hand to the button of his jeans before unzipping them. Like me, he's not wearing any underwear, and his dick immediately springs free. He's even bigger than Delaney.

"Jesus, Irish. I take back what I said about the Old Spice. Maybe your ma really was just after your da's big dick." I snicker as I take it in.

He smirks, then stands and waits while my eyes drift slowly over him. He's tall, and his smooth, muscular upper body tapers to a narrow waist and slim hips. He definitely never misses leg day.

"Sorry for staring, Irish, but you're sinfully fucking beautiful."

He laughs as he joins me on the bed, pinning my body under his, causing his erection to press against my thigh and dampen my skin.

"Not as beautiful as you are, darlin'." His mouth covers mine once more, silencing me.

His hands caress my body, leaving no inch undiscovered, and mine do the same. Reaching for his dick, I feel its weight and thickness in my hand. The tip leaks with pre-cum, which I spread around the tip, causing it to twitch in response. He growls loudly in appreciation.

His fingers drop to my pussy, and he thrusts two fingers inside me before adding a third, moving them deliciously back and forth while I slowly stroke his erection.

"Irish. I can't wait any longer." I groan against his mouth.

Breaking our kiss, he maneuvers his hips between my thighs, then, leaning on one elbow, he runs the blunt head of his dick up and down my slickness before using it to circle my clit. My hips raise instinctively, screaming for more, but he does it over and over again.

Tempting me, teasing me. Playing fucking games.

"Irish!"

"Look at me, Jaine."

My eyes gaze into their blue depths as he thrusts inside me.

I groan in appreciation as he fills me completely, my legs circling his waist and anchoring around him. Finally, he's fucking mine.

His face grimaces in pleasure. "Jesus, Jaine. I knew it would be fucking perfect being inside your sweet pussy."

"Well, now you're finally in there. Show me what you got, Irish."

Pushing my legs back so they're against my torso, he pulls out almost completely, then drives straight back in. I groan in pleasure and pain at how deep he's gone and how stretched I am.

Then he fucks me. Long, deep, hard thrusts have his dick massaging my sweet spot and his groin rubbing against my clit. His movements are deliberate and precise. Jesus Christ, he knows what he's doing with that cock. Using my slickness, his finger drops to my asshole, which he circles and presses against.

"You ever been fucked in the ass, Jaine?"

"Irish, do we need to have this conversation now while I'm concentrating on getting off?" I clench around him deliberately, causing him to curse.

"You little bitch," he snickers as he punishes me with faster and deeper thrusts.

I growl at the pace as all my blood starts to accumulate in the center of my body.

"No, I haven't." I groan as my center tightens.

He fucks me harder and faster, his movements becoming more erratic the closer he gets.

"Then your virgin ass is mine, darlin'."

"Oh, you think so." My nails dig into his back.

"I fucking know so. Jesus, Jaine. I'm about to blow. Where do you want me?"

"Come inside me, Irish." The thought of him filling me with his cum turns me on even more.

"Shit, I've never done this before." His voice is guttural, hot and breathy in my ear, causing me to shiver.

"What, fucked someone? For a lie that big, you'll be saying Hail Marys for the rest of your goddamn life," I whisper breathlessly.

"I've never fucked anyone bareback. Fuck... Jesus... Christ."

With a thrust that bangs against my cervix, he comes, his wet heat filling me, his face contorting with pleasure, and his eyes fixed on mine. My own expression matches as my center contracts, and I clench around him as the orgasmic waves release through my body.

We lie there, sheened in sweat and panting, his face pressed against my neck. I don't want to move. It was fucking perfect. He's fucking perfect.

I know then how much I really do love Padraig O'Connell.

Eventually, he pulls out, and our cum runs down my thighs onto the bed. Rolling over onto his back, he pulls me onto his chest, and I tuck my face into his neck, breathing him in. I press my lips against his salty skin and sigh contentedly.

I'm not sure how long we stay there. Do we need to rush? Can't we stay here all day? Fuck the cameras. I just want to be with Irish.

His arms tighten around me as I shiver, our bodies now cooling.

"You know we'll get out of here, right?" he whispers against my hair. "Someone will come for us, whether it be one of the MCs or the Dusters."

"I know," I say quietly. I'm not so convinced, but I don't want to tell him that.

He's humming a tune I've never heard.

"What's that you're humming?" I ask as I raise my head and look down into his blue eyes, my fingers trailing gently down his jaw as I take him in. I could never tire of looking at him.

"Firstly, I need to tell you that I love you, Jaine Jones. I always have." He kisses me softly on the lips.

"I love you too, Padraig O'Connell," I whisper against his mouth with a smile. And I mean it. I truly do. The problem is, I also love Ace, although that asshole only loves himself.

I exhale in frustration as my thoughts drift fleetingly to him.

"It's a song called *Kiss Me*, by a ginger-haired fella from England. Ed somebody."

"Oh, Ed somebody? How many Eds are there in England, Irish?" I laugh at his vagueness.

"Never mind that. When you hear it, I want you to always think of me. Of this moment." He looks subdued momentarily. "Will you do that for me, Jaine?" His smile returns.

"I will."

"Now, do as the song says. Fucking kiss me." He flips me onto my back, his hard-on poking me in the stomach.

I laugh out loud, and then I do.

Let's face it. Tomorrow we could be dead.

CHAPTER THIRTY-ONE

ACE

Location Unknown

STANDING WITH MY BACK RESTING AGAINST THE BARS, I LOOK around the sparse cell with its solitary bed, desk, and fridge.

PJ's is three up from mine and on the same side, going by where Padraig focuses his attention most of the time. Of course, that's if all of them are similar-sized.

I pace the floor, trying to stop my brain from thinking about her. About them. About what they're doing. He's fucking her. She's fucking him. Let's be honest. It's more than one fuck. They've been gone for ages. Then again, maybe they're just talking.

"Who the hell am I kidding?" I mumble to myself.

How do I act when they come back? Like nothing's changed when everything has? Like I'm not jealous when it's all I can feel flowing through my veins?

Every time I think of her with someone else, I get so reactive.

How the fuck did we end up here? It should never have come to this. How do I fucking fix this? Can I fix this? Do I want to fix this?

I don't know is the answer to the first two. Yes, to the last.

Then again, will I ever get the chance? We might never make it out of here alive.

I know she loves me. I've heard the words now from her own goddamn mouth.

So, how do I get her to forgive me for something when there's nothing much to forgive?

Ten Years Earlier (Age Eighteen)
The Angels of Hellfire Clubhouse, Rising, California

I GENTLY LIFT PJ'S ARM FROM ACROSS MY CHEST AND GET redressed. Now that we've committed to each other by getting our tattoos and sleeping together, there's something I need to do once and for all. I place a soft kiss on her cheek so as not to wake her and make sure her nakedness is fully covered, then I leave the room and close the door behind me.

"I CAN'T FUCK YOU ANYMORE, EM." I'VE BROUGHT HER INTO MY old man's room to tell her. The place smells of coal tar soap and leather, and a huge king-size bed dominates the space. It's not that I owe Em an explanation as we were never together. It was only ever fucking. I'm just trying to do the decent thing by letting her know, so she doesn't hear it from anyone else.

"I'm going to ask PJ to be my old lady," I tell her firmly.

She laughs exaggeratedly. "Are you serious, Jace? Plain Jaine is ugly. Everyone will laugh at you for scraping the barrel with her. I

mean, are you sure she doesn't have a dick? She looks like a boy."
She smirks at me.

"Don't be stupid, Em, and stop being so goddamn mean. My
mind's made up. I'm just letting you know." I fold my arms and
stare down at her determinedly.

She walks over to me, uncrosses them, then tries to wrap them
around her waist, but I drop them to my sides.

Her pretty face turns ugly when she scowls, which is what she's
doing now. She drops her hand to my dick and starts to rub me
through my jeans, but I push her away.

"I'm not interested, Em. I've told you I want to be with PJ. I
love her."

She walks across and sits on my old man's bed. I can tell she's
thinking about what to say in retaliation. To get me to change my
mind. To get me to choose her instead. I know that's what she's
been angling for all this time. To be the old lady of the next prez of
the Angels.

"I thought you said she was going off to school."

I frown at that comment. I wish I'd never mentioned that Jeremiah had told my old man PJ had been accepted into Yale, which is
where he studied. For some reason, PJ never even told me she'd
applied. Not sure why. I guess I'll have to ask and find out. Maybe
she just forgot. She'll have a good reason, I'm sure. It's not because
she doesn't care about me.

"She is," I reply quietly, but doubts are already creeping in and
starting to plague my mind.

"Well, she can't love you back if she was just going to go to
Connecticut without telling you. I reckon she just wanted a bit of
biker rough before she heads off to hang out with all those fancy
boys at Yale. She'll leave this two-bit town and won't ever look
back." She snickers nastily.

"She'll have a plan, Em. We've been friends since we were kids.

PJ's not going to go and forget about me. She'd never do that," I say, but I already feel a lot less confident. Would she leave and never look back? Does she love me? Maybe she doesn't. Maybe Em's right.

"Anyway, I'm just letting you know where my head's at, and about my decision," I say firmly.

I leave my old man's room just as Clay is walking past.

"You seen Duke, Jace? Gusto says he's looking for us."

I shake my head as I walk towards my room just along the corridor.

"Nope, not seen him for a few hours," I reply, not really paying much attention.

He stops and stares at me. "What were you doing in his room, then? Who's in there?"

"Em," I reply distractedly.

He smirks knowingly. "Jesus, tell me you didn't fuck Plain Jaine? Em said you looked like you were thinking about it but I didn't believe her. There's no way you would…"

"Shut up, asshole." I hiss, interrupting him. I know what he thinks about PJ. He's forever saying how unattractive she is.

Clay laughs out loud, like it's the funniest thing in the world that I would want to have sex with her.

"Holy shit. You really did. What the hell were you thinking? I mean, you're lowering your standards, Jace. PJ's a nice girl, but she's no looker, is she?"

"I said shut up!" I want to punch the fucker for saying that about her.

Clay snickers, refusing to let it go. "Well, I didn't have our future prez down for the type who hands out pity fucks." He glances at my old man's bedroom door, then smirks. "I mean, that's bad enough, but to fuck PJ, then move straight on to Emilia. Shit, even I wouldn't be that disrespectful."

I go along with it, even though I never touched Em. It's just easier that way with him.

"It's PJ's birthday. I could hardly say no when she came on to me. Plus, I'm never going to turn down free pussy. Anyway, she's keeping my bed warm, so I may see if she's up for another round or two before morning." I spout out any old bullshit to shut him the fuck up. I'm about to walk off when I hear my bedroom door click.

Did PJ hear that? Shit. I need to go explain. Let her know I was only going along with what he said to get rid of him.

"Jason, I need to speak to you, Clay, and Jefferson in my office, please," my old man announces as he walks through the door from the communal area.

"Can't it wait until tomorrow?" I groan.

"Now!"

I roll my eyes and follow him reluctantly, knowing it'll be to do with our patching in.

While he's talking and I'm only partially listening, I hear song forty-two being played. *Creep* by Radiohead. Mine and PJ's song. Who's playing that? No one ever does apart from her and me. I hate it when she calls herself a creep and a weirdo. She's neither. She's growing into herself. She's beautiful to me. Inside and out.

Eventually, we're allowed to leave the office, and I go straight to my bedroom to find PJ gone. I go into the bar area, hoping she's there.

"She had a run-in with Emilia and then she left." Gusto shrugs when I ask him.

I call her, but I get no reply, so I leave a voicemail. I tell her I love her. Tell her I want her to be my old lady. It's late, so I decide to leave it until the morning to message her. When I do, I still get no answer, so I get on my hog and ride to her house.

"She's gone to Connecticut to get settled before the first

semester, Jason," Jeremiah explains. He's dazed and seems as confused as I am.

I message her and call her, leaving voicemails over and over.

Nothing.

I explain what happened just in case she heard what Clay and I said. I tell her I love her again. Tell her I miss her.

Nothing.

A week later, I try to call her, but her number is no longer obtainable.

Jeremiah says she doesn't want me to contact her when I go to her house to confront him. He's not allowed to give her new number out either.

I go back to the clubhouse and sit on my bed. I thought maybe PJ loved me too. It turns out, Em was right. She never gave a fuck about me. I didn't even matter in her plans. Figures. That'll be why she never bothered to tell me what they were.

She burned her bridges with me and this town simply because we don't matter to her. Not anymore.

I guess I never meant anything to her. I guess she never loved me after all.

Our song? Covered up. Hidden from sight with a warning issued to all that anyone found playing it would meet their maker with my bullet between their eyes.

CHAPTER THIRTY-TWO

JAINE

Location Unknown

ACE HASN'T SPOKEN TO EITHER OF US SINCE WE GOT BACK, SAVE for a grumble here and there. It's awkward as hell.

It's the dawning of a new day. I've lost track of how long we've been held. Two days? Three? Four? Fuck knows. I keep wracking my brain trying to think of something I can do to change the pre-determined fate that's been very kindly mapped out for me by the Bratva, but there's nothing. In the absence of someone breaking us out of this hell hole, we're trapped. I'm trapped. My future's definitely not bright. Still, even if my destiny is fixed like the equivalent of a Russian mail-order bride, Ace and Padraig will be released unharmed. Or at least, they better be. If Lebedev or Sokolov lay a fucking finger on either, I'll kill them.

That's not a threat. That's a promise. And fuck the consequences.

Padraig's tried to include Ace in conversation several times. He does reply, but with a grunt instead of anything resembling a word or legible response. I don't even bother attempting to speak to him anymore. All we do is bicker. There's no point. They say there's a thin line between love and hate. Have we crossed it now? Is that what *this* shit is?

They both know how I feel about them. Some might find it strange that I'm in love with two men. I don't make the rules, though. It's just how it is. How it's always been. I didn't get to choose.

In turn, I know Padraig loves me back. He's told me so. Jesus, he's asked me to marry him. Whereas, Ace? Fuck knows. He's jealous as hell, but that doesn't mean jack shit. Some people get envious of what others have, even when they don't want it for them-selves. That's what Ace is like over Padraig's relationship with me. He doesn't want to speak to me or have anything to do with me, but he doesn't want Irish to either. Selfish fucker.

After showering, I change into the fresh clothes sans underwear that have been provided and that are almost identical to those I wore before. The only difference is both are in black. I still have to keep yanking the goddamn jeans up.

I lie on my bed, stare at the white ceiling, and wait. I know it's only a matter of time before Sokolov comes to fetch us. My skin crawls whenever the Russian scum looks at me. It's clear he was hoping Ace or Padraig would refuse to oblige or do the necessary so he could step in and save the day. I'd have to kill the fucker with my bare hands if that happened. There's no way his dick is coming anywhere near me. I doubt that would improve our already precar-ious position, though.

Given how Ace is behaving this morning, I'm concerned that's the path we may be heading down. I've got a feeling he's not going to be quite as obliging as Padraig was. Hopefully, I'm wrong. Can I convince him if he says no? It's not likely, knowing how unsatisfactory my performance must have been the first time around.

I curse myself for letting my mind replay that night over and over again. Why do I keep punishing myself? Delaney had no complaints, or Padraig. Like Ace, I'd sooner not be heading into a room for *take two*, and definitely not under these circumstances.

Padraig's gone quiet now. We all know what's coming. I try to imagine what it must be like for him. If it were another female and me with either Padraig or Ace.

Jealously fires up in my gut. I'm not sure I could handle it. Not when it's so in your face like it is here. Not when you know exactly what the other two people are up to. Their marked absence letting you know for exactly how long.

I've never seen Padraig with another woman. Ever. I'd want to shoot any potential WAG, as Sasha calls them, between the eyes on the goddamn spot. I know I would. With Ace? Well, I had to bear witness to watching him with Emilia for most of my teenage life, so I guess I'm hardened to that visual. I'm not sure I could so easily tolerate that shit if it were with someone else, though. My trigger finger would twitch for sure.

The door at the end of the corridor opens, and the sounds of footsteps fill the silence. It's not Sokolov as the steps are from someone with a longer stride, and they're louder, so perhaps a heavier body mass.

"Miss Jones, the obshchak is on the telephone, so he has asked me to collect you and Mr. Steele." I look at the goon who's now standing in front of me. He's got to be six feet six tall and likely the same wide. He's an ugly fucker. His face is impassive, with watery blue eyes, bushy brows, and fat lips that resemble two slimy slugs. His brown buzzcut finishes his overall unattractive exterior.

Placing cuffs on me, he leads me out of my cell, and we walk in the direction of the recording room. I'm guessing we'll be taken one at a time like we were yesterday, in case we try to over-power him. Could I take this big asshole? Probably not, but I'd still give it my best fucking go if I weren't cuffed. The bigger they are, the harder they fall.

Yesterday, they took Padraig first and me second, reversing it on the return journey. Today, it's my turn to go first. I glance in Padraig's cell on the way past, but he has his back to the bars. I'm guessing he doesn't want to bear witness to what's about to happen. That it's all too painful for him. Out of sight, out of mind appears to be his approach today.

I sigh and follow the goon to the same room. Everything is as before. The only difference is the silk sheets are now white as opposed to grey. As I wait, I notice the red lights aren't lit yet. They must wait until we're together before switching the recording devices on, maybe so there's less material to edit. Who the fuck knows? What I do know is that it's allowing me to seize what may be our only opportunity.

The goon removes my cuffs and leaves, locking me in.

I use the time to try the white door again, praying it's unlocked. By some miracle, the handle pushes all the way down, and the door clicks open. Quickly stepping inside, I glance around the damp-smelling, cupboard-like space. I'm conscious I have a minute at most.

I'm sure I can hear Sokolov. Walking to the far end, I press my ear against the wall. I can. He's on the phone.

"Mr. Tyler, we appreciate your patience, and we're also fully aware of the pressure you're under, but we must follow due process. The benefactors are insisting on the video evidence being with them before they will consider placing their bids. That is their preroga-tive, as I'm sure you can appreciate. The only alternative we have is to proceed with no payment in place. That decision is yours and yours alone. As you know, our organization is not benefitting financially from this."

There's a pause. Sokolov is obviously waiting for the other party to respond.

"Of course. Then we will proceed with the plan as it stands. We would expect the recordings to be concluded by tomorrow at the latest, and we will then review all content and have the material edited, so please allow two or three days for everything to be in place."

I hear footsteps approaching the room and quickly make my way out of the closet, but not before I notice both my suit jacket and shoes in the confined space.

I close the door quietly just as the other opens, and Ace walks in with the goon.

Not sure why I bothered to rush as the unobservant Russian barely glances in my direction before uncuffing Ace and leaving, locking us both in.

The red lights immediately come on, signaling the recording devices are now active.

Dare I tell Ace? How can I without being in his personal space? The last place he likely wants me to be. I look at him, and he's standing there in a black muscle tee and black jeans. His long hair hangs down way below his shoulders, and his blue eyes look almost black. Jesus Christ, he looks like Lucifer himself. The type of boy your mom told you to stay away from.

He's scowling at me. If I thought Padraig didn't want to be here yesterday, that's nothing to how repulsive and distasteful Ace is obviously finding this whole sorry situation.

I walk over and stand in front of him.

He looks menacing. Like someone who shouldn't be messed with. His expression is almost daring me to put my hands on him. Touch him. With my fingers. My mouth. My body.

Do I accept the dare? What choice do I have? Do *we* have? None.

What Ace and I have is different from Padraig and me. With Irish, the connection is loving and caring. With Ace? It's intense. Dangerous somehow. It's like it wants to chew us up and spit us both out the other side. Dead or alive. It's a ravenous craving that just wants its hunger to be satisfied.

My heart pounds in my chest, and my stomach fills with a combination of excitement and fear as I search his blue eyes. I'm not scared of Ace. I'm afraid of where this may lead. We're inches apart now, our mouths so close I can feel the heat of his breath against my lips.

I'm fully aware I'm so fucking wet.

My eyes roam his face. His tanned skin is complemented by the facial hair he wears. My hands itch to grab hold of his mane of hair and run my fingers through it. It's like the asshole can read my mind, as he smirks briefly, and then it's gone. He knows I want him. That I think he's fucking beautiful.

"You want me to fuck you, PJ?" The growl with which he says it makes it sound like a dark threat. It turns me on so much I suddenly feel light-headed and breathless as the blood carrying the oxygen around my body spirals straight to my center.

I lick my lips, but the ability to speak has gone, so I simply nod.

He lifts his tee over his head, and my eyes immediately drift to the defined lines of his upper body and the tattoos and scars that caress it. It has to be the single most spectacular visual I've ever seen in my goddamn life. He's looking at me like he's feral. Like a wild beast looking at its prey. I've decided I like that look. I like it a fucking lot.

I raise my hand and touch his abdomen with my fingertips, and his muscles tense. He grabs me painfully by the wrist.

"Don't lay a hand on me until I say you can. Now, take off your top."

I lift the tank top over my head. My arousal will be evident as my nipples are swollen and painful. Screaming for his touch.

His darkened eyes drop to them, making them scream louder.

"Jeans off."

I undo the button, then pull down the zip, and the baggy denim falls to the floor. I step out of them and stand before him, naked.

I raise my chin defiantly. Big mistake.

He growls, and his nostrils flare as though in outrage. "Get on your fucking knees."

I'm tempted to argue, but I don't. I've decided I like him telling me what to do.

I do as he says and then look up at him.

"Unzip me and take out my dick."

I do as I'm told and pull out his leaking cock. He's ramrod straight and huge. The veins feel like they're pulsing against my hand. His flesh is smooth as silk and hot as hell, and his musky smell makes me desperate to taste him.

"I like it wet." He watches as I gather saliva in my mouth, his eyes never leaving mine.

I flick my tongue over the tip and lick off the bead of pre-cum, and I watch his Adam's apple move as he swallows in response. My tastebuds savor the salty taste, my mouth watering for more.

His size is similar to Delaney's, so I know what to expect. I open my mouth and take him deep. I watch as his eyes close, and his face grimaces as the blunt head of his dick touches the back of my throat. I don't gag. He grunts and lets his head fall back briefly before his eyes open, and he watches me. Holding back my hair from my face, he starts to thrust in and out of my mouth, hard and fast. I let the saliva build up and mix with the pre-cum until it's dripping down my chin as he fucks me.

I want him to come in my mouth. I have an urgent need to taste him. I look up and take in his flushed cheeks and his slack jaw. I'm in complete control. My mouth is the most important thing in the world to him right now as it's getting him off and is the waiting receptacle for his cum.

It's as though he can read my mind.

"You want my cum in your mouth, PJ?" He grunts.

I nod.

"Squeeze my balls."

I lift my hand and squeeze them hard. He growls and closes his eyes.

I tighten my grip. His thrusting increases as he fists my hair painfully, his dick getting even harder as he gets closer.

With a curse, the first shot of cum hits the back of my throat, and I quickly swallow, gathering the rest in my mouth before drinking his saltiness down.

He watches me as I lick clean his still twitching dick before standing, then tenses as I slowly snake my arms around his neck. I'm doing it for one good reason. I need to talk to him.

"I know you don't want me in your space, Ace, but the recording devices are on, so you'll just have to tolerate it." I run my hands through his hair, relishing in the feel of it between my fingers. "I need to ask if you know anyone with the surname Tyler." I place kisses down his throat, and he shivers in response. I've found a sweet spot right on his collarbone. I smirk to myself as I run my tongue along it, causing him to groan.

"I can't fucking think straight when you're doing that, PJ." He grunts.

"Sorry." I snicker, then purposely do it again.

"Jesus Christ." He growls as he snakes one arm around my waist, pulling me tight against him. He uses the other hand to fist my hair and yank my head back.

"You asked me a question, and I'm trying to think. You want an answer or not?"

I nod and bite my lip.

His eyes darken at the gesture. "If you do that, I won't be able to think either."

I roll my eyes, my lips twitching upwards in a victorious smile.

"Why do you need to know?" he whispers in my ear as he punishes me by biting hard on the lobe.

"I just do, and stop biting my ear like that."

"Why? Is it turning you on, sweetheart?" His hot breath makes me shiver.

"No." Completely the wrong thing to say when I'm naked. He drops his hand down to my pussy. It's obvious how aroused I am.

"I'll think. You come."

I groan as he thrusts two fingers deep inside me, then moves them back and forth, his thumb circling my clit. I spread my legs to give him easier access, causing him to chuckle against my hair.

"Well, a girl has needs too, you know," I whisper.

"Yeah, and I'm about to see to them right about now." He increases the pressure against my clit, and I come pretty much instantly.

"Fuck, Ace." I groan against his neck as he tightens his grip around my waist to keep me upright.

"You good for now, PJ?" he says smugly. Asshole.

I don't reply. I rest my head on his shoulder. I find myself wishing it would take a lifetime for him to find the answer. I'm good right here.

"I think Bomb's second name is Tyler. Think his first name is Martin," he answers eventually as he kisses my neck. For the camera, obviously.

I run my hands through his hair again as I whisper back. "The door at the end of the room leads into a large cupboard. It's unlocked, so I went in. I heard Sokolov on the phone to a Mr. Tyler. Apparently, he's the third party who stands to receive the monies from the benefactor, not the Bratva."

I can feel him tense. Is he angry? Annoyed?

"Anything else?" he asks, his grip on me now borderline painful.

"Yes. When I was in the cupboard, I saw my jacket. My burner phone is in the lining." I press my lips to his, and he kisses me, his mouth hungry and demanding, his tongue probing and searching. For the camera again, obviously.

"And?" He breathes against my swollen lips.

"I can turn on the location finder, and Delaney will be able to trace where we are. I can message to say not to tell Bomb and to speak to Duke as he knows everything."

"What if he's responsible or involved?"

"Guess it's a chance we'll all have to take."

He squeezes my waist. "Let's get dressed and tell them we're done. We can pick up where we left off another time."

I feel cold when the warmth of his body abruptly leaves mine. I'm conscious of his eyes drifting slowly over me as he pulls up his jeans and buttons them, my skin prickling in response.

Grabbing my chin, he tilts my head up, his eyes searching my face. "And we *will* pick this back up where we left off, PJ." His mouth drops to mine, and he kisses me. Hard.

Once we're dressed, Ace knocks on the door. The red lights go off, and the goon cuffs him and takes him back to his cell, locking me in.

Rushing to the cupboard, I take my burner phone out of the lining of my jacket.

I message Delaney.

Jaine: *No time for questions. Will switch on location. Taken*

*by Bratva. Three Russians here minimum. Bomb responsible
plus one other. We don't know their identity. Trust no one
except Duke. He knows everything. Am here with Ace and
Padraig. Don't reply.*

Switching on the location finder, I place the burner phone back
in my jacket just in time for the goon to come and collect me and
take me back to my cell.

I can only pray Delaney has brought the receiving phone to
California with him.

CHAPTER THIRTY-THREE

DELANEY

Previous Day
The Angels of Hellfire Clubhouse, Rising, California

For the past three days, Duke has insisted I use Ace's office. I'm scaring the shit out of the women and kids because I'm walking around flicking my blade constantly. No one feels safe. They're all worried my foul mood and irrational behavior will see me slit their throats one by one. Right now, I can't rule it out.

They should have kept her safe like I fucking asked them to.

The office is small, but it's functional. The desk is dark wood and scratched, and the battered grey leather chair squeaks in protest every time I move. It's the complete opposite of mine. Material items are obviously unimportant to Steele. I've always been surrounded by the best money can buy. Always wanted to be. Always *had* to be. I can offer *her* the world, but I know that sort of shit's unimportant to her too. They're the same, him and her. They value people as opposed to possessions. They value living and making memories above all else.

Maybe my priorities are all wrong.

I stare at the Angels of Hellfire emblem contrasting on the white wall facing me.

She spent her youth in this clubhouse with him. I've been to the house she grew up in. Seen photos of her with her pop. Countless pictures of her with Steele. Been into her town and met some of the locals who have known her since she was in single figures. I can't imagine her living here, but then, am I just fucking kidding myself? Does she belong here? I'm not sure I know the answer. Or maybe I'm choosing not to see it. Not wanting to face the harsh reality that's staring me in the goddamn face. That she wants him and not me.

When Bomb said the Irishman was coming to help her carry out a hit, he couldn't have got it more wrong. Deep down, I knew it was all bullshit. But I still let him put doubt in my mind about her loyalty to me. It was clear the asshole wanted me out of the way by suggesting I stay in a hotel. It didn't work, but I still arrived too late. Their abandoned vehicle was found less than two miles from Rising PD. According to the detective, he'd received a tip-off about Steele, who was then picked up with O'Connell in tow. Jaine bailed them out, and then all three of them vanished. Lebedev is behind this, of that I have no doubt. And Bomb? That fucker's been feeding the Russians the intel. It's clear as day now.

I've spoken at length to Cillian O'Connell, and a meeting *was* scheduled to take place between the Dusters and the Angels. He was meant to attend, but Padraig offered to instead. The Irish don't know who Jaine is, either as Jaine Jones, an ex-girlfriend of Padraig's, or as The Exterminator. Not that I asked them about the latter. If they'd been aware of that, I'm sure they'd have mentioned it since the sniper always operates through the Scorpions.

By all accounts, no one else knew about her and Padraig's ongoing relationship until a few days ago—just the two of them. Sasha and Cherry know now. I think Duke might know too, but I've not asked him directly.

So how the fuck did Bomb find out? Who told him about this ongoing nine-year relationship? About the fact Padraig switched places with Cillian at the last minute? No one knew that part aside from the Dusters and Ace. I haven't pressed the lying asshole for the name of his disloyal fucking informant. I need to keep the lowlife sweet. For now, at least. I need him to think he's safe until I find Jaine. Why have they taken her? Where is she? If they've harmed her, I'll fucking end them. Each and every one.

I flick my knife again and run it across my fingertip, causing the skin to split and bleed. I imagine it's the disloyal fucker's throat. Soon it will be. He's lied to me and signed his own death warrant in the process. If he hadn't, I'd have been with her, and she would never have been taken. Have they kidnapped her to get at me? Or was she just in the wrong place at the wrong time? Do they know what she does in her spare time?

I flick my knife again and run it down the next fingertip. The skin splits. It bleeds.

Someone knocks at the door.

"Come in," I say gruffly as I fold the blade back in and put the knife on the desk. I press a tissue against my bleeding fingers.

She opens the door and walks in. Ace's old lady, Emilia. I don't know what the idiot was thinking, but she doesn't compare to Jaine. She couldn't lick her boots. If anyone's plain, it's this fake bitch.

"Can I get you anything, Razr? Food? Beer? Something stronger." She looks at me and licks her lips.

Is she drunk? High? What she wants is for me to eat her pussy and fuck her, and that isn't happening.

"Is that all that's on offer, sweetheart?" Playing with her, I lean back in the creaky old chair. I watch as she walks around the desk, leaning her ass against it, then moving deliberately so her short dress rises farther up her thighs. I can almost smell her goddamn arousal.

"What else did you have in mind, Prez?"

"What are you suggesting?"

Her attention drops to my dick, letting me know exactly what she's after.

"Aren't you meant to be Ace's old lady? Not too sure he'd be happy at you eyeing up my cock like that and offering me your pussy on a plate."

"I'm not his old lady." Maybe she thinks I'll take her up on her offer now I know that.

I can tell she wants to chat, so who am I to stop her from spilling her drunken guts, hopefully with something beneficial.

"He doesn't have one?" I raise my eyebrow at her.

She shakes her head. "He's been waiting for your old lady to come back home." She smirks. "There's no accounting for taste, is there, Prez? I mean, look at her compared to me."

I do just that and look at the pretty enough girl in front of me who's wearing way too much make-up, showing way too much skin in a short dress that skims her pussy, and tottering around on silly heels. Then I compare her to the fresh-faced Jaine, who seldom wears anything on her skin and dresses down in tank tops, cargo pants, and scruffy high-tops most of the time. There's no fucking comparison.

"Jaine isn't my old lady," I reply, closely watching her reaction.

She looks surprised briefly, but then she smiles and moves closer. "You know, we used to call her Plain Jaine."

I narrow my eyes at her. "Yeah, I do know that. Bit mean, wasn't it, sweetheart?"

She shrugs. "Well, she was always after Jason, and I claimed him first. Anyway, she got what she deserved in the end."

"Oh, is that right? And what was that?"

"I told her the night before she left that he'd pretty much asked me to be his old lady, but I lied." She laughs at the part she played in getting Jaine out of the picture. "No one knows that but you and me, Prez. So, it's our little secret. Worked out for the best for you, though, as she went to Connecticut and didn't bother coming back."

"As I said, she's not my old lady, and she won't let me wife her either. You think maybe Ace has something to do with those decisions?"

I pick up my knife and flick it back and forth, getting more and more agitated. I want to cut this scheming bitch.

"Maybe. She loved him. He loved her. Maybe now she's disappeared and gone for good, he'll realize I'm the best thing for him. Then again, I did always want to live it up in New York." She smiles and moves even closer, then runs her hand up my thigh. I stop it just before she reaches my dick.

"Maybe she's in love with someone else. Not me or Ace. Anyone else I should be concerned about?" I rub the back of her hand like I'm waiting for a goddamn genie to appear. Still, she seems to like it. Hopefully it'll see me get my good fortune. She leans towards me. The smell on her breath lets me know it's tequila she's been drinking, and it seems to have liberated her mouth.

"Well, there is an Irishman. I overheard Ace talking to him on the phone. Padraig somebody. Apparently, they dated way back when she first started Yale, and he still loves her. I mean, why does everyone fall in love with her? She's Plain fucking Jaine. Anyway, I told your VP about his planning to come to California, and he said he'd reward me for sharing what I knew." She cackles like a witch and rubs her hands.

My eyes narrow as I take in who I know now to be Bomber's very loose-lipped informant. Once we get them out from wherever the fuck they are, Bomb's mine. Ace or Jaine can take care of this twisted little bitch. If they don't, I gladly will.

"Well, thanks, sweetheart. Don't suppose you could fetch me a bottle of tequila from the bar? I'm just going to have a chat with Duke. See if he's heard anything."

She smiles like the viper she is and leaves. She's either too drunk or too stupid to realize she's just dug her own fucking grave.

Present Day

"Duke?" I knock on his office door, then walk in without waiting for a response.

"Razr?" He peers up at me from over his glasses. He looks like shit. Like he hasn't slept in days. He probably hasn't as his boy's missing, as is the girl who's been like a daughter to him.

I pass him the burner phone. As he reads the message, I take in the image behind him—the one of him and Jeremiah.

Jaine: *No time for questions. Will switch on location. Taken by Bratva. Three Russians here minimum. Bomb responsible plus one other. We don't know their identity. Trust no one except Duke. He knows everything. Am here with Ace and Padraig. Don't reply.*

He nods. "Use Clay and Jefferson. They're completely trustworthy." He hands the phone back to me. "Chase and Ink can leave separately in a cage. We need to make sure we don't arouse

Bomber's suspicions or he may try to make a run for it. Worse still, he may try to contact the Russians to alert them."

I take the phone from him and put it in my pocket.

Thank fuck she's alive.

Bomber? He's a dead man walking.

CHAPTER THIRTY-FOUR

JAINE

Location Unknown

I'M BACK IN MY CELL. MY HANDS GRIP ONTO THE BARS, AND MY face is pressed against them so tightly it's probably causing indents on my skin.

Should we tell Padraig about the message to Delaney?

My immediate thought is to say nothing. What if the Russians are listening in? I don't want to tempt fate. If Delaney picks up the message, and there's no reason to think he won't, then the cavalry will be here soon enough. Without horses and with hogs instead. That is provided he's got the burner phone with him.

At that point, depending on who's said what to Delaney, I may, quite literally, lose my head. Or, as a bare minimum, my throat. Still, at least then I won't have to marry Bratva scum.

Every cloud.

I stand there and wait for Irish to appear, but he isn't receptive.

He's avoiding me. He isn't ready to face us yet. Face me. Yesterday, he and I were quick to judge Ace's lack of response with eye rolls and raised eyebrows, wondering why he was making such a big deal out of things. But when the shoe's on the other foot, the reaction is mirrored. It's all too much to bear.

I can still taste Ace in my mouth. The salty male muskiness of his cum. I want more of him. I'd be kidding myself if I said I didn't, and one thing I'm not is a liar. Not even to myself. *Especially* not to myself.

Love is a curse. I know that only too well. More so when it's unrequited. Still, we'll be out of here soon and then reality can take over. Proper decisions can be made, or we can just forget about the whole sorry shitshow and go our separate ways. At the moment, we've developed a fucked-up take on Stockholm Syndrome, which is making us believe this situation, what we're doing here, is borderline acceptable. Like we're playing happy families. A murderous MC president, an Irish mobster killing machine, and a vigilante serial-killer sniper. A match made in hell, whichever way you look at it.

I lie on my bed. Fidget. Pace the floor. Look through the bars. Then I go through the process again.

Lie. Fidget. Stand. Pace. Look. Repeat.

Over and over.

I'm not sure how many times I go through the same motions until, finally, he's standing there.

"Irish, are you okay?" I whisper as I rest my forehead against the bars.

He doesn't reply. He just stares back.

"They're coming for us, Irish."

He frowns.

"PJ's right." Ace backs me up from farther down the corridor.

"So, now we just sit and wait?" he asks in disbelief.

I nod.

I HEAR THE FIRST GUNSHOT AROUND TWO HOURS LATER. THEN again, it could be two minutes or twelve hours. You lose all track of time when you're confined in a concrete prison. Maybe it's just a car back-firing. But then I hear it again.

Gunshots. Shouting. More gunshots.

I'm sure I can smell the gunpowder. Taste it even. Its meaty-sulfur aroma mixed with metal. Maybe the metallic smell is blood. I'm sure there will be plenty of that getting spilled.

Or maybe it's all just my imagination. That the familiar scent isn't really seeping under the door. Perhaps it's wishful thinking.

The entrance at the end finally opens, and several sets of feet come pounding towards us down the corridor.

I sob out loud when I first see Delaney, who's closely followed by Clay and Jefferson, all of them carrying Glocks. There were times when I thought I'd never see him again. My eyes take in the welcome visual. His long strawberry blonde hair has blood on it, as does his white Henley, but it's not likely to be his. His green eyes are fired up with adrenaline.

I shouldn't cry. Emotions are a sign of weakness. But right now, just for a few seconds, I allow myself that respite—a small release of the build-up of everything that's been going on. We weren't beaten or abused, but sometimes being left to your own thoughts can drive you stir crazy. Sometimes that shit's even worse.

Our cells are unlocked, and I step straight into Delaney's embrace.

I may not be in love with him, but he's been there for me these past four years. More than most. More than anyone, truthfully. I only hope when what's done is done, and when I say what I need to say to him, that we can still be friends. That he'll find it in his heart to forgive me for wasting his time.

"I'm so sorry, baby. This is all my fault," he whispers against my hair as he holds me close.

I shake my head. "It wasn't your fault. It was me they were after, so they'd have got to me eventually. They know I'm The Exterminator. Or at least Lebedev and Sokolov do. Bomb must have told them."

His grip on me tightens painfully, bruising me. He's not deliberately trying to hurt me. He's being eaten alive by rage and guilt. He told Bomb in confidence, and this has happened as a direct result. Deep down, I always knew Bomb would never show me his loyalty, but I didn't expect him to betray Delaney. Not to this extent.

Bomb now has an invisible *cut here* line across his throat. While Lebedev? Well, he's sporting an invisible X on his forehead. I know I'll have to take that fucker down personally. No one else will be able to get close.

I lift my face from Delaney's chest, look up at him, and he places a gentle kiss against my forehead. I'm conscious Padraig and Ace will be watching, but I don't feel guilty. I owe my thanks and gratitude to Delaney. He saved me. He saved all of us.

"We need to get the video evidence. I also need to get my jacket and my shoes. I can't leave my burner phone."

We find the recording equipment in the non-descript room behind the cupboard—the one where Sokolov was talking on the phone. The room's been ripped apart. Furniture upturned, and there's a splattering of blood on the floor. He's not dead, though. If Razr had cut him, the walls would be sprayed red with all ten pints of the fucker's lifeblood.

I take the tapes from the machines and put them in my jacket pocket.

Delaney watches, likely wondering what's been going on.

Now's not the time. That conversation will need to take place sooner rather than later, though. He needs to know. I also need to let him go. End what we have. I can't put that off any longer. I refuse to lead him on anymore. Not that I ever intentionally did.

He's a good man. Well, as good as you can be when you're a murderous bastard. He deserves someone way better than me.

CHAPTER THIRTY-FIVE

JAINE

The Angels of Hellfire Clubhouse, Rising, California

WE TRAVEL BACK TO RISING IN SILENCE. WHAT THE FUCK IS THERE to say? All three of us will be doing the same thing. Filing what happened away in a box, padlocking that shit up and pushing that fucker to the back of our minds.

It turns out we were being held in an old, converted warehouse just outside Fielding. Someone local must have given their insider the details as it's not like our town or the ones surrounding advertise vacant buildings for rent in the press. Everything is word of mouth in these parts. News travels faster that way.

I look at Padraig and Ace, who are sitting across from me in the back of the cage, but we don't make eye contact. It's a large black van, and the back's decked out with wooden seats on either side. Towards the rear doors and on the floor is Sokolov. The goons are dead. Once we've been dropped off, Clay and Jefferson will go back, remove the bodies, and burn the place to the fucking ground.

We can donate the monies back to the owner in some way as a charitable community gesture. Make sure they're not losing out financially. Simons will know something's gone down, but he'll appreciate that gesture for sure and likely then brush it under the carpet. He knows what side his bread's buttered on.

Sokolov's black, soulless eyes stare at me. He can't speak as his mouth is taped, and he can't move as he's trussed up like a Thanksgiving turkey with old yellow rope. He knows he hasn't got long. His hours, maybe even minutes, are numbered.

I'm not sure who'll kill who and in which order, but by close of business today, he'll have met his maker, as will Bomb. The other informant? If they've worked out who that person is? Well, I'm not holding out much hope they'll see tomorrow either.

I'll enjoy watching the demise of all three.

Too much damage has been done. Too many secrets almost spilled. In this life, both disloyalty and betrayal are met with death. No matter how sorry you are afterward, how much you plead for fucking forgiveness, there's no other outcome. You betray either MC or the Dusters, and your card's marked.

The surface we're driving over is uneven, and the van's tossing us around. We're no longer on a smooth road, so I know we're close to where we need to be. We pull up a short time later.

We'll be at the shed. It's located to the rear of the clubhouse, quite a way back. The whole property used to be owned by a farmer, and the lambing shed was where they birthed the lambs and where they also ended their lives. It has all the relevant drainage channels built in to drain bodily fluids away. The MC even keeps sheep on the seventy acres of land to substantiate the need for the building to remain fully functioning. Sheep blood looks like human blood, as does their piss, and the smell of shit is the same no matter what asshole it comes out of.

The rear of the cage is opened, and blinding sunlight streams in, causing me to shield my eyes. Jesus, it feels like forever since we saw the sun properly. Clay smiles at me sympathetically as he and Jefferson yank Sokolov out of the vehicle.

I don't want sympathy. Fuck that shit. I want revenge.

Ace and Padraig follow them, leaving me in the cage on my own. I eventually make my way out and stand staring across the open space. I breathe in. Petrichor and wildflowers. I'm home. There were way too many moments I never thought I'd see it again. Smell it again.

A pair of arms wrap around my waist from behind.

"Thank you for coming for us, Delaney." I turn in his hold and look up at him.

He shakes his head. "Bomb betrayed you. Betrayed us. If I hadn't told him about your other role, you'd have been safe, Jaine. If I hadn't listened to the lies he spilled when I got to California, I'd have been with you and not waiting for the brothers to pick me up. You'd never have been taken."

I look up at him. "What exactly did he say?"

He shrugs. "That O'Connell was flying in so you and he could kill me, Ace, and Duke because you held us three responsible for your pop's death. I mean, it all stacked up. It was the first I'd heard about you and O'Connell, so that made me even more suspicious. At that point, I never knew a meeting was planned between the Dusters and the Angels until I spoke to Cillian, and he confirmed it was all pre-arranged."

I nod. "I should have told you about Padraig. About our past. That I spoke to him most days. Well, every day, in fact. He's a good friend. A confidant. I'm sorry I never mentioned him. I never really felt the need as we weren't doing anything wrong. He's just someone from my past that means a lot to me and helps me see clearly at times when no other fucker can."

"I know you'd never betray me or be disloyal, Jaine. I'm sorry for even doubting you," he says, lifting my chin to look at me.

"Delaney, what they made us do," I say quietly, then bite my lip, trying to word it, but how can you beautify what happened? "The Bratva intended to auction me off with the bidders being their three main benefactors. The fuckers were going to have me marry the winner and then have me carrying out hits on their demand."

His grip on me tightens.

"They wanted a video of what I could offer. That's what's on the tapes. I... we had to *perform* on camera. I don't think any of the evidence has been seen by anyone as they were going to edit it at the very end. I just want you to know that none of us had any say in this. I had to perform with Ace and Padraig, or else Sokolov was going to oblige. He pretty much told me he'd rape me if he had to." I shiver as I say it all back.

Delaney punches the side of the van, growling with rage. At what, though? At what I'd gone through? What the Bratva did? Or was it in jealousy? The fact that I had to perform with Ace and Padraig. I'm not stupid enough to ask. Not when he's so wound up. Not unless I have a fucking death wish.

I walk away and rub my hands up my arms. "I only told Duke about The Exterminator as I was concerned Bomb wouldn't back me up if anything happened to you. That he'd just hand me over to the pigs. Only us three and Bomb knew. I have to be honest with you, Delaney, for a moment, I was worried you'd betrayed me. Given how you'd behaved when you arrived in California, I knew something was up. That someone had said something about me, and you were deliberating and deciding whether to believe it or not. But when I found out it was the Russians, I knew you couldn't be involved. You'd never side with them. Then I overheard Sokolov speaking to a Mr. Tyler. Ace told me that's Bomb's surname. The Bratva weren't benefitting from my sale. All the monetary proceeds were going to Bomb."

Delaney walks over to stand beside me, and I watch as his jaw clenches and unclenches in perfect timing with the flick of his blade.

"I've no idea how they found out about Padraig. Until I came back to Rising, no-one knew," I mutter.

He nods. "Bomb had someone on the inside. Not that they were a deliberate informant. They were just stupid. They overheard the conversation between Ace and Padraig and then told Bomb. Still, they betrayed both MCs by divulging, so their life ends today with Bomb's and Sokolov's. Knight and Blaze are bringing both of them here now."

"You know, I thought I saw Bomb in Rising a few days before I was taken. I was going to ask you about it when you got here... but then you never arrived. It all makes fucking sense now."

I raise my hand in a wave as Clay and Jefferson get back in the cage and drive off to go and take care of business at the Fielding warehouse. As they pull away, the other cage pulls up.

"Who was the other informant, Delaney?"

He looks at me.

"Emilia."

CHAPTER THIRTY-SIX

ACE

The Angels of Hellfire Clubhouse, Rising, California

WE DON'T USE THE SHED OFTEN. MOST OF THE TIME, WE TRY TO avoid shitting on our own doorstep. We have no choice this time, though. There are too many people involved, and there are too many lives needing to be ended.

It's a red brick building, and the walls are thick. No one wants to hear the screams from lambs when they're being slaughtered. No one will want to listen to the excuses or cries of the two disloyal fuckers whose throats will be slit here today, either. Or those of the Bratva scum. Not that I think he'll make a sound.

We watch as Clay and Jefferson drag Sokolov across the concrete floor, then rip the tape from his mouth. He doesn't speak. Doesn't put up any resistance. Proud even in death. You've got to respect him for that.

I glance around. Everything inside the shed is easy to hose

down. It will undoubtedly look like a massacre has taken place by the end of today if Razr and his switchblade have anything to do with it. By tomorrow, once Chase has carried out a full cleanse, it will look like nothing's happened. Back to business as usual.

The building is deathly cold and silent. Lighting is by way of fluorescent tubing. Any windows have long since been boarded up, so there's no natural light. My skin crawls as it does every time I enter this goddamn place. It gives me the fucking creeps. I'm sure I can hear the death gurgles of the guilty fuckers whose lives I've taken within these confines. Like the walls have captured and held on to the sound. It smells of death, if death has a smell. A combination of bleach, Lysol, piss, shit, blood, and fear.

We've left PJ in the cage. It was clear Razr wanted to spend time with her. Likely to talk about what's been going on. Will she tell him everything? Will she end things with him now she has it clear in her head that she doesn't love him? Now she's had a chance to reflect.

She loves me. Shit. PJ fucking loves me.

I shake my head. I can't believe it. Even when Padraig told me over the phone, I hadn't been convinced. But the words came out of her own mouth. *PJ loves me.* The only problem is, she loves Padraig too.

I look across at him. We haven't spoken much. What the fuck is there to say? We're both in love with the same woman, and we're both battling our inner demons over what's happened these past few days. He's dressed the same as me in a black tee and jeans. The only difference is I'm wearing a cut. We could be brothers with our dark hair and blue eyes. Our body shapes are even similar. Is that why she fell for him? Because he looks like me? Or is it just that she has a type? Personality-wise, we couldn't be any more fucking different.

My thoughts drift to Emilia. Stupid girl eavesdropping like that and spilling her guts to Bomb. It's going to result in something else being spilled today—her blood. Of course, I feel guilty. In her own way, I guess she was in love with me. Did I lead her on? Not intentionally. I never promised her anything, but she was always hoping. It's her hatred of PJ that's led to her demise. She knows I have feelings for her. Strong ones. So, yeah, I feel bad. But she's brought this on herself. She grew up in the life. She knows what happens when you talk about shit you shouldn't. She knows in order to stay alive; you mind your own goddamn business, avert your eyes, and keep your mouth shut. Now she's going to pay the ultimate price for her betrayal.

I turn my attention to Razr and PJ as they walk in. His hair has blood on it, and there's more on his Henley. He's knife happy today and itching for more judging by the scowl on his face and the repetitive way he keeps flicking his blade. My gaze moves to his other hand. His knuckles are bleeding and bruised like he's just punched something. Has PJ told him about what happened? My eyes connect with his, and I can feel the venom in his stare. The fucker hates my guts because, deep down, he knows she and I have unfinished business, and there's not a damn thing he can do about it. Money can buy a lot of things, but it can't buy her. He knows his harsh reality is that he's going to fucking lose her.

It makes me almost feel sorry for these fuckers facing the death penalty today. Only fleetingly, though. But it's guaranteed Razr's going to take out his bad mood on them.

My attention switches to PJ. She takes my breath away every time I look at her. She's lost weight these past few days, and the jeans the Bratva provided her with are hanging low on her slim hips. She must be able to feel my eyes on her as she shifts her gaze and looks at me. My eyes capture hers before slowly drifting down to her tits. I watch her nipples pebble in response, which brings a slight flush to her cheeks. She bites her lip, and my gaze drifts to her mouth. My mind goes back to seeing her pouty lips wrapped around my dick. I'm not small, but she deep throated me like a fucking pro. I can feel myself grow hard in my jeans just thinking about it. Her eyes drop down, and she smirks.

I scowl at her, and she scowls back. Both of us know we'll pick up where we left off. Of that, there is no shadow of a doubt. She'll pay for making me hard. That thought makes me even harder. The fact that she gets off on me telling her what to do. On me dominating her.

"Bring those other two fuckers in," Razr hisses.

He immediately starts pacing the floor, flicking his blade back and forth as Blaze and Knight leave to fetch Bomb and Emilia from the other cage.

I watch as they drag them in. They're cuffed. Unlike the Russian, who shows no fear, Bomb is sweating profusely, his eyes darting around, taking everything in. He's going to come out with all sorts of lame fucking excuses to try to save his sorry ass. There's no point in him wasting his breath. Emilia? Well, she looks at me and smirks. She probably thinks this is some sort of game and she'll walk out of here alive at some point.

"Get all three of them on their knees." Razr points to the floor.

Blaze and Knight push them down so they're all kneeling in front of him.

He paces. Back and forth. Back and forth. Back and fucking forth. Jaine's right. He's a Jekyll and Hyde character.

He stops directly in front of his VP, his top lip curling.

"Bomb, Bomb, Bomb. WHY THE FUCK DID YOU BETRAY ME, BROTHER!" He's right in his face, screaming at him, the veins on his throat popping out. He stands upright again and looks at PJ, then he closes his eyes briefly before running his hand through his hair. "You deliberately put my woman in the hands of the fucking Bratva. Why the fuck would you do that, brother?" he says quietly, disappointment etched over his face. "You've been my best friend my whole goddamn life. So, you answer me. WHY!" He's screaming again, and the blade's flicking back and forth.

"She was changing things, Prez. She was getting under your skin. You wanted her on council. There's no way a woman should ever be allowed. It breaks all the goddamn rules," he rasps.

I listen to his shitty excuses. Rules are made to be broken. With Jaine being The Exterminator, I can understand why Razr would want her on council. If she were part of the Angels, I'd want her on too.

"BULLSHIT! You were jealous of her, Bomb. Of what she did for the Scorpions! Of what she represented! Of what she meant to me! JESUS FUCKING CHRIST, YOU KNOW WHAT I HAVE TO DO NOW!" He runs his hand through his hair, yanking at the strands. He looks possessed. "Pull out his tongue." He motions for Blaze and Knight to do the honors. Knight prizes Bomb's mouth open, and Blaze pulls out his tongue.

Razr walks across, and he cuts into it, hacking at it and slicing the fucking thing clean off. Bomb immediately starts to choke on his own blood. "NOW YOU CAN'T TELL ME ANY MORE FUCKING LIES!" He stares into Bomb's eyes, absorbing his pain and fear like a fucking trophy, fueling his adrenaline further. He rams Bomb's tongue between his teeth before forcing his mouth closed. His hands are coated in blood, and it drips down and pools onto the floor.

"Swallow it."

Bomb's panting and choking. He shakes his head.

"FUCKING SWALLOW IT, YOU SON OF A BITCH." He spits in his face.

Bomb closes his eyes tightly, then swallows, gagging as he does. Razr takes in the sight. He glowers at his best friend since school, then his gaze softens as he tilts his head to admire his handiwork. Yup. He's fucking insane. He makes his way behind him, his nostrils flared. He's in complete Razr mode now. Paul Delaney has left the building. He puts his hand over Bomb's forehead and tilts his head back. His blade sinks in just under Bomb's ear and then he pulls it down and across his jugular before finishing his cut right below his other ear. Blood sprays everywhere as his heart pumps it out of his body. The organ meant to keep him alive is now killing him. Emilia and the Russian are left kneeling in the dark puddle as Bomb's lifeless body slumps forward to the ground.

She immediately starts to scream, now fearing for her life. Now realizing this is no fucking joke. She's going to pay the price for what she did.

Razr starts to pace again as he turns his attention to her.

"And you. You scheming little bitch. You never told Steele what you told me, did you? How you told Jaine that he'd asked you to become his old lady. You wanted him for yourself, so you needed to get fucking rid of the competition, and you succeeded. DO YOU HAVE ANY IDEA OF THE DAMAGE THAT DID TO HER?" He's spitting in her face with rage, but my anger immediately surpasses his. She told PJ that?

I hold my hand out for the blade, and Razr passes it to me and nods. It's hot from his hand and sticky with Bomb's blood.

I walk around and stand in front of Emilia. She's almost hyper-ventilating. Her eyes are wide and darting about, possibly looking for an escape route. There is none. Her time's up.

"You tell PJ what happened that night, Emilia. You tell her exactly what I said to you," I say quietly, anger coursing through my veins.

She stares at me like her brain can't connect with her mouth.

"YOU FUCKING TELL HER!"

She starts to wail. Her face is covered in tears, her nose running. She falls forward, and her hand connects with the puddle of still-warm blood. She grimaces as she jerks it away and then stares as it runs down her wrist. She wails louder.

"TELL HER, GODDAMN IT!"

She squeezes her eyes closed and speaks through her sobs.

"He told me he wasn't going to fuck me ever again... that he was going to ask you to be his old lady. That... that he loved you." I can't see PJ's reaction as I have my back to her. I know exactly what I have to do now, though.

I walk behind Emilia, and, as Razr did with Bomb, I place my hand across her forehead and tilt her head back.

"Please, Ace. I'm sorry. Please don't do this... I'll do anything." She's sobbing and saying it half-heartedly, but she's accepted her fate. She knows her pleading is falling on deaf ears. PJ stares down at her, then looks at me. I can see tears in her eyes. They won't be for Em. She fucking hates her guts. I'm not sure what they're a sign of. Regret? Relief? I keep staring into them as I sink the blade into Emilia's skin, and I cut her from ear to ear. She gurgles as blood sprays from her neck. Her body tenses fleetingly, then she goes limp. I remove my hand, and she slumps to the floor beside Bomb.

Adrenaline pumps through my body as I pass the blade to Padraig.

The Irishman takes it and grins. He's like some sort of fucking smiling assassin. I'm surprised he doesn't do a jig.

He walks around and stares at the Russian. He knows the Bratva won't beg for his life, and we've nothing to ask him.

"Well, I'd say it was nice meeting you, Sokolov, but it wasn't, so I'll just bid you farewell and take my penance from The Almighty for slitting your throat and sending you straight to the bowels of hell."

He smiles and salutes, then walks behind him. The Russian tilts his own head back. Padraig sticks in the blade and slices him ear to ear, wearing a grin the entire time.

The Russian falls forward.

Padraig hands the blade back to Razr. "I'm sorry, Jaine, that you never got to cut any of these feckers."

She chuckles, then looks to make sure Blaze and Knight are out of earshot.

"It's fine, Irish. An X marks the spot on the forehead that I need to claim, and I need to do so ASAP."

"Who?" I ask, not liking the sound of this.

She stares back at me, her expression soft for once. "Lebedev. I need to take out the pakhan before he realizes what's happened and tells the world my secret."

"There's no way you're fucking doing that," Razr rasps. He resumes pacing and flicking his knife again.

"Oh, I am, Delaney, and if anyone tries to stop me, they'll be met with their own engraved bullet for their fucking trouble."

She walks across to the corpses lying on the floor, and she spits on them.

"See you all in hell," she says before she turns and leaves.

I call Chase. "Can you come clean out the shed, brother?"

"On my way, Prez," he replies.

I hang up.

Now, how the fuck do I approach things with PJ?

CHAPTER THIRTY-SEVEN

JAINE

Jaine's House, Rising, California

I DON'T GO TO THE CLUBHOUSE WITH THE OTHERS AFTERWARD. I can't face the relentless stares or the continual questions.

Who? Why? Where? Repeat.

No, thanks. At least, not yet. Not until I come to terms with this clusterfuck of a situation in my head beforehand.

Instead, I make my excuses, then I have young Lincoln collect me from the shed and drive me home. We don't speak. I don't even make eye contact. I think he can tell I have no interest in chatting or taking part in any unnecessary small talk. I don't even look out the window to take in the scenery. I just stare at my fidgeting hands, lost in my thoughts. Hiding in them even. At least for now.

As much as I feel awful for thinking it, I'm grateful when I can finally get out of the cage and wave him off. I'm sure he realizes. I'm sure he also understands. I just want to be on my own. I need to be. It may seem strange having spent so much time doing just that these past few days, but this is different. I need to regenerate. Recapitulate everything in my head. Keep the good parts and file the other unnecessary shit away permanently.

Sasha and Cherry have been staying at the clubhouse for their own safety, so the place is empty when I get there. I'm grateful for that too, although the house looks unlived in. It also feels sad and unloved somehow without Pop's presence. I can tell someone's been here, though. Photo frames have been moved. It's as if they wanted to delve into my past. Was it Delaney? Someone else?

Picking them up one at a time, I gaze at the images they hold and smile. There are lots of me and Pop, and lots of me with Ace. So many photos of my beautiful boy and me from when I was seven right through until I was seventeen. There aren't any after I left Rising the day after my eighteenth birthday.

I look around at the dated interior—all bland and beige. I need to sort it out. Change it so it doesn't look like it belongs in the seventies.

Sighing, I strip off. Throwing the clothes provided by the Russians straight in the trash, I step into the shower. I need to wash away the smell of that place. Rose-scented disinfectant will forever bring back memories that, in the main, I'd sooner forget. I grimace. I'm sure I can still smell it. Taste it on my tongue.

I'm not saying the memories were all bad, but being held captive against your will isn't something you can ever look back on fondly, at least not in my opinion.

I don't regret what happened with Padraig or with Ace, though not even under the circumstances they happened under.

Scrubbing myself until my skin is red raw, I then wash my hair over and over.

Once dried, I finish dressing just as the doorbell goes. I know it's going to be either Delaney, Ace, or Padraig.

I feel kind of annoyed that whoever it is has shown up unannounced. They could have messaged. Then again, would I have ignored it or turned their visit down? Most likely. I just need a chance to gather my thoughts after what took place earlier. That fucking bloodbath. Do I feel sorry for Bomb? Do I fuck. Do I feel sorry for Emilia? Maybe a little. She acted the way she did because she was in love with Ace. Still. She should have known better than to spill her guts. She has no one to blame for that shit but herself.

I need to digest what she said. That Ace loves me. Or should I say loved me? He said that ten fucking years ago. He might not feel that way about me anymore. Yes, he wants to fuck me, but that means nothing. I used to want to fuck Delaney, but it doesn't mean I love him.

Used to. Past tense. I won't fuck him again.

I open the door to find Delaney standing there. He's wearing a black Henley with black jeans. His hair's wet and hanging down his back, no doubt after a much-needed shower. His familiar sandalwood cologne teases my nostrils, along with the leather scent of his cut.

"Can I come in, Jaine?" He smiles softly and asks quietly. His inner beast is calm, at least for now.

"Sure." I nod and open the door wide for him to walk through, closing it behind him. "Let's go sit on the porch," I suggest with a small smile. Deep down, I can tell he knows what's coming. Usually, he'd have dragged me straight to bed like a neanderthal. Fucking would be the only thing on his mind. Everything else could wait. But he hasn't even attempted to kiss me.

He sits in Pop's old rocking chair, and I lean against the railings, reminding myself that I need to get them painted. Picking at the flaking surface, I watch as a piece flutters to the ground.

We remain in silence for a while. It's not awkward. I guess we're both just finally getting the opportunity to reflect on things.

"I'm truly sorry about what happened, Jaine, and about my unintentional involvement in all of this. I hope what I did this morning in some way lets you know how much I care about you." There's no apology for how horrific it was. Then again, he knows I'm used to creating scenes just as brutal. I guess he means the fact that he slit the throat of his best friend for me. That he killed for me. In my honor.

I frown. "Delaney, I…"

He lifts his hand and interrupts me. "Let me say what I need to say while I'm able to say it, baby."

He pauses briefly, then exhales and runs his hands through his hair. "You know we've been together a long time. Over four years now. And in all that time, you've never once told me you love me." He's flicking his blade and staring into the distance. He's not going to use it. It's a coping mechanism. It's to give his hands something to do as he gets whatever this is off his chest.

"I realize now that's because you don't. You don't love me. I also understand you've never said it because you never wanted to lead me on." He pauses again. "It still doesn't stop it from hurting like a bitch that, no matter what I do, you'll never be mine."

He turns to look at me, and I can see the pain etched across his face. "When you first said you were headed to Rising, I swore to myself I would kill anyone who came near you. Anyone who tried to take you from me. In my mind, you were mine, regardless of whether you loved me or not. I realize now how goddamn selfish that was. More so when I look around this place and see so much of you here. With your pop. With Steele. See, I always knew you coming back would change things. Open up old wounds. Let him back in. I selfishly tried to keep you away for as long as I could because I knew in my heart you and Steele had unfinished business.

"Now, I don't know what will happen with you and him. Or with you and O'Connell, either. But what I'm telling you is if you want to end what we have right here, right now, then I won't hold it against you."

His knife is flicking back and forth as he rocks steadily in the chair but I don't feel threatened by it. It's just his coping mechanism.

"If you can't see yourself ever loving me or ever wanting to be my wife, then I'll accept that, and we can both move on. It'll break my heart. Well, as much of a goddamn heart as I have, but I can't expect you to stay with me if you love someone else. You and I have been through a lot, so regardless of whether you're my woman or not, I'd like to think we can still work together. That you'll still represent the Scorpions and still consider the council position. Then again, I also realize that would be impossible if you decide to move back to Rising."

He pauses, and I look at him. He seems defeated. He's fought the battles over and over and still lost the war.

My heart sinks in my chest. I realize now how much my loving him would have meant, but you can't force feelings, just like you can't switch them off.

I turn and focus on the horizon and take a long deep breath of air that smells of wildflowers and dust. I breathe in my home. I fill my lungs with the familiar fragrance. Welcome it. Let it cleanse my condemned soul, even if only fleetingly.

"Delaney. Regardless of Ace, or Padraig, or my feelings for either, I think this is the right decision. But for you, not for me. See, I don't think I'm old lady material. Not wife material, either. You need someone who'll do your bidding and birth your seed, and I'm not that person. I'm not sure I've even got it in me to be that for anyone. I'm too stubborn, too pig-headed, maybe even too selfish also. Deep down, you know we're not the right fit. I know you do. We never have been. We've just been trying to mold ourselves into what the other person wants, but that will only make us miserable in the long run. There's only so long you can keep up a pretense." I turn to look at him. "I care about you so fucking much, Paul Delaney, but I know I'll never love you the way a wife should love her husband."

We stay where we are, absorbing what's been said. I'm not sure how long passes when he finally stands. He walks across to me, the porch creaking under his weight, and he wraps his arms around my waist.

See, it would be so fucking simple to kiss him right now. Take him inside. Fuck him. But it's just a habit, and it won't help either of us. It won't solve anything. We need to leave it. Right here. Right now.

He kisses the top of my head and breathes in the smell of my hair.

"Will you stay in Rising, or will you come back to Manhattan?"

I press my face against his chest, and his grip tightens. We're both so tempted right now to carry on. Because it's hard. It's so fucking hard. Letting go of someone who still means so much. We've been such a big constant in each other's lives for such a long time.

"I don't know what I'm doing, Delaney. After everything that's happened these past few weeks, I don't want to make any promises or commitments to anyone. I need to give myself a chance to heal and to think things through, you know? A chance to breathe."

I also need to speak with Ace and with Padraig. Make decisions with them or without them.

First things first, though. I need to take out Lebedev.

CHAPTER THIRTY-EIGHT

JAINE

Jaine's House, Rising, California

I HANG UP ON OLD MAN POTTS, THE LOCAL UNDERTAKER. I'VE finally had word from the authorities that Pop's body is to be released, so I've scheduled the burial for ten days' time at Rising Cemetery. I should be back by then. Either alive or in a wooden box. If the latter, they can put me to ground with him.

It's not an occasion I'm looking forward to, but he needs to be laid to rest. He needs to be back in Rising where he belongs. I've asked the funeral parlor to let the MC and the townsfolk know and also to put a note in the local press. I'm guessing there'll be a lot of people who'll want to attend. He died for the Angels' patch, so as a hero.

I exhale loudly, feeling at a loss. I'm deflated since my conversation with Delaney. I probably don't feel anywhere near as bad as he does, though. Still, it's all out in the open, and I kept my neck, so

I guess I should be grateful. He can move on now and find someone who's better suited. Maybe he and Sasha will get together. Who knows?

I'm sure we can remain friends. At least, I hope we can. I'd never want the murderous bastard anywhere but on my side. He's not someone you'd want to make an enemy of. I was reminded of that fact witnessing the ease with which he cut his childhood friend's throat. It means nothing in this life. Friendship. It's all about respect, honor, loyalty, and living and dying for your patch and club. Nothing else matters.

He is right, though. It would be a shame for us to throw away four years. I'd miss him. A lot. I know how he ticks better than any other fucker likely ever will. We just have to make sure it never slips into friends with benefits, or we'll be back at square one. I'm fully aware he's cut me some slack this time around, probably because of what I've had to go through on account of Bomber's betrayal. I'm not so sure he would be as forgiving if there were a next time. Not without another neck being offered as a sacrifice to his blade as appeasement.

I stare at my phone. I mean, even though what Delaney and I shared wasn't love, it was still better than nothing in a lot of ways. It was still a connection with another person. Physically as well as emotionally. Now I've got nothing tangible. I haven't even heard from Padraig or Ace since this morning.

Padraig: *Stop being so anti-social.*
Jaine: *Speak of the devil.*
Padraig: *Were you just speaking about me?*
Jaine: *Yes. To myself. No one else would want to listen.*
Padraig: *Why? I'm tall, dark, and handsome, and the women love me. Even you love me. You said so yourself.*
Jaine: *Stockholm Syndrome sucks.*

Padraig: *That hurts.*

Jaine: *Not as much as Sokolov's neck hurts him.*

Padraig: *He can't feel it. He's dead.*

Jaine: *You need to go to confession.*

Padraig: *Flying home tomorrow, then heading straight to church. Father O'Reilly will be waiting. I have him on speed dial. You need a lift?*

Jaine: *Not sure I can trust you. You might come on to me.*

Padraig: *You've fucked me already. Several times. We can join the mile-high club together.*

Jaine: *Don't try and tell me you're not already a member.*

Padraig: *Okay, I won't, but I'm not a member with you. That's what counts.*

Jaine: *I've seen all your moves already. Why would I want to repeat them while I'm flying in a tin can?*

Padraig: *You've not seen anything yet. I was camera shy.*

Jaine: *You? Shy?*

Padraig: *I'll have you know I'm extremely sensitive, darlin'. Anyway, I've still not shown you what my tongue can do.*

Jaine: *I thought I told you to keep that thing in your goddamn mouth.*

Padraig: *I prefer it in yours.*

Jaine: *Eww, your slutty tongue's been in my mouth.*

Padraig: *Now, now. What have I told you? If you've nothing nice to say.*

Jaine: *You told me the ladies love your cunnilingus. I agree. Sometimes things are better left unsaid.*

Padraig: *I can bleach it?*

Jaine: *It'll still smell fishy.*

Padraig: *I just breathed into my hand, and it's minty fresh. Cherry agrees.*

Jaine: *What do you mean Cherry fucking agrees?*

Padraig: *I asked if I could kiss her, just to check, of course. She said yes.*

Jaine: *Shut the fuck up.*

Padraig: *You jealous?*

Jaine: *No. Fuck you.*

Padraig: *You are. I can tell.*

Jaine: *Fuck you. You're not getting two-word answers. I refuse to fall into that trap. See?*

Padraig: *She's sitting on my lap. Jesus, she has a lovely peachy arse.*

Jaine: *Are you shitting me right now?*

Padraig: *She doesn't mind my fishy breath, and she's happy to fuck me mid-air. I might ask her to come along for the ride.*

Jaine: *Fuck you.*

Padraig: *You see? Two words. Like taking candy from a baby. You okay?*

Jaine: *I'm fine. No, wait. In fact. I'm fucking perfectly fine, you Irish asshole. There. Seven words.*

Padraig: *You're being reactive. That means you're jealous. Do you want to join the mile-high club?*

Jaine: *You're an asshole.*

Padraig: *Terms of endearment will get you everywhere, darlin'.*

Jaine: *Go away.*

Padraig: *Another two words. The offer of a lift is there.*

Jaine: *Asshole. Appreciated. Now go away and take your tongue with you.*

Padraig: *If I keep it in my mouth, you want to join the mile-high club?*

Jaine: *You're pathetic. Delete my number.*

Padraig: *I can't. It's imprinted on my Irish heart.*

Jaine: *Bet you say that to all the girls, so they'll let you show them your fishy tongue trick.*
Padraig: *Nope. Just you.*
Jaine: *I love you.*
Padraig: *I know you do.*
Jaine: *Cocky Irish fucker.*

PADRAIG

The Angels of Hellfire Clubhouse, Rising, California

"Cillian, book the flight for tomorrow evening." I know I sound like a grumpy asshole, but having finally got to fuck the woman of my dreams, I've a feeling she's going to vanish for a second time. Not sure if my heart can take it again.

"For how many, Paddy?"

"Book it for three people. I'll let you know if it changes."

"Will do. Da wants to know about this Jaine Jones, by the way. Razr's old lady. The one you used to see when you were at Yale."

"She's not Razr's old lady. From what I hear, she's recently dumped him."

"Jesus, has she got a death wish?"

If only he knew who she was.

"The split was amicable as far as I'm aware."

"So, you used to fuck her while you were at Yale? Small world, Paddy."

"I never fucked her. We dated."

"You never fucked her?"

"No. She wouldn't give me access to her pussy."

"Someone actually turned you down?" He snickers in disbelief.

"Fuck you, Cill."

"Sweet baby Jesus, you sound like you're pussy whipped. You love her?"

I don't reply. That's all the answer he needs.

He lets out a long whistle.

"Well, you best make sure she's a practicing Catholic as you know Da will insist. You can't be bringing someone into the fold that Father O'Reilly won't be accepting of."

"Just book the damn flight, Cill, and fuck off."

"All right, all right, you cranky fecker."

I put the phone down.

I thought it best to offer Jaine a ride. If she wants to take down Lebedev, she needs to get back to New York. I thought it best to also offer Razr a ride. It would be rude not to. Manners cost nothing, and I've seen first-hand how handy he is with that blade of his. I need to keep on his good side.

Then I say a silent prayer to The Almighty that Jaine chooses me.

If she doesn't, I don't know what the fuck I'll do.

CHAPTER THIRTY-NINE

JAINE

The Angels of Hellfire Clubhouse, Rising, California

THE HEAVY COMPOUND IRON BARS CREAK IN FAMILIAR COMPLAINT as a smiling Lincoln prizes them open only long enough to let me ride through. I nod at him in a gesture of thanks. Parking up my hog, I take off my helmet and, staying seated, I check my phone, using my hand to stop the glare of the sun reflecting off the small screen. Padraig has been messaging me non-stop. It's like he doesn't want me to forget about him. How the fuck could I ever forget about my Irish?

> **Padraig:** *Send me a selfie.*
> **Jaine:** *No. Weirdo. Anyway, I look like shit.*
> **Padraig:** *I want to have you as my screensaver.*
> **Jaine:** *You know that sounds creepy as fuck, right?*
> **Padraig:** *See? It's a sign.*

Jaine: *What is?*

Padraig: *We're both creeps and weirdos. Just like in that song you like. It's proof I'm the yang to your yin. I need that selfie.*

I sigh, then laugh and shake my head. Jesus Christ, he can be painful at times. I raise my phone, take the pic, and look at the image. I'm sitting on my hog, and I look exhausted. It's totally unflattering. I'm way too thin again. A sure-fire sign that the past few weeks have taken their toll on me physically as well as mentally. I smooth down my black tank top and leather pants. Then I think of Padraig, and I can't help but smile. What the fuck would I do without him to brighten my days?

Jaine: *Sent.*

Padraig: *Jesus, Jaine. You're beautiful. First time I've seen you on your bike. I think I need to go fuck my hand.*

Jaine: *My hog, you mean. Your dick's already been in my pussy, so there's no need for all the flattery. It won't get you anything you haven't already had.*

Padraig: *That wasn't through choice, though, was it?*

Jaine: *What do you mean?*

Padraig: *We had to fuck. We didn't choose to fuck.*

Jaine: *I have no regrets.*

Padraig: *You sure about that?*

Jaine: *Yes. I never lie. You know that.*

Padraig: *You're at the clubhouse?*

Jaine: *Yeah, I just got here. I need to speak to Ace and Duke, and I also need to catch up with the girls. That's if they're around and not off fucking their biker boyfriends. Then I'll be setting off for the airport. Delaney's already at the hotel. I think he's staying in the same one you are.*

Padraig: *I'll see you tonight, then, darlin'.*

You could hear a pin drop. All eyes are on me the moment I walk into the clubhouse. I can feel each pair trying to search my goddamn soul. I don't even look around to see who they belong to. It's like I'm wearing a tee that says *I was Kidnapped by the Bratva and Survived.* I'm pretty sure every fucker's holding their breath. How much do they know? How much has Ace told them? Or Delaney, for that matter? My mind's working overtime trying to figure it out. Do they know about Bomb? Emilia?

I don't make any eye contact. I simply walk past and make my way to Duke's office. I need to find out exactly what's been said before I engage in any conversation, so I know how much or how little to divulge.

Knocking on Duke's non-descript office door, I curse when there's no answer. I bite my lip. It leaves me no choice but to go to Ace's door. I only hope he's not got a cum slut in there with him. I'm not sure I could cope with that visual. The memory of what I did to Bailey when she ground her pussy on Delaney's dick immediately springs to mind. It feels like a lifetime ago now. The only saving grace is that Ace can't be fucking Emilia. Then again, better the devil you know. It would be easier to cope with that sight than to catch him with someone new. Still, he's a free agent.

We will *pick this back up where we left off, PJ.*

Did he say that in the heat of the moment? When we were in the captivity bubble, where everything that was so wrong felt so incredibly right? Now that we're back in reality, has he forgotten that comment? Maybe he even regrets saying it.

I can feel my heart rate rise as I knock on the familiar dark grey metal door, and I run my now sweaty hands down my tank top.

"Come in." His voice is deep and dark, like melted fucking

chocolate, and my nipples immediately spring to attention, which won't go unnoticed, I'm sure.

I push open the door. He's facing away from me, looking out the window. He's only wearing a pair of blue jeans, and his midnight hair is wet. It's mid-way down his back these days. Its thickness and texture would make any woman envious. He's obviously just showered as there are beads of water on his skin. My eyes caress his taut, toned flesh, which magnificently displays his Angels' tattoo. My traitorous gaze drops further to his ass. I lick my lips. I can't help myself.

He turns around. He knows precisely where I've been looking. I trail my eyes slowly up his muscled form. I've already been caught staring, so where's the goddamn rush? More beads of water cover his torso, and I have to fight the overwhelming urge to walk over and lick them off. He should pierce his nipples. They'd look so fucking good pierced. It would add to the angsty bad boy image he carries off so well. Wetness pools in my underwear as my one-track mind tries to convince my body to cross the room and bite down on that full bottom lip of his. The one I'm staring at. The one I want on my fucking skin. Along with his hands and his tongue. My eyes finally rise to meet his. The room crackles with sexual tension. This boy. This man who I've loved most of my life is staring back at me like he wants to eat me alive.

His eyes darken as they drop to my peaked nipples, and I can see lust blazing in their blue depths. He crosses the room like a panther pouncing on its prey.

I can't remember how to breathe. I'm going to pass out.

Using his body, he presses me hard against the door. One calloused hand grips my hip painfully. The other pushes my hair back from behind my ear before gently tracing the outline of my tattoo. What does he think when he looks at it? Does he like the fact that I wear his mark for the world to see?

"Razr says you and he are done. Has he got that right, PJ?" His lips hover over mine, the heat of his breath almost sucking the life out of me. I stare at his mouth, then drown in his blue gaze. Over and over, my eyes flick from one to the other. He's hypnotizing me without even trying.

I lick my lips, and his eyes drop.

I can't speak, so I simply nod. I'm a free agent now too. He knows exactly what that means.

He presses his lips to mine, and his tongue immediately takes ownership, thrusting deep into my mouth. Searching. Tasting. Remembering.

I welcome his familiar taste, running my hands across his pecs and shoulders and relishing in the feel of his hot, sculpted flesh under my fingertips. He bites my lip painfully. I curse him against his mouth, and he growls in response like a wild animal, making me even wetter. His hands drop to grab my ass, pulling me firmly against his erection. Pushing his leg between my thighs, he spreads me and massages my clit through my leather pants. When his mouth leaves mine, I groan in disappointment.

Please don't stop.

He smirks at me. Then I realize I said that out loud.

"Lose the clothes, PJ." He watches me with dark eyes as I strip. Not sexily. I just want to be naked as quickly as possible. I need him inside me. Right now.

He pushes me back against the door, and I shiver. Is it the cold metal? Or is it what's about to happen? What I've been waiting for these past ten years?

I press my mouth to his again, but this time, I force my tongue past his closed lips. I need to taste him. Savor him. Never stop fucking kissing him.

He growls as his hands drop to my ass, spreading my cheeks. His fingers come from behind to rub against my slit. I'm drenched. I should be embarrassed, but I don't give a fuck. I'm well past caring. There's no hiding how aroused I am and how much I want him.

"You're so fucking wet." His voice is husky, like a sensual caress, and my clit throbs painfully in response.

He thrusts two fingers inside me, and I groan, pressing my nose against his neck, drowning myself in his masculine smell. My teeth connect with his skin, and I suck and bite on him as he fucks me hard with his fingers.

Sliding his hands under my ass, he lifts my legs off the floor, and I immediately wrap them around his waist.

"Let's finish what we fucking started." His breath is hot against my lips, his eyes boring into mine.

I stop him from saying anything else by pushing my tongue back into his mouth. I don't want conversation. I need his hands on me. I need his dick inside me. Every drop of blood in my body has rushed straight to my clit, and I feel faint.

"Ace, I need you to fuck me right fucking now," I growl as I rub myself against his hard-on like a bitch in heat. His hands drop to my swollen folds, and I groan as he thrusts two fingers back inside, scissoring them, preparing me for his massive dick.

"You want my cock in your soaking pussy, sweetheart?" He growls as his fingers pick up the pace.

"Fuck, yeah." I can barely speak.

He unbuttons his jeans and pushes them down, and I can feel the smooth heat and wet slickness of his dick as it rubs against my inner thigh.

Reaching down between us, I run the blunt tip up and down my folds before impaling myself on him, gasping as he stretches me and fills me completely.

Nothing has ever felt so fucking good. Nothing. It's been ten years too long.

Positioning my legs over his elbows, he fucks me against the door. My back scrapes against the metal, but I don't care. He's not gentle. This isn't nice boy Ace. This Ace is all grown up. He's one hundred percent man and a fucking killer. Like me. Both of us are taking exactly what we want and need from this because that's how we live our lives.

Like each day is our last.

He drives in and out of me hard and fast. His mouth connects with my neck, and he licks and sucks and then bites. I scream out and curse him again. But I love the combination of pleasure and pain, and he knows it. His skin is hot and damp with sweat, and my mouth immediately connects, my tongue licking the saltiness off, the raw taste of him turning me on even more.

"Watch me fuck you," he grunts. I rest my forehead against his and watch his thick dick, its length glistening with my slickness, drive in and out of me, hitting every single perfect spot.

"You like that, sweetheart? You like how I fuck you? You want it harder? Faster?

"Yes." I can barely speak.

He quickens his pace, driving hard and deep, his dick banging against my cervix.

"Rub your clit, sweetheart. I'm not going to last much longer."

I do as he says and drop my hand to get myself off.

"Shit, Ace." My voice sounds pained as the climax rattles through every single part of my body. I feel myself clench around him, my pussy gripping onto him so tightly, never wanting to let him go ever again.

His movements are erratic now, no longer precise as he reaches his own end.

He grunts and swears, his face contorting with pleasure as I feel his dick twitch inside me, filling me with his beautiful fucking cum.

We stay that way for a minute, maybe more, sweating and

panting against each other. He lowers my legs to the floor, and his seed runs down my thighs.

WHEN I RETURN FROM SHOWERING, HE'S ALREADY REDRESSED, AND he watches as I do the same. Both of us are silent. What happened needed to happen, but now's not the time to dissect what any of it meant.

Walking across the room, I stare out the window. The view is pretty much unchanged in ten years.

"Old man Potts has told me about Jeremiah's funeral. I'll let everyone know."

"Thank you."

"No one knows the details about what happened. All they know is we were taken and Razr got us out. No one's asked about Bomb and Em. About where they are. I think they already suspected they were traitors and deserved everything they got."

I nod.

I walk across and stand in front of him. My eyes take in every last detail. He wraps his arms around me as I press my nose against his throat and inhale his scent. Imprinting everything about him to memory.

Jason Steele. Ace. My beautiful boy.

I may never see him again.

Pressing my mouth to his, I kiss him. A kiss that tells him how much I've missed him and how much I fucking love him. He kisses me back. Hard. He knows I love him. I've said it out loud.

He's never told me.

Maybe he never will.

Maybe he doesn't.

Anyway, now's not the time. The Exterminator needs to go take care of business.

"If I don't get out of this alive, Ace, then you bury me with my pop."

I can tell he's going to say something. Probably tell me everything will be fine. That I'll survive all this. But he stops himself. We both know that's in no way guaranteed. I'm about to attempt to take out the Bratva's top man, and that shit isn't going to be a walk in the park.

I hug Sash and Cherry on my way out. We don't speak. I wasn't really looking for them when I came here. I did what I subconsciously came to do. Fuck Ace. Why? I might never get the opportunity again.

I'm blinkered now. My focus is on one thing and one thing only.

Killing Lebedev.

CHAPTER FORTY

PADRAIG

Los Angeles, California

Cillian: *Did you get a pic of your woman?*
Padraig: *She's not my woman.*
Cillian: *Okay, the woman you want to be your woman.*
Padraig: *Jesus Christ.*
Cillian: *What? Am I lying?*
Padraig: *No. I just don't want to tempt fate by sending you her fucking photo.*
Cillian: *You really think she'll turn you down?*
Padraig: *She might.*
Cillian: *What will you do if she does?*
Padraig: *I don't want to think about that.*
Cillian: *So deposit the other fucker in the Hudson. Limit her choices to one.*

Padraig: *You want me to kill the prez of the Angels of Hellfire?*

Cillian: *Okay… so we hire The Exterminator to do it, then. Incognito.*

Padraig: *If she wants to be with me, she will be.*

Cillian: *But if she doesn't?*

Padraig: *Let's just say I'm quietly confident.*

Cillian: *Send me her pic, then.*

Padraig: *Sends pic.*

Cillian: *Jesus, Paddy. You're punching, aren't you?*

Padraig: *You say the nicest things.*

Cillian: *I can't believe you've kept her hidden for nine fucking years.*

Padraig: *We were just friends. It was no big deal.*

Cillian: *Were? Are you more than friends now?*

Padraig: *It's complicated.*

Cillian: *I say shoot the other fecker and take the prize. I'll pay The Exterminator personally.*

Padraig: *It's complicated, Cill!*

Cillian: *You know, while you've been away, Da's been talking about marrying you off. Like an arranged marriage.*

Padraig: *He needs to be doing that shit with Eoin. He's the eldest. He's going to be the future lord and master of it all one day.*

Cillian: *The intended bride is only sixteen, so the marriage would need to take place two years from now. You're closest in age, being youngest and all. Anyway, she's perused our images, and you're the chosen one, so I'm led to believe.*

Padraig: *Am I fuck getting married to a teenager.*

Cillian: *He'll throw something at you if you don't.*

Padraig: *Aye? Well, I'll just duck as usual. It's Jaine or no one for me.*

Cillian: *You really do love her, don't you? But what will you do if she turns you down and chooses the other fella?*

Padraig: *She fucking won't. Tell Da to get the five million dollars ready.*

Cillian: *What for?*

Padraig: *The Exterminator has agreed to take out Lebedev.*

Cillian: *He'll be fucking delighted. It'll be like all his Christmases have come at once.*

Padraig: *Aye, I know. It'll be the first time this year the old fecker's cracked his face with a smile.*

Cillian: *You'll be the favorite. Well, until you tell him you don't want to marry the Sicilian, that is.*

Padraig: *A Sicilian? There's no way I'm marrying into the mafia. Is he fucking nuts?*

Cillian: *I'm just telling you what's been discussed in your absence.*

Padraig: *Listen, I'll speak to you when I get back to New York. Is Dylan still picking me up at the other end?*

Cillian: *Yes, and he can pick up your future wife too and drop her off. The American one, that is.*

Padraig: *Very funny. You should have been a comedian. You're shit at being a mobster anyway.*

Cillian: *Have a safe journey, Paddy.*

I haven't told Jaine that Razr has already flown back to Manhattan. I don't think the poor fecker could handle having his nose rubbed in it by being in such a confined space with me and her, so he made his excuses. He'd most likely have spent the entire journey flicking that switchblade of his back and forth like a metronome.

By all accounts, he was grateful for the offer, though. Or at least that's what I thought I heard when he said it through gritted teeth. If

I'd been anyone else, I'm sure he'd have slit my throat as a proper thank you since I'm one of the *other* men. He possibly didn't as we share a business arrangement. That and the fact I'm a Duster and my da would skin him alive. No one messes with Fergal O'Connell's family apart from old Fergal himself. Well, at least not anyone of sound mind.

I look at my watch. She's late. My pet hate. We need to take off in half an hour.

Pacing the runway, my thoughts are of her.

Jaine, Jaine, fucking Jaine. Since I was nineteen years old, all I've been able to think about is Jaine Jones. My brothers and I have women throwing themselves at us. Not her, though. Oh, no. I had to wait two dates before I was even allowed to kiss her, and then it was with no tongues. She captivated me with that librarian look she had going on and her determination not to let me anywhere near that sweet pussy of hers.

It was always more than that between us, though. It was always going to be more than just fucking. We connected immediately. Fate? Fuck knows. Maybe. If you believe in that sort of shite. We both came from the life, yet we were able to separate things out in those days and live relatively normally. School, studies, friends. At Yale, we were the same as everyone else. Jaine was a breath of fresh air in a world that, at that age, both scared me shitless and bored me rigid. A world where I had to torture and kill, but in return, I could have anything or anyone I wanted.

Well, apart from her and her pussy.

Women queued up for me to fuck them. Men feared me. Jaine? Well, she didn't care who I was. I was as much a non-entity to her as the next person. I neither impressed her nor scared her. She wasn't intimidated by what I did as it was all she knew too.

When she told me about *him*, the one who had spurned her, I thought my luck was in. Show her care and attention, and she'd be mine. It was in the bag. That was all she wanted. Well, it didn't quite work out that way. I made the asshole move that I've cursed myself for every day since. The one that will no doubt haunt me for the rest of my life. I fucked someone else just because I could, and for the first and only time in my life, I got dumped.

Nine years later, and I represent the Dusters legally and kill for a living. Jaine does the same for the Scorpions.

Razr? That fucking eejit should have tied her the fuck down when he had the chance. He had four years.

He didn't—his loss. Ace didn't—his loss.

It's my turn to claim what should now rightfully be mine. If she agrees, I'll have her in front of old Father O'Reilly within the week and my baby in her belly on our wedding night. We O'Connells don't mess about. When we make a decision, it's a done deal. Go big or go home.

I look at her photo on my phone. She's fucking beautiful without even trying and she doesn't even realize it. What you see is what you get with Jaine. She doesn't give two flying fucks what you think of her. Take her or leave her. Well, I intend to take her.

Running my hands through my hair, I curse silently. Where the feck is she? I need to get back by tonight as I've got back-to-back meetings tomorrow and some concrete shoes to fit to a host of people who've pissed off my da. He's created a list that's been building up in my absence. Being taken hostage by the Bratva is no excuse in his eyes. He called me a slacker. A lazy bastard. Apparently, I just wanted to sit in a cell with my feet up to avoid having to do any real work.

It's then I see her. Wearing a tank top and combats, she still manages to look like she's on a fucking catwalk. Most women would have a trolley filled with luggage and a face full of make-up. Jaine has a backpack, and the only thing she's wearing on her heart-shaped face is her bright green eyes, upturned nose, and pouty lips.

All of that flattered by that natural long blonde hair of hers. The only thing marring her physical perfection is that fucking tattoo behind her ear. The one of *his* initial.

I'm getting hard just thinking about how perfect she is for me. Jaine challenges me. She's my intellectual equal. We can talk for hours. We *do* talk for hours. I don't want a wife that looks pretty and decorative with nothing going on behind the facade. My brothers might settle for that, but it's not for me. Jaine ticks every box. And now I've been inside her, I need to make her mine. Her pussy was made for my dick. This woman is a keeper. She can take care of my needs in the bedroom, confidently stand by my side in front of any audience, and she also accepts the fact that I'm a murderous bastard who takes lives most days. She can accept that because she's the same.

She's the female equivalent of me.

"Irish." She hugs me, and I hug her back, making sure my hard-on doesn't brush against her. I look her up and down. She's glowing. I've seen that look on her before, and it was right after I fucked her. It can't have been Razr, so it must have been Ace.

Swallowing back my raging jealousy, I force a smile on my face and lock our fingers, most likely gripping hers way too tight. "Let's go, darlin'. We'll be taking off shortly."

I want to kill the fucker. Not Jaine. Ace.

We Irish would never hurt our women. We're brought up to provide for them, show them love and respect, and fill them with our seed. In my grandfather's time, all that was expected from them in return was to keep house and look after our bellies, offspring, and dicks. In those days, the womenfolk were kept out of the business side of things and were never expected to get their hands dirty. Da's now blathering on that we need to find wives who can handle themselves and who are from the life. Like our ma, Roisin. Even my da wouldn't mess with her. She's as insane as he is.

Any proposed union now needs to be beneficial to the Dusters by increasing our wealth, building a powerful alliance, and improving our reputation and position amongst our outlaw peers. He doesn't fucking want much.

None of us have taken his ramblings seriously, but with Cillian banging on about arranged marriages, maybe the old man's more hell-bent on the idea than we first thought.

Old Fergal would think he'd died and gone to heaven if I married the vigilante sniper. He'd think of it as being almost as grand an event as the second coming of Jesus Christ himself.

It doesn't look like she and I are going to be joining the mile high club, thanks to Ace, though.

Maybe I should take Cill up on his offer and drop the moody fucking biker in the middle of the Hudson.

CHAPTER FORTY-ONE

JAINE

Los Angeles, California

TRY AS HE MIGHT TO HIDE IT, PADRAIG IS CLEARLY PISSED OFF. Then I realize he can tell. Fuck knows how, as I'm sure it's not inked on my forehead. He must have some Irish sixth sense, but he knows I've just fucked Ace, and he is *not* happy about it. I don't acknowledge his mood or react. I just let him deal with it. It's his problem, not mine.

His grip on my hand is tight. Possessive even. He runs his other hand through his inky black hair in agitation as we board the plane.

It's spacious. All cream leather seating and a mini-bar area with drinks and snacks. The smell of new leather permeates the air, as does the savory aroma of the complimentary food. There'll be a bedroom too, no doubt. Not that we'll be using it. I'll struggle to sit through the journey, let alone do anything else given how hard Ace fucked me earlier.

This private flight must have cost a small fortune to book. Then again, the aircraft is likely owned by the Dusters outright. Irish is a billionaire, after all. His family is one of the wealthiest in Manhattan.

"Where's Delaney?" I sit down and watch as he walks to the bar and pours himself a whiskey. Holding the glass up, he offers me one, but I decline. I'm not much of a drinker as he well knows, so I'm not sure why he even bothered. Politeness maybe. Shrugging, he swirls the pale amber liquid around the crystal, then throws it back in one.

"He took an earlier flight. Said he needed to get back."

I wonder why Irish didn't let me know that beforehand. It's not like Delaney would have canceled last minute. He might be insane, but he still has manners.

I take him in. I've only ever seen a smiley, happy-go-lucky Irish before. But right now, I can feel a dark side emanating from him. I have to admit that finally seeing elements of the Duster side of the man is quite intriguing. A turn-on, in fact.

I watch as he pours himself another drink, repeating the same process. Should I say something or let him drink himself into jealousy-fueled oblivion? I decide to say nothing. It's none of my business. I'm not his mother. Or his girlfriend, for that matter.

I haven't made any commitments to anyone. I can't. I'm not in a position to. I could be dead tomorrow. I refuse to feel guilty about fucking Ace. It's not like I haven't already fucked Irish. Plus, it's not like I cheated on either. For the first time in over four years, I can fuck whoever I goddamn choose.

In advance of being told by the pilot, I fasten my seatbelt. I'm exhausted, and it's suddenly overwhelming and drowning me. Proper rest has escaped me for days. I guess it's only to be expected when you've recently been kidnapped. I'm constantly trying to sleep with one eye open. At least while we're in the air, I can relax.

I AWAKE MUCH LATER AND JUST IN TIME TO LAND. IRISH IS IN A brighter mood. I'm not sure if it's due to the passing of time or the volume of whiskey he's consumed while I've been comatose.

"You feeling better, sleepy-head?" he says with a warm grin as he sits across from me. He's tied his shoulder-length hair back, and my eyes use the opportunity to take in his striking features.

"Was I snoring or drooling?" I chuckle and smile at him.

"You were doing both." He kicks my foot teasingly.

"Fuck you." I stretch out and watch as his eyes drop to my tits, which are no doubt pressing against my top.

"Not sure we have time for that as we'll be landing shortly." He smiles, but it doesn't reach his eyes letting me know he's pissed off about that fact.

He exhales while releasing his hair, combing it through with his fingers. I take him in once more. Do I have a type? On the surface, he and Ace could be brothers. The most noticeable difference is that Irish is fair-skinned due to his Celtic ancestry. Both of them are fine fucking specimens of men.

Personality-wise, they're poles apart. Irish is full of charm and wit. The proverbial life and soul. I wonder if I'm only seeing the side of him he wants me to see. I've caught a glimpse of his darker alter-ego today. In comparison, Ace is the opposite. Moody and sullen. He wasn't always like that. Melancholy. He has no alter-ego. Jason and Ace are one in the same. What you see is what you get. If you don't like it, fuck off.

"How are you feeling about what's coming up?"

"I don't feel anything about it." My response is immediate, and my tone is clipped and sharper than it needs to be. I don't discuss any of my hits before they take place. Not with anyone. Or my mindset in relation. I've always been concerned if I involve third parties, then I may start to rely on them for guidance, reassurance, or, in the case of Irish, even just good fucking luck.

That would be a mistake. Perhaps a deadly one. They won't be there. It'll just be me, my gun, my target, and Lucifer himself, waiting for a soul. Mine or theirs.

"My brother is picking us up from the airport." He announces it like it's no big deal.

I frown. I'm not sure I'm ready to meet another Duster. Am I about to be assessed? Interrogated? Has he told his family his plans for me? Am I to be evaluated on whether I'm worthy of their youngest? Irish has made his intentions quite clear. He hasn't repeated it since escaping the Bratva, but I know he wants to make it official. Make *us* official.

I nod. "Which one?"

"Our Dylan."

I feel relief of sorts. My recollection is he's the second youngest and the quiet one, so he's not likely to barrage me with a host of intrusive questions that will make me want to blow his brains out in annoyance.

New York

I take in Irish eyes that are a shade darker than his brother's. More sapphire. The other clear difference is they're not smiling. They're staring at me and looking for any reason to condemn me and deem me untrustworthy. That's sensible. I'm doing the same fucking thing. The face that wears them is paler and clean-shaven. The hair is just as black, but it's cut short. Dylan is slightly shorter than Padraig and not as well-built. I'm guessing he doesn't get out much, which is probably through choice more than anything else. He doesn't strike me as the friendly sort. Looks like a grumpy fucker, judging by the permanent scowl on his face. He's handsome, but I'm guessing all the O'Connells are in their own unique way. He's wearing a white button-down shirt and dark grey pants, which seems a tad over-dressed. Maybe he's classing this pick-up as a social event, so he thought he'd best prepare for the occasion. Maybe he's trying to impress me. Then I realize I'm being a bitch. Maybe he's been somewhere beforehand or is going somewhere afterward. I sincerely doubt it, though.

"It's nice to meet you, Dylan." I deliberately ride shotgun and stare across at him. I might as well grab the bull by the horns. I'm not one for shying away from a dance with the fucking devil.

We're in a massive black SUV with a matching all-leather interior and blacked-out windows. No doubt the spec will mean it's completely bullet-proof.

"And you, Jaine." His voice is cagey.

We drive off. I push the boundaries. "So, what is it you do for the Dusters, Dylan?"

He doesn't turn around.

"This and that."

"Oh, this and that? Well, that answers *this* question and *that* question."

There's a pause.

"Dylan deals with our security, among other things, darlin'," Padraig answers from the back seat. I pull down the visor and look through the mirror into his smiling eyes. I watch as his brother glares at him through the rear-view one. It's obvious he's not happy with Padraig's big reveal.

"Jaine is completely trustworthy, Dyl."

Dylan doesn't look convinced. Then again, if the shoe was on the other foot, I'd be the same.

"So, you keep a watch over the people, the properties, and the city itself, then, Dylan? A bit like Batman?" The corners of his mouth twitch upwards. "Is there any particular light I need to shine into the night sky to get your help and attention? A leprechaun? A four-leaf clover," I add, taking full advantage of his somewhat receptive mood.

Christ Almighty strike me down if he doesn't laugh out loud. "I'm sure our Paddy can tell you how to contact me if you need to do that."

"Paddy? Is that what your family calls you? Jesus, you kept that nickname quiet." I snicker as I turn around to look at him.

"Well, I like you calling me Irish." He rolls his eyes, but he clearly loves the banter and being the center of attention.

"Oh, is that right, *Paddy*?" I laugh at him.

We're five minutes from my apartment now.

"It's just up here on the left, Dylan."

We pull up outside the building. It's a good area. An extremely wealthy one. I know Dylan will be relieved that I'm not some sort of gold-digger. I have all the fucking money I'll ever need, and I've earned every last dime.

"Well, it was nice to meet you, Dylan," I say as I wait for the countless door locks to unravel.

"You too, Jaine." He smiles at me. Jesus, we've come on leaps and bounds. My guess is Dylan O'Connell doesn't smile at many folks.

I open the door, and Irish is already there on the sidewalk, offering me his hand to help me down.

We stop at my apartment entrance. We both know this is as far as he goes. I don't need any distractions. I can't afford to have any today.

"I love you, Jaine. You know that don't you?" His eyes are earnest. He's open, and he means every fucking word.

"I know. I love you too, Padraig." My eyes roam over his face, absorbing his visual, then inhaling the familiar smell that is my Irish. Old Spice. I laugh inwardly as I press my mouth to his.

Like I did with Ace, I need him to know how much he means to me.

He growls softly, then his tongue immediately pushes past my lips and explores every part of my mouth. He kisses me like a man who's been denied the touch of a woman's lips against his for all fucking eternity. Drinking me in, he absorbs my very soul. I groan into his mouth, and he hungrily claims the sound by deepening the kiss. His lips and body let me know exactly how much he wants me as he drops his hands to my ass and pulls my front snugly against his.

Perfect fit.

I'm conscious that Dylan will be watching, but I don't give a fuck. Our lives are short in this game, and the laws of probability would suggest mine is currently shorter than most. Way shorter. Every second in this life has to fucking mean something. Time is a luxury we can't afford to waste.

He presses his hard-on against my clit, and I pull my mouth away. We need to leave it there. I need to focus. I rest my forehead against his.

"You let me put my tongue in your mouth," he whispers cheekily.

I laugh. "Yeah. I don't know what got into me. In fact, yes, I do. It was your slutty, fishy tongue, as you say."

"I'd much rather put something else into you, darlin'."

"You have no idea how much I want that, Irish, but you need to go," I whisper.

He nods as he places a gentle kiss against my lips before walking away.

I turn and enter the building without looking back.

Tomorrow?

It's kill or be killed.

DYLAN

"What did you think of her?" Paddy's tone is indifferent, like he doesn't care, but it's obvious from the way he's been speaking with Cillian about her that he fucking does.

He's gotten in the back seat again, treating me like I'm some sort of taxi driver, which pisses me off. I grit my teeth but say nothing.

"It's difficult to say. I only spoke to her briefly."

"It was long enough for a first impression, so fucking tell me what you thought of her."

"Why is it so important to you?"

"You know why."

I look at him in the rear-view mirror. The youngest of us brothers and the first one looking to stand in front of old Father O'Reilly and take himself a wife. I can tell how much she means to him, and I guess the feeling's mutual as I've just had to bear witness to them eating each other's faces off outside her apartment. It was like they were never going to see each other again. Something's going on. I know they're hiding something. Or Jaine is and Padraig's party to it.

"I liked her."

He looks at me. "Is that it?"

"What else is there to say, Paddy? We were in the car together for just over half an hour, so it's not like we had a full-blown conversation."

"Do you think Da will like her?"

"Now you're asking. Does anyone know what goes on in that lunatic's head half the time? Does he even know? It changes every five minutes. You do know he's talking about marrying you off? And he doesn't like to change his plans, being the great outlaw chess master he thinks he is."

"Do you think he'll like her, Dyl?"

I look at him. "Aye. I think he will."

I'm being honest with him. Jaine was completely unfazed sitting in a car with two Dusters. Then again, she was as good as being Razr's old lady for four years and used to pretty much live on the Angels' compound in her younger days. That's important. Women-folk marrying in from the outside never survive this life mentally. We've witnessed it time and time again, hence why Da's forbidden any of us from getting wed to anyone not already part of it.

Jaine comes across as pretty fearless. Padraig just has to convince Da to meet her. Usually, once he's made up his mind about something, he won't budge though. He's already had all the paper-work drawn up detailing the alliance with the Sicilian mafia. Paddy should be grateful that the don's teenage sister is at least pretty. Who knows who the rest of us will end up with.

It's just as well he's Irish as he's going to need all the luck in the world trying to convince the old man to change his mind and go back on his already given gentleman's handshake with Luciano Ruocco. An agreement signed in blood that says our Padraig will marry his baby sister, Sophia.

You see, that's the shit that happens in your absence when you let yourself be kidnapped by the Bratva.

You give that nutcase free rein with your life, which he then proceeds to sign away just because he can.

CHAPTER FORTY-TWO

JAINE

Jaine's Apartment, Upper East Side, New York

"So, EVEN THOUGH I'M KILLING HIM FOR PUTTING MY POP IN AN early grave and for what the fucker did to me, the Dusters are still going to pay five million dollars?"

"That's what Cillian's told me, Jaine."

"Jesus Christ." I lean back in my leather chair in my home office. Like the rest of the apartment, and all the furniture is black with all the accessories in silver.

I'm on the phone with Delaney. It's business as usual where me, him, and the Scorpions are concerned. Until I decide what my future holds, if indeed I have one, I'll continue as I was before— representing the MC legally and carrying out my hits via Delaney. If it's not broken, why fix it? Just because we're not fucking anymore, doesn't mean we can't still work together. That's what he wanted, and that's what he's getting. If it becomes too much for him, I'm sure he'll let me know.

"I'm surprised. I mean, Irish knows I'm going to take out Lebedev anyway, so there was no need for them to pay. This one's on the house for everyone's sake." I won't say no to the payment, though. That would see us donate a huge sum to charity.

"I'm just telling you what I've been told. I've received an email from Cillian to confirm the amount and the name of the target. Once the deed is done, they'll transfer the monies across."

I exhale. "Well, that's all good and well, Delaney. The current problem we're facing, though, is where the fuck is Lebedev?"

"Well, as far as we know, he's not aware of what's happened or the fact that you're no longer a hostage. I spoke to Ace this morning, and there have been no missed calls on Sokolov's phone. The warehouse you were being held in has been cleaned up, but it's still intact. They'll raze it once the hit has been carried out so as not draw any unnecessary attention."

"So, there's been no recent sightings of Lebedev at all?"

"Nothing in the last week using the network of contacts and cams we have available to us."

"Jesus." We ponder in silence for a minute or two.

"Listen, Delaney, you keep checking. I'm going to put a call out to someone, see if they can help. Ideally, it needs to take place today. It's been forty-eight hours now, so it's time-critical."

"Will do, Jaine."

Jaine: *You about, Irish?*

Padraig: *I'm fitting some concrete shoes at the moment, darlin'. It's not a good time. It's a bit messy. You know—a combination of bodily fluids and wet cement.*

Jaine: *Do you have a contact number for Dylan? I need to ask him a favor.*

Padraig: *Don't tell me you prefer my anti-social brother to me now?*

Jaine: *Stop being a dick and give me his contact details.*

Padraig: *Not until you tell me you love me.*

Jaine: *I said, stop being a dick and give me his contact details!*

Padraig: *Not until you tell me you love me!*

Jaine: *You're busy.*

Padraig: *Never too busy to hear that.*

Jaine: *Fine. I love you.*

Padraig: *Say it like you mean it.*

Jaine: *WTAF? How can I say it like I mean it on a message?*

Padraig: *Record it so I can play it back.*

Jaine: *No! You'll play it back when other people are within earshot.*

Padraig: *So? Are you ashamed to admit it?*

Jaine: *Irish, I don't have time for this.*

Padraig: *Say it or I'm not giving you Dylan's details.*

Jaine: *You're a dick.*

Padraig: *You say the nicest things, now say the damn words, Jaine.*

Jaine: *Ooh, are you bossing me around?*

Padraig: *Would you want me to?*

Jaine: *Not answering that.*

Padraig: *You want me to dominate you, Jaine? You'd get off on that?*

Jaine: *Not answering that.*

Padraig: *You've just given me a hard-on. I can't even fuck my hand as it's covered in intestines.*

Jaine: *That's too much information.*

Padraig: *Your ass is mine. Once this is over, I'm going to bend you over, and I'm fucking taking it.*

Jaine: *Promises, promises.*

Padraig: *If you don't stop cock teasing. I'll come there now, slimy hands or not.*

Jaine: *I've sent the recording. Now give me the details and keep your slimy hands and your cock away from me and my virgin ass.*

Padraig: *Jesus Christ. Don't say that, darlin'.*

Jaine: *What?*

Padraig: *Virgin ass.*

Jaine: *Well, that's what it is.*

Padraig: *Fuck... Jaine! I'll send you his details now. I'll let him know you'll be in contact. What do you need him for?*

Jaine: *I need him to check his Batman files. Thank you. Love you, Irish.*

Padraig: *Love you too.*

Jaine: *Dylan, I need your help with something.*

Dylan: *What do you want?*

Jaine: *Charming.*

Dylan: *So, I've been told.*

Jaine: *Listen, I need you to check your Batman paraphernalia and see if you can locate Lebedev for me. We've reviewed our regular material, and he's not been sighted in the last week.*

Dylan: *Why do you need to know where he is?*

SHIT. DYLAN DOESN'T KNOW ABOUT MY OTHER ROLE.

Jaine: *You there?*

Padraig: *I'm always available for you, darlin'.*

Jaine: *We can't find Lebedev, and I need to carry out the hit asap. It's been forty-eight hours, so he's going to find out what's happened soon. Delaney spoke to Ace today, and there haven't been any missed calls on Sokolov's phone, so I'm guessing he's allowing time for the footage to be edited.*

Padraig: *And? What's the problem?*

Jaine: *Dylan is asking me why I need to know where he is.*

Padraig: *So? Tell him.*

Jaine: *I can't do that.*

Padraig: *He's my brother. I would never betray you. He would never betray me. He's not likely to pass over any intel without knowing why, Jaine.*

Jaine: *Fuck.*

Padraig: *I promise you on my ma and da's lives, neither he nor I will ever breathe a word. Not even to the rest of the family. Pinkie promise.*

Jaine: *Pinkie promise? What are we, five?*

Padraig: *Just say it.*

Jaine: *Okay! Pinkie promise. I'll call him. I can't put it on here.*

Jaine: *I need to call you Dylan.*

Dylan: *I'm busy.*

Jaine: *It's fucking urgent.*

Dylan: *No need to swear.*

Jaine: *Just answer the goddamn phone.*

I CALL HIS NUMBER THREE TIMES, AND HE DOESN'T ANSWER.

> **Jaine:** *?*
> **Dylan:** *You didn't say please.*
> **Jaine:** *Are you kidding me right now?*
> **Dylan:** *Nope.*
> **Jaine:** *Please!*

If he asks me to say it like I mean it like his asshole younger brother by fucking recording it, I'm going to put a bullet in his stubborn skull.

I call him again.

"Hello, Jaine." Over the phone, Dylan's Irish accent is stronger and more pronounced than Padraig's.

"Jesus, Dylan. This is important and time-critical!"

"Is there any need for all the swearing?"

"Yes. Yes, there is!"

"What do you want?"

"I need to know where Lebedev is, and I need to know where he is right fucking now."

"Why do you need to know that?"

"Because your *da* wants me to put a bullet between his eyes, Dylan. That's why."

"He wants The Exterminator to kill him."

"Yes, and to do that, I need to know where the fucker is."

"There's no way you're The Exterminator."

"Please feel free to verify that with Delaney or your brother."

There's silence.

"I'll phone you back."

"Please make sure you get it confirmed verbally, Dylan."

He calls back two minutes later.

"I'm looking for details now, Jaine. I'll call you back when I have any intel."

"Thank you. Oh, and Dylan?"

"Yes."

"This goes no further, or you know what will happen. A bullet engraved with an X will have your fucking name on it."

"No need for threats, Jaine."

"It's not a threat. I'm of sound enough mind to know not to threaten a Duster. Think of it as you and me being on a promise."

"I'll contact you when I have the intel."

"Appreciated."

Jaine: *Duke, have you got Ace's number?*

Duke: *I'll send it now.*

Dylan: *I have the details. They'll be with you within half an hour.*

Jaine: *Thank you. It's appreciated.*

Jaine: *I miss you.*

Ace: *Who the fuck is this?*

Jaine: *PJ.*

THERE'S A PAUSE. A SECOND. A MINUTE. AN HOUR? ANOTHER TEN fucking years?

Ace: *I miss you too.*

The right thing to do or not? I don't know, but I needed to send it. I can't lie to myself anymore. Or to him.

DYLAN

The Hudson Dusters' HQ, Manhattan, New York

"Paddy, you never told me your woman was The Exterminator."

"I only found out recently myself."

"You know if Da knows, he won't force you to marry the Sicilian. He'll be dead happy for you to marry The Exterminator. He'll think he's king of the hill if he adds the sniper to his brood."

"I know that."

"I can't believe the sharpshooter's female."

"What do you think of her now?"

"Same. I like her. Maybe a wee bit more now she's threatened to shoot me between the eyes if I tell anyone."

"That's my girl."

"Is she, though? Cill says she's also in love with a biker called Ace."

"Thanks for reminding me."

"Welcome."

CHAPTER FORTY-THREE

JAINE

Jaine's Apartment, Upper East Side, New York

THE INFORMATION PROVIDED BY DYLAN IS COMPREHENSIVE AND precise. I pull out the rest of the detail from the plain A4 brown envelope delivered to my apartment within half an hour of our telephone conversation. Efficient as fuck. I like it—a lot. Like me, it's clear he doesn't trust email.

I take in the images of the short, rotund man, whose bald head gleams above a ruddy face that looks like it wears a sneer permanently, as he's wearing one in every shot. Life has definitely not been kind to him if he's only my age. Either that, or he seriously needs to consider making better lifestyle choices.

"Why the fuck are you staying at the Russian Consulate, Lebedev?" I whisper to myself. Normally, I'd pander to my curiosity and try to work it out, but I have no time right now. I put the question to the back of my mind. I have other more pressing matters at hand, like simply working out how best to discretely shoot the child-molesting fucker.

I slam the palm of my hand down on my desk in frustration. I know for a fact that all the surrounding buildings will be heavily monitored, and there will be cameras everywhere, obviously in anticipation of any assassination attempts on any influential Russians.

Spoil fucking sports.

It will make it impossible for me to build a nest in a neighboring property, taking away the opportunity for me to shoot the fucker while he's still within the confines of the building. I have no choice. I'll have to nest further afield and hit him in the skull when he's outside the property and on the sidewalk. So, in full view of members of the public depending on the time of day. As a moving target, this also means the chances of me missing are significantly higher. I also have no control over when and *if* he leaves the building, which means having to stake him out until I can see him clearly through my scope. I can't pull the trigger beforehand. I can't afford to shoot the wrong person or hit an innocent bystander.

I could be waiting days, and my window of opportunity may only be seconds. If I get one.

And if I miss?

Shit, that doesn't even bear thinking about. He'd know it was me, and my secret would be revealed to the fucking masses.

Hit or miss, Russian vermin will start to spill out of the building like angry ants escaping a burning anthill, meaning I'll need to get out of dodge pronto.

This is not good. Nope. This is far from fucking ideal.

My rifle is ready, and I have several scopes packed. The case also contains enough energy bars and water to last three days.

There's a fleece hoodie for warmth, plus a pair of fingerless gloves to keep the heat in my hands, so they stay flexible and reactive. I'm dressed in blue jeans, a grey tank top, and a pair of old white sneakers. The days are warm, so I can't wear my usual all-black ninja-looking attire because I have no control over the timing of the hit, and I can't afford to stand out. I need to be able to blend in with the regular joes on the sidewalk. There will be zero opportunity to change.

Padraig: *Have you left yet?*
Jaine: *I'm just leaving now. Tell Dylan thanks again for the intel.*
Padraig: *Will do. Be careful. Let me know the address, and I'll have the cleaners there the minute you leave.*
Jaine: *I will. I'll be as careful as I can. I've done this hundreds of times, remember.*
Padraig: *My phone isn't leaving my hand.*
Jaine: *Glad to hear it's your phone. It usually your dick that never leaves your hand.*
Padraig: *This is no time for joking around, Jaine.*
Jaine: *Yes, Dad. You know the rules. Don't contact me. I'll contact you.*

For some reason, his concern is making me feel emotional to the extent I have to blink back tears. Self-pity? Time of the month? Goddamn hormones. I've never thrown myself a pity party since I was eighteen years old. I swore blind I'd never partake in another. That shit's for the weak and foolish.

It's nine a.m. Locking up my apartment, I swing the battered guitar case over my shoulder and make my way down in the elevator.

Russian Consulate, New York

I WALK TO THE TARGET AREA. IT'S NOT TOO FAR, AND IT ALLOWS ME to scope out the immediate vicinity more discretely. Walking past the frontage of the five-story limestone building, I slow my pace to get my bearings. Distance isn't the critical issue, although, the closer, the better when trying to hit a moving target. I need to build a nest that affords me the most prolonged timeframe to take aim and fire, so preferably from side-on.

Shielding my eyes from the morning sun, I look around.

Walking on a few blocks, I stop at a tired-looking grey stone property. Most of the windows are cracked or broken, and all of the frames need re-painting. The apartments look empty, at least from the outside, with the exception of the fifth floor.

"This will do me just fine," I mutter to myself. I press the door entry system.

"Hi, sorry. I'm meeting someone to view the apartment on the ground floor." I keep my voice chirpy and upbeat as I blatantly lie through my teeth.

I'm met with a grunt, and the door release button is pressed without question. Hopefully, the man who emitted the noise will keep himself to himself. I have a knife tucked into my shoe, and I know how to use it. You don't spend four years of your life with a flick blade-happy killer and not know how to use a sharp piece of metal, whether in self-defense or for murder. You do what you have to when it comes to survival.

The inside of the building smells of stale beer and piss, and I can't help but wrinkle my nose in disgust. My eyes are met with pale blue walls, which are poorly painted and adorned with graffiti. I don't pause to look around. Instead, I try the handle to the ground floor unit, only to find it locked. Making my way up the bare concrete steps, I try the handle on the first-floor apartment. The door clicks, and I push it open. As it looked from the outside, it is empty apart from some loose pieces of discarded furniture. I close the door quietly behind me. The air is stale, like it hasn't circulated in months, so it's obviously been empty for some time.

There's an old leather sofa and a table and chair set. Stuff that looks second or maybe even third hand. Beggars can't be choosers. I immediately get to work setting up my nest using what I have available and making sure I'm set far enough back from the window not to be seen by residents in any of the neighboring buildings.

Checking my scope to make sure I have a clear, uninterrupted view of the front of the Consulate building, I wait. And wait. And fucking wait.

My shoulders are tense, and I need to stretch, but I daren't move. It's been hours. I glance at my watch briefly. It's three p.m. I eat an energy bar. I need to go to the bathroom, but I daren't leave my position.

I keep my wits about me and stay focused. It's mentally exhausting doing nothing while having to concentrate. Another hour passes and then I see him. He looks exactly like the images. My hands are suddenly sweaty, no doubt caused by the fact my heart is now pounding. I have no choice but to wipe them down my jeans. I can't afford my fingers to slip. I take in the rotund child-abusing fucker. The one who would have married me off without a second goddamn thought to one of his chief funders. Who would have had me kill on demand on his behalf. I squeeze my finger on the trigger, but the scope fills with condensation as my face starts to flush, so I release it.

He steps into the waiting limousine, and he's gone. I've missed my opportunity. My heart sinks. How long until the next fucking one? What if he doesn't come back?

"For fuck's sake, Jaine." I tell myself off frustratedly. "You had the fucker in your sights, and you blew it." Tears prick my eyes again.

What the actual fuck is going on with me? Is it because I know this is a life and death situation? That if he spills his guts, I'm as good as dead? All the vermin that I've killed in my time, all of their contacts and *business associates,* will be after me. Rotting in jail or not, I will have a hefty price on my head given the atrocities I've carried out. I'll be lucky to survive twenty-four hours inside or out.

I have no choice but to wait. What else can I do?

Hours pass. Two a.m. Three a.m. Tick fucking tock. I desperately need to use the bathroom and end up pissing into an empty bottle. My legs keep cramping, my shoulders ache, and my brain is steadily going numb. Now I know the true meaning of brain dead since I've almost reached that point.

A car pulls up in front of the limestone building, and I check my sights. It's him. Lebedev. I rejoice internally, then curse myself as my heart starts to pound again. I say a silent prayer as I look through the scope. This is it. He walks briskly towards the entrance. Well, as briskly as you can for a fat fuck. I try to fix on him. Then he suddenly stops, and he looks straight at me. I know the fucker can't see me. But it's as if he knows I'm there. Like he can sense my presence. He knows his time's up. I squeeze the trigger, and I can almost see my engraved bullet parting the goddamn air as it makes its way forward to connect with his skull.

He falls to the ground. I don't look. Is he dead or not? I don't know. I just need to get the hell out of here.

I pack up as quickly as I can. I've no time to lose.

My hands are shaky as I take out my phone and send Padraig the address.

Padraig: *Got it. I'll have the cleaners there within five minutes.*

Jaine: *Thank you, Irish.*

Padraig: *I'll pick you up.*

Jaine: *You sure?*

Padraig: *I'm already here.*

CHAPTER FORTY-FOUR

JAINE

Russian Consulate, New York

TAKING ONE FINAL LOOK AROUND THE ROOM, I MAKE MY WAY
outside. In contrast to when I arrived, the temperature is frigid as
the night sky is so clear. The vehicle Dylan used previously is
already there and waiting, and its engine sparks to life.

Padraig obviously had me tailed today. By others, or did he do it
personally? Am I happy about it? I'm not too sure. I'll reflect on it
once this is over.

I walk across, open the door, and get in. A feeling of safety
immediately envelopes me. I lean across and place my guitar case
on the back seat as we drive off.

Inside, I'm shaking like a leaf, but I try to maintain my compo-
sure on the outside. Even with Padraig, I can't let my guard down
entirely. I can't let him see, for whatever reason, how much this hit
has affected me.

Flashing lights and wailing sirens pass us. Ambulances. Pigs. You name it. They're on their way to assist the deviant lying in a pool of his own blood on the sidewalk. The one that may or may not be dead. The one that doesn't deserve to be fucking saved.

"I'm not sure if it was a success or not, Irish. I had no way of telling." My voice is surprisingly calm and steady, even though I'm so wound up I could puke. A feeling of sickness almost overwhelms me, and I breathe as deeply and discreetly as I can in an attempt to make the need to heave pass. Maybe I'm coming down with something.

Padraig doesn't reply. I glance at him, and he's focused on driving and checking the mirrors. More and more, I'm starting to see the Hudson Duster in him. I can't help but admire him. He's so easy on the eyes. Insanely so. My stomach flips. My adrenaline is fired up, and I need a release.

I notice we're headed out of town. I don't mention it. There's no need for me to question why. He knows what he's doing. I trust him completely. We take a turn off the highway and then we're on uneven terrain, pulling up eventually in front of what looks like a small boating lake. I have no idea where we are. I don't care. I'm not in that stuffy apartment having to piss in a bottle while I go slowly insane listening to the tick-tocking of a clock that doesn't exist.

Unknown Location, New York

HE SWITCHES OFF THE CAR ENGINE, AND WE SIT IN DARKNESS. IT'S just us and the dashboard lights. That thought makes me smile, then tears prick my eyes again. I have a brief recollection of the song being played in the Angels' clubhouse what feels like a lifetime ago. My pop's face was grimacing in distaste at the words, and I shrugged because I didn't know what Meatloaf was referring to at the time.

"Now we sit, and we wait for news," Irish mumbles as he leans back against the headrest.

He's right, of course. That's the priority. If Lebedev isn't dead, we both know that I soon will be. I'll become a dead person walking.

I stare across the lake in front, watching as the moonlight kisses the surface, resulting in its watery silver reflection being bestowed back on itself. A lone owl hoots. It's peaceful. Tranquil. Still. Padraig reaches across and takes my hand in his, locking our fingers together. We sit in silence as they announce that a man has been gunned down outside the Russian Consulate.

No fucking shit, Sherlock.

"Why did you wait nine years, Irish? Why did you wait so long to tell me how you felt about me?" I ask the question that's been bugging me for weeks. I blurt it right out there. No time like the present. When death's staring you straight in the face, scythe in hand, you've got nothing to lose.

He squeezes my fingers.

"I thought you didn't love me, Jaine. Or at least not enough. That your heart still belonged to the boy from your childhood who didn't love you back." He turns to look out the window. "I couldn't let you go, though, so I made do with being your friend. Your confidant. The person you'd turn to when there was no one else. I needed to have you in my life in any way I could in the hope that maybe one day our friendship would turn into something more."

I nod. Did I feel the same? Is that why I never let him go either? He cheated. That was proof paramount that I wasn't enough. Plain Jaine was always second best, wasn't she?

"I mean, we've always flirted since. But when you went to Rising, when you said you wanted to Facetime and that you wanted to meet up, I guess I hoped that your feelings for me had changed and that you thought of me as more than a friend. More than just an Irishman who made you laugh and cheered you up every day.

"I'm aware I fucked up, Jaine. It's the single biggest regret of my life. But for that one fucking mistake, I've paid a nine-year penance. Surely that's enough."

I turn my attention out the window. The clear night means the sky is filled with a festoon of stars.

Is it enough, though?

Can I grant him his redemption? The peace he so clearly still seeks after all this time?

Once a cheater, always a cheater. Isn't that what they say? I know I can't ever forget, but can I forgive, or will I always feel inadequate because of it? I mean, I wasn't enough then, so why should I be now? I'm still the same person on the inside. Will I always doubt him? Can I trust him to be faithful? Even if he is, will my brain allow me to believe it, or will I start to think of him not only as a cheat but also as a liar? I'm certain he loves me, and I know I love him, but is that enough when the trust has gone? Will its absence see it peck away at the love between us until nothing remains? When not even our friendship can be salvaged? Am I willing to take a gamble and risk the latter? Will our friendship survive if I turn him down?

If I were to marry Irish, that would be it. The only way I'd leave that relationship would be in a wooden box. His family are strict Catholics. Marriage is for life. You also don't get to simply divorce a Hudson Duster if it doesn't work out. You don't get to throw in the towel and walk away, that's for sure.

Hours pass. It feels like days. My brain has ceased to function. My eyes no longer know how to blink as I've been awake for almost twenty-four hours. I look across at Padraig, and he's wide awake and staring straight ahead. Waiting. Like me. The next news update could be life changing.

Did I kill the fucker, or did I not? My brain is screaming now for the answer. Stop playing with me, God, and just fucking tell me. Put me out of my goddamn misery. I'll have done the world a favor by ridding it of the perverted scumbag. Please let him be dead. Forever fucking silenced. My secret will then remain so.

The news updates.

The individual gunned down outside the Russian Consulate is confirmed as an Igor Lebedev. Regrettably, he was dead on arrival at New York Presbyterian Hospital.

Irish switches the radio off.

I exhale. I feel like I've been holding my breath underwater since I left my house yesterday morning. Slowly drowning in the black abyss of my unknown future. Relief flows through me. I turn to look at Padraig. He's pushed his chair back, and his eyes are dark and dangerous. I squeal as he grabs me by the waist and yanks me across onto his lap, his mouth immediately covering mine. Hard. Demanding. Bruising. I groan in response, parting my lips to allow our tongues to tangle. My hands reach for his hair and pull on the inky strands as his roam my body. Touching. Teasing. Our mouths part only briefly as he lifts my tank top over my head. I groan as his hands unclasp my bra before cupping my tits and squeezing the nipples, causing my clit to throb painfully in response. Our lips part once more as I yank his black Henley off, and I groan as my hands come into contact with his smooth, hot flesh. My mouth drops to his neck to taste him, my teeth connecting to bruise him, causing him to flinch and growl in response.

He unfastens my jeans, and I push them down my legs and onto the floor while I unbutton his dick to freedom. He feels enormous in my hand, and his silky length throbs between my fingers, the tip dripping with pre-cum, which I rub around the crown. I kick off my underwear. No foreplay necessary. I'm fucking soaked. I rub the blunt head of his cock up and down my folds as he digs his hands into my hips. I lower myself onto his dick and let gravity take me all the way down, groaning as my pussy stretches to take him in. Fuck, he fills me so perfectly.

My pace is fast and furious. I wrap my arms around the headrest, and I fuck him hard. He curses and tries to slow me down, but I need the orgasmic fucking high, and I need it now. I position myself so my clit is rubbing against his groin as I ride him. The silence is filled with the sounds of our appreciative groans and our naked flesh slapping together.

I increase my movements, causing him to swear further, and I gasp as my center explodes, the spasms of pleasure radiating throughout my body. My pussy clenches tightly around him, and he roars his own satisfaction as his dick twitches in response and empties inside me.

We stay there, my head resting on his shoulder, and our sweaty bodies still joined until we start to cool. I place a kiss on his neck, licking the salty taste from my lips. In silence, I move back across to the passenger seat, cleaning myself off as best I can with my underwear before discarding it and pulling my clothes back on.

Both of us redress. I clamber back to sit in his lap, my arms around his neck and my face pressed against his throat. I need him close. No matter what the future holds for us, I know I need this man as much as I need air to breathe.

He wraps his arms around me, and I feel safe. I've never truly felt safe before now. Not like this. Not since I entered this fucked-up outlaw world. I inhale the smell that is my Irish, and I feel content.

"Our souls have always been intertwined. You feel that too, darlin'?"

I nod. I can't speak. My emotions are a fucking mess right now, and I know I'll sob. But yes, I feel it. He's my Irish. I love him. Want him. Need him.

But I know I don't trust him with my heart. Not yet. And I'm not sure I ever will.

Silent tears run down my face. I know he can feel them, but he doesn't mention them. We don't cry in this life. We both know that. But I can't seem to stop them from falling.

Sleep takes us.

I rest peacefully for the first time in weeks and wake to find myself still on his lap, our arms still wrapped around each other.

He's already awake and holding me close. Casting my eyes over him, I take in every last detail, and he does the same. Then, placing a gentle kiss against his lips, I slip back to the passenger seat.

It's time to go back.

Lebedev is dead. The next stop is Rising.

The next date on my calendar is for me to say goodbye to my pop.

And to see Ace.

CHAPTER FORTY-FIVE

ACE

The Angels of Hellfire Clubhouse, Rising, California

"COME IN."

I enter my old man's office and take a seat on the chair facing him. Sunlight streams in through the window. At least he's started opening the curtains again. Started living again. I even caught Darla sneaking out of his bedroom this morning.

"You see the news, Ace? About Lebedev?"

I nod. "Seen it. I'll set Clay and Jefferson on with razing the warehouse in Fielding. We'll make it look like an electrical fault. It's been valued, so we'll be able to donate the sum to cover the cost of the property and rebuild, plus a little extra for the owner's inconvenience."

He nods, looking thoughtful. "Anyone been asking questions about Bomb or Em?"

I shake my head. "Nothing. I guess they all suspect they were behind the betrayal now, so what's to ask? All the corpses have been fed to the pigs, and anything left has been turned into soup and drained away. Chance has taken care of cleaning up the shed, so it looks like the bloodbath never happened."

He nods again. "Well, Jainie did good. Lebedev can't have been an easy target to hit right in the middle of New York and at street level. The Dusters are paying five million dollars for the privilege. Old Fergal is over the moon with the sniper and is looking to hire *him* for other problematic business acquaintances. Let's hope he never classes us as one, although I think we'd be safe from lil Jainie's bullets."

He chuckles, then rests his feet on his desk and shakes his head. "I still can't wrap my head around it, son."

I exhale. "Me neither." I don't think it will ever fully sink in what PJ does in her spare time. I didn't want to tarnish her with the blood I have on my hands, but shit, she's wearing more than me. "It's not been announced yet that The Exterminator killed the Russian, so we have to keep that to ourselves for the time being."

He frowns as he looks over at me. "How you holding up, son?"

I shrug. "About Em? She got what she deserved. She spilled her guts. If I hadn't cut her throat, Razr would have."

"Is that the only reason you did it?"

I shake my head. "Nope. She betrayed me ten years ago by lying to PJ. Not saying that it would have made any difference to the eventual outcome between us, but it won't have helped the situation."

"You going to try to win her back?"

"Damn right I am. Shouldn't have let her go in the first place."

Ace: *You there?*

Jaine: *What, at the end of my phone? Where else would I be?*

Ace: *I heard the news.*

Jaine: *That's not a discussion for this number. I'll message from the other.*

Jaine: *This is my burner phone.*

Ace: *You want me to save the number.*

Jaine: *I'll leave that up to you, Ace. You're a big boy now. You can make grown-up decisions.*

Jaine: *Was that all you wanted to say?*

Ace: *Kinda.*

Jaine: *Kinda? Wow? Could you be any vaguer?*

Ace: *I'm sorry.*

Jaine: *For what? There's a long list of shit you should be sorry for. Which one do you want me to offset that lonely single apology against?*

Jaine: *Ace?*

Jaine: *?*

Ace: *For all the shit with Emilia. For all the hurt I caused you.*

Jaine: *So, you want me to allocate that one apology to every occasion you behaved like an asshole?*

Ace: *Yeah.*

Jaine: *I'll have to spread that fucker so thin it'll be transparent.*

Ace: *I realize that.*

Jaine: *Anything else?*

Ace: *The funeral's confirmed. Will you get here before, or will you arrive on the day?*

Jaine: *I haven't decided yet. I'm just taking some time off. I need to clear my head after all the recent events.*

Ace: *You seen Padraig?*

Jaine: *Yesterday.*
Ace: *Right.*
Jaine: *Why do you ask?*
Ace: *No reason.*
Jaine: *Right...you sure you're not...?*
Ace: *I'm not what?*
Jaine: *Doesn't matter.*

THERE'S A PAUSE.

Ace: *Sorry, I'm no good at small talk, PJ.*
Jaine: *You don't say.*
Jaine: *Sorry, Ace. I take that back. That was unfair of me.*
Ace: *It's ok. I deserve it.*
Jaine: *No, you don't. Turns out you didn't actually do anything wrong. Turns out I hung an innocent boy judging by Emilia's last words.*
Ace: *I know. I told you that at the time.*
Jaine: *?*
Ace: *In the messages I sent and voicemails I left. I explained everything. You just didn't listen. Couldn't or wouldn't. Likely wouldn't because you're stubborn like that.*
Jaine: *Then I guess I'm the one who should be sorry, Ace. I'm the one who should be apologizing, not you.*
Ace: *It doesn't matter now. What's done is done. Clay and Jefferson are taking care of the warehouse. You may need to smooth things over with Simons, but everything else has been cleaned up.*
Jaine: *Thank you.*
Ace: *No problem. Well, guess I should get going. Good-bye PJ.*
Jaine: *Goodbye, Ace.*

I stare at my phone. I'm no good at messaging. I'm no good at talking just for the sake of talking, either. As much as we may look alike, Padraig and I are complete opposites when it comes to being sociable and saying what needs to be said. I don't have the gift for conversing easily like he does. Not anymore. I used to when I was younger. Before *she* left. Before I stopped caring about anything.

There's so much more I want to tell her. So much I need to explain, but I don't know how or where to start. I don't know how to put into words the shit that's floating around in my fucked-up head. I tried in the voicemails and messages, but that moment's passed. It's all ten years too fucking late.

Am I jealous she saw him yesterday? Probably fucked him. Damn right I am.

But then, would she want to be with me? I mean, what can I offer her? I'm not poor by any means, but I don't have the billions that Padraig has. Even if I did, what would I spend it on? I live in Rising. I always will. There's nothing here. Nothing changes. With him, she could live a flash life in New York. Be part of *the* celebrity legal couple of Manhattan if that's what she wanted. They have so much more in common.

Both intellectuals. Both people persons.

She'd never want to give any of that life up, would she? I've nothing to offer but me and a life she left behind ten years ago.

I run my hands through my hair in frustration. I wish I'd had the chance to go off and do something different, but my fate was mapped out when I was born the son of a president of an MC. You do what your father did before you in this life. You don't get to decide. Do I resent it? Hell yeah. But I can't change it, so I've learned to accept that it is what it is.

Is it enough? Am *I* enough?

I mean, I love her. Have done since I was eight years old when she stood in front of me, all bashful and shy.

I remember the day like it was yesterday. She thought her smile wasn't pretty and that I'd make fun of her, but all I saw were big green eyes the color of a meadow and hair like spun gold.

She was tall for a girl even then, and she was the prettiest thing I'd ever seen.

"I'm Jason, and I'm eight." I'd held my hand out to her. I'd taken the scowl off my face first so as not to scare her, then smiled the best I could, even though after losing my mom I didn't really have much to smile about. I'd kind of forgotten how.

"I'm Jaine, and I'm seven," She stared back at me all wide-eyed, then after running her little hands down her pale blue summer dress, she shook mine. Hers were clean, and mine were dirty. I could tell she wanted to play and get hers dirty too.

She looked over at our pops, and I'd turned to look at them too. They were smiling, slapping each other on the back, laughing real loudly and looking like they hadn't seen each other in forever.

"My pop's not smiled in ages. Not since my mom went to heaven," she said quietly, and a tear ran down her little face.

I looked at her and saw her pain. She was living a torment that mirrored my own. I walked closer and lost myself in those big green eyes of hers that were full to brimming with unshed tears. I wiped the fallen ones from her cheeks.

"My mom's in heaven too, so maybe they're best friends now?"

She smiled shyly, obviously liking that idea. "Yes, for sure they are." Then, forgetting, she'd accidentally shown her teeth, she looked really cute when her cheeks went red, and she put her small hand over her mouth.

"What you hiding your smile for, Jaine? It's real pretty," I told her, trying to make her feel better.

She'd smiled back at me, and her cheeks went even redder, which made me feel real good.

"You think if our pops are best friends, and our moms are, that we could be best friends too?" I'd asked her. Suddenly, I felt shy. I never felt shy, but I wanted her to say yes more than anything. What if she didn't?

"Sure." She answered so quietly I could barely hear her. I was so goddamn relieved.

"You want to go to the river? I can show you how to skim stones." She'd looked at me, her face full of longing, and I knew she desperately wanted to go play. Maybe she needed a friend as much as I did.

She nodded and smiled, showing her teeth without trying to hide them this time.

"Race ya, then, slow poke!" I ran off, leaving her to play catch up.

It was right then I knew I loved Jaine Jones.

JAINE

Jaine's Apartment, Upper East Side, New York

I STARE AT MY PHONE. I KNOW ACE IS NO GOOD AT MESSAGING OR at conversing these days. A far cry from the teenager who used to spend his life with his face in his phone. He's the type that only speaks when he has something worthwhile to say now, and only then if he feels comfortable saying it. He's the complete opposite of Irish, who loves the sound of his own voice so much I'm sure he holds conversations with himself just so he can hear the damn thing.

I frown—these voicemails and text messages. I need access. I need to know what Ace said when I ran away all those years ago. I'm kicking myself now for not reading or listening to them, but was it for the best? What would have happened if I had? We'll never know. In some ways, it was maybe a Godsend. Being apart allowed us the chance to develop and grow as individuals. We'd never have been able to do that joined at the hip the way we were.

I type in the number for the mobile phone company. Better late than never.

"Yes, good morning. This is Jaine Jones from Jones & Associates Legal. I need some information on a number. The details I need are from around ten years ago. Text messages and voicemails, etc. Are you able to provide this, please?... Yes, it's for legal purposes." I blatantly lie. "You are? That's fantastic."

PADRAIG

Padraig's Apartment, Hudson Yards, New York

Dylan: *Your woman did good, Paddy.*
Padraig: *Jesus Christ, are you dishing out compliments, Dyl?*
Dylan: *To her. Not to you.*
Padraig: *Cheers. So, you approve of her?*
Dylan: *What's not to approve? You're punching.*
Padraig: *Nice to know.*
Dylan: *Are you still thinking of introducing her to Da?*
Padraig: *After she buries hers this weekend.*
Dylan: *Will you be going?*
Padraig: *Aye. He was the lawyer for the Angels. Cillian will be going too.*
Dylan: *I'm not sure introducing Jaine to the old man is such a good idea unless you're planning on dropping The Exterminator bombshell.*
Padraig: *You know I can't do that, and neither can you.*
Dylan: *I gave my word. I will honor it. Da's looking to*

*speak to you about your arranged marriage with Ruocco's
sister, just so you know. I overheard Eoin on the phone
with him.*

Padraig: *I'm not marrying her. You marry her.*

Dylan: *She's seen us all, and you're the one she's got her
heart set on. Plus, you're closest in age. Apparently, what
Sophia wants, Sophia gets. She's a spoiled brat, but a stun-
ning one.*

Padraig: *Then she'll just have to be disappointed. She'll
need to accept someone else.*

Dylan: *Have you told Jaine about her?*

Padraig: *Why would I?*

Dylan: *Da will want it done now he's given his word to
Ruocco. He'll expect you to court the girl and get to know
her over the next two years.*

Padraig: *Well, that's tough, because as soon as this funeral's over and we're back in Manhattan, I'll be asking Jaine
to be my wife.*

Dylan: *You're dancing with the devil, Paddy. This is all
going to blow up. I really wish it wasn't as I like Jaine, but
don't say I didn't warn you.*

CHAPTER FORTY-SIX

JAINE

Oak Lodge Hotel, Depling, California

I HAVEN'T SPOKEN TO ANYONE FOR DAYS. I JUST NEEDED SOME ONE-on-one time with myself ahead of today's big event.

Burying my pop.

The world news is The Exterminator took the Lebedev trash out. Delaney's confirmed old Fergal has now paid his dues. Apparently, he's got a list of people he wants rid of. No surprise there. I've told Delaney to agree in principle that I'll take a look at the names, but I'll only consider them if they're scum. I'm not getting rid just because he's got a personal vendetta against someone. Given how easy it is to piss the old Irishman off, I'd wind up having to eradicate half of Manhattan. I refuse to become his personal sharpshooter, no matter how much Mr. O'Connell Senior is willing to pay.

I'm staying in a hotel in the larger town of Depling, which is around fifty miles outside Rising. I collected my hog from home yesterday when I handed my house keys to Jethro, the local handyman. He'll pack up the contents and place them into temporary storage, then give the property some TLC both inside and out. New electrics, plumbing, and any other building work that needs doing, all finished off with white walls and dark grey floors. The pool will also be replaced in its entirety. All this is to take place over the next four weeks. My pop was a wealthy man, but he didn't like to spend.

So, the place will be a blank canvas. A new start. That's if I ever decide to move back to Rising.

I'll worry about that tomorrow. Let's get today over with first.

Checking my appearance in the mirror, I take in the tall, too-slim blonde. I'm wearing black jeans, long leather boots, and a black tank top, finished off with my old leather jacket bearing the Angels' patch.

I won't stand out. There'll be bikers galore from all over attending Pop's funeral. The Angels will be there, and I suspect many of the Scorpions too. The Dusters? I'm not sure. Since taking out the Russian trash, I've kept my messages to Padraig down to one per day. Just to let him know I'm alive more than anything. He hasn't pressured for more which I'm grateful for. I figure he's realized I needed a break. From everyone and everything. Including him.

I take in the scenery as I ride to the cemetery. Familiar sights and the smell of wildflowers bring back memories of my childhood. I blink back the emotional tears. I can't cry, even though it's all I seem to be doing these days.

I know I'm running late, but I don't care. There's only one person who matters, and he's not going anywhere. He's waiting to be lowered into his final resting place. Everyone else? Well, as much as I appreciate them attending to pay their last respects, today isn't about them. Most will use this as an excuse to get drunk and fuck the cum sluts until they can barely walk.

I pass the signs for Rising and head towards the cemetery. The streets are empty. Everyone will be attending. My pop was Catholic, so old Father Reynolds will be conducting the service. Not sure I've ever told Irish I was raised Catholic. I'm not practicing. I'm sure the church would burst into fucking flames if my condemned soul were ever to enter the holy place.

Rising Cemetery, Rising, California

THE FAMILIAR GREY STONE PILLARS OF THE ENTRANCE ARE AHEAD. The overhanging black wrought ironwork twisted to say Rising Cemetery lets me know I've reached my destination. One day, hopefully not too soon, it will be my final one.

As a child, I always loved the peace and tranquility of this place and spent hours rubbing the moss off some of the older headstones and reading the inscriptions. The poignant final words spoken silently between the living and the dead. Telling them how loved they were and how missed they'd be. I never thought I'd be burying my pop when he was still a relatively young man.

Having recently purchased a large family plot, I ride straight down the small road which leads to the area farthest from the entrance. It has fabulous uninterrupted views of Rising, and I've made a considerable donation to the church funds to ensure that sight is never spoiled. Not for the dead's benefit. For the living. For those who may or may not choose to visit. I'll be laid to rest here one day, and there's space for Duke and Ace too, plus several others.

I guess funerals make you realize nothing is forever. It's not morbid. It's just the harsh reality of life. At some point, we all fucking die, and we have to prepare for that eventuality.

My heart swells with pride when I take in the hundreds of bikers who have shown up to pay their last respects to my pop. I swallow the lump in my throat as I also take in much of the adult population of Rising. It's then I see the casket cloaked in a flag bearing the Angels' insignia. I wish he could see this turnout just for him—this visual. Maybe he can.

"I love you, Pop. I miss you so fucking much," I whisper, my voice breaking.

All eyes turn in my direction as my Softail makes its way down. There's a space reserved for me between Duke and Ace. Duke's wearing dark glasses. This day will be as hard for him as it is for me. He's lost his best friend. It would be the equivalent of me losing Ace or Irish. Neither bear thinking about. The entire Scorpions' council is in attendance. Padraig is also here, and I'm guessing the striking red-haired man beside him is Cillian. Not that I've ever met him, but he's the only brother who has the auburn hair of his ma, or so I'm told.

Switching off my hog's engine after I've parked up, I remove my half-helmet, kick down the stand, and get off. I leave my avia-tors in place. It's easier to hide that way.

Duke embraces me in a fatherly hug, and I almost lose it there and then.

"How are you holding up, Jaine?" Father Reynolds asks me quietly as he wraps his arms comfortingly around my shoulders.

"I'm doing okay, Father. Thank you." I nod and smile at the tall, slim man in front of me, who I've known since I was seven years old. To me, he's always been as old as Methuselah himself. He's never changed. His aged complexion and sparkling blue eyes compliment his kind, concerned smile, while the gentle breeze almost dislodges his thinning white comb-over.

Sasha and Cherry make their way over and stand beside me, dressed head to toe in designer black. Each holds one of my hands, which they squeeze encouragingly. It feels like I haven't seen them in ages, but it's only been two weeks or so. A lot has happened in that time. Much of which I'd sooner forget.

I look at the dark walnut casket that contains the earthly remains of my pop, and I listen to Father Reynolds. I try to take in what he's saying. I try to believe. I try to find my faith. In the end, my bitter and twisted soul can only take comfort from the fact I put his killer to ground. When I get to hell, I'll end the fucker over and over again.

When the service is over, everyone who carries raises their gun to the sky. Three shots are fired. As his kin, I walk across to Pop's casket, and I wrap a St. Christopher around my Glock and place it on top. Both will be buried with him to keep him safe on his travels, wherever they may take him.

The crowd starts to filter away. Rising's residents back to their homes. The bikers off to the Angels' clubhouse.

"We'll see you back at the compound," Sasha says as she hugs me close, covering me in whatever designer fragrance she's wearing these days.

"Take all the time you need, Jaine," Cherry adds as Jefferson and Blaze flank her. I'm guessing she's fucking them both now.

I nod.

"I'm so sorry, baby." Delaney wraps his arms around me, and I feel comforted momentarily by his familiar scent. I look up at him, and he kisses my forehead. Again, I feel overwhelmed with the urge to cry. I watch as Sasha leads him away. I find myself wondering if they're together now, or if they ever will be.

Finally, it's just me and Pop's casket, which, once I've said my goodbyes, will be lowered into the ground. Earth to earth. Ashes to ashes. Dust to fucking dust.

I don't speak. I just rest my hand on top, and I let the memories filter through my brain, storing them away as safely and securely as I can, knowing I can't ever make any more. My pop will always be fifty-eight. He'll never get any older. That fucking sucks.

I'm not sure how long passes. Minutes. Hours.

I drift back to my shitty reality and notice the cemetery workers still waiting patiently, their expressions kind and understanding. They're not rushing me or anything, but the sun is setting, and they have families to go home to. Unlike me. I have no one.

I suddenly find myself flanked by Ace and Padraig. Have they been here the whole time? Did they leave and come back?

I'm in love with two men. I mean, how is that even possible? As if my life's not complicated enough. How can I ever choose between them?

I turn, and I look at my beautiful boy with hair like the midnight sky and eyes as blue as the bluest thing ever. My eyes drift over him. I step forward and press my lips against his, parting mine to allow his tongue to thrust into my mouth. I savor the taste of him and the pain caused by his fingers digging into my hips. I groan as he pulls me against his erection. Finally, our mouths part, and my gaze drifts over his swollen lips, resting on his eyes that are now dark with desire.

I turn then, and I look at my Irish. He looks hurt and confused. I smile softly, then walk across and press my mouth to his. His hands immediately snake around my waist as he kisses me hard, his tongue filling my mouth as he growls against my lips, cupping my ass to pull me against him. I'm panting when he finally lets me go.

I look between them both.

"I'm going back to my hotel. Are you coming or not?"

CHAPTER FORTY-SEVEN

JAINE

Oak Lodge Hotel, Depling, California

"Keep the boots on, darlin'."

I turn to look at Padraig, and he's wearing a smirk on his face, which I can't help but return. Cheeky Irish fucker that he is. He's discarded his suit jacket and shoes and is sitting on the cream two-seat leather sofa with his hands behind his head and his feet resting on the small glass table in front like he owns the fucking place. If this hotel were in Manhattan, he probably would. The appearance would also be considerably more appealing if it were a Dusters' establishment. Still, this is as good as it gets in these parts. The hotel has this one suite which consists of a double bedroom and a living area with the whole color scheme finished in shades of seventies-inspired bleach your fucking eyeballs beige. A bit like my pop's home before I instructed the essential makeover.

Said boots are shiny zipped black leather and finish well above the knee. I guess the four-inch heels do add a bit of sexy to my overall look of the day. Not that I was aiming for that by any means, but still. I switch my attention to Ace. As usual, his impassive expression gives nothing away. A man of so much fucking hot action, but so few words. I'd love to know what's going on inside that beautiful bad boy head of his. Maybe if he shared it, we wouldn't be in this shitty situation. Then again, he did, and I just didn't listen.

"Ace? You have a preference?"

He shrugs, then he and Irish make brief eye contact before smirking at each other. "Well, they definitely are fuck-me boots, sweetheart."

I roll my eyes at them as I make my way into the bathroom, trying to keep the smile off my face. I need to shower off the smell of Rising Cemetery first.

When I asked them to come back to the hotel, they had stared at me, then each other, most likely wondering if I was being serious or not. It wasn't pre-planned. Maybe it was a rash decision, but my thinking was, depending on what my future holds, I may never get to fuck one or perhaps either of them ever again. Ever again could prove to be a long time. That shit's not a fairytale ending by any means. Not that I expect one. Or deserve one. But still. You also only live once, and you don't get to decide for how long. If nothing else, today proves that. So, if an opportunity comes your way, grab that fucker with both goddamn hands. If it comes your way twice in one day, then grab both.

That's what I'm doing—grabbing both. Rightly or wrongly.

This is a first for me. Being the meat in a very hot outlaw sandwich. It won't be the first time they've shared a woman, though. Even as a nineteen-year-old, Irish would regale me with stories of what his brothers got up to. Meaning he had done in the past too. Not that he ever admitted as much. As for Ace? It's an everyday occurrence in the MC world to witness the cum sluts having all three holes filled at once. Hands and tits too, when they were needed, depending on the number of dicks they were servicing at any one time. He'll have shared with his brothers more times than I'd be able to count. Thankfully, I haven't had to bear witness to that sort of visual with Ace as a willing participant, but I've seen plenty of the other brothers share a cum slut on way too many occasions.

I dry myself, then put on a pair of black lace panties and my boots. I leave my wet hair hanging down my back. It will take too long to dry, and I don't want to wait. I'm pretty sure they don't want to either.

Staring at myself in the full-length mirror, I take in my almost naked body. I wish I had fuller hips and bigger tits, but overall, I'm happy these days with what God gave me now I've filled out a little. I do my best to look after it too.

I'm about to open the bathroom door when I suddenly feel anxious. Is this the right thing to do? Am I blurring lines? Confusing myself? Confusing them? Will any good come of this? Who knows? Maybe I'll regret it in the morning. Maybe immediately after. Perhaps they will. Perhaps we all will. All I know is, in my gut, this feels like the right thing to do. For some reason, I just know the opportunity will never arise again.

Opening the door, I step out and walk to the middle of the room. Two icy blue gazes trail over my flesh, making my skin feel red hot while causing it to prickle and shiver at the same time. I look at Ace, who's stripped to just his black jeans. He's staring at me with eyes filled with so much carnal lust I instantly feel light-headed as all my blood heads to my core. My eyes graze over his taut and beautifully inked upper body, then drop to where his slim hips and muscular thighs are displayed to perfection in the snug-fitting denim. My hands are itching to touch him. My mouth is watering to taste him. He walks across slowly until he's inches from me.

"You sure about this, PJ?" He bends his head down so his mouth hovers over mine, his breath so hot it almost scalds my lips.

I nod.

"Say the damn words." Intense blue eyes bore into mine, waiting for me to give him the green light. Asking me to confirm that I'm okay with what we're all about to do.

"I'm sure, Ace."

He gently pushes back my hair and traces the outline of my tattoo before pressing his lips against it. I shiver in response. Moving his hand, he splays his fingers across the nape of my neck before pulling my lips against his. His mouth is hard, and his tongue immediately takes ownership. I don't fight him for control. I give it willingly. We both want the same thing.

Abso-fucking-lution.

Our tongues tangle and taste as he steals the oxygen from my body. Fisting my hair, he pulls my head back and places wet kisses from my jaw down my neck before his tongue dips lower and flicks over my nipple. I groan, pushing my tits against his mouth. Wanting more. Needing more. He chuckles softly, tickling my skin with his warm breath, then tugs on the needy tip with his teeth before biting it painfully, the resultant bolt of desire causing my clit to throb.

I open my eyes and let them drift to Padraig. I swallow as I take him in. He's sitting in black suit pants with his shirt fully unbuttoned. The contrast between the crisp, clean whiteness of the fabric and the dirty darkness of his inked skin looks all kinds of wrong and all kinds of fucking right. A saint on the outside with a murderous sinner at the very core. My mouth waters just looking at him.

"You just going to sit there and watch, Irish?" I'm almost breathless. Fuck, I want him. I gasp as Ace sucks on my neck while running his fingers slowly down my sides, causing my core to flutter. Deliciously. Uncontrollably. His hand drops further to cup my pussy through my now drenched underwear. I close my eyes and embrace the sensations as he circles my clit torturously slow.

The hair from the back of my neck is moved, and warm lips gently caress the sensitive flesh, making me shiver. I gasp as Irish's hands move to cup my tits, his thumbs rubbing the tender buds into hard peaks. His fingertips slowly trace down my spine, causing me to arch my back and press my ass against his very evident hard-on.

"You going to give me what I want, darlin'?" His breath is hot against my ear as his hands drop to my ass. He kneels on the floor, then slowly slides my underwear down my legs, letting me step out. Pulling my cheeks apart, he runs his fingers slowly between them.

"You're fucking perfect, Jaine, you know that?" His voice is husky, and my skin tingles in response. He parts my cheeks further, his tongue rimming my asshole. The sensation feels strange as he kisses and sucks there before gently pressing his tongue against the tight opening. I'm not a prude. I've just never had anal sex, and I know that's what Irish is chasing. I close my eyes and allow the unfamiliar sensations to flow through me. I want to give him what he craves. Ace drops to his knees. He deliberately tortures my clit with his warm breath. So near. So far.

"Ace, don't fucking tease me."

He sucks it into his mouth and thrusts two fingers inside my slick pussy. I gasp and grab his hair, our eyes remaining connected as he feasts on me. My legs begin to shake as his fingers thrust faster and deeper, and he stands and snakes his arm around my waist to hold me steady. I part my legs further as the orgasm approaches, and as I reach the dizzy heights, Irish stands and pushes a finger inside my ass, causing the feelings to intensify. I gasp loudly in satisfaction as he replaces one with two. It no longer feels like an intrusion, more a sort of unknown pleasurable pressure that I don't yet know where it will lead.

"You like that, darlin'?" His breath is hot in my ear.

I groan in response as he increases his finger thrusting as Ace removes his. Closing my eyes, I lean my head back against Irish's shoulder, welcoming the feel of his hardness behind me.

"Ride me, sweetheart." Ace motions to where he's now sitting on the sofa.

I straddle him, and he pulls me forward, his tongue filling my mouth, his leaking, throbbing erection pressed between our naked bodies. Positioning his cock at my entrance, I lower myself down onto him, groaning loudly as he fills me. Holding onto my hips, he immediately starts to thrust upwards, staking his claim. His tongue tangles with mine before his mouth drops to suck in my nipple, causing me to grind harder against him.

"Lean her forward, Ace."

Ace pulls my upper body towards him, adjusting my position so my legs are slightly more parted, all the while continuing to relentlessly drive into me.

A cool liquid is poured between my ass cheeks. I've no idea what it is. Lube probably. I'm past caring.

Fisting my hair, Irish pulls my head back, his lips seeking mine, his tongue filling my mouth.

"If it hurts, we'll stop, darlin'." His breath is warm against my now swollen lips.

Spreading my cheeks apart with his hands, I feel his erection press against my rear.

"Don't tense up, Jaine. Just relax." I hold my breath as he pushes into me. "Breathe, darlin'." His voice is thick with desire.

It feels strange, and my instinct is to push the intrusion back out, but he inches forward until his thickness is fully sheathed inside me.

"Fuck, you're so tight." He grunts and pants almost like he's in pain. "You okay, darlin'?"

I nod. I can't speak. I'm so fucking full of dick.

His thrusts are short and steady to begin with, and his movements cause both their cocks to press against every single erogenous zone I have down there. The first orgasm hits me unexpectedly, causing Ace to curse loudly as my pussy clenches tightly around him.

Padraig grips my hips and drives harder and faster, knowing my body is now receptive to his dick being in my ass. I groan, and he leans over me and presses a kiss against my shoulder, his sweat dripping deliciously down my back. I so want to lick it off him.

Ace thrusts deeper, and that slight movement causes his dick to rub against my sweet spot. Every part of me clenches as another orgasm rips through me, decimating every single one of my nerve endings. I whine loudly as I drown in waves of pleasure.

Padraig swears and thrusts harder, his fingers moving to circle my clit while Ace sucks painfully on my nipples. Padraig fists my hair with his other hand and yanks my head back, biting hard on my neck.

The combination of pleasure and pain pushes me over the edge, and I cry out as I tighten around Ace again, causing him to growl and swear loudly in his own satisfaction as he empties deep inside me in short, steady thrusts.

Padraig's fingers dig into my skin as he slams into me, reaching for his own end. The sound of flesh slapping against flesh fills the room. He roars and curses, his movements becoming erratic before they slow as he spills his hot seed.

I'm fucking spent. I can't move, and I'm literally filled with cum.

"Jesus," I whisper.

"It's Padraig, actually." He chuckles as he wraps his arms around my waist and places gentle kisses behind my neck. Ace grabs my hair and pulls my lips down to meet his, his tongue filling my mouth possessively.

"You're an asshole, O'Connell." I snicker as I nuzzle into Ace's neck, my tongue flicking out to lick the saltiness off his skin.

"I may be one, but yours has just been well and truly fucked."

I laugh out loud. "Jesus Christ."

"I've already told you, Jaine, The Almighty had nothing to do with it." He chuckles again as he gently pulls out. He walks naked to the bathroom and brings back a towel, then we clean ourselves down before redressing in silence.

The heady endorphins are starting to leave my body, and I'm coming down from the natural high I was on. I think that applies to us all. What happened was a one-off. It will never be repeated. We all know that.

Maybe it wasn't such a good idea after all, though. Or perhaps I'm now just in a melancholy mood. My emotions are all over the place these days.

I think they can both sense that I want to be alone.

They leave at the same time—Ace heading back to Rising on his hog and Padraig to the airport.

I'M STILL AWAKE AND STARING AT THE CEILING TWO HOURS LATER.

Padraig: *I'm on my way back to New York now. You've been quiet. Is everything ok?*
Jaine: *Yes.*
Padraig: *Did I hurt you?*
Jaine: *Mentally?*
Padraig: *No.*
Jaine: *Physically?*
Padraig: *Yes. In fact, either?*
Jaine: *No.*

Padraig: *Why am I getting one-word answers?*
Jaine: *No reason.*
Padraig: *Do you regret what happened, Jaine?*
Jaine: *I'm not sure.*
Padraig: *Jesus Christ.*
Jaine: *What?*
Padraig: *It's what you fucking wanted to happen.*
Jaine: *You didn't?*
Padraig: *No.*
Jaine: *What do you mean?*
Padraig: *I don't want to share you with anyone else, darlin'.*
Jaine: *Oh. Do you think Ace felt the same way?*
Padraig: *I don't really care how the other fella felt. I'm telling you how I felt.*
Jaine: *I'm sorry. It seemed like a good idea at the time.*
Padraig: *And now I'm linked to one of your regrets?*
Jaine: *I said I'm not sure if it's a regret.*
Padraig: *Shall I ask them to turn the plane around?*
Jaine: *I don't think there's any need for that.*
Padraig: *There's every fucking need if you're full of regret over what just happened.*
Jaine: *Why all the drama?*

My phone vibrates and I immediately answer. If I don't, he'll keep calling until I do.

"Do you have any idea how much I fucking love you, Jaine Jones? Do you? I just wanted you to hear me say it out loud once more, so maybe you'll finally be convinced. I don't want you to have *any* regrets where I'm concerned."

"You sound angry, Irish. I don't think I've ever heard you angry before." I chuckle and try to lighten the mood. It doesn't work.

"Of course I'm fucking angry! You made me share you with

another man, and we O'Connell's don't share our women. And now, to top it all off, you have regrets over it."

"Then why didn't you say no?" I'm yelling now.

"I did it for you! It was what you wanted! Once we're married, that will never fucking happen again. Every part of you will belong to me and only me!"

"Oh yeah? Well, who says I'm going to marry you and become your goddamn possession, you arrogant Irish Duster fucker!"

"I say it, Jaine!"

"Well, you can kiss the ass you just fucked! I wouldn't marry you if you were the last man in fucking Manhattan!"

"Stop being childish. Sweet Baby Jesus, what's gotten into you recently, darlin'?"

"Don't you darlin' me!"

"I'll do more than fucking darlin' you!"

"Promises, promises… darlin'!"

"I. Will. Turn. This. Fecking. Flight. Around."

"Yeah! Well, I'll just go to the airport right now and fly anywhere so I can get away from you, so don't waste your goddamn time or mine!" I pause. "I'm hanging up!"

"No! You'll stay on the phone until you've calmed the fuck down, Jaine."

"No, I fucking won't!" I hiss, disconnecting the call.

What the fuck has gotten into me? I'm never this reactive or immature.

Jaine: *Ace, I'm sorry if what we did tonight made you uncomfortable.*

Ace: *It's ok. It wasn't an ideal situation, but if it's what you needed to happen, then I guess I owed you that much.*

Jaine: *You don't owe me anything. You didn't do anything wrong, Ace.*

Ace: *Doesn't matter if I did or not if it's what you wanted. I'll always prioritize your needs over my own.*

Jaine: *Sash, can you and Cherry come see me tomorrow?*

Sasha: *Sure, my beautiful BFF, what's wrong? Anything we should be concerned about?*

Jaine: *Yeah. I think I might be pregnant.*

Sasha: *Oh dear. We'll be there at eight a.m. I'll bring an assortment of tests.*

Jaine: *Thank you, babe. I love you.*

Sasha: *I love you too. Can't wait to be an auntie. Who's the daddy?*

Jaine: *Your guess is as good as mine.*

Sasha: *Cherry's just called you an undesirable name. I won't repeat it. It began with an 's'.*

Jaine: *Pot. Kettle. Black.*

CILLIAN

On Route to New York

Cillian: *Did you know our Paddy is in love with this Jaine Jones?*

Eoin: *Who the fuck is Jaine Jones?*

Cillian: *Razr's ex. The one Paddy went to Yale with.*

Eoin: *His life's been signed away in an arranged marriage with Sophia Ruocco now. She's chosen him specifically.*

Cillian: *No one's fully explained that to him yet.*

Eoin: *Oh, I'll explain it all, Cill. Leave it with me.*

Cillian: *Eoin, I don't think you fully understand how much he really loves this woman. He's just spoken with her on the phone. They had a right go at each other. He threatened to turn the fucking plane around so he could go back and calm her down.*

Eoin: *The old man won't care if he fucking loves her, Cill. Business is business, and it always comes first. Paddy will have no choice but to marry the Sicilian.*

Cillian: *I'm not so sure, you know.*

Eoin: *I said leave it with me.*

CHAPTER FORTY-EIGHT

JAINE

Oak Lodge Hotel, Depling, California

THERE'S A KNOCK ON THE DOOR. IT'S SASHA AND CHERRY. I KNOW before I open it as the smell of Chanel No. 5 has already wrapped itself around my olfactory senses, and the only way to get that fragrance in these parts is via mail order.

"We're here! Don't panic! The BFF cavalry has arrived, bringing goodies!" Sasha singsongs as she bursts into the room, her arms filled with shopping bags that no doubt contain a selection of pregnancy tests. I instantly feel brighter as her joie de vivre fills the space. Someone should bottle whatever aura Sasha emits. They'd make a goddamn fortune.

She places the items on the floor, then pulls me in for a tight hug.

"I'll wrinkle you, Sash," I mutter, staring at her pristine white pantsuit and the matching designer aviators holding back her perfectly styled chestnut locks.

"Oh, wrinkles, sminkles. As if I'm bothered about this old thing."

My eyes drift down the suit that probably cost as much as a small family car.

"Where's Cherry?" I question, looking past her for my other BFF.

"She's fetching lattes and muffins from that quaint little coffee shop on the corner." I watch as she investigates the lounge area, wrinkling her nose up at the place, then shrugging and smiling to herself. I'd love to know what goes inside that head of hers at times.

I hear the clicking of heels in the passageway outside. Cherry enters the room balancing three large to-go coffees in a cardboard cup holder and a paper bag, which I'm assuming holds a selection of muffins.

"Oh, are you allowed to drink coffee? If you're... you know?" Sasha frowns and stares at my stomach.

"I might not be, though."

Can I drink coffee? Shit, is there a list of dos and donts?

"The question is, who have *you* been fucking, Miss Jones? We want *all* the deets!" Cherry's baby blues stare at me over the top of the black cat-like sunglasses she has perched on the end of her nose. Like Sasha, her red hair is perfectly styled and complemented by the little white playsuit she's wearing, displaying her pocket-sized hourglass figure to perfection.

She places the drinks tray on the tiny table before closing the door.

"Okay, in which order do you want things, girls?"

"Start at the beginning. We can take all day if we need to." Sasha removes her shoes, then passes out the lattes. Getting herself comfortable on the floor, she then breaks off a piece of her chocolate muffin before popping it in her mouth. Some things never change. There'll be crumbs everywhere.

I sit on the sofa, and Cherry sits beside me. After taking a sip of my caramel latte, I tell them everything. Well, apart from The Exterminator-related elements. It's safer they don't know. And the Bomb and Em parts. No one needs to hear that gruesome shit. What they don't know can't hurt them.

"So, let me get this straight. You had to fuck Padraig and Ace on camera as the Russians wanted to auction you off based on your sexual performance? Damn! How exciting!" Cherry looks envious. She's weird like that. She's read way too many taboo novels over and above the reverse harem shit.

"How was the Irishman? Was he good? Worth the nine-year wait?" Sasha asks as she stares at me, wide-eyed.

"If you want to know if he has a big dick and if he knows what to do with it, then yes on both counts." No point beating around the goddamn bush. She won't stop asking until I tell her anyway.

"So, you had unprotected sex with Padraig while you were being held hostage, but all poor Ace got was a blow job?" Sasha sounds disappointed on Ace's behalf. Like I need to make it up to him somehow.

"Well, yeah, but I fucked him at the clubhouse to make up for it."

She nods thoughtfully. Obviously, that's now acceptable, although maybe she'll make a mental note that I now owe Irish a blow job.

"But you were always so careful, Jaine. You've always been the sensible one out of us," Cherry says.

I shrug. "I realize that, but I couldn't take my pill the whole time I was held captive. I guess I hoped as I'd been on it for so long that it would be okay."

Sasha shakes her head. "Well, someone obviously has super determined sperm. Are you sure it can't be Delaney's?"

I shake my head. "Nope. We haven't fucked since we were in Manhattan."

"Anything happened with Ace or Padraig since?" Cherry asks.

I exhale. "Well, I fucked Padraig in his car, and then I fucked both of them last night." I just get that shit right out there in the open.

"What, at the same time?" Cherry's eyes light up.

"Yeah, at the same time."

"Did you enjoy it?" She's like a dog with a bone. This is her thing. I'm in her territory. She'll likely want to compare notes.

"Yes and no. I think I did it for all the wrong reasons. My gut told me to do it, even though I think deep down I knew they wouldn't get any real enjoyment out of it. Well, apart from the obvious physical pleasure. They both did it for me."

"What do you mean your gut told you to do it?" Sasha asks, sipping on her coffee.

"I can't explain it. It's like I just know something is going to shift, maybe permanently, and that it'll mean I lose one, maybe even both of them." I can feel the tears prick my eyes at the unwelcome thought, and I blink them back.

"Do you love both of them, Jaine?" Cherry asks quietly.

I nod.

"Do you love one more than the other?" Sasha asks.

I shake my head.

"Can't you have them both? You know a *why choose* scenario?" Cherry asks. No doubt this is a common theme in her smut books too.

I laugh softly. "Neither of them want to share, babe. Plus, there are other factors to consider. The distance is a key one. Padraig is a New York Hudson Duster, so he can't leave Manhattan, and Ace is prez of an MC in California, so he can't leave Rising. Then there is, of course, Irish's family. They're practicing Catholics who go to church every week. They believe in the sanctimony of marriage and spending your life with that one person once you've committed to them and taken the vows. There's no way they'd ever condone or be accepting of a relationship of that sort, even if Irish was, which he most definitely isn't."

We sit in silence for a bit. Then, finally, I eat my muffin and finish my coffee.

"You know, I'm in a similar situation with Blaze and Jefferson," Cherry adds quietly.

I look at her and take her hand in mine, squeezing it gently. "What are you going to do, babe?"

She sighs. "Well, I don't want to leave Manhattan, so I'm going to ask Jefferson if he'd consider moving there, maybe joining the Scorpions. I mean, they've got a council position going now Bomb's disappeared, and word is he won't be coming back any time soon. So maybe they could shuffle things around to include him."

I nod. I'll never tell them about what happened to Bomb and Emilia. There are some things it's safer for ordinary folks never to know. "You know, you need to run that past Blaze and get him to approach Delaney on it. It's a good idea. All you then need to do is convince Jefferson to leave his hometown. If he loves you enough, I'm sure he will."

"What about you, Sash?" I turn my attention to my model-like friend. "You still got your sights set firmly on Delaney?"

She shakes her head. "No. He's still hung up on you and probably will be for some time. He's just taken to fucking the cum sluts for now, from what I hear. That new one, Bailey, has got her claws into him."

I grimace when I recall my altercation with her. She's pretty if you like the plastic Barbie look. "There's no way Delaney will wife a cum slut, but I'm glad he's moved on all the same. As much as I don't love him like that, I still love him in my own way."

She exhales, then smiles. "I do think I'm going to see how it goes with Clay, though. I'm considering moving to Rising so we can give things a proper chance." She crinkles her nose, and her smile widens. "He told me he loves me and wants to do that WAG thing. You know, where I have to sit on the back of his bike."

"You mean he wants to make you his old lady and have you riding bitch." I chuckle at her.

I smile inwardly and feel relieved. So, my past is colliding with my present, and regardless of where I end up, I'll at least have one of my BFFs with me. That makes me happy inside. Of course, I realize it's totally fucking selfish, but still.

"So, Miss Jones. We won't be able to find out who your baby daddy is, but we can find out if you do have a muffin in that little oven of yours."

My heart starts thudding in my chest. Is it PMS that's making me emotional? What if I really am pregnant? Do I tell Ace or Irish? Do I not?

I nod. "Let's do this."

Twelve tests later, and they all show the same result.

Positive.

It turns out I'm one to two weeks pregnant. So, that I now know.

What I don't know is whether it's an MC baby or a little Hudson Duster.

Can I put off making any decisions about Ace and Irish until after I find out? Then again should I allow that to ultimately dictate who I spend the rest of my life with?

My gut is telling me it's not going to be my choice to make anyway. Something's going to go down, and I'm not going to like whatever it is. I just fucking know it.

I can feel the doom of that shit in my goddamn bones.

CHAPTER FORTY-NINE

PADRAIG

The Hudson Dusters' HQ, Manhattan, New York

"I'M NOT FUCKING MARRYING HER."

My eyes go around the table, taking in my brothers and my da. All of us are wearing the ridiculous fucking tailored suits and ties he insists upon to try to hide the fact that we're nothing but murderous mobster bastards.

"I have given my word to Mr. Ruocco that you will wed his sister when she turns eighteen. I have given my word, Padraig, so that's the end of it! The paperwork has been duly signed in blood by both parties on that basis, my lad, so don't be giving me any more of your backchat!"

"So, you decide my future while I'm being held hostage by the Russians? Without consulting me?" I slam my hand against the tabletop. "I could have been fucking killed, and meanwhile, you've been planning my nuptials to the teenage sister of the Sicilian mafia don? Are you fucking insane?" I glare at my da across the table.

"We already know the answer to that," Dylan whispers to me from the corner of his mouth.

"I heard that." Da wags his finger at him, and Dylan, having been caught, sinks down in his seat. He's lucky. If I weren't the center of attention right now, something would have been flung at his head for that truthful remark.

"The Russians were just messing about. They were never going to kill a fucking Duster. I don't know why they took you, but you're back. You were always going to be returned relatively unscathed. It's unfortunate that you weren't available, but the decision had to be made. The young girl was given no choice in the matter either. All she asked was that she could choose between the three of you." He's wagging that fucking pointer finger at me now.

Eoin smirks. He escaped the line up what with him being the future Da Duster. Gets away with everything that one does.

"Well, it's a crying shame that she chose me because I'm not fucking marrying her. I'd sooner shoot my brains out." My tone is aggressive. I wouldn't normally be so blatantly disrespectful of old Fergal, but he's gone too far this time.

I don't add that my refusal in the main is because I'm in love with someone else, as that will just incur a plethora of questions I refuse to answer. I've decided I'm just going to drag Jaine in front of old Father O'Reilly and get him to marry us on the spot.

"You listen to me. The Exterminator and I are on good terms these days after he took out that annoying Gorbachev fucker on my behalf, so I can quite easily arrange for him to put his bullet in your thick skull, my lad. Save you the bother."

I smirk at that comment and look at Dylan, but he doesn't make eye contact. He's got sense. Da's as perceptive as fuck. If he thought we were hiding something, he'd torture it out of us if he had to—family or not.

"Aye, you do that, Da. You fucking do that."

I stand up from the table and leave the room, slamming the door behind me. I need to speak to Jaine urgently.

There's no way I'm marrying Sophia fucking Ruocco.

EOIN

"Eoin, my lad, you need to talk some sense into your baby brother. I have given my word. My fucking word. My word is sacred. Like the Holy fucking Grail, son."

His hands are fidgeting, so he's going to throw something or punch someone. I'm only glad there are no weapons to hand. "I hear you, Da, and I'll get it sorted one way or another."

"You make sure you do, laddie, as I will not be made to look a fool by my own flesh and blood. You hear me?"

"I hear you, Da."

"I mean, who is this Jaine Jones that he's all puppy-loved over? He's still not mentioned her. Is she even from the life?" He looks at Dylan because he knows he's met her. Poor Dyl looks like he wants to disappear even farther under the table.

"Aye, she's from the life, Da." Dylan speaks slowly, choosing his words carefully. Wise decision. "She went to Yale with Paddy, and they had a thing way back when they were nineteen. Her background is MC. She was Paul Delaney's old lady, but rumor has it she's let him go recently after four years together."

Da looks thoughtful for a moment.

"Shame we didn't know about her. She might have been a good fit for Paddy. Still, he shouldn't have kept her hidden like a dirty fucking secret, should he? It's all his own fault. My word has been given, and I will not have it under-mined. Eoin? You take care of it. There's a good lad." He closes his notebook to let us all know that he's not discussing this or any other matter any further. Decision made. Discussion closed. Paddy *will* marry the Sicilian.

"Will do, Da," I assure him, grateful that no paperweights were slung during today's family meeting.

JAINE

Jaine's Apartment, Upper East Side, New York

THERE'S A KNOCK ON THE DOOR. IT CAN ONLY BE SASHA, CHERRY, or Delaney, and it's unlikely to be the latter given where things currently stand between us. I think if he were going to show up, he'd let me know in advance.

When I open it, it's neither of the females I expected to see.

Familiar eyes look at me. Irish ones. My unexpected visitor's hair is jet black, perfectly styled in a short fashion and sprinkled with silver at the sides. I'd guesstimate him to be in his late thirties. He's handsome, like GQ model handsome, and he's well aware of that fact. He's lean, panther-like. Power radiates from him, making his presence seem larger and more menacing somehow.

Is he trying to intimidate me? It won't fucking work.

"Come in, Eoin." I motion for him to enter my apartment. There's no point asking who let him into the building. He's a Duster. He can get in anywhere. I'm just curious why he's paying little old me an unscheduled visit.

He enters, and I close the door behind him. He'll know my apartment was expensive. He'll know everything about me. My outlaw background. My company and career. My past relationships.

My fucking bank balance. I recall how efficient Dylan was when I needed the lowdown on Lebedev.

There's only one thing he won't know. That is unless Dylan or Padraig have betrayed me. For some reason, I don't think they have or that they ever would. The Dusters are fiercely loyal and trustworthy. They pride themselves on it. It's ingrained in them and stems from their patriarch, Fergal. His word, when given, is gospel. You could inscribe that shit on a goddamn stone tablet and deem it to be another commandment.

He sits on the sofa, not waiting to be offered, then relaxes across it, stretching his arms across the back. I take in the fact that the length of his reach is almost as long as the piece of furniture itself—his finger taps on the leather as he scrutinizes me.

I'm just showered and wearing camo combats and a white tank top. My hair is hanging wet down my back. I'm not dressed up. I seldom am unless I'm working or going to a function.

"I'd offer you something to drink, Eoin, but my gut tells me this isn't a social visit."

I stand and look at him. I'm not in a defensive pose because the fucker doesn't scare me. My hands are slung low in my pockets.

"You know who I am?" His voice is much deeper than Padraig's and way more sinister sounding. My guess is his impassive expression is meant to instill fear in people. Might work on others. Not me. Does he practice in front of a mirror, I wonder? I snicker inwardly. He's eight years older than Irish, so he'll have had way more time to master his mobster craft, and he'll also have significantly more killings under his belt. Then again, does Padraig sound different when he's talking to someone else? When he's flicked that internal switch of his and entered Duster mode.

"It doesn't take a rocket scientist to work out who you are. You look like an older version of Padraig. I've met Dylan. I've seen

Cillian. So, by process of elimination, that means you're the eldest O'Connell."

He's wearing a suit and tie, so they've obviously just had their family meeting. Irish says it's like *Reservoir Dogs*. I smirk, thinking I'm doing so inwardly. I'm not.

"Something amusing, Miss Jones?"

"Just wondering which Mr. you are. From the Tarantino movie. Mr. Blonde, perhaps? Are you going to have me looking like Da Vinci by the end of whatever the fuck this is?"

His eyes narrow as he takes me in. I stare back at him. Two murderous killers assessing each other. Not that he knows that about me. Well, hopefully not.

"So, would you care to explain the purpose of this unexpected visit, or are you going to keep me in suspense? I have things to do. I'm sure you have people to visit and... things... to be getting on with too." He knows I'm referring to illegal activities. He might wear an expensive business suit, but he's not a businessman in the traditional sense of the word.

He stands up and walks towards me, so we're inches apart. He's taller than Padraig. Maybe six feet five. I'm tall, and I have to tilt my head. Up close, his eyes aren't bright blue like Padraig's. They're aquamarine. His face also wears more lines, no doubt caused by living longer in the life. He's striking. Unbelievably so.

I raise an eyebrow.

"If you're trying to intimidate me, Mr. O'Connell, it won't work."

"It's not my intention, Miss Jones." He looks down at me.

"Then why are you looming over me and standing so close? You're either trying to intimidate me or kiss me. We've already decided the first won't work, and I wouldn't suggest you attempt the latter. That is if you want to be able to produce the next heir to The Hudson Dusters."

His eyes drop to my lips fleetingly, and my stomach flips in response. They then slowly graze my face before staring back into mine. Do I detect a hint of admiration in them?

"Pretty girl." It's barely audible, as though he's speaking to himself.

He turns around, and I'm left staring at his back.

"My brother. Padraig."

My blood immediately runs cold and that recent feeling of doom envelopes me once more. "What about him?"

He breathes in and out slowly, like he's trying to work out how best to deliver what must only be shitty news. "I need to ask you to cease all contact with him."

I feel like I've been sucker-punched. Of all the things I was expecting, it wasn't that. All my memories of Irish flash in front of my eyes like some sorry-ass slideshow. The nineteen-year-old boy, the twenty-eight-year-old man. The countless conversations and message exchanges spanning nine years. I realize I haven't got anywhere near enough to ever be able to let him go. I'll never have enough. Please, God, let me make more. Please.

"Why?" I'm surprised at how calm I sound.

He turns back around, exhaling loudly. "He's been entered into an arranged marriage that my da thinks will be beneficial to the Dusters. It's become apparent that Paddy won't go through with it if he thinks there's a chance you'll have him."

My mouth is dry. I can hear thudding. I realize it's the sound of my heartbeat pounding against my eardrums.

"When was this arrangement made?" My voice remains surprisingly steady, even though, inside, I'm slowly falling apart.

"When the Russians were holding you."

I nod. "So, it was all agreed without his consent? When was Padraig made aware of this… marriage?"

"Just after you were released."

I nod again and frown. Why didn't Irish tell me about this? We could have discussed it. Looked at the alternatives if there were any to be found.

"Who is it? Who is he to be wed to?" Jealousy flows through my veins to add to the pain and anger that's already coursing through them. Who the fuck is going to take my Irish from me?

"Sophia Ruocco."

I laugh out loud. "She's a fucking teenager."

He narrows his eyes. "She's just turned sixteen. The wedding is to take place when she turns eighteen. Once he is married, the Dusters have no issue with you and Paddy resuming talking to each other."

Because when he weds, it will be until death.

"Two years? You expect me not to speak to him for two years?" I sound confused. Am I misunderstanding? But I know I'm not.

"Yes. My da has given his word to the Sicilian don that Padraig will wed his sister. He won't go back on it, even though Paddy is insistent he won't go through with it. As you know, my da is a man of his word. Cillian overheard your conversation with Paddy when they were flying back from LA. It's clear Paddy's in love with you, so it's safer if you keep your distance. For your sake as well as for his."

Is this my fault? If we hadn't bickered, would this ridiculous ban be put in place? I curse myself. I curse my fucking hormones. I curse my stupid fucking rash decisions.

I turn away from Eoin. I'm no longer bothered about this posturing competition we seem to have going on. Who wins is no longer fucking important. Irish being the equivalent of dead to me is. There's no way we could just pick up where we left off after that length of time, and there's no way his new wife would allow it, even if we wanted to.

I shake my head. "I've spoken to Irish every single day since we were at Yale together," I whisper. To myself? To Eoin? To God, if he's even fucking listening? "I won't be able to do that."

He's already anticipated my response.

"Do you love him, Jaine?"

I nod slowly.

"Then let him go."

I immediately start to pace the floor. "And if I don't?"

"Well, as you know, we have ways of removing you from Paddy's temptation. We've recently taken care of Lebedev, which I'm sure you're aware of, so we do have The Exterminator on our books now."

I smirk at that, then run my hands through my wet hair. I stop and stare at him as he stands there, thinking he's all Mr. Big and Intimidating. He fucking wishes.

"So, you would have The Exterminator plant an engraved bullet in my skull if I don't do your fucking bidding?" I laugh out loud at the absurdity of that comment. Oh, if only this asshole knew. "Surely little old Jaine fucking Jones isn't worthy of the famous sharpshooter's attentions, Eoin?"

He merely stares in response. So, I'm guessing the Dusters really do see me as a threat to their plans.

"And if I still don't give him up despite being threatened with a bullet between my eyes?"

"Then you'll put Paddy at risk as the likelihood is he'll refuse to go through with the marriage. There's no telling how the mafia will react if the Dusters are deemed to publicly disrespect their don's sister." He retakes his seat on the sofa.

I laugh and start to pace again. "Their don? Luciano? He's an incompetent asshole."

"You know him?" He sounds interested.

I stop and glare at him. "I know a lot of people, Eoin, given what I do for a living. My client list is extensive. I don't only represent the MC. I have the personal contact details of several high-ranking politicians and many influential people of significant power. I've met Luciano on more than one occasion. If he ever laid a hand on Padraig, I'd kill the fucker personally."

He stares at me. His expression is thoughtful. Maybe even regretful.

"Are you prepared to take the risk, Jaine? Risk something happening to Paddy?" Eoin's voice is quiet. He knows my answer. The fucker's played the top trump card and has me over a barrel, and he's fully aware of it.

I'm not prepared to risk Irish. Not for anything.

I walk toward the window and gaze out over the city. My emotions are all over the place. Heartbreak is definitely a trigger for unwelcome tears. More so when pregnant. I refuse to let this asshole bear witness to my emotional breakdown, though. I blink to fight them back.

"No."

"So, you will cease all communication with my brother?"

There's a pause. Minutes? Hours? Fucking days? How to reply to a question I never want to answer.

"Yes."

I rub my hand across my tired eyes, suddenly feeling drained. "I will have to end things properly with Padraig. If I simply stop speaking to him, he'll just turn up unannounced, much like you have today."

"Of course. Please make sure he understands your mind is made up. That there's no coming back from this."

"I will."

"Thank you."

I hear him stand and make his way to the door.

"One last thing, Eoin." I compose myself before turning to look at him.

Our gazes connect, mine full of unhidden loathing. This is all in a day's work to the eldest O'Connell. Coercing people into doing the Dusters' bidding using whatever means necessary. The impact on me? On my life? It's irrelevant to him. It means nothing. I mean nothing. I simply represent a problem that needs solving.

He thinks he's solved it. Big fucking mistake.

Don't shoot the messenger? That's exactly what I will be doing when the time is fucking right.

"You will pay for this. Not the Dusters. You personally. They say revenge is a dish best served cold. It is. Today, you have underestimated who you're dealing with. That's a mistake on your part. A grave one. Mark my words, Eoin. One day I will make your life as miserable as you have made mine."

He nods, thinking it's an empty threat, then he leaves and closes the door behind him.

It's not empty. He will pay. Me and him? We're on a fucking promise.

———————

Jaine: *Dylan, I need to speak to you.*
Dylan: *You know the number.*

"I'VE JUST BEEN PAID A VISIT BY BIG BROTHER EOIN," I MUTTER.

There's a pause. "So, you know."

"Yes, I fucking know. Why didn't Irish tell me, Dylan?" I'm yelling. It's all I seem to be doing these days. Fucking hormones.

"Which part?"

"Oh, the fact that he's been entered into an arranged marriage with Sophia Ruocco?"

"Oh... that part." He sounds decidedly sheepish.

"Oh, that part. Are you guys insane? Which fucking century are we living in?"

"It's da. He sees these arrangements as bettering our social standing and building strong alliances."

"Yup, he's a lunatic. Building a better social standing by getting into bed publicly with the untrustworthy Ruoccos? Even then, to build a better one, you'd need to have one in the fucking first place."

"It's clear you're not happy with the news."

"Not happy? Not fucking happy? Not happy is getting home and realizing you've picked up the wrong type of milk at Walmart, Dylan. Not happy doesn't constitute the emotions you feel when you're told you can't have any communication whatsoever with someone you've spoken to every day of your life for the past nine years. Not happy is the understatement of the goddamn century."

"So, you've been told not to contact Paddy at all?" he asks in disbelief.

"Yes! Not for the next two fucking years until he's safely married to Sophia Ruocco."

"Jesus Christ."

"Yes, Jesus Christ. I could have coped with the fact that he was to be married off. I could. Really. Nothing surprises me in the life. What will be will be. We've spent most of our lives as *just friends,* Irish and me, so if we were destined to be dear old buddies for the rest of our days, then so be it. I may not like it, but I'd accept it. But the big brother ban that says I'm to ignore him for the next twenty-four fucking months? Which effectively means I'm going to lose him from my life forever? Give him up completely?"

"He loves you, though, Jaine. If he thinks there's any chance with you, he'd never go through with the marriage to Sophia."

"Yes! And that's why I've agreed to it! Because I don't want the mafia to fucking harm him!"

"So, what's next?"

"Well, now I have to break my own heart and your baby brother's by telling him it's all over between us. That we can't even be friends. That we can't be anything. That's what's next, Dylan." I can hear the tears in my voice as it breaks.

"Jaine..." His tone is sympathetic

"I don't want your pity. I'll have my fucking revenge, I assure you. I should tell your da to stick that list of people he wants taking out up his Irish backside, but I won't."

"Well, that's good to know." He breathes a sigh of relief.

"So, you'd better get yourself a burner phone, as The Exterminator will be dealing with you personally when it comes to any hits for the Dusters. No one else. That fucking arrogant asshole Eoin must never know who I am. In return for my work, you'll pay all monies to the Scorpions as before, but you'll also keep me informed on how Irish is getting on. Agreed?"

"Agreed."

"Do you know what the funniest thing was?"

"What?"

"Your brother threatened to have me shot by The Exterminator if I didn't do as I was told."

We both burst out laughing. A brief moment of escapism from this most current fucked-up situation.

"If we told my da who you were, Jaine, I'm sure he'd manage to extract Paddy from the mafia arrangement."

"It's too late for that. I could never live with myself if the mafia retaliated, and I ended up with Irish's blood on my hands."

"You love him enough to give him up?"

"Yes, I do. I'd die for him if I had to."

At this precise fucking moment, a brutal death would be less painful.

CHAPTER FIFTY

JAINE

Jaine's Apartment, Upper East Side, New York

ED SHEERAN. THAT'S THE ED IRISH WAS TALKING ABOUT. I'VE spent the last twenty-four hours with his songs playing on a loop while staring at the wall and throwing myself a pity party. I haven't moved since Eoin's visit. Bathroom stops and bottles of water. That's about it. I can't eat. I feel sick. I can't sleep. My brain won't shut down.

Padraig tried to call me countless times back-to-back yesterday. I didn't answer. Was it urgent? Who knows? Does it matter now? It's not like it will change anything. Next time we speak, I need to break the news. When I do, his name won't light up the screen on my phone anymore. The visual that's been a constant these past nine years.

I don't want to let that go just yet. Pathetic, I know. Selfish, I know. I don't want it to be permanently gone. For him to be forever silenced.

I also don't want to let him go from my life. But I will. I have to force the issue too. So, he lets go of me and moves on with Sophia like the Dusters want. Like the mafia want. In the end, I'll just be someone he used to know. A distant memory for a short time until I'm completely forgotten about.

I'll never be able to forget him, though. My Irish.

I'm still not sure I can go through with it. But I have to. I have no choice.

Eoin says it's for two years, but we both know it's for good. There's no coming back from this.

So how can I willingly answer? How can I break his heart? And my own? How can I make him hate me? Because he will. Of that, there is no shadow of a doubt. He'll never speak to me again after I do what I have to do. Say what I have to say.

I sit contemplating it over and over, hoping that by delaying the inevitable, big bad brother Eoin will have a change of heart. That he'll change his mind. That I won't be plunged into a living night-mare forevermore.

I've only just stopped crying. How many tears can one body produce? I've likely only run out temporarily as I'm not giving them enough time to replenish. They'll start again soon enough, I'm sure.

I've considered calling to drop the bombshell, but he'll know I'm lying. He's a fucking lawyer, same as me. You can't pull the wool easily over our professional eyes. Plus, it's something I never do. Something I pride myself on, in fact. I'd never pull it off.

So instead, I'll have to resort to messaging to tell him the pack of lies. By doing so, I'll make him feel I care that little he's not even worthy of a fucking phone call. Like the past nine years meant nothing to me in the grand scheme of things. I only wish that were true. Then it wouldn't hurt quite so much. My phone flashes with a message. I pick it up, and it's from Irish.

There's no time like the fucking present, I guess. I can't put this shit off any longer. I can only hope one day he'll forgive me for what I'm about to do and that he understands my reasons. That his beloved big brother left me with no choice.

That, in the end, I did all of this for him.

Padraig: *I tried to call you several times yesterday.*
Jaine: *Sorry, I was busy.*
Padraig: *Too busy to speak to me, darlin'? When have you ever been too busy to talk to me? It was urgent, Jaine.*
Jaine: *Was it? Sorry. I have a lot on.*
Padraig: *Yesterday was the first day you haven't spoken to me since we were at Yale.*

Does he think I don't fucking know that? I rub my hands over my face and my cheeks are wet. I'm crying again. God, I can't do this.

Jaine: *Was it? I didn't realize.*
Padraig: *Jaine, what the fuck is going on?*
Jaine: *I don't think we should contact each other anymore.*
Padraig: *Very funny. In fact, you're fucking hilarious.*

There's a pause.

Padraig: *Jaine, please tell me you're joking?*

There's another pause.

Padraig: *Fuck! You're serious? Why?*

Jaine: *I've had time to think things through and reflect, and I realize I don't love you. I just thought I did because you remind me of Ace.*

Padraig: *You're fucking joking, right? Tell me you're joking, darlin'?*

Jaine: *I'm serious, Padraig.*

Padraig: *There's no way you don't love me. I can tell you love me. There's no way this connection we share isn't love!*

Jaine: *I guess I was showing you the love that belonged to him all along. I love Ace. I want to be with Ace. I'm sorry, Padraig.*

Padraig: *Can I call you? Please?*

Jaine: *There's no point. My mind's made up.*

Padraig: *Nine years, Jaine. I've loved you for nine fucking years. I'd do anything for you. Be anything, change anything to be what you need, what you want.*

Jaine: *You can't change the fact that you cheated on me.*

Padraig: *No way! Do NOT use that as the catalyst behind ending things. Do NOT fucking destroy me by throwing something in my face that I can't fix. That I can't change. Something I've regretted every fucking day since.*

Jaine: *Why not? I'm still the same person. You cheated on me then. Why wouldn't you do it again?*

Padraig: *I thought it was because you didn't want me, darlin'. That you didn't love me enough. That you loved him more.*

Jaine: *I do love him more.*

Padraig: *But you said you loved us equally. I thought I had a chance.*

Jaine: *I realize I love him more. I guess I've just used you as a substitute for him all this time.*

Padraig: *A substitute?*

There's a pause. I realize how much me saying that must have fucking hurt and I hate myself for it.

Padraig: *So that's it. You're drawing a line under the past nine years just like that? Throwing it all away?*

Jaine: *I'm sorry, but it's for the best. I don't want to lead you on. We both need to move on with our lives. Stop wasting time.*

Padraig: *Is that what you think you've been doing with me? Wasting time?*

Padraig: *Are you saying we can't even be friends?*

Jaine: *No. We've muddied the waters way too much now to ever be just friends, Padraig. We can't go back to the way things were.*

Padraig: *Was it because of the other night? With Ace?*

Jaine: *Yes. That made me realize it's him I want. Look, I need to go, Irish. I'm sorry, but it's easier if we just make a clean break and don't drag things on. The right girl is out there for you. It's just not me.*

Padraig: *Fuck, no! Not like this, Jaine. Please don't do this, darlin'. I'm begging you. I'm literally on my hands and knees fucking begging.*

Padraig: *Jaine? Please? You're breaking my heart, darlin'. I love you so fucking much. For fuck's sake. Please don't do this to me.*

Padraig: *Jaine?*

Padraig: *Jaine?*

I'm not sure how long passes. Fuck knows.

Padraig: *If that's how you want it, then so be it, but know now that you are dead to me.*

So, it's done. What Eoin wanted. Bravo, Jaine. Well fucking done.

My shaky hands try to place the phone on the table, but it falls to the floor with a clatter. The screen is blank. It will remain so. Silent tears continue to run down my cheeks. Eventually, they'll be invisible to the outside world, but they'll always be there. They'll always be falling. Every minute of every fucking day and for the rest of my goddamn life, they'll fall for my Irish.

PADRAIG

Padraig's Apartment, Hudson Yards, New York

I STARE AT THE BOTTLE OF WHISKEY. IT'S THE THIRD, I THINK. Maybe fourth. Who's counting? Who the fuck cares? This one's almost finished. I drain the glass, then throw it at the stone fireplace, where the crystal smashes into tiny pieces.

I take another off the silver tray beside me, and I fill it to the top.

No matter how much I drink, it's not numbing the fucking pain. It's never-ending. Will it ever pass?

It will. In time. Time's a healer, so they say. Or does its passage just make you more angry, bitter, and twisted? Time will also tell.

I stare at the amber-colored liquid in the glass, then swirl it around and drink it down. I can't taste it anymore, but I'm not drinking for enjoyment. I'm drinking to forget. To try to eradicate the last nine fucking years of my life. To drown out the memories of *her*.

I look around my apartment. At the luxury and wealth. What the fuck does any of it matter when I can't have the one thing, the only thing I've ever truly wanted?

"It means fuck all," I growl as I throw the empty vessel at the stone fireplace and watch it smash into tiny pieces like the others before.

Like my fucking heart.

The empty space in my chest where it used to be will close up eventually, I'm sure. Then hard scar tissue will form over the top and cover it. Impenetrable. Nothing will ever touch me there again. I won't fucking let it.

EOIN

Three Days Later
Padraig's Apartment, Hudson Yards, New York

"PADDY, WHAT THE FUCK ARE YOU DOING? I'VE BEEN TRYING TO get hold of you for fucking days." The apartment is in darkness when I walk in. It smells of whiskey and body odor.

"How the fuck did you get in?" The grumble comes from the direction of the sofa.

"I have a key," I reply, throwing open the curtains.

He grimaces and swears as he holds his hand over his eyes while they adjust to the daylight that's now flooding the room. I look at him sitting there in nothing but a pair of stained grey jogging pants. I take in the plethora of empty bottles and the smashed glassware. He looks at me briefly, and his head wobbles. He's drunk. His eyes are bloodshot. He's not shaved. He looks like a fucking tramp and smells like one too.

"You need to get in the shower, Paddy. You stink." I look down at him.

"Fuck do I care," he stutters, not looking back at me.

"Come on. It can't be that bad," I try to joke.

He scowls up at me. "It can't be that bad? What the fuck would you know? The woman I love with every part of me, who I've loved for the past nine years, has told me she doesn't love me back. When you love someone as much as I love her, Eoin. When you experience that kind of deep-rooted fucking intense love where nothing else matters, then you tell me how you would feel if the woman you had feelings like that for told you she didn't love you back?"

He swallows the whiskey, then throws the glass at the fireplace.

He sobs in despair and runs his hands through his disheveled hair. I walk across, sit down, and wrap my arms around him. Then I let my baby brother cry his fucking heart out.

Jesus Christ, what have we done?

See, this is our fucked-up life. This is our sick existence. Every move is like playing a deadly game of outlaw chess.

And how the fuck is Paddy going to react when he finds out? Which he will. At some point, he will know we threatened her. *I* threatened her. By using him as the pawn to checkmate her out of his fucking life.

CHAPTER FIFTY-ONE

JAINE

Four Weeks Later
Jaine's House, Rising, California

I TAKE IN THE WHITE WALLS AND ANTHRACITE TILED FLOORS OF THE property and breathe in the smell of fresh paint. It's a pleasant smell. A new start smell. The place looks completely different inside and out. It's amazing what a little TLC can do. It can turn an almost forgotten house back into a much-loved family home.

Jethro has tidied up the gardens and lawns too. I've told him looking after the property is a job I'll need doing on an ongoing basis, and the rate agreed means he'll be paid handsomely for his efforts. I can afford it. With three young ones under five, he needs all the goddamn money he can lay his hands on.

I'm not trying to eradicate any memories from these four walls. I don't have enough of those as it is. I guess I just wanted to put my mark on the place. I want to make it feel loved and lived in like it was ten years ago. Before I left.

See, I understand now. I realize that, for my pop, when I left Rising, time stood still. That's why he never changed anything. Why everything was in limbo. He was living in the hope his daughter would just walk out of her pink girly bedroom that was filled with sparkly, feathery, glittery things. That she'd just reappear. She left in such a hurry he never had time to adjust. He didn't know how to. He never recovered from that.

For him, every day was all just some big bad Groundhog Day fucking nightmare.

And I get that now. I truly do. The hurt and pain caused by having someone who means everything, someone who's the center of your universe, ripped from your life with no prior notice, with no time to say goodbye. I know because it's what I've had to go through with Irish.

The ramifications are devastating to those left behind. I can vouch for that. Now I fully fucking understand the domino effect my selfish teenage actions will have had. The hurt I caused Pop? I can never make that up to him. The hurt I caused Ace? I can. If he'll let me.

Karma is being served back to me extremely cold. That fucking bitch has been in the freezer for ten goddamn years. Lesson learned. I will never take those close to me for granted again. From now on, I will treat every day with them like it's the fucking last.

One day it will be.

After the exchange with Irish, I needed time to heal, so I holed myself up in my apartment for days on end. I then realized the emotional roller-coaster I was on, I needed to get off, and quickly. It was too damaging. Now? I've come home to Rising.

My phone beeps.

Dylan: *You there yet?*

Jaine: *Just arrived. I'll send you some images.*

Dylan: *How you feeling?*

Jaine: *I'm fine, Dad.*

Dylan: *Now, now, Jaine. I'm being serious.*

Jaine: *I know you are. I appreciate your concern. Are you still coming to visit next week?*

Dylan: *For sure. I'll personally hand-deliver the list of dead people walking.*

Jaine: *Jesus Christ. I hope there's no one on there I fucking know.*

Dylan: *You're a sniper. It's not like they'll see you before your bullet smacks them between the eyes.*

Jaine: *I still have a conscience.*

Dylan: *Tell that to St. Peter when he knocks you back from those pearly gates. 'Let me in. I had a conscience, I tell you'.*

Jaine: *LOL! Shut up. I'll message you later, dour face.*

Dylan: *Thank you. You say the nicest things.*

Jaine: *Fucking welcome.*

I speak to Dylan every day now. Have I slotted him into my life as a replacement for Padraig? Not at all. He just keeps me up to date with how my Irish is getting on. Just in terms of his general wellbeing. Nothing more. The rest I don't want to know. It's not any of my fucking business. I'll only find it upsetting hearing how he's moving on with his life without me in it. Then again, I have to do the same. Would hearing about that upset him too? I guess I'll never know.

Does he miss me? Talk about me? Wonder how I'm coping without him? Does he love me still? All questions I would *never* ask

Dylan. That wouldn't be fair. Doesn't stop me from wanting to know the answers all the same.

And me and Dylan? He's a bit of a recluse, so he seems glad of this friendship we've fallen into. It suits us both. We get on well. Really well.

I still find myself picking up my phone without thinking most days, though. Well, every day. Ready to message or call my Irish when I've heard something funny or when I just need some advice. Then I remember I can't. I tell myself it's just a habit, but I know it's more than that. It always will be.

Habits don't hurt.

Still, I have to be strong for both our sakes. And I will. This is my penance to pay. For what, I don't know, but I've accepted it now. Irish is safe. That's all that matters. He will remain so for as long as I stay away.

But life goes on, and for however long I've got left above ground, I need to start living it. It's not just about me anymore. I've been to see an ob-gyn, and it's all been confirmed. It's time to start making some roots.

Ace? We've been talking and messaging every day, trying to fill a ten-year void. He knows Padraig and I are no longer in contact. He hasn't asked why. Ace isn't the type to ask questions when he doesn't think the answers are any of his business. He just gets on with life. He lives it day by day, taking nothing for granted. I'm going to take a leaf out of his book. Or at least try to.

I've seen all the messages and voicemails now—the ones from ten years ago. There was only one that mattered in the end. It was left on my phone from that night. The night before I left for Connecticut. It was the only one I could be sure was sent without influence. Not impacted by regret or simply because he felt guilty or just missed having me being around.

"Hi, PJ... um, it's me. I came back to the bedroom, and you had

left for some reason. I wasn't sure if your pop had picked you up or... well, um. It was just that I wanted to tell you something. Ask you something too. Um, I just wanted to let you know that I... that I love you, PJ. And that if you would think about it, I'd like you to be my old lady. That's if you want to. Anyway, I should go. It's late, and you'll be asleep. I'll see you tomorrow."

But he didn't see me the next day. I ran out on my best friend and didn't look back until ten years later. I know now how much I hurt him. How much I hurt myself. Now, I could and maybe should have regrets, but I don't. See, I'd never have met Padraig then, or if I had, it would only have been in passing. Things happen for a reason. No matter what's going on between me and Irish, I was always destined to love him. I'm as sure of that as I am of anything. I guess this is all just part of God's fucking master plan. Fuck knows what's around the corner for any of us. Still, I've accepted my past and my failings and have come to terms with both now.

The future is all that matters.

So, I'm still in love with two men and I will always love them equally. You can't simply switch that goddamn emotion off. Padraig is gone now. He's out of my reach. For two years at least, probably forever. Could we become friends again? I'd love it if we could, but it's unlikely. I'm sure his teenage wife would have something to say about that. She'd never condone our weird, dysfunctional relationship. I'm not sure his family would, either.

I miss him, though. So much. *Too much.* I could think up something overly sentimental to say. I miss him like the deserts miss the rain. Like the flowers miss the sun. But I'm not that eloquent. I just miss him lighting up my phone screen a million times a day. I miss hearing that beautiful Irish lilt of his. I wish I'd spoken to him more. Sent more messages. Met up sooner. But I can't change the past. I can only hold on for dear fucking life to the memories and never let them go.

Do I have regrets? Our paths crossed, and for that, I will be eternally grateful. Even though the pain of losing him has been almost unbearable, I'd do it all again in a heartbeat.

I step outside, stand on the newly painted porch, and gaze up at the Californian sun. I breathe in the familiar smell of petrichor and wildflowers and smile as I scan the horizon. I know I'm doing the right thing.

Deep down, I knew it always was.

Straddling my Softail, I set off on my surprise visit to the Angels' clubhouse

The Angels of Hellfire Clubhouse, Rising, California

"PJ, WHAT YOU DOING HERE? WE WEREN'T EXPECTING YOU, WERE we?" Clay looks at me in confusion from where he's sitting at the bar, chatting to Rio. The barman passes me a bottle of room temperature water, and I smile in thanks as I take it from him.

"Just coming to pick up the keys to Pop's house," I reply, dangling them in front of his face. "I've had Jethro working on it for the past four weeks, giving it a make-over. You missing Sash yet?"

"Shit, yeah. But she'll be back soon, and she's hopefully staying for the long-term. See if we can make a go of it. You here to see the prez?"

I smirk at him. "Maybe."

"He's in the office with Duke."

I nod. "I'll get his attention, don't worry."

My hands suddenly feel sweaty. I rub them down my leather pants, but it doesn't help.

I walk across to the jukebox and take in the lights flashing at me in welcome recognition and the initials engraved in the top right-hand corner. JS and JJ. I smile as I press song forty-two.

Creep by Radiohead springs into life, and I let the melancholy lyrics wash over me.

I do belong here. This is my home. This is where I did my growing up. Where I want my baby to grow up. Living the life I did, with hopefully a best friend as special as the one I was lucky enough to be blessed with.

The door leading to Duke's office is thrown open and Ace steps into the communal area and looks around. My eyes scan over his black jeans and Henley, his prez cut over the top. His hair's tied back, and it emphasizes his beautiful face and his J tattoo. He fixes his gaze on me, and he frowns in that scowly sort of way he does. The one he throws me when he thinks I'm deliberately trying to piss him off. Maybe I am. Maybe I always have been. Do I do it over and over just to see that fucking expression on his face? I smile to myself. Most likely, yes, as the angsty bad boy look sure suits him.

"PJ? You never said you were coming to Rising." His voice is deep and dark.

"Is that a problem? You got a cum slut hiding in your bed or something you don't want me knowing about?"

His scowl deepens at that comment.

I realize then I'd give anything to see that scowl on the face of a beautiful little eight-year-old boy with shoulder-length wavy hair that's as inky black as the midnight sky and with eyes as blue as the bluest thing ever. His face will have been turned brown by the sun, so it has a small smattering of freckles, and he'll have a little dent in his chin that will make it look like a little butt. He'll be covered in dirt from playing out, and when he shoots the little girls that crooked smile of his and shows off his two pointed teeth that make him look like a wolf, they'll instantly fall in love with him.

Like I did. With his father.

I gulp back the sob that's threatening to overwhelm me as I walk towards the bar. Fucking hormones.

All eyes are on us now.

"I was just passing by, Ace."

He crosses his arms in front of him, causing his pecs and biceps to bulge impressively. I can't help but lick my lips as I look at them, which doesn't go unnoticed by him. He ignores my reaction like he always does. "No one just passes by Rising, PJ."

I nod. "I was picking up the keys from Jethro. I wanted to see the house. Then I thought I might take myself down to the river. To the spot where you taught me how to skim stones."

He looks confused. "You want me to go with you?"

I nod and smile. "Yeah, I'd like that."

We walk outside into the yard.

We stand inches apart, and I gaze up into the face of Jason Steele.

My beautiful boy. My Ace. My future.

"Shall I meet you there?" he asks quietly, realization beginning to dawn on him, his eyes now filled with hope.

I shake my head and smile. "I'd like to ride with you, Ace, if that's okay."

His lips curve upwards, and he smiles wolfishly back. My heart floods with so much fucking warmth and love I swear I could explode with happiness.

"You sure, PJ?"

"I've never been surer of anything in my life."

We get on his ride, and I wrap my arms tightly around his waist. Closing my eyes, I press my face against his cut, inhaling the drug that is his familiar scent.

We ride to the river. It's not far, so we don't bother with helmets. The wind blowing through my hair makes me feel alive and free. Like I'm seven years old again. I'm home, and I'm happy just to be little old Plain Jaine Jones for the first time in my life.

· · ·

The River, Rising, California

WE DISMOUNT, AND ACE TAKES OFF HIS CUT FOR ME TO SIT ON.

"You letting me sit on your leather, Ace?" I look at him questioningly.

"My old lady is more important than my cut." He smirks back.

"Not sure when I agreed to be your old lady, or are you referring to some other woman you've offered that grand position to?" I snicker.

"Your ass was on the back of my hog, so that means you now belong to me, PJ."

Before I can reply, his mouth covers mine, his tongue pressing against my lips and asking for entry, which I give willingly. I groan as they join, tangle, and taste.

He slowly undresses me. He's not rough like he usually is. He's taking his time and savoring the moment. His lips move gently over mine and then drop to place soft kisses down my neck as his hands drop to caress my nipples, causing the peaks to tighten in response.

Naked, I stand and watch as he removes his own clothing, our eyes never breaking contact.

He leans his forehead against mine and closes his eyes, breathing me in before lowering me onto his cut. His lips find mine again, his tongue filling my mouth as his hand drops to my pussy, running his fingers up and down my slickness before sliding two inside. I gasp as his thumb presses against my swollen clit, my body already on edge.

"Come for me, sweetheart," he whispers softly in my ear, and as the orgasm's still releasing through my body, he thrusts into me, filling me and making me his.

His movements are slow and unhurried, our mouths tasting. Our breaths inhaling with whispered words of encouragement and exhaling with soft groans of pleasure. Our hands tracing and caressing warm, bare flesh. The build-up is so slow we're both sheened with sweat when we finally reach the pinnacle, and I anchor my legs around his hips as he releases inside me, our foreheads pressed together, his eyes gazing into mine.

Do I have any regrets? No. Not when everything that's happened in my life so far has led to this single moment that truly defines perfection.

ACE

WE LIE BY THE RIVER IN THE EXACT SPOT WHERE I SHOWED HER how to skim stones when she was seven years old. My heart is beating so fast as my brain tries to come to terms with the fact that PJ is actually fucking mine.

I pull her body closer and relish in the warmth of her skin as she rests her head on my chest. My face drops to her hair, and I inhale the fresh, clean smell that always surrounds her. Nothing fake. Nothing added. Just her.

"I love you, PJ." I force the words out of my mouth. I want to say them. I need to say them. Yeah, I said them ten years ago, but I haven't said them since, and she needs to hear them, no matter how exposed it makes me feel. She needs to know that I've loved her since that very first fucking moment.

She tilts her face up, and I take in her big green eyes the color of a meadow, and her hair like spun gold. She smiles her beautiful smile, the one that was perfect even before she got her braces fitted. The one she always tried to hide. "I love you too, Ace. Always have. Always will."

I kiss the top of her head and wrap my arms around her so

tightly I'm probably crushing her, but she doesn't complain.

For the first time in my life, I feel content. I've finally got my PJ. My old lady.

Nothing else matters to me but her.

I don't know how long we've got together. Life can be short in this outlaw world, so I'm going to cherish every moment I have with her. I've waited ten damn years, and I'd do it all over again just so I can spend the rest of my time, however fleeting that may be, with my Plain Jaine in my fucking arms.

EPILOGUE

JAINE

Twelve Months Later
The Angels of Hellfire Clubhouse, Rising, California

Dylan: *At least Sophia doesn't threaten to shoot me in the head every day.*
Jaine: *Stop exaggerating. I don't say it every day. I only say it when you piss me off.*
Dylan: *Oh, so just every other day.*
Jaine: *Don't piss me off, then. It really is that fucking simple. It seems to be a knack you Irish have. I'm sure you all try to surpass each other.*
Dylan: *You're just tetchy.*
Jaine: *And you're just a gobby fucker.*
Jaine: *Oh, and old Fergal still owes me for the last hit. I had to fly to Mexico for that one too. Delaney's told me to*

chase you up. You wouldn't want to make that murderous bastard's blade hand twitchy, now, would you?

Dylan: *I'll have a word with Eoin. He's the money man.*

Jaine: *He's the asshole, you mean.*

Dylan: *Aye, he's that too. Da's on at him to find himself a wife, but it's difficult when the woman will have to be big bad Ma Duster. There's a lot of responsibility with that role. It's not for the faint-hearted.*

Jaine: *What's not for the faint-hearted is having to face a lifetime of putting up with him. It's difficult for him to find a wife because any sane woman would run for the hills as soon as she realizes he's an arrogant fucker with zero personality.*

Dylan: *Anyway, enough of you picking on my big brother. Shouldn't you be getting on your way? You're supposed to be marrying your biker boyfriend today. I wish you both all the luck in the world, by the way, Jaine. A dozen crates of the best Irish whiskey will be with you Monday, courtesy of the Dusters.*

Jaine: *Thank you, Dyl.*

I'M STANDING IN MY CHILDHOOD BEDROOM, STARING AT MY reflection in the mirror. Ace and I have taken to living in my family home more often than not these days.

My floor-length dress is simple and understated in full cream lace and with long sleeves. My blonde hair hangs down my back. It's almost waist length now, but there's no urgency to cut it. There's no urgency to do goddamn anything in Rising. One day simply rolls into the next.

I'm embracing it while I still can. Soon, I know it's all going to change. When I have no choice but to return to Manhattan.

I'm wearing a headdress made up of the cream poppies that grow wild in these parts, and their floral notes fill the air. Over the top of my dress, I'm wearing a cut. It's something I swore I'd never do, but I want him to know how much he means to me.

How much I fucking love him.

On the back, it says Property of Ace.

The service is being held at the clubhouse so all the brothers and their old ladies can attend. It's a bit of a free for all, so half the town will undoubtedly turn up too. Everyone will come out to celebrate the two young people they've known since they were children take the vows together. There's so much love in Rising today it's almost fucking tangible.

These past twelve months have been some of the happiest days of my life.

"Stop daydreaming, Jaine. We need to go." Sasha grabs my arm. She's giddy with excitement. She's handled most of the arrangements now she lives in town. You'd think it was her who was getting married today and not me. Although, that's not likely to happen anytime soon. She and Clay are no longer together as he recently stuck his dick in one of the new cum sluts. Some nineteen-year-old. He denies it, of course. I'm selfishly hoping it won't see my BFF rush back to New York any time soon as I've gotten used to having her around.

We walk outside to our hogs, where Cherry's already sitting with her engine running. She's only here for the weekend as it's all the time away she can afford. She's taken over the reins of Jones & Associates Legal in my absence, which means she's also having to handle Delaney's business portfolio, including the Iron Scorpions' account. In return, Delaney has offered Jefferson an open-ended seat on the Scorpions' council, although he's yet to take him up on a position. It turns out the prospect of leaving Rising is a bigger deal to him than anyone first thought. Cherry's convinced he doesn't love her as a result of his reluctance to accept.

Her rapport with Detective Prescott isn't quite as amiable as mine was either, and he's not as accommodating with her. She reminds me daily of how anxious she is to pass the reins firmly back into my far more capable hands. I'm just not sure how I'm going to be able to juggle it all. Still, I'll worry about that shit tomorrow.

My BFFs look fabulous in short black leather dresses. The bikers will come in their pants when they see them, that's for sure. Pulling my skirts up to my knees, I straddle my Softail. My mind drifts to my pop, and I blink back tears. He should be walking me down the aisle today, but it wasn't in God's plan.

Sasha is on the phone, her face set in a grim line, no doubt as she has to converse with Clay to tell him we're on our way. When we set off, my eyes scan the horizon, taking in the familiar spots and reminiscing. It's a day for doing that. My thoughts drift to my Irish, and I smile. Time is a great healer. My memories of him are fond ones although I have good days and bad days.

Life moves on. It has to, or else that shit will just pass you by.

We pull up at the compound. It's been decked out with bunting and flowers. For once, it looks pretty. All the old ladies and cum sluts are working together in harmony, arranging all the food and trying to keep the younger children contained and entertained. They stop to shower me with their blessings while Sasha and Cherry arrange my dress. The ceremony's taking place at the rear of the building, where there's ample space to hold all the guests.

I walk inside the clubhouse I've known since my childhood, and I take in my pop's best friend. Duke wipes the tears from his face with the back of his hand.

"Jainie, I wish Jeremiah could see you right now, baby girl." He sounds like a broken man. I know he misses him as much as I do.

I put my arms around him. "I'm sure he and Mom will be looking down."

In my heart, I know they will be.

We make our way outside. Sasha and Cherry walk down first, and the brothers holler and whistle as they take in their barely-there biker dresses, no doubt receiving disapproving frowns and elbows in the ribs from their old ladies or WAGs, as Sasha still likes to call them. Then it's my turn. I smile at Duke as I take his arm, and he pats my hand proudly. This is everything he ever wanted. The song I'm walking down the aisle to? *Creep* by Radiohead. I wouldn't have it any other way.

Tears prick my eyes when I take in my beautiful boy. My first love. Standing there in snug black jeans, a black shirt, and his cut. I see him blink back his own in response.

He holds my hands in his as Father Reynolds takes us through the formalities, and we exchange plain silver rings at the end.

He smiles wolfishly as I rub my hand over my tummy. The one that now holds a precious new life. The one we've still to tell anyone about.

Then he kisses me, his tongue filling my mouth possessively, causing everyone to cheer and holler.

I am his and he is mine. Only death can part us now. We were always fated, Ace and me. I realize that now.

My father-in-law's old lady, Darla, stands with tears in her eyes as she passes me my sleeping little boy. My heart fills with a love so strong I never thought it possible.

I immediately close my eyes and press my nose against him, inhaling his perfect baby smell. My lips caress his pale skin while my fingers smooth back his hair, which is as black as coal. When he opens his eyes, they sparkle blue, just like his father's.

Baby Finian.

His full name? Finian Fergal Jeremiah O'Connell Steele.

He's named after his Irish great-grandfather.

I told Ace that day at the river I was pregnant, but that I had no idea which of them was the father. How could I know? He vowed to stand by me regardless, which was what I expected. The baby was part of me, and that was all that mattered to him. Finian's paternity was clear at birth. There was no avoiding it. No testing was necessary as my little man was born looking the spit of his Irish daddy and with the O'Connell birthmark that all the males have - a little horseshoe on his inner wrist.

Ace has raised him as his own, and he loves that little boy as if he were. Now he's going to have a little brother or sister to grow up with.

No one else knows about Finian's parentage. Not even Cherry or Sasha. It's easy to pass him off as Ace's son as he and Padraig have the same coloring. There's no knowing what Irish would do if he found out. Probably drag me to church and insist I marry him on the spot, earning himself a bullet in the head from the Sicilian mafia for being dishonorable as a result.

I can't take that risk. I can't have his blood on my hands.

Once Padraig is married, I'll return to Manhattan and introduce the next generation Hudson Duster to his biological father and the rest of his O'Connell family.

For now? I'll continue to live my life here in Rising with my husband, my little boy, and our new baby when they arrive.

In twelve months, give or take, I'll return to New York and pick up my business reins on a part-time basis and with Ace's blessing.

Then I'll sit back and watch as the shit hits the fan.

Author's Note

_____

I hope you enjoyed Ace's story. His isn't the end of the journey, it's only the beginning.

ACE is NOT standalone.
ACE is BOOK 1 of a SERIES which contains an ONGOING STORYLINE that CONCLUDES in BOOK 6, DIRTY PADRAIG.

These books contain MULTIPLE POVs from characters across the entire series.

Due to the nature of the CONTINUING STORYLINE, these books MUST be
READ IN ORDER.

The Outlaw Chess Reading Order

ACE

DIRTY CILLIAN

RAZR

DIRTY DYLAN

DIRTY EOIN

DIRTY PADRAIG

These books are NOT standalone.

Due to the nature of the CONTINUING STORYLINE

PLEASE READ IN ORDER.

Acknowledgments

_____

To Karen. To Ashton.
Two words. Thank you. For believing and encouraging.

To the writers
whose books I have read. You are my forever heroes and my
ongoing inspiration.

About the Author

Harley Diamond is a writer of romance novels with plot twists that will leave you begging for more. In every dirty story, an angsty bad boy and a badass queen lead the cast.

When Harley's not reading, she's writing. When not doing either, she's plotting to unleash her next novel on you from her non-working farm in West Yorkshire, England, surrounded by her faithful but very needy companions. Her seven rescue dogs.

Facebook Group: Harley's Hangout
Facebook Group: Harley's Spoilers

www.harleydiamond.com

Printed in Great Britain
by Amazon

62752698R00251